Pure Jade

PAINTING THE MISTS, BOOK 4

PATRICK G. LAPLANTE

Published by:

Patrick G. Laplante

Second edition, 2020

ISBN: 978-1-989578-09-4

Other Painting the Mists Books

Clear Sky

Blood Moon

Light in the Darkness

Dedication

*To those who feel guilty: Trust in your conscience;
the rest will solve itself.*

Author's Note

Wow. Time flies.

It's been eleven months since I started writing casually, and Book 4 is undergoing final touches before being published as an eBook. At the time of writing this note, I've already written the outline for Book 5. Further, I wrote four chapters of Book 5, scrapped the outline, and started over again.

For the first time since writing Book 1, I've finally taken the opportunity to slow down and write at a comfortable pace and with a comfortable process. It has made a world of difference, and I hope it comes across to you as you read this book.

Those of you who read the eBooks might not have noticed, but I paused online releases for over a month to make this happen. I expected loads of backlash—after all, web serial readers are notorious for their impatience. Yet to my surprise, not a single follower on Royal Road has complained this entire time. For that I thank you.

Before we head into Book 4, entitled *Pure Jade*, I would like to direct your attention to two things: confidence and conscience. In life, people have many possible choices that they can make. Therefore, it is natural to doubt and to regret. Sometimes people instinctively know they have made the wrong decisions. They know this because of their conscience, and their guilt helps determine their choices later in life.

Values take a lifetime to figure out. No one is perfect, and each bad decision adds guilt to a person's heart. Each misstep adds a layer of polish to the rough stone that is a person's soul. Given enough time, it isn't long before the soul becomes resplendent.

Like pure jade.

Prologue

It was a cold autumn day in the Silverwing Mountain Range. The fresh breeze caused Xi Ling to shiver as she ran through the wilderness. She was careful to avoid poisonous plants, disgruntled beasts, and annoying insects. Her cultivation robe stubbornly clung to her body as she weaved through the cluttered trees. She didn't have the luxury of caring.

Out of five companions, only three remained. A chance encounter with an early-purification demon beast had devastated their small group. Frightened and bleeding, the human cultivators had been a very attractive target.

A piercing shriek caused Xi Ling to look back reflexively. She saw Meng Huan, her Dao companion[1], collapse to the ground after being struck down by a demon bear's mighty claws. Her heart clenched when she saw the last of his life drain away. She bit back her tears and forced herself to remember Meng Huan's last words: *If I die, live on.*

Yet the love of her life had just died, and she longed to join him.

She and Meng Ruxing, her last remaining companion, quickly retreated to a small abandoned cave. The younger man dutifully started a hidden fire, bringing much-needed warmth to their shivering bodies. He said nothing. She knew he liked her, but he

---

[1] Dao companions in Xianxia novels are martial cultivators who have chosen to embark on a lifelong journey of seeking the Dao together. It's effectively marriage but for cultivators.

had reined himself in once her relationship with Meng Huan had solidified. He was Meng Huan's elder brother, and she trusted him with her life.

Her fingers soon thawed. As did her bottled-up feelings. She cried like she'd never cried before, so Meng Ruxing erected a qi barrier to prevent the nearby demon beasts from hearing. She soon fell asleep.

The next day, they found themselves wandering through a cold, dark tunnel. Neither of them bothered to use a light source, as their incandescent force provided them with basic visibility. Besides, using light in dark places could attract ground-dwelling demons. Their last encounter had crushed any hopes they had in escaping a second time.

"Why are we wandering down here again?" Xi Ling asked, her voice hoarse from all the crying the previous night.

"To find a safe place to heal our wounds," Meng Ruxing replied softly. "It's hardly safe to stay near the entrance of the cave, and it's equally unsafe to stay in a cave without knowing what's in it. We need to scout this place out to make sure it's suitable for us to rest and recover. We'll make a break for it when we're ready."

What he said made sense. It was just that Xi Ling didn't want to *do* anything. She just wanted to lie down and die and join Meng Huan in the afterlife.

Unfortunately, she had no choice but to go along with the young man. Whenever she felt like stopping, she heard that delicate voice telling her to live on.

Meng Huan, my love, she thought. She fingered the jade ring on the fourth finger of her left hand. Meng Huan had a matching one. He had said it bound them by karma, so that they would be together in this life and the next.

An hour later, the tunnel widened, and the darkness lifted. It opened into a glowing room filled with various crystals. Purple, clear, and green. And blue. Blue had been Meng Huan's favorite color. She sobbed softly as she walked but was soon silenced by Meng Ruxing's outstretched hand tapping her with alarm.

We're not alone, he said to her mentally. They both pulled their weapons. His was a dagger, an unusual weapon for a man. It suited his rare wind attribute. She had lost track of the amount of times he had stealthily stabbed stronger opponents in the back. At least thirty.

Xi Ling used a pair of elegant swords. One was green while the other was blue. She was a healer, dually proficient in wood and water. Wood and water cultivators were known for their superior defense, one of the reasons she'd managed to survive their deadly encounter.

Scratch. Scratch. Scratch.

Xi Ling paused. It was the terrible sound of claw on stone. She steeled herself and struck out first, her twin swords aiming to restrain the fierce beast and buy enough time for Meng Ruxing to land a killing blow. The beast roared and lashed out with claws the size of her face and teeth the size of her forearms. She prepared herself for the inevitable backlash of crashing against the powerful demon beast.

To her surprise, her swords slashed through the teeth and claws with ease, instantly slaying the beast. It was just a low-level badger, working diligently to expand its cave dwelling. Meng Ruxing hadn't even rushed forward.

What's wrong with you? he sent mentally. For some reason, she felt sick to her stomach. Killing demon beasts would have never caused such a reaction in the past, but her emotions were unstable due to the death of her lover. She started dry heaving, and Meng Ruxing ignored her as he gutted its corpse.

He still wasn't done by the time she recovered, so she took the chance to explore the room where the badger had been digging. She focused her incandescent force but noticed that it stopped suddenly near where the badger was digging. The dark space that was only dimly illuminated by the crystals in the other room. She frowned and took out an illumination stone to better observe. The walls were covered in gray, brown, and green stone. The bulk of the brown and gray stone had been scratched off by the innocent badger, leaving the hard green stone untouched.

She couldn't help but reach out and touch it. A warm feeling shot through her arm when she did. *Is it something valuable?* she wondered.

Her instincts as a cultivator kicked in. She scratched away the remainder of the brown and gray rock. Afterward, she used her sword and began cutting out large chunks of the green stone. It seemed like some sort of jade, a worthless material used for mortal jewelry. The same material her ring was made of.

Meng Ruxing approached her as she continued to cut out chunks, some measuring a cubic foot. She ignored him as she worked, cutting block after block. And then her blade stopped. She frowned. Magic weapons could cut through ordinary stones like butter. Therefore, she had widened the excavation and began removing larger and larger segments to reach the impenetrable obstacle. Meng Ruxing soon began to help her. He stabbed away quickly and efficiently, storing brick after brick of pure jade.

He's always been miserly, even with family, she thought.

It wasn't long before the jade was completely removed. What they discovered shocked them. The wall, which had previously been solid green, now glowed with resplendent green, white, and yellow colors. There was even a spot of purple and a spot of blue. The color was creamy and opaque, much like the stone before it. However, it seemed purer. More substantial.

"What do you think it is?" Xi Ling whispered.

"I think..." Meng Ruxing said hesitantly. "I think it's immortal jade."

She furrowed her brow. "Why have I never heard of such a thing? Is it a treasure?"

"More than that," Meng Ruxing replied. "It's a treasure so valuable it could cause a civil war."

She gasped. "What is it used for?"

"It's used for advancing past core formation," he explained while walking up beside her. "It's also used to make top-grade core-formation equipment and alchemical products. It's not something we can dig out and sell ourselves. We must find someone with sufficient political clout and negotiate a payout."

She nodded and touched the stone wall, admiring its multicolored surface. "It's too bad the others aren't here. We came here to find our fortune, and now they are gone forever. With this, we wouldn't have had to worry about riches for a lifetime. Meng Huan and I could have moved to the south, where it's always summer and never winter. We could have lived the rest of our lives in peace."

Meng Ruxing paused. "Do you miss him?"

"More than anything," she whispered, still staring at the wall. "I wish I could join him in the otherworld. We could reincarnate together and find each other again in the next life."

There was naught but silence. Silence followed by a sharp pain between her shoulder blades. She sank down to her knees, unable to move any of her limbs.

"Why?" she asked as her vision blurred.

"I think you know why," he said. "It's nothing personal. I wouldn't even trust my own brother with this secret, much less his Dao companion. Besides, didn't you say you wanted to join him?"

Xi Ling was angry and shocked, but as her lifeblood left her, she took solace in the fact that she would soon be reunited with her lover. She had tried to fulfill her promise to live on but had failed.

Knowing that his brother did this to me would devastate him, she thought. *I shall not tell him. What use is there in telling him if we'll forget everything when we drink Aunty Meng's tea?*

Her life faded as her soul was pulled toward the unknown. She didn't resist, and when she opened her eyes once more, she saw a desolate shore near a small yellow creek. There stood the soul of her lover Meng Huan. He was handsome and well kept, his eyes bright and full of intelligence.

"See? I told you she'd be here soon," a cloaked figure said. He smiled as the two lovers reunited.

They hugged each other tightly before looking at the cloaked man, who hadn't moved since she had arrived. "Must we step into the Yellow River?" Xi Ling asked.

"Alas, this is the law of the universe. Your souls must be cleansed before being sent into the cycle of reincarnation. You will forget everything after you drink Aunty Meng's tea."

Tears flowed down Xi Ling's translucent face. "Do you mean we won't find each other in the next life?"

"There are no absolutes," the cloaked figure said. "Luckily, you purchased these jade wedding bands. Wonderful things. I have a friend who makes a killing selling them."

Xi Ling glanced at her finger where she saw a faint jade glow where the ring had been. She also felt a soft line connecting her to Meng Huan. "The rings have bound you by karma. You will meet in your next life, for better or for worse. The rest is up to you."

The couple's worries evaporated. They nodded to each other before stepping into the yellow stream, hand in hand. Their souls transformed into white balls slightly tinged with yellow. They were connected by a jade tether, entangled and inseparable.

"Mortals lead such beautiful lives," Yama said, sighing. "It's a pity they are so short, like flowers that bloom only to wilt the next day."

Unlike those two youngsters, he was aeons old. He was destined to be forever alone as he watched the streams of reincarnation. No one would ever want to share his immense burden.

Besides, the Underworld was filled with a bunch of gold diggers. Sifting through the crowds of women that fawned over him every single day was a near-impossible task. Even the most sophisticated dating apps in the universe hadn't yielded him any convincing results, causing him to completely give up on finding a Dao companion.

Yama teleported back to his office after finishing the round of inspections. His assistant appeared shortly after. As the ruler of the Underworld, he had a special exemption to the strict no-teleportation law that applied to the entire city. However, he could only teleport to his office from outside the city and vice-versa. Failure to adhere to this rule would result in fines. Fines that would impact his operating budget.

It is as I feared, he thought. *A new universe war is coming, and there is nothing I can do to stop it.*

The Underworld had always been neutral. They treated souls of mortals, angels, devils, and demons. Only buddhas and evil spirits were outside his control. They were a bunch of cheaters that didn't play fair.

"Have you booked today's appointment?" Yama asked his secretary. She wore a designer suit-top with a tight skirt that rested just above her knees, her blonde hair kept in a tight bun.

She wore red glasses today, he thought. *She must be in a good mood. No way she'll ask for a raise again.*

"Of course, Your Excellency," the secretary replied dutifully. "I've taken the trouble to compile an update to his file since his latest promotion."

Subtle hint drop, Yama thought. *Very subtle.* "We're old friends. Why would I need an update?" Yama said while batting away the file.

"But you know that he is rather pedantic," she said. "This promotion is quite substantial."

"Nonsense," Yama said with an air of finality. "I'll have none of it."

He ran down the stairs in a fashionable jogging suit. The elevator was the fastest way down the 666 flights of stairs, but he was in dire need of exercise. His aging limbs were stiffening. He panted as he ran toward his dear friend's residence, which was fortunately quite close. The tall tower, his destination, was made of pure obsidian. The eye-shaped fire atop it was wedged between four angled stones for dramatic effect.

Large guardians appeared as he approached the massive black gates. They recognized his aged figure and began pushing large steel wheels. The doors opened at a slow, calculated pace. His friend had always loved drama, which was why his recent foray into show business was quite successful.

All to stoke his gigantic ego, Yama thought.

He arrived in the courtyard a short while later, and seeing that his friend had not yet arrived, he dematerialized his sweaty jogging suit and resummoned his traditional black robe and cloak.

An Underworld hour of jogging is surely sufficient for the remainder of the week, he thought.

"My friend, you made it!" a joyful voice called out. A tall figure wearing an imposing-looking black helmet was walking toward him. The impressive piece of headgear incorporated many spiky bits and deep eye sockets for extra effect.

"Cut with the theatricals, my dear lord—" Yama started.

"It's marquis now," the tall figure cloaked in black interjected.

"Oh, I'm sorry, *Marquis* of the Rings," Yama said in an annoyed voice. "Does this mean that your father—"

"No, no, he's quite all right," the man said while removing his spiky helmet. His figure looked boyish and immature. His thick square glasses didn't make things better.

Yama had always encouraged his mysterious dressing habits, as they made him look less like some dweeb who got stuffed in lockers. Layers of armor soon disappeared, revealing a skeletal frame. A single golden ring covered in runic characters glowed brightly on his middle finger. It was the one wedding ring that he'd forged for himself many aeons ago.

"I just recently married into a noble family, so I'm a marquis now. I was never satisfied as a lord. Now I can flaunt it like I always dreamed of."

"Fair enough," Yama said, chuckling. "You *are* the best jewelsmith in the Underworld. And here I was, wondering what you would do with all the money you earned by marketing those fancy limited-edition wedding rings of yours. It turns out you were amassing a dowry. Remind me, there were nine for mankind?"

"And some of the elves and the dwarves," he replied. "And for some reason they all ended up killing each other over them. I just don't get it. Regardless, it made for a very good story. I made a killing off the movie and merchandising. I have no regrets."

"I don't suppose you have a bit of that fortune left?" Yama asked.

That was why he was here, after all.

"Money is a bit tight, I must admit," the Marquis of the Rings said. "But I can always spare something for an old friend. What do you need it for?"

"I'm promoting a candidate for mayor," he said. "I need him and his policies to get more workers to manage the upcoming flood of souls. Can you do it?"

The Marquis of the Rings hesitated. "I can contribute a little, I suppose... with a sponsorship ad of course. Does ten billion work for you?"

"Ten billion?" Yama snorted. "More like ten trillion. Elections aren't cheap nowadays, you know. It's money that wins elections now, not the platform."

"You may as well bleed me dry," the man said with an aggrieved expression. "That's my entire life savings. I'd be a pauper!"

"You know that's not true, you big whiner," Yama said. "Besides, I have some good news. This mayor, he really hates many of the pieces of bad art in the city."

A gleam appeared in the man's eyes. "Do continue, my dear friend."

"Well," Yama said, "it just happens that we need to nominate ten million pieces of terrible art for destruction. Now as you know, *terrible* is a very subjective term. If I were to have your competitor's advertising statues destroyed..."

The Marquis of the Rings fell silent, pensive. "Fine. I'll do it. But I have one more condition."

"Oh?" Yama said. "Pray tell."

His friend had always been this way, trying to milk the most out of the situation with the least amount of effort. It was no wonder a few halflings he had short-changed had melted down his wedding ring once. That practical joke had stung his friend deeply.

"I want the statue of the white wizard gone," he said gravely. "I've always hated that jerk, ever since he humiliated me in school."

"But it's a work of art!" Yama protested. "It's truly a beautiful statue."

"I don't care!" the man yelled back. "This is personal. It's this or no deal. I want to be able to talk about his destroyed statue at all the balls and parties."

"Just because you're not man enough to fight him yourself, doesn't mean I need to indulge your petty grudges," Yama said sternly.

"It's not petty and you know it!" he said. "Do you have any idea how many of my shadowfire demons he's killed? Do you have any idea how many orcs he's slain, just because he feels like it? And he cloaks it all in a mantle of righteousness. I really can't stand that prick."

"Can't you think of anything else you want?" Yama said. "How about I arrange a date with the elf queen. You've always wanted to—"

"I'm married now!" the Marquis of the Rings exploded. "Do you have any idea what it's like to have to put up with that she-devil? All for the sake of this title? She doesn't even let me go to bed late. Lately, she put me on a stupid diet. Don't you *dare* bring up the elf queen again."

A moment of silence ensued. "Fine," Yama admitted. "I stepped over the line there." He walked toward the man's beautiful flower bed, the one he personally grew, watered, and weeded. Despite his despotic reputation, the man was truly a kind and caring fellow. "Is there truly nothing else you want?"

"None," the Marquis of the Rings said with his arms crossed. He wasn't budging.

"Fine," Yama said. "It's a deal."

Chapter 1: Crumbling and Hardening

Cha Ming carefully adjusted his position while he sat cross-legged in his temporary accommodation. He held three things in front of him: the Clear Sky Brush, a stack of talisman papers, and a tall gray candle. The gray candle was inscribed with incomprehensible runes and was mounted on a bronze platter. Its wick was whiter than alabaster and gave off a relaxing fragrance. It was the same comprehension candle he had received in Fuxi's Library. He would soon light it for the first time.

His cultivation was advancing far too slowly for his liking. The difference in cultivation time between half-step foundation establishment and initial foundation establishment was vast. It was unlikely that he would progress soon.

He had one last way of strengthening himself before trouble came knocking: creating magic talismans. However, he had no formulas; the knowledge gleaned from Fuxi's Library could only take him so far.

What he needed now was inspiration. Inspiration in the form of a gray, runed candle. He lit its white wick, watching it burn with a black flame. The candle vaporized as the heat of the flame ate away at it. The resulting gray smoke invaded his nose, eyes, ears, and mouth, but he felt no urge to cough or wheeze. His surroundings faded as he entered a deep trance.

Cha Ming was dreaming. His surroundings were lifelike and vivid, to the point where he could see and feel everything around him. At the same time, he maintained his lucidity. He was experiencing the best of both worlds: the boundless imagination of the sleeping world and the mindfulness of the waking world.

It took him some time to realize that he was now standing in an open field. A circle of large giants held up a massive sphere. It was as large as a planet, and it was held up with the communal efforts of the entire group.

The large men all sat cross-legged, their dreams projecting a massive hand above them. Some hands were filled with visions of conquest while others were filled with hopes of a peaceful life. Others dreamed of their children growing strong, living a fulfilling life, and supporting their parents. All of these were fantasies, as unreal as the lifelike vision he was currently witnessing.

Time passed, little by little. After what seemed like a lifetime, he noticed a single crack appearing on one of the hands. It was miniscule and seemed inconsequential, but it was there. Another lifetime passed before the strain of the world it supported took its toll, forcing the crack to widen.

Another lifetime passed. One crack became two, and two became three. Before long, the hand was covered in countless cracks. The fragile hand was only held together by the giant's iron will.

However, this was far from enough. In his effort to maintain the hand, cracks appeared on his body in the same way. The thought of his dreams disappearing brought tears of magma to the stone giant's eyes. He gritted his mountainous teeth as he mustered every fiber of his being to contain the damage. But the weight of the world was merciless. The cracks continued to multiply, and as the cracks propagated, the stone giant let out a mournful howl. Finally, both his body and his dreams crumbled away into nothing more than the finest dust. The giant and his dreams were no more.

With the disappearance of this one stone giant, each of the other giants' burdens increased by a small and almost unnoticeable amount. Yet just like the one before them, two giants began to weaken. They struggled heroically, but soon enough, they too crumbled under the weight of the world. What seemed like years passed by. Every few months, the number of falling giants doubled.

Finally, the last giant shattered, and the world fell into the void. Their task seemed impossible to begin with. Cha Ming, in his lucidity, observed that all the giants that had cracked and broken had one thing in common: Their foundations were too weak to support their dreams. Each foundation had a fatal flaw, and once enough pressure was applied, the giant would inevitably crumble.

Do you understand? a voice asked.

Cha Ming woke from his deep meditation with a start. Suddenly, he remembered the heavy burdens that had weighed him down over the years.

He was burdened with Huxian's fate—if he died, the baby fox would as well. He had been burdened with disability, which had caused him to lose all hope for a short time. Finally, he had been burdened with slavery, and with the fate of the people in Crystal Falls. All these burdens were very real, and their weight exceeded the strength of his foundation. Given enough time, his will would have shattered just like these stone giants.

Hands shaking from this sudden feeling of fragility, Cha Ming took up his brush and began writing. Dark brown ink flowed across the sheet of paper as he poured his feelings of vulnerability and near-collapse.

The weight of the world crumbles countless dreams;
Man's foundation is ever brittle.

To Cha Ming, these verses seemed like a universal truth. He decided to call it a Crumbling Talisman. It was a poetic talisman, just like Elder Ling's Ode to Mr. Mao Mao. As such, he had no idea what power it might hold, but he was sure that it far exceeded that of an ordinary mortal-grade talisman.

Having finished his new creation, he collapsed in the tent, shivering. He wasn't sick, nor was he physically injured in any way. However, he couldn't shake that feeling of helplessness, that feeling of almost failing. He could feel his own cracks widening.

"Your hands are shaking," Li Yin said to Cha Ming as the younger man tried to steady his needle.

Cha Ming was currently stitching a cut on one of the many carpenters who was new to the village.

"It's nothing," Cha Ming said, preparing to insert the shaky needle into the man's arm. Just as he was about to proceed, he felt an old worn hand grasping his arm. There was no power behind Li Yin's grip, only undeniable firmness.

"Let me take care of this one," the doctor said authoritatively. He proceeded to stitch the wound in only a few minutes and sent the carpenter on his way. Then he closed the door to their shack, one of the few wooden buildings in town.

"What happened?" Li Yin asked.

Cha Ming sighed and sat down on one of the three chairs in the room. "It just seems like I was so close to failing, so close to crumbling in the mines. Dr. Li, it was my mistake that caused so many people to suffer. And if a lucky chance hadn't come about, I wouldn't have been able to escape and kill the bandits. Everyone here would have eventually suffered a miserable fate." He looked up at Li Yin with red eyes. "How can people still trust me?"

The doctor looked at him compassionately. "I'll admit that many don't," the doctor said. "But many also realize that people make mistakes. You could have run away after escaping, but you didn't. You owned up to your mistakes. And tell me, will you make that mistake again?"

Cha Ming shook his head.

"Then quit worrying about it."

Li Yin placed a hand on Cha Ming's shoulder. "You're strong, Cha Ming. You've withstood what many people can't. Yet you overcame all that. Are you really going to forget this and crumble now that the pressure is gone? How laughable would that be?"

Cha Ming couldn't bear to look at the doctor.

"Today is not your day, it seems," Li Yin said. "You're useless to me here when your hands are shaking. Go outside and get some sunshine. Don't come back here until you've straightened yourself out. You're better than this. I know you are."

Cha Ming spent the rest of his day performing manual labor. Nothing skilled, just brainless hauling of wood and stone. Many people gave him odd looks as he trudged on like an ox, but he took pleasure in being able to perform these simple tasks.

If I have the strength of an ox, he thought, *I may as well use it.* Meanwhile, he agonized over his failure in raising Huxian. He hadn't even tried looking for him, and the poor little fox was all alone in the wilderness. Was he all right?

Cha Ming wiped the sweat off his brow as he pulled a load of stone to the newly built frame of the future inn. It was a priority building, as it would accommodate the many workers they had brought in from neighboring villages. After a bit of looking, he spotted the chief mason.

"Where do you want this load?" he asked as he pulled the wagon up to the middle-aged man.

"Just over there," the man said, pointing. "Are you free right now? We could use a hand setting up some large beams. They are heavy as all hell, and without you, we'll have to set up a pulley and waste a few days."

"My hands are a little shaky today," Cha Ming said hesitantly.

"It doesn't matter," the mason said dismissively. "All we need is someone who can hold the weight up. We'll take care of the shaking. If you can pull a cart, you can hold up a beam."

Cha Ming helplessly followed the chief mason, who continued to give orders as they walked. The workers moved quickly as he barked out directions. Soon they arrived at a large pile of thick tree trunks. They were spirit trees, judging by their size. Each trunk had been shaved of bark and branches.

"Each trunk weighs three thousand jin," the man explained. "I want you to pick one up and walk up the stairs we built, then down the central beam. You can lay it down at the other end. Once you get there, do your best to hold it in place, and my men will fasten it down. Piece of cake."

"It's no problem as long as you keep people out of the building in case I fall," Cha Ming said. "No need to worry about me. I'm sturdy."

"Done," the man said. He took a minute to shout a few dozen offensive words at the workers. They hustled out of the building like their life depended on it. He then looked to Cha Ming. "It's all clear."

Cha Ming nodded, grasping the first beam, using a sling. It creaked and strained as he lifted the beam off the ground, and the soil sank as he walked with it. After carefully checking his balance, he walked up the makeshift steps that led to the top of the building.

The massive central beam creaked only slightly as he traversed it, carefully standing firm despite the blowing wind. It was a strong beam, worthy of being this large building's foundation. It would last at least a hundred years if properly maintained.

Sweating, he walked steadily until he arrived at the predetermined location. To his surprise, the large beam wasn't shaking. It was likely due to its massive weight.

For some people, he thought, *a larger load is best. A king can easily bring ruin to a small household. However, he works best under the pressure of a nation.*

At his signal, a pair of men scrambled onto the roof and fastened the large log. He helped them with the next nine, successfully aiding them in installing the roof's foundation. He ended the day tired but satisfied. However, once he got to his tent and saw the gray candle, he couldn't help but shiver and recall the emotions he had poured into the talisman.

Surely there is a balancing concept, Cha Ming thought. He hesitated slightly before shutting the flap of his tent and taking out talisman writing materials. Then, wincing, he lit the wick on the gray candle once more. The black flame roared to life.

This time, Cha Ming saw an entirely different scene. He saw a young boy whose family's finances were crumbling. His father and mother could no longer take the pressure, and it was evident that they would lose their home and be forced to live on the streets.

The boy had many younger siblings. He couldn't bear to see his parents in such a state, and he could only imagine what would happen to his siblings should he hesitate. Therefore, he decided to leave school to support his family. He became a carpenter, and he toiled away day after day, barely making enough to feed them.

Unfortunately, it wasn't enough. His third brother was rather intelligent, and only with proper schooling and private tutoring would he be able to bring out his full potential and become a government official. So the carpenter badgered his boss repeatedly, and eventually he was appointed as assistant manager. After one year of stellar performance, he was promoted to manager. Then, using his influence and his newly improved finances, he managed to put his brothers and sisters through school.

Unfortunately, his success was short-lived. The kingdom was thrust into a war that he knew nothing about. They conscripted him into the military, and he was forced to kill men on the battlefield to survive. Many of his brothers in arms fell before he eventually became a captain. Even as a captain, there was little he could do to alleviate the suffering.

Decades passed. After much hard work and determination, he became a general. He defeated the kingdom's enemies, earning much praise and riches from the king upon his retirement. But unlike many of his contemporaries, he didn't move to the capital or take many wives to start a large family. Instead he returned to the small town where he grew up.

The town had been stricken with poverty and drought ever since his departure. His parents had long since passed away, but many of his brothers and sisters remained. After seeing their plight, he used everything he had earned in the military to purchase food and building supplies. He poured his sweat, blood, and tears into improving the village, and soon, it was prosperous again.

He spent the rest of his days with his friends and family, and when he finally died, the entire village mourned. It was the story of a man who, despite having been through so many things in life, just wanted to feed his family. And that's what he did until he breathed his last.

Do you understand?

Cha Ming awoke to tears of joy and satisfaction. He recalled the misfortunes he had overcome. He recalled fighting against the heavenly tribulation with Huxian and becoming crippled in the process. Despite the setbacks and subsequent depression, he discovered a way to save his life and recover his cultivation. Eventually, Li Yin took him on as an apprentice.

Later, an impulsive decision brought the bandits to the village. He was enslaved, and he lost his mind to the vicious chains that imprisoned him. After escaping, he strengthened himself and came back to eliminate Wei Chen and his lackeys, freeing the villagers.

With these thoughts in mind, he painted the next talisman with light-brown ink. His stone-like will was infused into the paper through the following verse:

Hardening through countless ages;
Never questioning his resolve.

He called it the Hardening Talisman. It was an obvious continuation of the first two verses, juxtaposing two opposite phenomena, crumbling and hardening. Hardening was defensive while crumbling was offensive. The verses belonged together, but he did not have the strength to combine them.

Looking down at his hands, he found that they had stopped

shaking. His emotions were no longer unstable. However, as he tried to paint another Hardening Talisman, he discovered that it wasn't possible. The same applied to the Crumbling Talisman. He had poured his emotions into these talismans, and his heart had yet to recover.

He slept peacefully that night. His dreams were filled with a field of rocks. Some were solid, while others were feeble. Some were cracked, others unbreakable. He woke to a funny thought: In more ways than one, people resembled stones.

Chapter 2: Resistance

In Quicksilver City, a large figure wearing a black cloak walked down the elegantly crafted streets of Central Square. Men and women alike practically dove out of his way, his baleful aura causing them to avoid him instinctively. Even the city guards shivered as they walked past him, maintaining as much berth as their dignity allowed them.

Xiao Heilong, the mountain of a man who led the Serpentine Sword bandits, didn't wear cultivator robes. Instead he wore a suit of black armor with a matte finish. Two weapons were sheathed at his side, large black daggers tinged with red. His black hair was trimmed short, emphasizing the man's practical nature.

He soon reached a tall black building standing opposite another equally large building made of white stone. The arrangement was obviously a deliberate show of their intense rivalry. Not that he cared. All he knew was there was someone in the black building who would take his money to perform simple services, regardless of their dubious nature.

A beautiful lady dressed in an elegant but revealing black robe welcomed him at a black-marble desk. Her mannerisms and appearance gave the impression that, like all the services offered in the building, she was also for sale. Not that he was interested. He wouldn't be caught dead frequenting a viper like her. He calmly ignored her coy behavior and tempting gestures while following her to a room upstairs, where a decrepit old man was waiting.

"What can I do for you today, little snake[2]?" the old man asked in a pleasant voice. He wore unkempt black robes that matched his unkempt hair. His large, greedy grin exposed a set of rotting yellow teeth.

A large purse plopped onto the old man's desk with the clink of coin. "I need you to find someone who killed a member of my group," Xiao Heilong said, ignoring the diminutive nickname.

"Excellent," the old man replied. "Do you have something that bears his presence, or the presence of your group member?"

"Of course," Xiao Heilong said while retrieving a jade slip. It was Wei Chen's life slip, and it was broken in half. "I need to find the one who killed him while the trail is still fresh."

The older man picked up the purse, his eyes glittering when he saw the amount inside. "How very wise of you to seek me out as soon as possible. The trail of vengeance fades with every passing day. Wait one moment while I perform some auguries. Do you want the location of the murder, or the location of the man?"

"I don't give a damn about the location of the murder," Xiao Heilong said. "I just want to actively track the one who killed him. He likely took my man's possessions after the fact."

The old man pulled out a dousing pendulum and walked over to a map of the Quicksilver Empire. After making a few arcane gestures, the silver pendulum darted out and landed on a point on the map. "That's not so bad. Only a few days away."

"I need to be able to track him long term," Xiao Heilong said blankly. "I don't know when my next mission will come, so it needs to be a semi-permanent solution. At least one year."

"Patience is a virtue, my friend," the old man said. He took the jade slip and carried it to an altar. There, he lit some incense and muttered unintelligible words. The air seemed to shiver as the man opened his eyes and shouted, "Evil spirits, heed my call, reveal the crimson thread of vengeful karma!" Several illusory threads, most of

---

[2] His name, Xiao Heilong, means little black dragon. Little Dragon is another way to say snake in Mandarin Chinese.

them black and white, appeared in the air. The man sifted through them before eventually finding the crimson thread he was looking for.

The old man reached out to pluck the string, but as he did, his hand jerked back. After looking at the thread fearfully, he turned back to Xiao Heilong with a frown. "Grasping this thread is far more dangerous than normal. I have no idea why. I will need double your original payment to do this. Alternatively, I can give you your money back, and whatever information you've gained thus far will be free of charge."

Heilong grunted and tossed yet another purse on the desk. "Old crook," he muttered.

The man ignored him. A look of resolve appeared on his face as he aggressively shot his hand out toward the thread. The air cracked and distorted as he fought against a massive pressure. The man coughed blood as his hand grasped the crimson thread. He wrenched it free and wrapped it around a needle, which he then installed on a fengxue compass.

Pale, the man handed the fengxue compass to Xiao Heilong, who stowed it away unceremoniously.

"Not worth it," the old man said while shaking his head self-deprecatingly. He crawled over to a bed in a corner of the room. "You may leave now," he said, waving his hand.

Xiao Heilong shrugged and left the black building and Central Square. He didn't particularly care about avenging Wei Chen. However, the man had told him that he had found something big, and that he would take care of it personally. Knowing Wei Chen's character, that meant that he had found something massive and wanted to keep it to himself. Just when Xiao Heilong had decided to go extort the small fortune Wei Chen had earned, the man's life slip had broken.

Having exited Central Square, he pulled out the fengxue compass, noting that it pointed eastward. He was about to head in the general direction when he felt a vibration from his bag of holding. Sighing, he withdrew a little black notebook through which he received his missions.

Just my luck, he thought. It was an urgent mission, one that he couldn't ignore for contractual reasons. *Vengeance will need to wait.*

Weeks passed. Cha Ming continued his routine of cultivating during the evening and helping the villagers during the day. Over the past week, he had used his ridiculous strength to clear large swaths of land to develop fields for the village. He had removed the large trees with his bare hands while they cleared the brush and dug out the roots. Now it was the oxen's turn. They plowed the barren fields in preparation for the farmers who had yet to arrive. Meanwhile, the wood he had gathered was used to construct houses.

Whether the land would be able to produce next year would depend on their upcoming outing. They lacked seeds and farmers. Seeds could be bought with money, but farmers could not. He would accompany the mayor across the river tomorrow to recruit ambitious young families looking to build a new future.

Cha Ming worked hard and ended the day exhausted and satisfied. As with most nights, he meditated and attempted to draw the Crumbling Talisman and Hardening Talisman, to no avail. These emotions, while powerful, were elusive to him now. They came and went as they pleased, like naughty children playing pranks on him.

Cha Ming sighed. It was the fourteenth time he had tried and failed. He still needed to increase his strength, and his cultivation was coming along far too slowly. It was time to seek new inspiration. He lit the gray candle once more after a moment of hesitation.

Cha Ming saw an ocean in the distance. It was neighbored by a sandy beach, where many people were swimming. Waves gently crashed against the shore while children and their parents played in the gentle waters. He smiled softly as he remembered such an innocent life. Their screams of joy were intoxicating.

Realizing that this scene was there for a reason, he indulged in it and walked down to observe the people more closely. The children were young. He guessed the youngest was around five and the oldest twelve. While some mothers were out playing, most of them sat on the beach with their fathers, enjoying a moment of intimacy while their children were distracted.

Suddenly, a crackle sounded from above. He saw a peal of lightning, and the winds began blowing more aggressively. His instinct told him that the calm-looking ocean would not stay this way for very long. To his surprise, however, the parents didn't notice, and neither did the children. The children only experienced greater enjoyment as the waves grew increasingly tall.

It didn't take long for the situation to run out of control. Two or three children were pulled beneath the waters by the waves. The other children's screams alerted their parents, who rushed out to the waters to save them.

The scene bothered Cha Ming greatly, but as he moved to save the children, an unknown force prevented him from approaching. It was only a dream, but the thought of doing nothing distressed him. He felt helpless.

He watched on in horror as the mighty waves pulled down twenty children in total. Only six of these were saved by their fathers, and the rest were lost forever. He saw grown men struggling, continuously diving in a futile attempt to save those who had disappeared. They knew it was meaningless to try, but they couldn't help themselves.

Finally, exhausted by their search, they swam back to shore. He saw the grown men weep, collapsing in tears of grief. Their spouses joined them in their sorrows. They could do nothing else, for this was their fate.

Do you understand?

Cha Ming woke from the vision with sweat beading on his forehead. The dream had been so lifelike that his heart was still crying. He could feel their pain. He picked up his talisman brush despite the tears in his eyes and slowly spelled out his emotions. He wrote the words in dark-blue ink, pouring his feelings of helplessness into the talisman paper through his ink and brush.

The ocean cares not for drowning children;
Man is a slave to the sea of fate.

He called it the Resistance Talisman, for obvious reasons. The words reminded him of a cruel reality, the helpless nature of mankind. So many unavoidable disasters wore away people's wills. Before long, they would feel helpless, incapable of changing their circumstances. It was the same for impoverished people. Hope became an unaffordable luxury. The resistance posed by the outside world and their inner thoughts were far too high.

Cha Ming felt something was missing when he finished the last stroke. It was as though the two verses were incomplete, missing their second half. However, he felt helpless to finish it. Could he really make the next talisman? More to the point, was he truly helping the villagers?

He questioned his actions over the past several weeks as he drifted off to sleep.

"You can't be serious," Li Yin said with disbelief. Cha Ming's eyes avoided the older man's as he felt judgment wash over him. "If I understand correctly, you feel helpless and unable to change anything. You feel this despite having just decimated a group of bandits, escaped slavery, and having literally rebuilt half the village.

On top of that, you've done nine-tenths of the work to open up new farmlands."

Cha Ming's face flushed red as he was berated by his teacher, who sighed and shook his head. "You really need to stop getting yourself distracted like this. Just keep yourself busy, and you'll recover. Eventually."

"Shouldn't I stay and help you in the hospital?" Cha Ming asked. The hospital was largely empty nowadays, so there was little damage he could do.

"Absolutely not!" Li Yin snapped. "I will have nothing less than fully confident hands on my patients. It's not just your manual dexterity that's important. Doctors play a very important psychological role, and I will *not* have you discouraging recovering patients."

Helpless, Cha Ming proceeded to the dock, where three men were waiting. One was the mayor, and two were newly appointed elders.

"Where have you been?" the mayor asked. "We were about to leave without you."

Cha Ming bowed in apology. "It won't happen again."

These submissive gestures caused bewildered expressions to flicker across their face, but only for a moment. Their experience and demeanor were why they had been chosen as elders in the first place.

A few hours later, they set up a booth in the largest nearby town called Jinyang.

"Free land for young couples in Crystal Falls. We purchase your starting seed, you farm without worries!" The elders hawked like merchants at every young man and woman who passed them. They continued for hours without success, as most people eyed their stall with suspicion. Cha Ming simply sat down and waited, ready for any trouble that might occur.

The day passed by uneventfully, so they stayed the night at an inn. Everyone but Cha Ming ate and enjoyed the local music while he sat in his room, half meditating and half brooding. He no longer needed to eat very often. Instead he spent his time attempting to replicate the Crumbling, Hardening, and Resistance talismans.

The elemental essence returned to his brush every time he failed, and after an hour, he gave up and began cultivating. He had no pills or supplements and could only cultivate slowly but surely while draining away the energy from mid-grade spirit stone ore. The ambient qi of heaven and earth was insufficient for cultivation at the foundation-establishment level.

Morning arrived. They set up their booth, and like the day before, no one came. The looks became increasingly suspicious, causing Cha Ming and the others to ponder what they had done wrong. Was there perhaps a local custom they were breaking?

"Did we step in cow excrement?" one of the elders asked. "Or did we somehow offend someone powerful? I just don't know why we would be ignored like this."

"Who knows?" the mayor replied. "We're not just getting ignored. People are looking at us as though we are thieves or murderers. We'll have to move on to the next town if we don't find anyone today."

Noon arrived when they finally received their first visitor. It wasn't a young man or woman like they expected, but a guard. He was dressed in leather armor and wore an exquisite sword. To Cha Ming's surprise, his cultivation was at initial foundation establishment.

Cha Ming rose to greet the guard. "Greetings, fellow Daoist," he said while clasping his hands together and bowing slightly.

"Greetings, fellow Daoist," the guard said, bowing back. "I see that the four of you are recruiting farmers for newly cultivated lands in a place called Crystal Falls. However, I have never heard of this village. Would you care to tell me where it is?"

"This..." the mayor said. "You have probably never heard of it as we have been quite isolated in the past. Our village is hidden in the woods across the river, near the largest waterfall. It is perpetually covered in fog. If you have a map, I would be happy to show you the location."

The guard nodded and continued his questioning. "Then why is it that you have a sudden need for farmers? Surely there are sufficient people in your village who could manage these lands."

The mayor shrugged. "In the past, we haven't done much farming. Recently, however, a disaster struck our village, and we felt the need to come out of isolation. We have never dared exploit the lands in the woods, but due some recent events, the spirit-beast population has decreased substantially. Now we have much land available but no one to cultivate it."

Cha Ming thought on this with sadness. The spirit-beast population had been decimated by the bandits when they had patrolled and foraged for food.

The guard looked doubtful. "Would you mind coming with me to confirm some things, then? My name is Captain Bao Tiehu, and I oversee the security of this village and the surrounding ones for the emperor. Circumstances as they are, we must ensure the legitimacy of your recruitment."

"Yes, we can do that," the mayor replied.

"Excellent," Bao Tiehu said. "Please come this way to meet the mayor." He immediately led them down the main street to a large manor. Cha Ming was surprised to spot two half-step foundation-establishment guards at the gate. They immediately joined their group at the captain's signal. They were taken to a study and brought tea and snacks.

"What do you think the matter is?" Cha Ming asked his companions. "Is it illegal to recruit workers in the empire?"

"I'm truly not sure," the mayor replied. "It has never been a problem to recruit workers in the past. There was no issue when we recruited the carpenters. I've also never had problems buying or selling in towns as long as I paid the appropriate duties and taxes." The mayor paused thoughtfully. "Something unusual must have happened recently to make them suspicious. And it must have been a high-profile occurrence given that even normal people refused to speak to us."

A quarter hour passed before the captain of the guard entered with another middle-aged man. A younger initial foundation-establishment cultivator wearing religious robes followed them inside. Cha Ming knew that two half-step foundation-establishment cultivators as well as many peak-qi-condensation cultivators were present outside.

"Please forgive my caution, friends," the middle-aged man said. "My name is Li Tai, and as the mayor of this area, I take the security of my residents very seriously." He motioned to the young man beside him. "This young man is an inquisitor from the Church of Justice, and he will validate the truth of your words. Will that be a problem?"

Cha Ming recalled the time in Fairweather when the issuers of the rescue mission had hired an inquisitor to verify the truth of their statements. According to Gong Lan, this was common practice with important transactions. It made sense that this also extended to security duties.

The three men shook their heads, and Cha Ming followed suit but added, "It's fine as long as the questions aren't too personal."

"Naturally," Li Tai replied. "Lai Zhi, will this be a problem?"

The young inquisitor's gaze rested on Cha Ming, and he shook his head self-deprecatingly. "This man's soul is two levels higher than mine. I will need him to slightly lower his soul defenses." He lifted his hands apologetically. "Please understand that I mean no harm to those who do no evil. However, some recent occurrences have rendered these precautions necessary. I will by no means take advantage of your lowered defenses."

Cha Ming relaxed upon hearing these words. "Since these are the words of an inquisitor, I am reassured that you aren't lying. I will cooperate." Cha Ming immediately lowered his soul's natural defenses by one level. "Is this sufficient?"

The young man nodded in response.

"Excellent," Li Tai said jovially. "My first question is this: Does the town called Crystal Falls really exist, and where is it located? You may use the large map on the wall to point it out."

Zheng Fang, the mayor of Crystal Falls, walked up to the map. "Crystal Falls exists, though it is currently being rebuilt after recent catastrophic events. It is located here, right beside the large waterfall where the clouds accumulate. It is surrounded by woods, and we have been secluded and difficult to find for many decades."

"Why was the town secluded for so long?" Li Tai asked.

"These are personal reasons. Please forgive me for not answering," Zheng Fang said.

Li Tai frowned but didn't press him. "Very well, that isn't relevant. I take it that the town's secrecy is no longer required?"

"That is correct," Zheng Fang said.

"Why are you in sudden need of farmers?" Li Tai asked.

"A disaster struck our village, which coincidentally decimated the local spirit-beast population. As such, we were able to open large tracts of land, for which we don't have enough population to farm. The trees are already removed and the ground tilled. We only need seeds and farmers to have a successful harvest next year."

Li Tai looked to the young man, who nodded. "Interesting. And you have no ulterior motives for these farmers?"

"Pardon me?" Zheng Fang asked, offended.

"Please entertain me and answer the question," Li Tai said. "Then I will explain everything."

"We have no ulterior motives for these farmers," Zheng Fang said. The mayor's gaze traveled to the other three, and they all replied in the same way. Li Tai visibly relaxed after hearing their answers.

"I apologize," the mayor said. "Please join me for lunch and an explanation, after which I believe I can help you get what you need."

They left the room and followed Li Tai. As they departed, Lai Zhi bowed and left in another direction. As he left, he sent a mental message to Cha Ming.

It's a good thing you weren't lying. Otherwise at least half of us would need to die to apprehend you.

Cha Ming chuckled inwardly but didn't correct the man. Indeed, if they had tried to apprehend him, Cha Ming could have slain them without breaking a sweat.

Chapter 3: Momentum

Li Tai's house was large, and the banquet he served extravagant. Fine wine, a delicacy from a kingdom to the north, was served along with the dozens of dishes. It was the finest meal Cha Ming or the elders had seen for over two years. He took a respectable helping of two vegetable dishes and ate as the mayor spoke.

"We never used to interrogate people," Li Tai said once they had finished eating. "One year ago, however, pockets of unrest appeared throughout the empire. Bandit groups multiplied, and devil cults began appearing everywhere. It was only with the help of the Church of Justice and the Imperial Army that many of the small towns survived.

"Many innocents mortals have been captured since then. What you were doing, offering free land with relocation, was one of the many schemes they used to entrap mortals. This specific scheme happened to be used here exactly one year ago. Over one hundred residents from this town were captured and brutally killed in devilish sacrifices, thus my caution. It is also why so many residents were suspicious of your motives."

Li Tai's eyes teared up. "Even my own daughter was captured. She disobeyed my wishes and married a farmer. It was difficult for them to make ends meet, so I tried to help, but they refused. They left for more prosperous, undeveloped lands, the same hoax I spoke of. The next time I saw her, she was dead."

The maids served tea once the meal was over. No one ate much after the mayor shared his story. The men from Crystal Falls only understood half his pain. They had been enslaved, yes, but their children hadn't been killed. They didn't even have the heart to ask about recruiting farmers for fear of upsetting the distraught father.

"Now then," Li Tai said, "there remains the issue of finding farmers. Truth be told, this isn't a problem. I own all the lands here, and there is a large surplus of farmers. They will flock over in droves as long as I give the word. However, nothing is free in this world."

Zheng Fang frowned. "What did you have in mind?"

"Nothing major," Li Tai said. "In fact, it will help you. You are an unregistered village. As such, you have not been paying taxes. You cannot remain this way, as the empire will eventually discover you, enforce the law, and appoint a manager. However, I have an alternative." The man's eyes glowed as he spoke. "Many of the towns around here have their own mayors but report to me. I take care of processing paperwork and taxes, and at the same time, I arrange regular patrols from the Imperial Army to deter crime. In addition, my people build and maintain roads to facilitate commerce.

"I propose that you become one such village. You would maintain your autonomy but will need to pay me taxes. In turn, I will register your village. Since taxes are based on a percentage of revenue, I will do my utmost to help you develop the village's economy. What do you think?"

The mayor of Crystal Falls hesitated. "Can we think on it?"

"Most certainly," Li Tai said. "No pressure, but I will need to report this matter to my superiors. I'm sure they won't penalize you, but as a bare minimum you will need to register your village independently. I'm just offering you a hassle-free way of resolving this issue."

They left Li Tai's house after lunch, and after two days of negotiations, the matter was settled. They left for the village with boats full of young families and bags of seeds. The young families didn't remain idle once they arrived at the village. They built houses next to their new plots of land and made preparations for the winter.

It didn't take long for them to fully integrate. Cha Ming helped where he could, but eventually he became fully redundant. He could only retreat to his tent and cultivate when the hospital wasn't busy.

The village had developed its own momentum. Given that his cultivation wasn't advancing very quickly, he was sure that it was time to leave. But before that, he had one last thing to do. He needed to learn the next talisman in the set, and he already had a good idea of its nature. He lit the gray candle once more.

Cha Ming was standing at the peak of a mountain. It was a wonderful spring day. The mountain glacier beside him was melting at a steady pace and trickling into a stream. He followed it as it traveled down the steep incline.

Eventually it was joined by another stream from higher up. Others joined in until it was no longer a stream but a raging river. He continued to follow it until it became a tall waterfall. The water stopped in a stagnant lake.

The lake filled in slowly, and what seemed like months passed. One day, Cha Ming noticed the reason for the stagnant nature of the lake: The exit of the river was blocked by a beaver's dam. Having nowhere to go, the water accumulated. Finally, the pressure exceeded the dam's limit and rushed out all at once, washing away everything in its path in its pursuit for equilibrium. It passed through various rivers and lakes before finally arriving at the sea's shore. There, it blended into the ocean and achieved its dream of eternal stability. Or did it? Little did it know that after mingling with the ocean, it would soon evaporate and condense back into rain and repeat the journey once more.

Do you understand?

Cha Ming was reminded of his past and current life. It seemed that fate was always dragging him forward, but he realized his mistake. It wasn't that fate was dragging him but his momentum that kept him going. Just like the momentum the village had established. Without hesitation, he started a new talisman. His brush flowed smoothly as he painted light-blue characters on the sheet of paper. The words he wrote resonated with his heart.

Flowing down from high to low;
Never questioning his direction.

This was the Momentum Talisman, and it was a continuation of the first two verses. It juxtaposed two opposite phenomena: resistance and momentum. Momentum represented the tendency of things to move and flow, while resistance opposed it. Their nature was complementary. He wasn't sure what the talismans did, but as he completed the Momentum Talisman, the feeling of despondency and depression he had been brooding over disappeared along with the ink in his brush.

Cha Ming contemplated for days. He had crafted four talismans—resistance, momentum, crumbling, and hardening—only to realize how deeply the emotions affected him. They reminded him that his entire cultivation journey had consisted of lucky chances and being led around by the nose.

His decision to cultivate was a choice, but at the same time, he felt such a choice was mandatory. Later, he fled through the woods and accepted the task to save Huxian. This was also a choice, but it seemed like a false one. He couldn't have chosen otherwise without betraying his morals.

The concepts of momentum and resistance danced around him. He felt trapped in an inescapable web. When the events in Fairweather unfolded, Wang Jun had said he was pulled there by fate.

But after discovering the atrocities committed, he had no choice but to act. He still worried about the fate of the Song Kingdom. Protector Song had been sent by Zhou Li, whose influence was far-reaching.

Perhaps this is my next task, Cha Ming thought. *I can't abandon the Song Kingdom without going against my conscience.*

He needed to contact Wang Jun as soon as he entered a city. He also needed to find Huxian. Was he okay on his own? What if he'd been captured? He was just a baby, and the decisions he made were impulsive and conceited.

Going back to his previous mental exercise, he remembered his choice to recover. It wasn't truly a choice—he knew that if he died, Huxian would as well. Besides, there was no reason for him not to try recovering. After that, helping Dr. Li was just a matter of course. He wasn't so selfish as to turn the man down after all the help he'd received.

Later, he had helped the thief Lei Dong. It was a foolish but necessary decision on his part. That wasn't to say that he would do it again—he wouldn't. But the him before didn't understand his current reasoning. The subsequent invasion and his enslavement forced him to harden his resolve to resist crumbling under the pressure. He had to. For the villagers' sake. For Huxian's sake.

Now he waited for the bandit leader to come, to eliminate the last threat to the village's safety. The documents in Wei Chen's bag of holding held a dossier on Xiao Heilong's mannerisms, deeds, and strength. Given the man's temperament, he should have come for Cha Ming by now.

Cha Ming sighed once more. *What is my goal in life? What is the reason I cultivate? Will I keep floating around in life without choosing anything like in my last life?* He had many short-term goals: finding Huxian, saving the Song Kingdom, protecting the villagers, getting Li Yin a medical license, and finally, fulfilling his favor to Wang Jun. The more he thought about it, the more depressed he became. All these goals revolved around others and not around himself.

Dejected, Cha Ming walked around the camp and observed the villagers who were busy rebuilding the village. He looked at the children who happily helped their parents. He saw groups of women preparing food and anything else the village required. Watching their smiles cheered him up somewhat.

"Something seems to be bothering you again, boy," said an older man behind him. Cha Ming looked back and saw Li Yin, who was walking toward the hospital with his portable medical kit.

Cha Ming joined him. "I'm just wondering about life and life goals. I'm not sure about my reason for existing. I just feel like I'm going with the flow, getting dragged along by a sea of fate. I never seem to have a choice in anything that happens."

"Oh?" Li Yin said, raising an eyebrow. "For a man so good at attracting trouble like yourself, I find this very unlikely. What particular event is bothering you?"

Cha Ming sighed and told the story of his current life and his perspective on it. It took him took until supper to finish the telling.

"I honestly don't see your problem," the older man said between mouthfuls of food. "It seems to me that you're leading an exciting and fulfilling life. You've made plenty of decisions, plenty of choices. But maybe it's easier to see it from the outside. Let me give you an example. In my life, I've become a doctor despite being crippled. I saved a man despite knowing it was a trap. I continued my practice despite a ban by the medical association. Do you think I've made many choices in life?"

"Absolutely," Cha Ming replied. "You didn't have to do any of these things, but you did. I admire you greatly."

"But it's rather funny, now that you mention it," Li Yin said. "I really don't feel that I had any choice in the matter. Becoming a doctor and helping people was my dream. I would not be Li Yin if I had made different decisions. Every choice I made didn't feel like a choice. Each one felt natural and unchangeable."

Cha Ming was silent for a moment. *If he had not made those choices, he would not be Li Yin,* he thought. Was he misunderstanding the nature of choice?

"You need to change your perspective, Cha Ming," Li Yin continued. "You need to realize that all this time, you *have* been making choices. For example, you could have chosen not to cultivate. For the you right now, it doesn't make much sense as a decision, but many people appreciate a peaceful and normal life. The decision made you who you are. It seems like you didn't have a choice, but I assure you that if you had made the other choice, you would feel the same way. But you wouldn't have been Cha Ming.

"The same applies to your decision to fight devils in Fairweather, the decision to save your fox friend, the decision to save the bandit, and finally, your decision to return to the village when you could have easily left it. Instead, you came back to save us.

"You seem to be upset because of a lack of choice that could go either way. Well, I hate to break it to you, but such choices don't exist. The makeup of a person will make them tend to choose certain things. It takes a person without morals or values to decide everything at the toss of a coin. Since you have morals and values, things aren't so simple. You weigh everything, and the math isn't exact. You make choices that only seem predetermined.

"Give up on the idea of having a life goal if you don't have one already. Let nature take its course. Settle for small-scale goals. Do whatever you feel you should in the moment. Who cares if you don't have substantial ambitions and run around helping everyone for the rest of your life? That's what *I've* done all my life. All my decisions were made not because I selfishly wanted to become a doctor. Rather, I did these things to help people in the way I knew best. And I have no regrets in my life. None."

Cha Ming spent the rest of the night watching the flickering flames where the villagers were gathered. It was true. He didn't need a long-term goal. He had five smaller goals, and his actions in the near term would be decided by them. To contribute to the Song Kingdom, he would need to contact Wang Jun. To do this, he would need to go to a city. And to succeed in anything else, whether it be Wang Jun's favor or protecting the Song Kingdom, he would need power and wealth. Therefore, he would need to pursue the next level in his craft. Pieces were moving, and that was good enough.

He slowly realized that this was, in fact, another form of

momentum. It wasn't that he was being dragged along by the river of fate, but rather, his goals were causing him to willfully move forward with purpose. It was all a matter of perspective. Each poetic talisman he made was also a matter of perspective. The Resistance Talisman could either slow down his opponent or stabilize his body for defense. The Momentum Talisman could either make it difficult for his opponents to control their movements or grant his staff arts unprecedented strength.

Even the Crumbling Talisman could either be used to break his opponent's defenses or to crumble his inhibitions. The Hardening Talisman could be used to bolster his defense and courage or to solidify his opponent's perspective and make their movements rigid. It was all a matter of perspective.

That was what made emotions so frightening. He could either ride them to great heights or let them break his will and shatter his resolve.

He aimed to do the former.

Chapter 4: Cash Cow

*T*ick. Tick. Tick.

Wang Jun's face was haggard and pale. He was tired past the point of exhaustion, trying to salvage his disadvantaged position. His family had given him an impossible task, one which he had no choice but to complete. His alternative was to give up his bid for the family's leadership, something his brother would relish greatly.

Brother... Wang Jun clenched his fists as he thought of that despicable excuse for a human being. Originally, he'd had no intent on competing with him. And neither did his sister, despite being much more talented than he was. Yet his cruel brother had felt the need to nip the threat she posed in the bud. That had changed everything. Unfortunately, Wang Jun had started too late. He did not yet have the power to contend with his elder brother. Only by risking his wealth and health could he make up for the deficiency.

This assignment was clear evidence of his lack of support in the family. The mission had originated from the council of elders and had been approved by the current patriarch, then ultimately reviewed by the grand elder. Those same people had said nothing about his sister's murder.

If they condone such cruel competition, then he isn't fit to oversee the family, Wang Jun thought. *My brother, the patriarch, and the grand elder... they must all be purged.*

Elder Bai entered the study at the hour he always did. However, he paused just after entering, giving time for Wang Jun to adjust his mental state. Wang Jun waved him in.

"Young Master," Elder Bai said, "are you sure you don't want me to come back later?" The fatigue on the old man's wrinkled face was evident.

"No need," Wang Jun said wearily. "What's our current status?"

"Our total profit to date is six hundred thousand," Elder Bai said. "However, our total liquid assets continue to dwindle. We have less than a quarter of this amount to invest due to our forceful acquisition of seventy-five percent of the weaponsmithing assets and half the mining capacity in the Song Kingdom.

"Even though we have some influence in the alchemical market, the nationalism in the Song Kingdom is apparent in their purchasing decisions. Therefore, we aren't making sufficient headway in this market. The crown prince and the Zhou family use their market share in alchemy as a continuous supply of working capital. The competition becomes stiffer with each passing day."

"What about the real-estate market?" Wang Jun asked.

"We've made no ground in real estate. The prices are currently over-inflated. That, and the third prince's influence is extremely shaky. If anything should happen to the king before the deadline, we will be forced to take heavy losses when pulling out of the market. I suggest we wait."

Wang Jun massaged his brow. The only thing that could save him now was war. In fact, most of the decisions he made counted on an inevitable conflict. The king's sickness was far too coincidental, and his condition would undoubtedly worsen in the near future.

"Continue as before," Wang Jun said with a sigh. "Continue purchasing our competitors' weapons and spirit medicine through intermediaries in as much discounted bulk as you can manage. Right now they are trying to starve out our businesses. They are willing to off-load their stored products on the market at a low price to choke us out.

"However, they do not yet know that this is a mistake. We will punish their shortsighted behavior. Meanwhile, we must focus on producing premium spirit weapons and magic weapons from our unique alloy blends and sell them at a premium to non-affiliated countries. We must ensure that we have a stock of high-quality weapons for immediate sale when the time comes."

"Isn't tying up so much working capital wasteful?" Elder Bai asked hesitantly.

"It *seems* wasteful," Wang Jun said. "However, my strategy is far-reaching. It is a high-risk but high-reward strategy. If things unfold like I believe they will, then we will have the advantage. We will have hope." He looked at Elder Bai. "Continue doing this, and I will ask the crown prince for yet another large loan."

"How much this time?" Elder Bai asked.

"One hundred thousand," Wang Jun replied. "However, we won't spend this capital. We will need it in the future, but we must borrow it now. Even if the interest costs us greatly, we *must* have this money available. There will soon come a time when it will be impossible to borrow, and cash will be king. This will be our turning point.

"Besides, there are people in the shadows who are preventing us from achieving our full potential. The rising nationalism interfering with the alchemical business, the pressure on our prices for exports, the difficulties in securing import partners. The king's poisoning. I believe a third party is meddling."

"You mean..." Elder Bai started.

Wang Jun nodded in response. The elder sighed but proceeded to pour tea for two. He then presented a second dossier. Wang Jun looked at him quizzically as he picked up the document. "You've been so stressed lately," Elder Bai said. "I kept the good news for last."

"Oh?" Wang Jun said while opening the package. It was a thick report, but he read through it with practiced ease. His eyes gleamed as he read. "Interesting. Such a cash cow truly exists in this small kingdom? Ah, but it is in the middle of demon-beast territory. The Silverwing Mountain Range is no pushover. I dare say that even the royal army would have trouble facilitating such a mining expedition."

"The difficulty is what presents the opportunity, Young Master," the older man said.

Wang Jun nodded. "What are the terms to purchase the information?"

"Instead of antagonizing one party or another, the seller of the information has offered it for fifty thousand high-grade spirit stones," Elder Bai said. "More than one party can purchase the information, which the seller has guaranteed by death vow and through verification with a high inquisitor. He swears it is enough for applying for a mining permit. However, we must move quickly. If we don't apply for the permit soon, the crown prince's group will automatically gain the rights to this lucrative find."

"Elder Bai, please purchase the information on credit using this seal," he said, tossing him a green jade slip. "In the meantime, I'll go to the third prince's residence to secure funding. No doubt he'll want a cut of the mine as well, but I can live with that. This mine is sufficient to solve at least half of our problems, assuming the information is correct."

Huxian yawned as he lounged in the sun on his mountain peak. He was bored. A few months prior, he had seen a glimpse of the beast called Silverwing for the first time. The beasts on the mountain said it was a regular occurrence. Every three lunar cycles, the large bird would fly from its mountain to feed. He was determined to catch it.

Like Huxian, no one had seen the bird's true form. At most, they had caught a silver gleam as its shadow rapidly flitted across the sun. It was a majestic sight. It made Huxian fearful but expectant. He smelled an opportunity.

A full boring day passed before Huxian began doubting the accuracy of the bird's schedule. As he waited, he wondered about Cha Ming and how he was doing.

I can't wait to show him how much I've grown, Huxian thought. *He's going to be very impressed. Though I hope he finds me before I become the monarch of the entire mountain range.*

It was noon again, and the sun had reached its zenith. Its rays rained down on the parched mountaintop, roasting away at any who dared stay exposed. Even Huxian, a mid-purification Godbeast, felt the urge to take shelter from the sun's rays.

This was exactly why he didn't. The timing was far too coincidental, so he figured Silverwing had waited for this very moment to make his exit, away from the watchful eyes of the beasts that hid away from the blistering sun.

As expected, a sharp cry cut through the air like a sword through silk fabric. It made Huxian's blood boil, something only possible with a higher-level demon beast. Not long after, a silvery glint flew from the nearest mountain and headed skyward before flying toward the next mountain over. A large gust of wind swept up the dust beside the small fox, cleaning the mountaintop in a single pass.

Huxian's interest was piqued. Using his superior movement speed, he dashed off toward the flying demon he could barely see. He was nowhere near as fast as it was and could only catch up because the bird was hovering around the mountain looking for prey. If he wanted to see it, he would either need to bait it or go visit it on its own mountain.

Huxian enjoyed a challenge, so baiting was the preferred method. He stealthily stalked the various beasts on the neighboring mountain, carefully analyzing each potential prey using his knowledge of such birds. Despite its impressive cries and the massive gusts of wind, his instincts told him that the bird was rather small. Therefore, he narrowed his search to demon beasts no larger than a small spirit wolf or spirit hog.

The mountain's construction was peculiar, with one side ending in a sharp cliff that prevented its inhabitants from taking shelter. The only suitable prey was roaming on the second quartile from the bottom of the mountain. While the lowest quartile met the size requirements, these beasts were much too weak to provide suitable nourishment for the powerful avian creature.

Huxian lurked near a pack of spirit hogs. Plump, small, and powerful, they were the most likely targets. The skies showed no indication of the avian demon. The sky was its servant, shielding its sovereign from the fox's prying eyes.

Suddenly he felt turbulence in the wind that caused his hairs to stand on end. A sharp sensation of crisis forced him to dodge into a nearby shadow, just in time to miss three dozen trees tumbling to the ground after being chopped at their base.

So fast! Huxian thought. *So sharp!*

He panicked. Never in a million years would he have thought that the prey the bird would choose was none other than himself. He looked to the ground, where a small silver feather had dropped. It was only six inches long. He smelled the feather, smelled the *presence* of the feather, which enabled him to instantly lock on to the bird in the skies. He couldn't see it, but he could now sense its presence enough to track it.

A loud cry pierced the skies as the bird dove down once more. This time, Huxian was ready. The black and white markings on his fur blended with his surroundings, forming a fifty-foot bagua around him. As the bird descended, Huxian feigned being paralyzed with fear. The surrounding winds slashed at his black and white fur. He held strong as his hunter swooped in for the kill.

It arrived in the blink of an eye. Then it stopped. The formation took effect, granting him a precious three breaths to do whatever he wanted. But he didn't pounce on the sovereign mountain beast. Instead he carefully observed it. The bird's wings spanned only twenty feet in width, making it impressively tiny for a peak-purification demon beast. Its brown body was highlighted with a slim row of silver feathers, the very same feathers that reflected the sunlight as it flew.

The feathers were *sharp*. Huxian sensed that even coming into light contact with them at the edge of its wings would split his tough skin open like paper. The feathers triggered a distant memory. He remembered an absurdly large bird that could fly ten thousand li in a single breath. Its massive silver wings could split mountains and cut apart seas. It was a Godbeast, the original Silver-Winged Roc.

The falcon, which was still frozen in midair, possessed a trace of its imperial bloodline. In this single breath that passed, Huxian firmly decided that he must possess it. The bird would become his general of wind.

But it's so powerful, he thought, sighing. *I can't forcibly convert him into a general like I did Lei Jiang. I need to deceive him to recruit him into my service. But how do I defuse this awkward situation?*

Another breath passed while he deliberated. Huxian decided to take a gamble. He swiftly grew to his original forty-foot-long size and pounced on the helpless bird. His attack broke the eight trigrams that bound it, and the bird's eyes widened in surprise.

Both figures tumbled as Huxian's claws gripped the falcon's small body, his teeth attempting to draw blood through feathers hard as steel. The falcon's talons repeatedly scratched his tough fur, but they weren't nearly as sharp as its wings, which were thoroughly restrained by Huxian's wrestling. It attempted to flee but was repeatedly pulled back into the fox's embrace.

"I surrender!" the falcon suddenly shouted.

Huxian, bewildered by the sudden reversal, swiftly freed the tiny bird. The both stood apart, viciously glaring at each other and projecting the strength of their bloodlines. They were equally matched. Huxian's bloodline was originally much purer than the falcon's, but the small winged beast was a peak-purification demon beast. Each step in the purification realm greatly condensed the strength of one's bloodline.

Seeing that their posturing was having no effect, both Huxian and the falcon suppressed their auras in tacit agreement. Huxian looked at the feathered beast curiously. A hint of frustration surfaced in the falcon's eyes.

"How dare you shrink your form," the falcon suddenly shouted. "Have you no shame?"

Huxian furrowed his brow in confusion, but the falcon continued berating him.

"It's so difficult to find sufficiently small high-level prey; how could I possibly resist attacking you? If you had taken on your original form, I would have completely avoided you. What? Speechless?"

Huxian was indeed speechless, but before he could reply, the falcon's tirade continued. "Not just that, but don't you appreciate your massive form? Did you shrink yourself just to mock me and my tiny stature? How dare you mock this sovereign!"

Black lines started to form on Huxian's forehead. "I wasn't mocking your stature. I just feel more comfortable in my reduced form," he said with a sigh.

The falcon's initially fierce expression suddenly transformed to one of excitement. "So, you agree that a small form is the best form too? How fascinating. Most of the brutes out there like to show off their massive build. That insufferable bear on the neighboring peak liked to flaunt his hundred-foot stature all the time. But he was unaware that I am proud of my small form. Smallest is most comfortable. Smallest beast is best beast."

Huxian shrugged helplessly. How could this bird possibly know that he was only a baby? He liked his smaller form because of his precious memories, the memories of Cha Ming holding and petting him. "Yes, this is truly the case," Huxian said in a calculated manner. "Smallest beast is best beast." To accentuate this point, he shrunk his size all the way down to the appearance of a month-old fox.

"So adorable!" the bird said. "I'm jealous. Here, look at *my* smallest form." The bird rapidly shrunk until its wingspan was only two feet wide. It was much smaller than before, but not as small as Huxian. "Aren't I cute? Aren't I handsome?" The bird adopted several poses to make itself look regal.

Huxian no longer knew how to reply, so he only shook his head and walked away.

"Wait, wait," the falcon yelled, flapping over. "Where do you live? Can I come see?"

Huxian shrugged. "Suit yourself. I live right next door, and I'm heading back now."

The bird nodded and began flying softly overhead. His words were mentally projected to the fox as he walked. "How impressive to be so strong at mid purification. It's too bad I have such a diluted bloodline, or I'd be much stronger than you are." The pride the falcon felt for his heritage was very apparent.

"Do your inherited memories not contain a blood-purification technique?" Huxian asked curiously. This was standard issue in any Godbeast's inheritance.

"Inherited memories?" the falcon said, blinking. "What are those? Are they tasty?"

The falcon's queries overwhelmed Huxian with two emotions. He was shocked and confused. It appeared that the beast's bloodline was not sufficiently dense for it to awaken the inherited memories hidden in its blood. This was both a tragedy and an opportunity for Huxian. After all, due to the bagua fox's general system, he had a vast multitude of suitable techniques to pass on to whomever he pleased. Perhaps he could convince the bird to become his general in exchange for the techniques.

The second emotion was appreciation. The falcon had a similar liking for tasty things.

"Yes," he said cheerfully. "They are very tasty."

As they walked back toward the peak of Huxian's mountain, they began exchanging names of delicious things and the ways to obtain them. For gourmets like them, this was the highest pursuit of a beast's life. There was no such thing as too much tasty talk.

Chapter 5: Departure

Two months passed uneventfully. The swift vengeance Cha Ming had expected from Xiao Heilong never came, and he began to grow nervous. During his idle time, he helped the village with its construction. When it seemed like houses wouldn't be built in time for the winter, he accompanied the mayor and a few others on a mission to recruit additional carpenters. He also bought food, clothing, and other provisions, enough to last them a year if need be.

After the first snow fell, Cha Ming knew that it was time to go. He had no way of helping the villagers further, and no way of increasing his strength if he stayed in this remote location. It would be better to go to a major city, both to find ways to surpass his limits and to find information on Xiao Heilong's whereabouts.

The next day, Cha Ming stood at the edge of the village. He wished goodbye to the many people he had befriended, hurt, and helped during his extended stay. Although he would miss the village's calm atmosphere and Li Yin's wise words, there were many things he needed to do.

"Are you sure you don't want to stay a little while longer?" Li Yin asked him. The fatigue that had accumulated over the years had finally faded from his aging face. He was no longer overburdened with injured and malnourished villagers.

"It's time for me to go, teacher," Cha Ming said. "I know there is a place for me in this village, but there's so much more that I can do outside. If I stay any longer, it will be to the detriment of my friends."

He didn't tell the whole truth about Xiao Heilong. It was best if he quietly found the man and defeated him without their knowledge.

Though sad, he found he was excited at the prospect of seeing and experiencing new things. Momentum was like that. Now that he had started moving, he didn't want to stop, lest resistance grasp him with its sharp claws.

Li Yin nodded. "It's good that you know this, and that you know your direction. You've grown up, Cha Ming. Before, you were in a pit of despair and self-blame. Now you've learned to take responsibility for your actions, and you know what it is you *should* do." Li Yin's eyes turned red as he began tearing up. He hugged Cha Ming tightly and whispered to him, "Take care of yourself out there. It can be a cruel world, but never give up hope."

Cha Ming couldn't help but shed a tear as well. He looked at all the villagers that had gathered, all the children who were sad to see him leave. He had treated half of them in his time as Li Yin's apprentice. He still felt a lot of guilt over the pains they had suffered these past years, but they seemed to have forgiven him. Over half the village had shown up to wish him safe travels.

After saying a few more goodbyes, he turned around and walked through the well-worn path that now led to and from the village. The path was both familiar and unfamiliar. It was lightly covered in snow, but he could see firmly pressed stones beneath the light dusting. It was the same path he had led Lei Dong through, the same path the bandits had taken on their way to the village. Yet as he walked through the woods, he passed three wagons and four horses. Such traffic would have been unimaginable only three years prior.

After leaving the woods, Cha Ming let out a deep sigh and summoned a flying sword, which he used to fly over the river to the next village on his way to the nearest city.

A few days later, Cha Ming was already halfway to Quicksilver City. He rested in inns as he traveled and ate meals at dozens of villages, enjoying himself immensely. After all, he had spent three years cooped up a small town and a mine. He yearned for discovery and variety.

He ate today's meal at a quaint inn, whose walls were built with a peculiar but fragrant wood. It also sported a large bar, which was currently occupied by a very large man.

"It's the twentieth time this week, I tell you," the burly man said softly. If Cha Ming didn't have incandescent force, he would have struggled to hear it. "Merchants don't want to come down here any longer. Whenever the Imperial Army makes the rounds to clear them out, they end up settling everything with just a few words." The bartender shrugged to avoid the conversation, but the man continued regardless. "This thieving can't go on. Otherwise, how will I continue my trade? I may as well pack up and leave!"

"Why *do* you stay around here, anyway?" the bartender said. "A spiritual blacksmith such as yourself doesn't need to live so far away from Quicksilver. Besides, the thieving isn't so bad. No one dies in these exchanges. It's just simple robberies, that's all. And they don't even take everything. They wouldn't even touch your iron."

"But I can't ship my weapons off to other villages," the blacksmith complained. "And what do you mean spiritual blacksmith? I'm just a failure, a second-grade spiritual blacksmith. I'm not worth anything near the capital, so I have no choice but to stay out here to scrape out a living."

The man took a long pull from his mug of ale. "Back to thievery, though. It's not enough that people don't die during the robberies. The merchants are never the same after they get robbed. It's like they lose their will to live. They return to the city, and their businesses go under. Most of them hang themselves afterward. No one wants to make the trip anymore because they fear for their very souls."

The bartender scrunched his brows but didn't reply.

Cha Ming, who had heard everything, sat down at the bar beside the man. He slapped twenty spirit stones on the counter. "Please buy this friend a drink," Cha Ming said.

Seeing the glittering stones, the bartender nodded and placed a pot of wine on the bar. "For yourself?" he asked.

"I don't drink wine," Cha Ming replied. "Tea will do. The best you have." He then turned to the blacksmith. The man looked confused. "No need to be alarmed, friend. I heard the conversation you were having just now, and I've encountered something similar in a faraway place. There was once a village where individuals bewitched soldiers. Have you heard descriptions of the thieves?"

The man hesitated, then nodded.

"Could you please describe them in detail?"

He nodded once more. After taking a swift drink, he spoke in a hushed voice. "It's no secret, and nothing I haven't told half the village," the blacksmith said. "There was once a merchant who was robbed, but instead of heading back, he came to this village. His face was pale. His hands shaking. It was as though he'd seen a ghost. So I asked him, 'What happened to make you look pale as a sheet?' To which he replied, 'I saw the devil. At the bridge crossing Salmon Creek. She was a bewitching beauty, her hair long and black as night, her skin pale as white jade. And her eyes—when I looked into her eyes, I lost a piece of my soul. Barely enough was left over, as though she fed on the feelings of despair that shook me.'

"Then he went on to describe the bandits. They were all women, and they only stole precious metals and spirit stones. The rest they left in the wagon, all packed up and pretty. The merchant and his guards didn't stand a chance. As they rode off, he was left with the great urge to return home and liquidate his assets, then send them to an account in the city. He was overwhelmed, so he stopped in the village for a drink.

"The man stayed for a few days, after which he hung himself in despair," the blacksmith finished.

Cha Ming frowned as he assembled the pieces of the puzzle. He had never encountered a creature that could devour souls, but he had fought some that could bewitch them. Then again, he'd only fought against devil cultivators below foundation establishment. Did their abilities change at higher levels?

He also remembered the gold-gathering formation in Fairweather. Stealing precious metals and spirit stones was something a creature like the Merchant would do. That being the case, it was highly possible that two devils were acting together.

"Do you know anything about the Imperial Army patrol that went out?" Cha Ming asked. "Like the strength of their leader?"

"I'm not sure about that," the blacksmith replied, "but I know that most patrols are headed by someone between initial and middle-foundation establishment. It's the requirement to become a captain in the Quicksilver Empire."

Cha Ming recalled the guard captain in the small village and his impressive cultivation. It seemed that he'd only been a frog in the well. From the maps that he'd seen, the Quicksilver Empire was several times the size of the tiny Song Kingdom. In addition, it was much wealthier. It made sense that the qualifications to be considered powerful here were much higher than his home kingdom.

"Many thanks," Cha Ming said. He drank his tea in a single gulp. He then walked out of the bar and took off on his flying sword toward the east. He didn't want to rush into their dwelling on the mountains, as that would be very dangerous. Instead, he opted for the safer approach.

And for that, he needed bait.

A merchant's wagon was racing swiftly toward the west, its horses sweating from exhaustion. They could sense the driver's fear as he whipped them, trying to speed them across the dangerous stretch of road. His friend, a spice merchant, had been accosted near that damnable bridge. Word had spread quickly, and the steady flow of merchants to the eastern parts of the dynasty had dried up.

In other words, demand had peaked while supply remained desperately low. Liu Hao sensed an opportunity, and a merchant so poor as himself couldn't turn down such a potential windfall. He figured he was smarter than the rest of them. He had bought the swiftest horses available and picked up several mercenaries before leaving. Heck, he'd picked up an extra one in the town just before the bridge to be sure.

The special enchanted cloth covering the wagon could resist fire and arrows. The wagon contained chests of holding to maximize its carrying capacity. He brought with him both expensive goods and bulk goods in large quantities. Even simple commodities had sky-high prices due to the decrease in shipments. Liu Hao figured he could earn three times his initial investment on this trip. He would also get to keep the horses, the carriages, and the chests to boot.

Suddenly his horses neighed. The wagon slowed to a crawl. Panicking, he whipped the horses bloody to get them moving, but they refused to budge. They stood there placidly like they were enjoying a good brushing. He had never seen anything so strange in his life.

In the distance, a dozen people approached from the side on horses.

"Dammit," he cursed softly. "You better all be ready to defend the wagon. If you don't, I'll report you to the mercenary association."

The men in the wagon shifted uncomfortably. Ultimately, they drew their weapons. Failing to accomplish a mission had dire repercussions in their line of work, where reputation was everything.

The opposing horses stopped fifty feet away. The merchant looked at their leader nervously; he had heard far too many rumors about what happened to the people they caught. The common consensus was that anyone who met them would go mad. Still, as he looked at her, he realized that things couldn't be further from the truth. A fair-skinned lady such as herself must be in dire straits to resort to a robbery. Perhaps it would be best to just give her his wares and be done with it. He could recoup his losses on the bulk goods he brought. Yes, that would be best.

As he continued looking, her charming blue eyes, deep like endless oceans, met his. He wished for nothing more than to lose himself in them, so he let himself go. He let himself float in the ocean in his dreams, only to realize that it wasn't such a calm ocean as he had imagined. Rather, it was an ocean filled with sharks and other dangerous creatures.

He felt a sharp stab of pain as something bit his foot off. A hideous aquatic creature surfaced and shot him a toothy grin as it munched on his flesh. Unsatisfied, it bit off his other leg and followed up with his arm. He could barely stand the pain. Unfortunately, he didn't faint. It was as though his only path of retreat—losing consciousness—had been cut off. He could only look on in despair as he was eaten alive.

Suddenly he felt a stirring in the ocean. The aquatic creature roared as it abandoned its attempt to devour him and plunged back into the waters. Relieved, he continued floating until he finally drifted off to sleep.

Chapter 6: Eyes of Pure Jade

Cha Ming was surrounded by an endless ocean. He floated there, seemingly helpless. He knew what lurked beneath the sea. The tentacled monstrosity's maw was wide open and ready to tear into his incandescent soul. That is, if it could get its tentacles on him in the first place.

This was a dream. To be more precise, it was a forced mental projection, a hybrid of his mind and another. The skies were white, unnaturally so. He wasn't worried, however. The white sky was his domain, and it shone much brighter than the ocean below. He harnessed the power of the sky and sunk down into the ocean, breathing it in as he would air. The pupils of the large creature below dilated as it saw his fearless approach. It struck at him with its large tentacles.

He could tell instinctively that these two worlds were a representation of their souls. His soul was much stronger. He imagined his surroundings covered in a black mist, and it was so. The water around him evaporated to nothing as it contacted the barrier of pure destruction that surrounded him. As the tentacles whipped toward him, they too were burned and disintegrated after striking the impenetrable shield.

The creature below roared in anger. He smirked at the evil monster, summoning the Clear Sky Brush and hefting it with two hands like a spear. He focused the power of his soul into it, elongating it forward a full mile and piercing the ocean-dwelling creature in the eye. It let out an aggrieved howl before the reality around him shimmered, then collapsed into nothingness.

Cha Ming woke to a woman's scream. He looked around himself calmly, only to see that the mercenaries in the wagon had all fainted. This was normal, of course. They were foolish in thinking that their cultivations, which were only at the peak of qi condensation, could allow them to withstand these "thieves."

As he walked out, he saw several women huddled around their beautiful leader, who had fallen from her horse. She glared at Cha Ming venomously, her right eye bleeding profusely. This development was intriguing to Cha Ming. After all, he hadn't expected the results of their mental battle to transfer so well to the physical world.

Seeing his nonchalant expression, she stood up and glared at him. "Surely there is a misunderstanding," she said in a high-pitched voice like that of a songbird. He swooned slightly when he heard it. "If sir would take the time to discuss, I'm sure we can come to an agreement."

His blood raced as he heard her voice. His heartbeat quickened. The thought of doing anything possible to please her flirted with his mind.

"No," Cha Ming said, thoroughly suppressing his urges. "I don't believe this is a misunderstanding. I know who I came to find." Then he materialized his Clear Sky Staff and pounced toward them. He headed toward the injured one, who was coincidentally the biggest source of trouble.

"Kill him!" the woman yelled.

As he closed in on her, his movements faltered as his mind was assaulted by ten others simultaneously. They were all top-class beauties, and the movements they made while approaching him with daggers drawn entranced him. Each step was seductive, and even the way they wielded their daggers seemed to have certain unwholesome implications. He almost didn't notice a tomboyish-looking figure that snuck behind him, threatening to tear him apart from behind. Almost.

His staff swung backward, smashing against the tender girl who thought she had caught him unaware. A soft ping sounded as a large amount of recoil shot up his arm. Dodging to the side, he saw that the girl's skin had turned golden, just like the Merchant in Fairweather. Her feet sunk into the soft ground below her.

"Support me!" she yelled. The ten others nodded, focusing their attention on Cha Ming as the girl rushed toward him with fists bared.

He clicked his tongue but didn't fight her head on. Instead, he bashed her with his lengthened staff from the side and used his Soft Staff Art to dive behind her toward his initial target, the mastermind behind the thefts. The beauty's face turned pale as a sheet as a quake staff crashed down and shattered her skull and spine. As soon as he struck her down, however, a searing pain blinded him, causing him to take a blow from behind his head.

The world was a blur. He couldn't see, and he could barely stand. The pain faded quickly, just in time for him to block a kick to his face that surely would have killed him. As he stood up, still dizzy from the trauma to his head, he saw an entirely different world.

All around him, he could only see various shades of gray. Curious, he looked at his own hand. It was covered in a slight shade of green.

An aged voice whispered through the wind. *Can you see what I see with these eyes of pure jade?*

Cha Ming saw ten yellow silhouettes and one shining with a malevolent ochre glow. It was the girl with the golden body.

Is she different from the others in some way aside from her golden body? he wondered. The ten others had similar abilities to the one he had just killed. *No, that isn't true. Their combined assault isn't even a fifth of her initial assault.* It was as though their technique was an empty shell, a piece of glass posing as precious porcelain.

Their pressure was still present, so he resolved to rid himself of it as soon as possible. After exchanging six rapid but jarring blows with the gold-bodied girl, he broke away from the ochre figure and instantly killed one of her bewitching assistants, who had clearly not broken through to foundation establishment or its equivalent.

She paused her assault, so he continued mowing them down one by one. But when he finally turned around to meet her in combat, he was horrified by what he saw. The pretty, tomboyish girl from before was now missing her entire hand. Golden blood oozed from the bones where the hand had been previously. She held the severed appendage as she chewed on its golden finger bones. Her aura climbed at a frightening pace as she devoured the golden flesh.

Cha Ming wasn't so foolish as to let her increase her fighting strength, so he rushed toward her with his staff, attacking her remaining arm with the strongest blows possible. Despite being made of metal, it bent unnaturally with every blow.

At this moment, he wished that he had a reliable fire technique. Fire was the nemesis of gold, so he suspected it would have a pronounced effect against her. Even water would have some effect, since metal fed water. Her resistance to physical blows was astonishing. Only his sword staff and plain physical attacks had much of an effect on her. Barely.

They continued fighting blow for blow, but despite his best efforts, Cha Ming was unable to obtain an advantage in their confrontation. His energy reserves were dwindling, and he had difficulty evaluating his opponent. She clearly didn't have the same limitations as a human. He began panicking, unsure if he could sustain his continuous assault. His clothes were drenched in sweat, his arms burned, and his hands were numb from the continuous recoil of his constant attacks.

The golden creature's speed and strength increased drastically. He smelled burning metal as its arm burnt away to its elbow.

Shit, Cha Ming thought. He quickly pasted one of his trump cards, the Hardening Talisman, to his chest. His skin turned hard and brittle, and his muscles and bones did the same. Just in time for him to receive a kick to the stomach that sent him tumbling backward. If it weren't for the talisman, he would have died from that blow.

Fine, I may as well go all out. Three talismans flew out at once and struck the golden monstrosity simultaneously. Her movements faltered as if unable to overcome her resistance. He could see the struggle in her eyes as she feebly raised her arm to deflect his staff as it bore down on her head.

Her arm barely deflected the strength of his heavy blow before shattering. Her body was now brittle due to the strength of the Crumbling Talisman. She screamed as what was left of her arms burned up to her shoulder, increasing her strength by another level. This time, she didn't attack. She darted off with greatly increased speed, and he was barely able to keep up with both his movement technique and Stormchaser Boots. To his dismay, he saw her inching away. His energy reserves were insufficient to keep chasing her.

Shit, it's now or never, he thought. *If I want to stop her, I need to use it.* He didn't think twice before throwing out the final talisman in his possession, Ode to Mr. Mao Mao. Like the non-poetic talisman from his fight with the bandits, it transformed into the stable phantom of a demon bobcat. This time, it was only a single foot long, just like the original Mr. Mao Mao he had met in Elder Ling's shack. He nearly puked blood after seeing the phantom's appearance.

What the hell? he thought. *You wanted to highlight the might of your feelings for Mr. Mao Mao, and you gave me this? What use is a kitten?*

To his surprise, however, the girl shivered and stopped escaping. A look of incredulity spread across her face as she began shaking and quivering. Cha Ming felt a mounting presence in front of him. He identified with the presence as "cuteness," but unbeknownst to him, the girl was experiencing something entirely different: suppression.

She backed away from the projection fearfully as the cat advanced in a lofty, imperial manner. The small bobcat was an incredibly cute sovereign that looked upon the world with disdain. Seeing his chance, Cha Ming rushed to the petrified golden girl, who now lacked two arms.

As he struck down, the phantom kitten let out a cute "meow" and set himself upon the helpless girl, who screamed as its claws tore through her golden flesh. Golden blood poured out only to be absorbed by the vicious kitten. At the same time, Cha Ming's staff came crashing down on her skull. Golden blood and brain matter sprayed about. That, too, was devoured by Mr. Mao Mao's phantom. It continued to eat away at the golden girl, and once the grisly task was accomplished, it let out a pleased mewl and disappeared. Nothing was left behind.

So this is the power of emotions you wanted to show me, Cha Ming thought. The talisman was significantly stronger than the last. If he hadn't been told they used the same amount of qi and ink, he wouldn't have believed it.

He was also pleased with the power of his four poetic talismans. One had protected him while the other three had rendered her helpless, unable to defend herself. The tough arms that he couldn't affect with his strongest blows easily shattered after she was affected by the Crumbling Talisman.

If only I could make them again, he thought.

Sighing, he sat beside the wagon to meditate as he waited for the mercenaries and the merchant to recover. When they came to, they ran off to the next village at Cha Ming's insistence. He wasn't sure if they had been inflicted with lasting damage, as he knew precious little about matters of the soul. He could only pray for their recovery.

The battle just now had also reminded him that he was still weak. He required better talismans and battle techniques to fight effectively. In addition, his cultivation was far too low. He also resolved to find out more about these monstrosities. If an eye technique from the Devil Sealing Scripture identified these creatures with a malevolent ochre glow, they must surely be devils.

Cha Ming left shortly after they departed. Unbeknownst to him, his eyes had transformed. His irises were now green like the purest jade. And on his irises, two runes had also appeared—one golden and one blue.

Intense pain shot through Huxian's eyes as he trotted through a forested mountain valley. After moments of debilitating pain, he opened his eyes to discover a world tinged in gray. It only lasted for a short moment, but he knew what it was.

Eyes of pure jade, huh? Huxian thought. *It looks like Cha Ming is getting closer and ran into a good bit of fortune. I'll need to find something for him as well.*

Their bond may have had its advantages, but there were a few disadvantages as well. Now he needed to watch out for how much sin he accumulated, otherwise they'd both lose their wonderful eyes. Demon beasts like himself usually didn't have to care about merit and sin. The moral obligations for demons differed greatly from that of humans.

After recovering his eyesight, Huxian carefully observed local fauna. He wanted something small, but it needed to be sufficiently nutritious as well. As he roamed, he emanated the pressure of his bloodline and forced the beings on the mountain to show themselves.

Too small. Too big. Too bony. He looked through the swarm of beasts like he would produce at a grocery store. Finally, his eyes settled on a grouse. It was a tier-two beast, a tier above most of the beasts on the mountain. Further, it was a seventh-grade spirit beast. Most importantly, it was small. Barely two feet in length. Perfect.

He exerted a tiny bit of his bloodline pressure, and the beast instantly committed suicide, leaving not a single trace of fear in its marbled flesh. He picked it up in his mouth and sprinted toward the peak of the neighboring mountain.

This mountain was strange compared to his. The woods ended a full mile from the peak. In addition, a spire jutted from the mountain, forming an obelisklike structure that overlooked the adjacent peaks. If he could choose any of the mountains, he would choose that one without a doubt. The overbearingly tall tower pleased him. Unfortunately, it was taken.

Before long, Huxian arrived at the base of the spire. A sharp screech sounded out from nearby as Silverwing flew out from his cave on the cliffside. His small body landed near Huxian, and he looked at the prey curiously.

"Is this for me?" he asked in beast language.

"I happened to encounter it while I was eating breakfast and thought you would appreciate it," Huxian said with his honeyed tongue. "Besides, I have a larger appetite than a taotie[3], and such a small, cute, delicious grouse would barely fill a small corner in my stomach."

"Quite right," Silvering said, salivating. "Such small delicacies should be reserved for little old me." The falcon immediately devoured the tiny beast. This decisive behavior caused Huxian to roll his eyes.

Like feeding candy to a baby, he thought. *Convincing him to become my general is going to be much easier than expected.*

The falcon finished his appetizer quickly and let out a loud burp that made the mountain tremble. "What are we doing for fun today?" he asked the small fox, who shrugged.

"We explored my mountain last time," Huxian said. "How about we see yours?"

The falcon's feathers ruffled in excitement. The small bird clearly liked showing off. "I have something great to show you, and it only appeared recently," the bird said excitedly. Huxian lazily followed him down to the base of the mountain and into a network of tunnels. As they dove deeper, a multicolored glow appeared. They were soon surrounded by glistening crystals.

"Truly pretty," Huxian commented, "but useless. I sure hope this isn't what you brought me here to see."

---

[3] A taotie is a fiendish Chinese mythical creature, basically gluttony incarnate. It is shown with only a head but often with no lower jaw, which some people have speculated means that it was so hungry that it devoured its own body.

"Of course not!" the falcon said indignantly. "My friend the badger used to live here, but one day he was killed by a human. I never found him, but in the process of looking for him, I found this multicolored stone wall."

They rounded the corner and arrived at a partially excavated wall. A small chunk was missing from it, but otherwise it was a perfectly smooth multicolored mosaic. Further, he recognized the substance. "Isn't this immortal jade?" he wondered aloud. "How can there be such a large amount here?"

The falcon bounced excitedly. "Did I do good? Did I do good?"

"Yes," Huxian said, frowning. "You did good, but I'm worried. This was clearly excavated by a human. Immortal jade means nothing to us, but it is very valuable to them. If they come back, it will cause us endless problems."

"Can't we just kill them as they come?" the falcon questioned.

The fox shook his head. "This is much too valuable. We might be able to defeat them a few times, but you underestimate their need for it. It will only be a matter of time until core-formation cultivators arrive." Then he sighed. "What a headache. I sure hope they don't come for a few more years. Though that's likely wishful thinking on my part."

"What do we do, then?" the falcon asked.

Huxian was pleased with the bird's increasing dependence on him. "We wait," Huxian replied. "We get stronger. While we can't use this immortal jade, it might be useful depending on who comes to claim it. This can either be a calamity or an opportunity. Only time will tell."

A tense silence followed.

"Have I introduced you to my follower, Lei Jiang?" Huxian asked.

"Follower?" the falcon asked, perplexed. "You have a follower?" His eyes bulged out when he saw the small mid-purification mouse appear atop Huxian. "So cute! Can I pet him?"

Huxian rolled his eyes. "How could you pet such a noble spirit beast? Lei Jiang might be my follower, but he's still a fifth-tier variation beast. His talent is even a step above yours. Of course, it's partially because I gave him a technique when he became my follower, but he's pleasant company."

"I'm Lei Jiang. Pleased to meet you!" the little mouse said. "Are you a friend of the boss too?" His glittering eyes would melt the hearts of most women, and his purple fur was equally adorable.

"Yes, of course I'm your boss's friend," the falcon replied. "A good friend, in fact. May I touch you?"

"This…" The mouse hesitated. "You promise you won't eat me, right? I'm a very important member of the boss's team, and he's taught me many things and fed me many precious herbs. He even taught me a technique to increase the purity of my bloodline. Therefore, I don't want to get hurt. I owe him everything."

The falcon's eyes narrowed, and his feathers ruffled in excitement when he heard those words. "Of course not. I wouldn't dare hurt Huxian's follower. But you mentioned bloodline purification?"

"It's boss's secret ability," the mouse said. "He has countless techniques at his disposal. Of course, the best ones are only available for his generals."

"Stop tempting him," Huxian said. "He is my friend. I can share a lesser refinement technique with him. Alas, I can only share the best techniques with my generals, but that is a heavy oath, and I can't make that decision for him."

The little mouse seemed aggrieved at the rebuke but nodded nonetheless. "My apologies, boss. I'll let him pet me to atone." Then he rapidly appeared beside the falcon's talon. The falcon pet the mouse's purple fur slowly. He was clearly deep in thought.

"Where are my manners?" Huxian said. "Since I've offered, I can't take it back. Here is a minor technique for you to use. I can't promise it will help you break through to the next realm, but you can still try."

A small black-and-white sphere came out from Huxian's glabella and floated up to the falcon's beak. The bird of prey chomped down on it and instantly became enlightened.

"How convenient!" Silverwing exclaimed. "And you even gave me a few combat techniques! I don't know how I'll ever repay you."

"No thanks needed," Huxian said. "You're my friend, so I'll naturally do my best to help you. I hope you'll understand that I'm helpless for other matters."

"Of course," Silverwing replied. A pondering expression remained on his face. Huxian observed him intently. The bait had been set, and it was only a matter of time until this proud bird submitted and became his general.

Interlude
Buddhas and Evil Spirits

A golden gleam lit up the sky as a female monk in a kasaya banished yet another spectre. It was the fortieth this month, and the third graveyard she had visited.

"Tell me again why we need to kill these ghosts?" Gong Lan asked, then uttered another mantra. The words flowed from her lips with great ease, combining with the thin light qi in her body. Her cultivation realm was far, far lower than the realm of her soul. However, that didn't matter. Buddhist arts didn't care much for the body or qi, only for the soul. It was a qualitative transformation. Few could match the might of a buddha's soul.

"I would hardly call these ghosts, little girl," the bodhi seed said to her. It appeared as a small projection on her shoulder. "They are evil spirits. Creatures that have accumulated far too much karma in their past life and thus remain bound to this plane. They are the exact opposite of buddhas, they who have shed their physical bodies and have rid themselves of all earthly karma. They linger. For that reason, they are a plague on this world."

"Are all spirits stuck in the mortal realm truly evil?" Gong Lan asked in a soft voice.

"Of course not," the seed replied. "Some especially strong souls stay with the intent to protect. If they have kept true to their vows and have not needlessly meddled in earthly affairs, they will remain pure. We call these holy spirits. Still, they are few and far between.

Holy spirits can be corrupted. You need to consider that it may be worthwhile to banish a spirit that has not committed heinous deeds, because it will prevent them from harming others. We are only sending them back to the circle of reincarnation, after all, not destroying them."

Gong Lan suddenly focused on an oncoming swarm of ghosts up ahead. "Grant me blades of light with the strength to banish these evil spirits and return them to Samsara," she uttered. Her resplendent force combined with the light qi within her and formed two sabers, not unlike those she had wielded in the past. Only, these sabers could not harm the living, only the dead.

She spun around in circles, much like she had in the past, dispatching one evil spirit after another. Each one she cleaved transformed into motes of light that were welcomed back into the Yellow River by the laws of the universe. As she banished them, rage flickered across her otherwise peaceful face. It wasn't uncontrolled rage. Rather, it was calculated rage toward these evil spirits that had tormented the residents nearby, feeding on their fears and sorrows and sometimes driving them to suicide. It was righteous indignation.

These emotions further fueled the power of her blades, increasing their length and width while making them lighter and easier to wield. Before long, one hundred evil spirits had been dispatched.

"You are learning well, child," the bodhi seed said. "It is not wrong to lash out against the evils in the world, to resent them. This resentment will give you strength, but you must be careful. You must keep yourself balanced, or your soul will lose its purity. Much like angels can swiftly become devils, buddhas can also become evil spirits. It is a dangerous path to tread, though sometimes necessary."

"Where to next?" Gong Lan said, seemingly ignoring him. Then, after looking at the tree's indignant expression, she chuckled. "I'm just teasing you. Of course I heard. I'll be sure to keep myself balanced."

The bodhi seed sighed in relief. "We have another hundred and five spirit accumulation points to visit before worrying about anything else. Whoever has been plotting in the Song Kingdom has been at it for over a thousand years. It's hardly feasible to crumble everything they've established in a single night."

Gong Lan sighed. "Very well. Let's keep traveling. The night is still young." With a resplendent soul, she no longer needed sleep and no longer needed sustenance. She could devote her full attention to her goals and never falter. She finally felt like she was making a difference.

I wonder how the others are doing, she thought before walking into the night.

Chapter 7: Quicksilver City

Veritable mountains and seas of people flooded the busy streets of Quicksilver City[4]. As the capital of the Quicksilver Empire, people traveled here to trade from across the continent. At a glance, its reputation as the city of engineering marvels was well deserved. Both the city walls and several buildings inside it were around two hundred feet tall. Running water was available to every building in the city.

Cha Ming had also seen several water wheels, irrigation pipes, and pump wells in small villages outside the city. It seemed the life of common people was much better in this nation compared to the Song Kingdom. It was little wonder that Li Yin's medical innovations had frightened the Spirit Doctor Association to the point of banishing him. They had likely seen shifts in the balance of power with each new emerging technology. Even simple technologies could undermine the utility of lower-tier members of any organization, thus reducing the influx of new members and their total revenue.

One day, your medicine will change the face of this continent, Cha Ming thought as he passed a spirit doctor hospital. The building was opulently decorated. Its ostentatious construction was a clear indicator of overabundant pride. Which was ironic, given that of

---

[4] 人山人海—People Mountain People Sea is a popular saying in China that describes large masses of people as far as the eye can see. It is used every day, but especially when national holidays like Spring Festival flood the streets.

all organizations, the Spirit Doctor Association should have stood for the benefit of the common people. As he directed his senses to the line in front of the building, he confirmed that the only people being treated here were cultivators, despite its location in the poor outskirts in the city, where many mortals lived.

Flight was prohibited within the city. There was also a clear limitation on physical traveling speed inside the city without relying on an approved means of transportation. According to the guard at the entrance, the penalty for breaking this rule was six months of imprisonment. That is, unless one's station was high enough to grant one an exemption from the rules. Over the course of his journey in the city, he saw only two figures traveling on flying swords or flying boats, indicating that such a privilege was indeed rare.

As he walked through the streets, a conspicuous set of tracks caught his attention, tracks that seemed to run all the way down the main street.

Surely they haven't already discovered the power of steam and steam engines? Such technology, especially when used as a common means of transportation, was incongruent with the rest of what he'd seen.

His curiosity was sated once he saw a large set of joined "wagons" skimming along the tracks at a swift pace. For the low fee of five low-grade spirit stones, he boarded the marvelous contraption at one of its many stops. Then, he extended his incandescent force, probing the various pieces of machinery within the vehicle.

To his surprise, there was no engine to drive the locomotive. Instead, a team of ten cultivators were taking turns operating a strange mechanism. It consisted of a set of gearlike contraptions that converted the power of a rotating device to the wheels below. They used only the naturally recovered powers of these metal-aligned cultivators.

The device spun, and the train carried thousands of people from the edge of the city to the center at a speed of fifty li per hour. Considering the many stops it made, it only took an hour for Cha Ming to reach the center of the city.

Central Square was a marvel to behold. The buildings were all at least four stories tall to accommodate the sky-high real-estate prices. To his surprise, only a few supporting pillars were engraved with runes. The remainder of the structures, while likely assembled by a geomancer, were all self-supporting, showing that the understanding of physics and construction in the Quicksilver Empire had reached an extremely high level. The building was a prime example of how cooperation between mortals and cultivators could allow society to flourish and propel itself to new heights.

"Step right up, step right up," a peddler said. "New from the revered alchemist's workshop, a pill that has a ten-percent chance of imbuing an untalented youth with first-grade talent. One child below ten years old can attempt to digest this pill up to three times, effectively giving your child a twenty-seven out of a hundred chance of developing cultivation talent. This is a large increase compared to version seven, which only granted an eight-percent chance.

"Come up now and purchase this life-changing pill! The revered alchemist wants nothing more than to see civilization flourish. The introductory price will be three gold per pill as version seven is eased out of production. Soon, version eight will be available for the low price of ninety silvers, once it reaches mass production. This amount barely covers the raw materials and the wages of the low-grade alchemists in the workshop.

"As if that weren't enough, this pill is still able to give a three-percent chance for anyone above ten years of age to develop cultivation talent. While it is very unlikely for you to break through to foundation establishment, think of your children! Everyone knows that cultivators have a higher chance of giving birth to children who cultivate. What we are doing now is setting up a firm foundation for their future. So think not only for yourself, but for your children and the empire. Come purchase this limited stock now while it's still available. Only ten thousand doses are available in this introductory batch!"

A crowd of well-dressed mortals instantly flooded the stall, which sold out in a hurry. Through his enhanced senses, he could hear that even though more gold was offered to cut the line or for purchasing in bulk, none of which was tolerated. Only those who lined up properly were given a pill at the cost announced. And only three pills were allowed per person.

Such a sight left Cha Ming astonished. What he had seen in other cities prior had not reassured him about the morality of the cultivation world. It was a relieving eye-opener to see such philanthropic deeds. Developing cultivation talent in even the lowest citizens of the empire would bring unprecedented prosperity to the entire city. It was like full child literacy. By increasing the education in the bottom rungs of society, the quality of the labor would be increased. As such, many prohibitively expensive projects would become reasonably priced. He longed to see the result of this social experiment.

Soon, the shock of the massive city wore away, and Cha Ming made his way toward one of the central buildings in the city: the Jade Bamboo Auction House. Like the one in Green Leaf City, it was of plain construction, adorned with nothing more than a green bamboo garden at the entrance. He noticed many guests entering and exiting, most of them higher-level cultivators. Foundation-establishment cultivators were not uncommon. Even the greeters at the entrance, who were effectively guards dressed in pleasant clothing, were initial-foundation-establishment experts. If even guards had this level of power, it was little wonder that this was also the minimum cultivation requirement for a captain in the army.

As he approached, the guards bowed with pleasant smiles on their faces, allowing him inside. While his strength was higher than theirs, it still wasn't enough for him to obtain preferential treatment. He walked in nonchalantly and lined up behind four others at a service desk reserved for foundation-establishment cultivators.

Time trickled by, and soon he was greeted by a beautiful lady with blonde hair, a very unusual color in the continent. It reminded Cha Ming of Wang Jun, who also had blond hair, albeit with some white streaks due to the time he helped out Huxian.

"How can I, Wang Bing, help you today?" she asked with a pleasant smile.

As I suspected, Cha Ming thought. *She really is from the Wang family.* "I would like to send a message to the Song Kingdom. The recipient is named Wang Jun. Could you help me with that?" He placed a jade slip on the desk, having learned what to do from his prior experience.

As she picked up the plate and scanned it, an awkward look flashed across her eyes. It was only for a moment, then her expression reverted to normal. "Please allow me to go to my manager to discuss."

She returned shortly with a middle-aged man who also had blond hair. But instead of greeting Cha Ming, he rudely used the strength of his soul to scan him. Cha Ming's incandescent force was helpless against this man's soul.

Is he a core-formation cultivator?

Then, the man picked up the jade slip and handed it back to Cha Ming while smiling. "I'm afraid this contract is not valid here. It is only valid within the Song Kingdom."

Cha Ming frowned after hearing this, as the terms of the contract stipulated that it was valid everywhere on the continent.

"I see," Cha Ming said. "Can I trouble you to send a message to Young Master Wang Jun? Surely that is something that the Jade Bamboo Conglomerate can accomplish."

"Of course," the man said with a grin on his face. "Sending a message to a high-ranking member of our clan is absolutely free and will be completed within the hour. However, please remember that his form of address is *Second* Young Master, and referring to him otherwise is disrespectful to his superiors."

Looking at the man's twitchy smile, Cha Ming finally realized what the problem was. There was in-fighting within the Wang family. This was likely the reason that Wang Jun had ended up in Green Leaf City to begin with.

"What is your message?" the man asked, still pleasant as before.

"Please inform him that I will be residing in Quicksilver City for a short while and that I would like to ask him how he is doing," Cha

Ming instructed. "Also, please ask him if he has heard any news of Huxian."

The man nodded. "Should I leave a name or perhaps some other details that he should be aware of? It seems like precious little to go on."

"I'm confident he will understand," Cha Ming replied. After confirming the contents, the man issued him a receipt, which Cha Ming verified in detail.

"You marked down the wrong date," Cha Ming said after looking at the paper. "It's dated three days from now."

"Is it?" the man replied. "My apologies, I was just negotiating a large contract due on that date. Please let me rewrite it."

This time, the receipt was correct. Cha Ming walked off without saying anything more.

The blonde-haired beauty, Wang Bing, walked swiftly beside the middle-aged man as they proceeded to the message terminal. She wore a doubtful expression, which the man picked up on instantly.

"Do you disapprove of my actions, Bing Er?" he asked. Then, seeing her nervous expression, he added, "No need to reserve yourself so much. This is as much of a learning assignment as anything else for someone with your potential."

"I think we might be causing a little too much trouble for our dear cousin," she admitted. "After all, while he is in a disadvantaged position, he is still *that man's* apprentice. It would not be wise to make a long-term enemy out of him."

"True," the man said. "It does come with its disadvantages. But little do you know that I've already committed far greater crimes against him, so this is like adding a drop to a lake. Besides, every opportunity I have to meddle with the second young master is an additional opportunity to ingratiate myself with the future leader of the family. Despite being *that man's* apprentice, he still needs to obey the family leader and the council of elders. I need to do as much as I can to push my station up. The young master's position isn't yet solidified."

"I understand," she said. "But wouldn't it have been wiser not to antagonize him and give the illusion of friendliness? If you had honored his contract and not attempted to delay his message or pry? He may have given us additional information to work with. At least until Second Young Master informed him not to trust us."

That comment caused the older man to pause for a moment. He shook his head self-deprecatingly. "Truly, the young will exceed the old with every generation. I'm glad the Wang family's education hasn't declined over the years but has instead improved. You will do well in the future."

They proceeded down a dark hallway to a stone room seemingly constructed from a single piece of marble. They passed by many shelves containing transmission jades before arriving at a much larger one that seemed more like a book than anything else. Then, after waiting till precisely the end of the hour, the middle-aged man transmitted the message.

Not orally, of course. That would have been much too quick. Instead he wrote it in the jade-covered notebook. There was no urgent marking or anything of the sort, and it was written exactly as the young man had said. He changed nothing—after all, this was according to the terms of the contract, and the Wang family paid great attention to fulfilling all contracts with care. Not that the young man's contract earlier was invalid. Rather, it hadn't been ratified by a core-formation cultivator, a requirement for continent-wide contracts. He was under no obligation to honor it.

Suddenly, Wang Bing felt a vibrating sensation from her bag of holding. She withdrew a black notebook, which she read immediately. "Uncle, it seems that he's taken residence just a few blocks away at the Quicksilver Hotel. Coincidentally, this is where we have the least influence in the city. He is registered under the name Du Cha Ming but left shortly after asking about the Talisman Artist Guild."

"Good work," the middle-aged man said. "Don't forget to fish for information on the man from our branch in the Song Kingdom."

"Already done," she said. She had always been systematic and professional about her work.

"All right, let's take off," the man said. "It should take a while for him to get the message, and if we aren't in this room for the reply, we can wait until the next routine check."

Just as they were about to exit the room, however, the clear sound of a bell caused them both to frown. They had no choice but to turn around and answer it, as doing otherwise was would have been a breach of their duties.

They walked back to the jade book, and after pressing a runic character, a jade-colored hologram popped up. It was a miniature image of the second young master, Wang Jun.

"How lucky to catch you both," the small illusory man said with a chuckle. "I just happened to be checking over our transmission book when I saw your message. Could you believe my surprise when you coincidentally sent a message that interested me?"

"Indeed, what a coincidence," the uncle said. Wang Bing knew, of course, that these were all pleasantries. The second young master's near-prophetic abilities were well-known. "Do you have any instructions?"

"Of course," Wang Jun said with a smile on his face. "First off, I wanted to pleasantly ask you to stop meddling in my affairs south of the border. It's against the family rules, and the moment I find concrete evidence, I will have you expelled from the family.

"Second, I am ordering you to deliver a core-transmission jade to Du Cha Ming, whom you have undoubtedly investigated. You likely know exactly where he lives and where he is heading. It's not that I trust in your abilities, old man. I trust in Bing Er's abilities."

The older man's face twitched. "A core-transmission jade is a precious family asset that you can't just give out at will. You will need approval to—" His voice was interrupted by a vibrating sensation from his bag of holding.

"Please check your transmission book, Wang Chen," Wang Jun

said. "I've already troubled my teacher for permission, so I doubt that you'll have trouble following my instructions."

Wang Chen grimaced after checking his book. "You know, Jun Er, you should really address me as uncle given our gap in age and cultivation. Since you have secured permission, giving him a core-transmission jade is not a problem. We will deliver it as soon as someone becomes available."

"You'll do it directly after this conversation, and you'll do it personally," Wang Jun retorted. "It is, after all, an important family asset, and we can't have just anyone delivering it. You will also inscribe my contact information on the jade prior to delivering it. Also, please don't call me Jun Er, as we are not so familiar, despite being family. It would be best if you remembered your station. Despite being a core-formation expert, you are still required to call me Second Young Master at my insistence, according to the family rules.

"Third, Bing Er, could you please check the message that just appeared in your transmission book?"

Hearing the sudden address in conjunction with a vibrating sensation, she immediately pulled it out and checked, causing her to groan softly at the troublesome nature of her opponent.

"I've taken the trouble of having all information on Du Cha Ming erased in both our files and other information networks," Wang Jun said pleasantly. "Please don't waste any more of our family's funds or time investigating him."

Then, as abruptly as the projection had appeared, it vanished.

Wang Chen shook his head but quickly retrieved a small jade orb covered with exquisite runes from the shelf. "I'll be off," Wang Chen said.

Wang Bing nodded in understanding. Orders from a superior in the family, when within the family rules, were absolute. Wang Chen couldn't delay the delivery without being punished.

The recent exchange with Wang Jun also made her aware of how frightening Wang Jun's abilities were. While they had been in the same class, Wang Jun had always been low key. The results of his examinations had never been publicized due to a request of *that man*, his teacher.

As she walked back to the desk she should have been manning, she began doubting the wisdom of her uncle's decision to oppose him.

Chapter 8: Status

"What a pain," Wang Jun said as he exited the small room and met up with Elder Bai. "Did you catch all of that?"

"Most certainly," the white-haired man said. "It's too bad we don't have any concrete proof of their meddling. The mastermind—who is surely not Wang Chen—is far too skilled and leaves not a shred of evidence behind."

"We should be thankful he is so careful," Wang Jun said. "Otherwise, his actions would be so aggressive that all our attempts to profit in this city would collapse instantly. Even if the failure could be justified, it would be difficult for me to secure my position as a contender for the family's leadership. The only reason that he hasn't interfered enough is due to fear of me and my teacher, and I need to make sure that fear remains. The message today finally gave me an opportunity to show off."

"How did you manage to get the information destroyed so quickly?" Elder Bai asked Wang Jun. They were now back at his office and brewing tea.

"Simple," Wang Jun said. "Cha Ming and Huxian disappeared almost three years ago, and I was convinced foul play was involved. I was also convinced that they hadn't died. In the event that they had survived, to reduce their likelihood of being found, I commissioned the destruction of their information. When my cousin went digging, I didn't have to do anything."

Elder Bai chuckled at the revelation, and they moved on to proper business. "How is the permitting process proceeding?" Wang Jun asked.

"With great difficulty," the older man said. "Despite all our best efforts, I can't put our chances higher than fifty-fifty. The crown prince is highly favored by the king, but fortunately the third prince cares deeply about his father. The king is hesitant in showing favoritism. This gives us an intangible edge. The administrative staff in the palace doesn't dare take sides too heavily."

Wang Jun sighed. "Fifty-fifty is still acceptable. If we don't win, it just means that fate is a treacherous lady who likes to string along every good-looking man that comes her way. Now, what about our purchasing plan? How is it going?"

"It seems they haven't noticed yet," Elder Bai said. "We've been able to secure a twenty-percent discount on our purchases. However, I suspect it's only a matter of time until they uncover the truth. What price are we willing to tolerate?"

"Five percent above market price," Wang Jun replied. "Higher than that, and our finances can't take the hit. Let's hope that they don't spot us for some time."

They drank tea for another half hour. Wang Jun looked askance at Elder Bai, who sighed and shook his head.

"There is no need to look into her whereabouts further," Wang Jun said with a tinge of sadness in his voice. "If she's truly part of my story, then I will see her again one day. If not, consider it my loss in life."

"Cha Ming," a voice yelled out from behind a crowd in Central Square. Cha Ming recognized it as the voice of the middle-aged manager who he met at the Jade Bamboo Auction House. The man he didn't leave his name with.

That was fast, he thought. *He wouldn't be here to cause trouble for me, would he?*

Understanding that the man was much more powerful than him, he stopped and turned toward him. He clasped his palms together in greeting. "To what do I owe the pleasure?" Cha Ming asked. "It's barely been an hour and a half since we last met."

"To make a delivery, of course," the man said. "The value of the package is substantial, so I must hand deliver it. It is a gift from the second young master. Take care not to lose it." He handed over a small wooden chest.

"What's this?" Cha Ming asked.

It's a core-transmission jade, the man sent to him mentally. *Don't open to box here, or you'll invite trouble. To use it, pour your incandescent force into it and focus on the single mark, which is Second Young Master's. The object will take care of the rest. Do make sure you use it in private, as it would be a shame to have such a precious treasure stolen.*

After saying these words, the man immediately left. Cha Ming put the box in his Clear Sky World, which was still under the guise of a bag of holding. He didn't return to the hotel immediately and instead continued to the Talisman Artist Guild. It was a relatively small building compared to many of the other guilds near Central Square. It wasn't as opulently decorated as the Spirit Doctor Association, nor as exquisitely crafted as the Spiritual Blacksmiths Association. It couldn't hold a candle to the Geomancer Guild, which obviously subscribed to the philosophy of building things that lasted millennia.

The only building that was comparable to the Talisman Artist Guild was the alchemy workshop. This was very surprising to Cha Ming, who had been told that most alchemists were insufferable and ostentatious. However, it meshed well with the philanthropic display he had seen when he entered Central Square. This was a good sign— it likely wouldn't be too difficult to secure medicinal pills.

Medicinal pills, wealth, and techniques, Cha Ming thought. *I need all of these to get more powerful. And to get these, I need status. Getting my talisman artist qualification should allow me to build sufficient status.*

While he had a small fortune in spirit-stone ore, he was reluctant to spend too much of it, lest he arouse suspicion. The preferred way was for him to generate as much of his own wealth as possible.

With this thought, he pushed open the door to the Talisman Artist Guild. The entrance of the small building was a storefront which displayed a large variety of wares. Hundreds of talismans were stored behind glass cases. They were separated by both element and grade, and anyone could walk around and inspect them freely— without touching, of course. Activating a talisman would not only lead to the loss of the product but could also cause significant damage to the storefront.

As he walked to the serving desk, the grade of talismans on display increased. As such, the amount of display space allocated to each individual talisman increased as well. Near the desk, he saw a display which contained twenty magic talismans. Twelve were least-grade talismans, six were low grade, and two were mid grade. There were no high-grade talismans. He wasn't sure if this was due to the lack of artists at a sufficient grade or if these items were too precious to display.

Curious, Cha Ming extended his incandescent force to the glass case, only to discover that it was being repelled. The clear material encasing the talismans was rejecting spiritual force like oil did water. Which was unfortunate, because without accessing the case, he would not be able to survey the talismans with great enough accuracy. As such, he could only commit the superficial lines and characters to memory for the Inferno Talisman, the Respite Talisman, the Earth Dragon Talisman, the Frost Dragon Talisman, and the Hundred-Blade Talisman. It was only a cursory examination; he knew that it would be difficult to replicate them without further study.

The other talismans were far too intricate to study on such a basic level, with intertwined lines and circular relationships that could not be represented in two dimensions. The characters posed no problems, of course, but even the simplest least-grade talismans took advantage of an array embedded within the sheet of paper that regulated the usage of the runic characters. Which, he noticed, were drawn with poor quality in all twenty talismans he observed.

"What can I do for you today?" a young man who had just ended a calligraphy exercise asked from the counter. He was about the same age as Cha Ming. A bronze badge with the number six was situated on his chest. The badge was inscribed with a variety of runic characters that said "Certified by the Quicksilver Talisman Association."

"I'd like to apply to join the association," Cha Ming said.

"Of course," the man said. "Please give me your qualification jade, and I will proceed with the application."

Cha Ming blushed slightly. "I'm afraid I don't have a qualification jade."

The man raised his eyebrows. "Have you never taken an exam before?" Cha Ming shook his head. "Are you knowledgeable in talisman arts?"

"Somewhat," Cha Ming said. "Is there a way to take exams here?"

"Of course," the man replied. "However, you will need to start from the first level examination. Exams up to sixth grade are conducted in groups, while the higher examinations are conducted on an individual basis. The fee for the first-grade examination is one mid-grade spirit stone, and you must supply your own materials."

Cha Ming thought the price rather high but was unable to determine if things were simply more expensive in this kingdom or if the occupation was simply lucrative.

Should I really be wasting my time like this? he thought. Taking exams one by one at his level was far too troublesome. He spread out his incandescent force softly and non-intrusively, sensing seven other people with incandescent force on the premises. One small location was completely isolated from his intrusion. Judging by the furniture outside, it was the office of the guild leader.

"Song Bao, I'll be taking care of this fellow Daoist," said a voice from a room in the back. It was transmitted using incandescent force, one of the seven Cha Ming had sensed. Before long, a man wearing red robes and long silver hair appeared. He wore a silver badge on his chest with the character for "middle" on it, symbolizing his status as a mid-grade talisman master. The man clasped his hands together and bowed slightly. "Greetings, fellow Daoist, what can I do for you today?"

Cha Ming bowed back. "My name is Du Cha Ming, and I would like to join the association as a talisman artist, but I have never taken an examination. Will this be possible?"

"It's definitely possible, fellow Daoist," the man said. "My name is Feng Huoshan. I can directly assess your capabilities all the way to ninth-grade artist. Is this sufficient for you, or will you be applying for another rank?"

"I believe I might be able to apply for master qualification, but I am unsure what an examination for this would entail," Cha Ming said.

"Very well. Explaining it to you is not a problem," Feng Huoshan said. "In order to gain your qualification, you must simply participate in an exam that takes place twice per year. The next exam is in two months. Within the span of three days, those testees must produce ten different magic talismans of, at minimum, least grade. The exam tests both one's versatility and one's ability to achieve a thirty-three-percent success rate while crafting."

Cha Ming scratched his head, embarrassed. "Unfortunately, I only know four types. Is there a place where I can learn additional talisman formulas?"

"Most certainly," the man replied. "However, you must complete a ninth-grade artist examination, and you must then buy a library card and library credit. If you have money, you can study in the library."

So straightforward, Cha Ming thought. He had expected the association to hoard its knowledge.

"I'll have to trouble you, then," Cha Ming said. "Do you sell liquified elemental essence here? If so, how much does ten taels cost?"

While he wanted to buy more, he only had a limited amount of mid-grade spirit stones left from the bandits' belongings. He also wasn't sure if exchanging ore was possible like it would be at the Jade Bamboo Auction House. That is, if he were inclined to trade it there.

"That would be 125 mid-grade spirit stones," Feng Huoshan said. Then, seeing Cha Ming place 125 mid-grade spirit stones on the table, he quickly pulled a vial out from his robes. "It's troublesome to get it from the back, so this is from my personal stock. Please, follow me to a room in the back where we won't be interrupted."

They passed a library, a common room, a brush maker, and what looked a board that listed assignments. Soon they arrived in a room containing a writing desk and a mannequin of sorts.

"You would normally need to take the exams one by one," Huoshan explained. "But we make an exception for foundation-establishment cultivators, as their strong souls allow them to master mortal-grade talismans very quickly." He motioned to the seat. "The exam is quite simple. You have one hour to craft ten different ninth-grade talismans. If you can complete these at greater than 60% peak effectiveness, you pass."

Cha Ming scrunched his brows when he heard this. He had never drawn ninth-grade talismans. Mortal-grade talismans normally contained between one and three complementary characters. While he knew a wide array of characters, he had never drawn them as talismans before.

Cha Ming sat down on the chair and soaked up liquified elemental essence into his brush. It drank greedily until there was nothing left in the large vial. It looked rather small for something containing ten taels, but liquified elemental essence was quite heavy for a liquid.

After filling his brush, he rummaged through his mental space, summoning the various characters he'd mastered in Fuxi's Library. With a wave of his hand, the weakest nine thousand disappeared. Then, the weakest nine hundred of these remaining ones vanished. Soon, he selected what he saw as the most powerful basic characters that could be imprinted onto a talisman. After all, not all runes could be used on their own for a desired effect. The word "massive" was hardly useable on its own, and neither was "miniscule."

He settled on characters like "absolute zero" and "sublimation," extreme characters that denoted powerful, high-energy changes. They were the most complex to paint, but they had the highest chance of qualifying as ninth-grade talismans.

Feng Huoshan was bored. He had brought this fellow Daoist here out of respect for his cultivation base, but now the young man had chosen to sit still for fifteen minutes, wasting his valuable time. Still, it was impolite to do anything else but wait, so wait he did.

Suddenly the young man moved. His brush flowed with elegant grace, painting a marvelous blue pattern onto the provided talisman papers. The character resembled calligraphy. *Unusual* calligraphy, because he did not recognize the character.

Is it truly a ninth-grade talisman that he is painting? Time would tell. The testing mannequins were very accurate, and regardless of the effect, they would assess it accordingly. Even something subtle like healing or weakening could be assessed.

A few minutes passed, and the obscure character was completed. The talisman paper turned a light shade of blue, complementing the mixture of blue and white that composed the talisman. The temperature of the room quickly plunged.

Natural phenomena on creation? he thought. *This shouldn't be possible before magic grade.*

The young man didn't pause and moved on to the next talisman, swiftly taking advantage of every moment. Huoshan didn't understand this character, either, but he knew it had something to do with earth. Many characters had commonalities, radicals that combined into characters. Just like before, the character solidified. The cold in the room was soaked up into the yellowish-brown talisman. The humidity in the air was absorbed as well.

Talisman after talisman produced their own phenomena. It

wasn't until the sixth that the man realized two frightening things. First, the young man could paint in five elements. This was a rare but prestigious thing in Quicksilver City. Second, he hadn't failed a single time in their production. This meant that his skill level was definitely at least master level. That is, as far as runes were concerned.

Cha Ming finished fifteen minutes before the time ran out, despite having taken fifteen minutes to do what Huoshan could only assume was adjust his frame of mind. "Congratulations, you've finished the first part. However, we must still test these talismans on the testing mannequin to validate the result."

"Must we?" the boy asked. He seemed pained at the thought of using these talismans.

He's a foundation-establishment expert for heaven's sake, Huoshan thought. *Why is he such a miser?*

"Yes, it's a necessity," Huoshan replied. Normally he could have used his spiritual force and knowledge of characters to determine the result. Unfortunately, he didn't know a single one of these characters. He was truly curious to see their effect. "You may begin."

Cha Ming was nervous. It wasn't that he was worried about money, but rather that he wasn't entirely sure what constituted a ninth-grade talisman. His education with Elder Ling had been cut short, and he was sorely lacking in what should be basic knowledge. Besides, even if these were legitimate talismans, he wasn't sure what the man meant by sixty-percent efficiency. Was there such a thing as efficiency? Why hadn't he heard about this before?

Gritting his teeth, he threw the first light-blue talisman out at the mannequin. The room was suddenly transformed into a freezing icebox. The mannequin was frozen solid, but a display at the back of the room showed measurements.

Half-Step Magic Talisman. Efficiency—97%.

Cha Ming was pleasantly surprised. He had indeed made a mistake—the characters he had chosen were too powerful. *What a mannequin,* he thought. *I wish I had one.*

One after another, he threw the talismans out. One absorbed moisture and power, another poisoned the mannequin. Another sliced it in half, and another burned it to ashes. The mannequin recovered quickly every time. Naturally, these talismans would not have such a pronounced effect against him personally, but he would still need to divert some qi to defend against them. He decided then and there that he would make a large number of basic talismans in his spare time, as their effects in large amounts could be devastating.

Finally, the last talisman was expended. Each talisman he painted had been a half-step magic talisman with an efficiency ranging between ninety-five and one hundred percent. Only one, an Inferno Talisman, had achieved a perfect score.

"Congratulations!" Huoshan said. Then he handed him a bronze medal with a nine on it. "Here is your qualification. With this, you can go get a library card and will have access to all our facilities."

"Excellent," Cha Ming said. "Thanks for the trouble."

"Not at all, the pleasure is mine," Huoshan said. "In the future, I wouldn't mind buying some of these talismans off you. Perhaps I could glean some insights from them."

Cha Ming instantly realized that the characters he used might not have been familiar to the man.

"Naturally," Cha Ming said. "Can I trouble you with something, however? I am looking to exchange spirit-stone ore for spirit stones. Is there a place I should visit?"

"Spirit-stone ore, you say?" The man contemplated for a while before replying. "With small amounts, you can go to auction houses. For quantities greater than one thousand jin, you can go to the commodity exchange in Central Square.

"Much obliged," Cha Ming said. "Then if you'll excuse me, I'll be back tomorrow."

Chapter 9: Catching Up

Cha Ming poured his qi into the single mark on the core-transmission jade. The green sphere glowed with a soft light, pulsing repeatedly as it sent a request into the void. After half an incense time, a jade-green hologram appeared inside Cha Ming's well-lit hotel room.

"My friend, it's been so long," the tiny transparent Wang Jun said.

"It certainly has, Brother Jun," Cha Ming replied. "Sorry to keep you waiting. I went to get my talisman-artist certification, and I only just returned."

"Not a problem, my friend," Wang Jun assured him. "What grade did you secure?"

"Only ninth grade," Cha Ming said. "I'm not far from master level, but I need some time to study."

"Not bad, not bad," Wang Jun said. "It's useful to have a profession, especially in major cities. From what I understand, you are allowed to fly in Quicksilver if you are a master in any profession. The savings on travel time alone are worth it. What have you been up to these past few years?"

Cha Ming proceeded to narrate his story, starting with overcoming the calamity, the interception by Protector Song, and the spatial transmission to Crystal Falls. He told him about his recovery, his enslavement, and the Serpentine Sword bandit group. And finally, he finished off with his journey to Quicksilver City.

Wang Jun listened intently, his face alternating between concern and anger. His face softened by the end of Cha Ming's tale. "I'll be sure to send someone to look over these villagers that took care of you. In addition, I'll look into these Serpentine Sword bandits to make sure they've been fully uprooted. We don't want them causing problems again."

"Much obliged," Cha Ming said. "Have you heard anything of Huxian's whereabouts? We were separated, and I can't sense him anywhere."

Wang Jun shook his head. "I haven't heard anything. Since I now know the range of the talisman, I'll dig more deeply into areas that fall inside its transmission circle. To be honest, it's amazing that both of you didn't die from the spatial storms."

Cha Ming nodded. "By the way, how is everyone else faring? How are things on your end?"

A complicated expression appeared on Wang Jun's face. "Feng Ming is doing better than ever. He keeps climbing up the ranks, and it won't be long before he becomes a general. Every operation he commands ends beautifully with minimal losses. He's quite favored in the capital.

"Gong Lan... I have not seen her since her brother took her away. She wasn't doing well, Cha Ming. Her bloodlust got a hold of her, and she ended up in jail. Her brother busted her out, though. Hopefully he found her help. I haven't seen them since.

"Hong Xin... I just don't know." Wang Jun's expression turned gloomy once he mentioned her name. "While you were gone, I broke up with her. She took it very hard, my friend. She ran away from home, and I haven't been able to find her. My divinations can't sense anything. I... I realized my mistake after we started dating. As you might have realized, the situation in my family is extremely complicated. I would hate myself if anything happened to her in the struggle for power. I was foolish to fall in love. I don't deserve such a thing."

Silence. Cha Ming wasn't sure how to console the man, and he also felt quite sad for Hong Xin. He was indebted to their whole family, but it seemed that he had brought them only pain. "Everything will be all right, my friend," he said, sighing. Hope was a luxury everyone could afford.

"As for myself, things are not going so well," Wang Jun continued. "As I said previously, I'm currently performing a task for the family, which is why I was in Green Leaf City to begin with. It's very important that I complete it, but it involves making an unfathomable amount of profit and gaining a large market share in key sectors. At this point, I'm basically counting on that bastard Zhou Li plunging the kingdom into a war to take advantage of the chaos.

"Fortunately, an opportunity has arrived in the form of a newly discovered immortal-jade mine. The profits would go a long way in meeting profit targets, and the capital obtained can be quickly reinvested. We're currently fighting over the mining rights. It could go either way, so Elder Bai and I are working night and day to make it happen."

Cha Ming finally noticed his friend's gaunt and fatigued expression. "You need to take care of yourself. Sleep is a key part of your foundation, even if you only need to sleep once a week. Even the strongest building will crumble with cracks in its foundation."

Wang Jun chuckled. "It seems you've grown a little wiser in the time we've been separated. But no need to worry. This brother is a late-foundation-establishment expert now. I do not tire so easily."

"I'll take your word for it," Cha Ming said. "By the way, you mentioned immortal jade. Does the deposit contain jade for each of the five elements and immortal jade core?"

"It will most definitely contain the first five," Wang Jun replied. "As for the jade core, it all depends on luck. There is a one in ten chance, given the information we've gathered. Why? Do you need some?"

"I need a jin of each of these for my body-transformation technique," Cha Ming said. Seeing the agitation on his friend's face, he added, "Relax, I'll pay for it. I won't let you suffer a loss."

Wang Jun's expression relaxed considerably. Cha Ming could only imagine the type of pressure his friend was facing, given his usual generosity. "Brother Jun, do you need me to return the core-transmission jade? It's a priceless treasure, and I'd hate to have reduced your working capital."

"It's not a problem," Wang Jun said. "It is not assigned a monetary value. Rather, it is counted as a key family asset. It is a core treasure. As such, its value is difficult to measure by normal financial means." Cha Ming nodded in thanks. "One last thing, Cha Ming. You need to be careful. Many people in my family hate me down to their bones. I've painted a target on your robes by sending you this jade."

Cha Ming shrugged. "They seemed to paint a target on me as soon as I said your name. It makes little difference."

Wang Jun shook his head. "You don't understand what I've gotten you into. Make sure you tell me if anything happens, especially with regards to purchasing magic weapons and magic pills. The branch in Quicksilver is strongest in these sectors, but I'll do my best to pull some strings and help you out."

"Noted," Cha Ming said, frowning.

A door opened in Wang Jun's hologram. "I need to go now, my friend. Do take care of yourself. I may also need you to do some things for me in Quicksilver if the most unlikely scenario occurs in the mining-rights negotiation."

The hologram disappeared.

After disconnecting from the call, Cha Ming stretched his limbs and willed his body to undergo a transformation. The bones in his face expanded, and his height shrunk. His arms widened, and his cultivator robes became mediocre clothes that fit him poorly. He quickly exited the inn under the suspicious stares of the staff and blended into the crowd. Little by little, he changed his features as he weaved through it. Sometimes, his nose would shrink. At other times, his chin would change.

He ducked in an alley some time later and walked out a completely different person. It wasn't a man he had seen before. Rather, it was an amalgamation of many different people. His clothes transformed to plain black cultivation robes, complete with a deep, hooded cloak that hid half his face. After this substantial change in appearance, Cha Ming walked out of the alley and calmly strolled through the large doors of the commodity exchange.

The exchange was noisy. People clustered together in groups around the well-dressed men who announced commodity lots and the asking prices. The asking price could either be the market price or some set minimum with a specific selling timeframe. Many things were traded. Rice was traded in tens of tons while herbs were sold in hundred-jin packages. Lower-grade spirit weapons and medicinal pills were sold by the hundreds, as were large quantities of iron ore or other crafting materials. Even liquified elemental essence was sold, but only in increments of 1,000 jin.

He absorbed this information as he walked up to a desk in the corner. "Greetings, esteemed guest," a young man said, bowing. He was at the peak of qi condensation, and his demeanor was impeccable. "What would you be putting up for sale today?"

Cha Ming looked around with an emotionless expression. "Is it possible to meet someone to have a private conversation?" he asked in a gravelly voice that was far removed from his own.

"Of course, sir," the young man replied. "Right this way."

He escorted Cha Ming through exquisitely crafted wooden doors. They traveled through a hallway built with seamlessly connected marble blocks. After a short walk, they arrived in a small room.

"Could the room be bigger?" Cha Ming asked.

The man's eyes widened, and he took Cha Ming to a room that could easily accommodate a thousand people. They were clearly ready for a transaction of any physical size.

"Please wait here one moment, and I will have my manager come in right away," the young man said.

Cha Ming sat calmly in meditation. His new face was gaunt and bald, but he kept it carefully hidden by his hood to maintain an air of secrecy. Before long, a graying man in a fine suit of silk clothes walked in.

"My apologies for the long wait," the man said. "My name is Xu Zhong, and I am the branch manager for this commodity exchange. Might I know your esteemed name?"

"You can call me Wen Ning," Cha Ming said. "It is not my real name, so don't bother looking into it. I am looking to make this transaction as anonymously as possible."

"Of course," Xu Zhong said. "Many clients opt for this, but please be aware that anything you present will count as newly produced and be subject to the kingdom's tax on whatever category of goods it belongs to. You will not be able to count these as imported goods, where you could pay duties instead of the tax with a proper certificate. Is this acceptable?"

Cha Ming, who didn't have such a certificate in the first place, nodded. Then he grasped his bag of holding under his cloak and poured pile after pile of spirit-stone ore onto the floor. Once the work was complete, he sat down in meditation, and Xu Zhong quickly gathered a few appraisers and began sifting through the goods.

A whole twelve hours passed, but to cultivators, this was nothing. Cha Ming's incandescent force strictly monitored the appraisers and their conversations.

"This lot is different than the rest," he heard a man say. "Is this a test?"

"It must be," another man said. "Sometimes our business partners do this to validate our appraisal services. Let's just make sure to note down this batch correctly and highlight it in our report."

"This is so much high-grade spirit-stone ore," the first man exclaimed. "It's worth far more than the rest of the ore in this room put together." His companion berated him for being a country bumpkin.

A light smile appeared on Cha Ming's lips. The year and a half of mining had yielded what he thought was 1.5 million unrefined mid-grade spirit stones. Now it seemed the amount was closer to 1.4 million mid-grade and over 100,000 high-grade spirit stones. One high-grade spirit stone was worth 10,000 mid-grade spirit stones. He thanked his lucky stars that he'd had the common sense to come to the building anonymously. Otherwise this fortune would have been far too large for him to swallow, as it exceeded the net worth of many core-formation cultivators.

Twelve more hours passed before the manager presented the final report. "As you might know, there are two things to consider when setting a selling price for these ores. First, the ore needs to be refined and cut into an optimal form. This leads to a loss of ten percent with mid-grade spirit stones, half of which is salvageable as spirit-stone dust. For high-grade spirit stones, this is reduced to five-percent loss, some of which is salvageable as spirit-stone dust. Overall, you can expect eighty to eighty-five-percent conversion on the mid-grade spirit stones and eighty-five to ninety-percent conversion on the high-grade spirit stones. This is naturally due to the need for buyers to turn a profit during the ore-refining process.

"Given that this is a cash-equivalent commodity, we recommend an asking price of 1,100,000 mid-grade spirit stones for the mid-grade ore, and 102,000 high-grade spirit stones for the high-grade ore. We would separate these into five batches to be auctioned over a week's time. The kingdom's tax will be five percent of the sale value, as this is a cash-equivalent commodity, while our transaction fee will be two percent. Is this convenient for you?"

Cha Ming nodded. "Yes, but I would like an advance."

Xu Zhong looked to be in an awkward position. "How much of an advance are you looking for?"

"Only twenty percent," Cha Ming said with a chuckle. The man's expression softened considerably.

Perhaps I should have asked for a little more, Cha Ming thought.

"Give me some time, and I will return with a contract and the advance," Xu Zhong said. Minutes later, he returned with a piece of paper, a jade stamp, two crystal cards, and a ring. "Here are two crystal cards worth 10,000 high-grade spirit stones and a complimentary low-grade storage ring filled with 22,000 mid-grade spirit stones. The cards can be exchange for the spirit-stone equivalents at charge with any currency exchange or bank on the continent.

"The contract is an anonymous sale contract. Given that you will not be signing with your name or blood, this stamp will be used to validate your identity after signing. It is a single-use item uniquely wrought with fate techniques beyond my understanding. You will need to present the stamp to receive your payment."

Cha Ming reviewed the contract. Upon seeing everything was in order, he pressed the jade stamp onto the contract paper, which left a jade mark on the document. The stamp in Cha Ming's possession immediately lost its luster, but he could detect a weak thread connecting it to the mark on the contract.

"I will return in one week," Cha Ming said in his gruff voice. He was escorted back to the exchange floor, which was just as rowdy as before. He didn't hurry to leave. Instead he sent his incandescent force out to listen to the various announcements by the auctioneers. After a few moments, he found what he was looking for.

"Bulk liquified elemental essence, 10,000 jin! Asking price is 160 high-grade spirit stones," someone announced in a corner of the room. He was surrounded by several other individuals that immediately began placing bids. Among them, he noticed someone with a silver talisman-artist badge.

"One sixty-three!" one shouted.

"One sixty-five!" another shouted.

The price eventually closed at 182 high-grade spirit stones, an eighteen-stone discount compared to the retail price. He continued to watch as several lots were sold for a similar price. After ten lots passed, a lot came up for 50,000 jin. This time, however, it auctioned for 880 high-grade spirit stones.

It seems that fewer people can bid for the larger lots, so the price is slightly lower, he thought. *But not too low; it's a cash commodity, after all.*

Using his incandescent force, he scanned the register until he found the largest lot to be auctioned: a 100,000-jin lot. The asking price was set for 1,600 high-grade spirit stones. He waited patiently for one hour until the lot finally came out.

"Bulk liquified elemental essence, 100,000 jin! Asking price is 1,600 high-grade spirit stones!"

"One thousand six hundred twenty!" one man shouted.

"One thousand six hundred forty!" another shouted.

"One thousand six hundred forty-five!"

The numbers continued to rise slowly until they reached 1,685. Given the previous bidding, Cha Ming guessed that a fifteen-percent bulk discount was the most they were willing to tolerate for such a large amount.

"Seventeen hundred!" Cha Ming shouted. No one added on to the total.

"Seventeen hundred going once! Seventeen hundred going twice! Sold! Please proceed to the desk with this jade slip to complete the transaction."

Cha Ming retrieved the slip from the man and proceeded to the exchange desk. He broke one of his crystal cards worth 10,000 high-grade spirit stones with the banker and received eight small crystal cards worth 1,000 each and 300 high-grade spirit stones in change.

After completing the transaction, Cha Ming walked out of the exchange. Sensing some cultivators tailing him, he shielded his presence using his incandescent force and disappeared into the crowd. He changed his appearance many times, causing people to look over their shoulders only to realize that they must have been imagining things. Eventually, he changed back to his original appearance, clothed in hooded blue robes. The hotel attendants looked at him in surprise as they wracked their brains to remember when he'd left his room.

Cha Ming collapsed on his bed with a smile on his face. The money problem had been resolved. All he needed now was status. The rest would take care of itself.

Chapter 10: Adventure

Huxian woke from his pleasant dream of massive riches and a human city. In this dream, he wasn't a beast, he was a man. These dreams had been getting more frequent of late. With a yawn, Huxian lazily stretched out and wandered out of his cave on the mountain peak. He saw Silverwing and Lei Jiang enjoying a bout of light sparring on the jade platform. Silverwing dominated, of course. They stopped just before he arrived and greeted him warmly.

"Congratulations on your breakthrough to late purification, Lei Jiang!" Huxian said to the small purple mouse who stood proudly beside his winged sparring companion. Silverwing looked at the small mouse with a longing expression.

"It's all thanks to the purification technique that Master gifted me," he said humbly.

"Nonsense," Huxian rebuked. "Your natural talent is quite high. If I gave this technique to just anyone, they would never be able to use it to full effect. Give it a few years, and I guarantee you'll be able to step into core formation."

Lei Jiang continued showing off for a bit longer before scampering off.

"I'm sorry you had to see that, my friend," Huxian said, shaking his head. "He might be inconsiderate at times, but he means well. I truly wish I could help you, but my hands are tied. Still, the technique I gave you is much better than nothing. You'll surely break through to core formation in five decades or so. That's nothing to demons like us."

Silverwing sighed. "What's the use? Even if I break through to core formation, what comes next? I won't have a formula to continue my advancement. I can't keep begging for techniques like this."

"Come now, Silverwing," Huxian said. "You're my friend, so you're not begging. I'm giving them to you because I can." Then, noticing the falcon wasn't convinced, he glanced at the jade plate behind him. "Maybe you can make up for it by trading information."

"Information?" the falcon asked.

"That's right," Huxian said. "For example, I was wondering what the story is about this jade plate. Do you know what it does, or its origins?"

The falcon nodded. "Its origins are linked to my ancestor. He was good friends with the monarch at the time. In fact, these mountains were named after my ancestor. Every generation in my family takes on the name Silverwing to honor him.

"I'm not too sure what the jade plate is for. No one is. Except maybe the monarch. All I know is that there are nine mountains, and each mountain peak holds a jade plate. It is rumored that there is a tenth plate in the valley between the mountains, but no one dares to go."

"Why not?" Huxian asked.

"It is a valley of death," Silverwing replied. "Only the monarch and his inheritor dares to go there. I'm surprised you don't know all this, though. The current inheritor is on your mountain peak. It's that True Seer Great Owl. The reason the old sovereign never touched him was because he's the progeny of the monarch."

"That's very interesting," Huxian said. "See? That information was totally worth those useless techniques. By the way, do you want to go have some fun today?"

"What kind of fun?" the bird asked suspiciously.

"I want to go tease the tiger," Huxian said. "I heard that he's guarding a yin-yang dragon fruit. It's been maturing for almost 108 years, the perfect maturity for such a fruit."

Silverwing hesitated. "I suppose this fruit is for you to break through to late purification?"

"That's right," Huxian admitted. "I'm worried that the humans will come here to make trouble, so I need to be as strong as possible before they arrive. Otherwise they'll end up taking over your mountain. I think we both don't want to see that happen."

"All right," Silverwing said. "But we need to be careful. He's a half-step core-formation demon beast. I have a very high defense, so I don't have much to worry about. He could kill you in a single strike, however. And by the way, he's actually a lion. There's a big difference."

"Don't worry, I'm very fast," Huxian said, rolling his eyes. He was touched by Silverwing's concern. "Lei Jiang, you run ahead to scout."

The three small beasts quickly moved through the forest that encompassed the nine mountains. The scenery changed drastically once they arrived at their final destination: Reptilian Mountain. The forest quickly turned hot and dry and the trees increasingly sparse. It became just like a savannah, a habitat filled with tall grass. It was ideal for hiding predators.

"Do you have any idea how he managed to terraform the forest?" Huxian asked Silverwing.

"It's a very impressive feat, but it makes sense given the lion's mixed bloodline," Silverwing replied. "What other animal can you think of that can change the terrain so easily?"

"A geomantic boa?" Huxian guessed.

"Wrong!" Silverwing said, chuckling. "It was a geomantic python, a much higher tier demon beast. He bragged about it just a few years ago. While he doesn't have the ability to lay traps, and his ability to terraform is mediocre at best, he was still able to change the terrain on this mountain to the most suitable climate for him and his pride.

"He's much stronger than a normal half-step core-formation beast, and his claws and fangs are naturally coated with a strong venom. His defenses are also absurd, so he can attack without worry."

"Then we should make sure we don't bother him," Huxian said.

"And how will we do that, given that we want to take the fruit he's been guarding for the last hundred years?" Silverwing asked.

Huxian was at a loss for what to say. If this lion was as strong as Silverwing said, they were courting death by stealing from him.

They soon arrived in a wide clearing surrounded by many feline creatures. Most of them were lions, all female, of course. A male lion would never tolerate other males in its den unless it was looking for an heir. They all sat patiently, awaiting the arrival of their king.

"How much longer until the fruit ripens?" a young cub asked.

"It will ripen when it ripens!" a lion that Huxian could only presume was its mother rebuked.

"No need to be so harsh on the little cub," an older female lion, presumably the mother of the entire pride, said. "The yin-yang dragon fruit is a fruit of balance. It will ripen today halfway between high noon and midnight. We are here both to guard it and to congratulate your father on his upcoming breakthrough to core formation. He will enter seclusion after retrieving the fruit. Then we will begin raising your younger brother to become his successor."

Huxian and his friends were hidden in a small shadow. Huxian's shadow abilities were very useful for clandestine operations. "How can we steal the fruit in such open terrain filled with lions?" Lei Jiang said. "It's basically impossible."

"It's better to turn back," the falcon said, nodding. "Our lives are more important."

Huxian shook his head. "We have to risk it. This is too good of an opportunity. Lei Jiang will run a distraction while I dive in to grab the fruit. What are your thoughts?"

"That's suicide!" the falcon cried. "I'm all for helping you, but I'm not for losing my life. Besides, I don't have a bad relationship with the old lion. Why antagonize him needlessly?"

Huxian sighed. "I see how it is. Very well, you can just stay back, and we'll try our best."

The falcon looked at him with a hurt expression but said nothing. Instead, Silverwing flew up and perched himself on a nearby tree, observing everything.

Hours passed while Huxian and Lei Jiang waited patiently.

I can't believe he's not helping you, Lei Jiang said. *What an ungrateful bird!*

He's not ungrateful, Huxian said. *He is being cautious, and the technique I gave him isn't worth his risking his life. This is perfectly reasonable of him. I don't want you causing trouble for him and ruining my plans.*

Lei Jiang wore a resentful expression. *Fine. I know I can get that fruit for you.*

Don't focus on getting the fruit, Huxian said. *I need you to be an annoying and flashy distraction. Even if you must die, I need him distracted until I get the fruit. If you're still alive by the time I get the fruit, try your best to escape.*

A look of determination flashed in Lei Jiang's eyes. *I am willing to die for you, Master.*

Huxian did not reply but instead continued to observe the pride of lions. The hour was drawing near.

A frightening pressure appeared in the sky a quarter hour later. A large scaly lion walked in the air from afar. He ignored all the nearby beasts as he gloriously pranced over to the maturing fruit. Purification-realm demon beasts could not walk in the air in this way; only core-formation beasts could. This was a small advantage the Reptilian Lion Sovereign had gained when forming his false core, a faint imitation of the true core he would condense to enter core formation.

"My pride," he roared, "it is good for you to be here during this glorious moment."

"We are joyful in being able to take part in my lord's[5] glory," the oldest lioness replied submissively.

"After I retrieve the fruit, I will retire into seclusion," the Reptilian Lion Sovereign said. "Pick a newborn male cub of your choosing and raise him as you see fit during my absence. You will naturally be in charge and may kill anyone who displeases you."

---

[5] In Chinese culture, an ancient way of referring to one's husband is to address him as "my lord."

"As you wish, my lord," the lioness replied humbly. The nearby lionesses trembled in fear.

"Beautiful," the Reptilian Lion Sovereign whispered while watching the fruit mature. It was like a normal fire dragon fruit, but the fruit's flowerlike husk was white and black, infused with the powers of light and darkness.

As far as Huxian was concerned, it was a waste for this lion to consume it. Huxian's attributes perfectly matched the fruit, while the lion's attributes did not.

An incense time passed, and the sun began setting on the horizon. "Almost there," the Reptilian Lion Sovereign whispered.

Now! Huxian yelled mentally. He slithered into the long shadows created by the setting sun while Lei Jiang transformed into a purple bolt of lightning that darted toward the fruit.

"What gall!" the Reptilian Lion Sovereign roared as he swiped at the Calamity-Swallowing Mouse. Lei Jiang didn't reply. Instead, the sky turned dark as he summoned purple lightning in the shape of a storm. It rained down and formed an offensive shield around him, which spread out and began attacking the scaly lion.

"That hurts!" the lion shouted in surprise. The lionesses nearby could only watch in fear and awe. They would be burnt to a crisp the moment they so much as touched the purple lightning shield.

Only a few more moments, Huxian said as he waited beside the fruit. It had almost reached its peak of maturity.

Not a problem, boss. I can handle him, Lei Jiang said. But he spoke too soon. Suddenly the pressure given off by the lion skyrocketed, and Lei Jiang found himself suppressed on a fundamental level. It was the power of the lion's false core that restricted him. The solidified bloodline present in a demon core was much more concentrated than a purification beast's bloodline.

"I will devour you for sustenance before eating the yin-yang dragon fruit," the lion said. "This way, my odds of success in core formation will double. Did you really think that your pathetic speed could contend with my false core?"

Lei Jiang, clearly suppressed by the lion's solidified bloodline, attempted to run away. However, the speed it was most proud of didn't matter in front of the gigantic lion, who swatted him aside with ease. Huxian heard breaking bones, but he steeled himself. Getting the fruit was most important. If one of his generals died, he could always replace him.

As the lion pounced on Lei Jiang, Huxian jumped from the shadows and swallowed the fruit whole. Its powerful energies did not immediately dissolve into his bloodstream but were stored away for a later date.

"How dare you deceive this sovereign!" the lion roared, appearing directly beside Huxian.

What shocking speed, he thought. He mustered every ounce of his power but soon discovered that the gravity around him had been amplified a hundredfold. An enormous, venomous claw came crashing down on him. He braced himself for his inevitable demise.

I'm sorry, Cha Ming, Huxian thought. *I tried.* He closed his eyes and waited for the inevitable 20,000-jin paw strike.

Peng!

The paw didn't land. He opened his eyes and saw brown and silver feathers. "Silverwing!" Huxian shouted.

"You dare meddle in my affairs and help these thieves, Silverwing?" the lion roared. "Do you think I would hesitate to annihilate every bird on your mountain in retaliation?"

"You can say whatever you wish," Silverwing said. "But if you dare do such a thing, I will eliminate every cat in the mountain range. We both know you can't kill me. Both because you don't dare and because you're physically incapable."

The lion hesitated, then looked to the side at the crumpled Lei Jiang. "Fine. But this one stays with me as an apology."

Seeing the blood running down Silverwing's beak, Huxian was ready to make this concession. However, before he had a chance, the large falcon spread its wings. "I'm taking the mouse with me, and you can't stop me. However, we are indeed in the wrong. In the future, I owe you an equivalent herb or fruit, and it will be much more suitable to your constitution. This will happen within the next ten years."

The Reptilian Lion Sovereign's eyes narrowed. He seemed about to yell out in indignation but suddenly held himself back. "Very well. You may take the mouse, then. I'll give you face for the sake of your ancestors."

Silverwing bowed his head slightly and calmly picked up both Huxian and Lei Jiang in his talons and flew off. They retreated until they arrived at Huxian's mountain, where Silverwing dropped them unceremoniously. Huxian, seeing Lei Jiang's dire state, coughed up a tiny bit of blood essence and fed it to his follower, whose erratic breath quickly recovered.

"Many thanks, Silverwing," Huxian said. "If you hadn't—"

Paff.

A wing struck Huxian across the face, sending blood flowing out of his mouth. "What's your problem?" Huxian asked, growling.

"What's *your* problem?" the falcon asked with a menacing glare in his eyes. "I warned you he was powerful, and you wouldn't listen. Not just that, you used your slave as bait. I saw it clearly. You were willing to sacrifice him for that fruit. I thought I knew you, but I was wrong."

Huxian gulped and was immediately filled with something he had never felt before: regret.

Seeing Huxian's expression change, the falcon shook its head. "You're just a kid. You know nothing. But you should appreciate friendship, Huxian. I saved you today because you are my friend. I risked my life today because you are my friend. And I saved Lei Jiang's life because he is my friend, too.

"I didn't have to save you two, but I did. You need to appreciate what you have. Otherwise you might lose it all one day. If you don't care for the people around you, even your closest friends and brothers will abandon you." Silverwing looked up toward his mountain peak. "I'm entering seclusion now to recover from my wounds. I don't want to see your face for a week. But when I do, I hope you'll have reflected on your mistakes."

Silverwing disappeared in a flash of silver, and Huxian was left alone on his mountaintop. He was dejected and confused. He felt regret. From what he understood, his ancestors had always treated his generals as disposable commodities. However, the more he thought about Lei Jiang, another new emotion surfaced.

Guilt.

Can I really recruit Silverwing as my general? he thought. *No. I could never do that to Silverwing. What a terrible thing to do to a friend.*

The Reptilian Lion Sovereign lounged next to the giant jade plate on his mountain. He was moping, and for a good reason. A large shadow approached him from afar before landing beside him.

"Why couldn't I just kill the mouse?" the Reptilian Lion Sovereign said. "Is it really so important?"

"The mouse is irrelevant," the figure said. "But it's Silverwing's friend. That alone should be enough."

"I know how you operate," the Reptilian Lion Sovereign said. "You wouldn't save the mouse just for Silverwing's sake."

A pause ensued. "You're right. I wouldn't," the figure said. Then, without further explanation, he vanished.

Chapter 11: Brush Maker

"ha Ming, it's so good to see you again!" Feng Huoshan said warmly. The attendant, who had paid little attention to him the first time he visited, now clasped his hands and bowed in greeting.

"My apologies on not making it sooner," Cha Ming said. "I needed to take care of some matters and wasn't able to come back until now." Dark circles surrounded his eyes, as his sleep had been restless. He had strange dreams where he was the sovereign of a mountain, overseeing the life and death of countless beasts.

Last night, he'd fought a frightening adversary—an incomparably powerful lion covered in scales. Only with the help of a silver-winged falcon did he survive. While the dream was very interesting, it made him long for the companionship of his little brother, Huxian.

"Not a problem," Feng Huoshan said. "Would you like me to show you around?"

"I would be in your debt," Cha Ming replied, smiling. He followed the older talisman master through the same hallway as before. But this time, instead of bypassing the different rooms, they stopped for a tour and an introduction. Their first destination was the mission board. It was in a large stone room and consisted of four large jade plaques that constantly displayed internal and external requests. The writing on the plaques continually shifted in a futile attempt to display all the information contained within.

"You can check the details of any posting by inserting your

incandescent force," Feng Huoshan explained. "The majority of the postings are internal. The guild has several long-term contracts and also requires a minimum stock of mortal-grade talismans for the storefront. We supply various sects and clans, and we even supply a set number of talismans to the royal family every month. Members can complete these tasks either for internal credit or cash renumeration."

"Senior Brother Huoshan, what can the credit be used for?" Cha Ming asked.

"They can be used to purchase guild materials at cheaper prices," Huoshan said. "Various inks and brushes can be purchased. Or you can pay for private lessons or tutoring from senior artists. For the most part, however, people use their credits to browse the library."

"Makes sense," Cha Ming said. "What about the external postings?"

"External postings are a little more complex," Huoshan said. "The simplest sort is when a sect requires a large batch of talismans over and above the regular contract. The rewards are more lucrative, but the timelines are usually extremely tight. This usually happens before large expeditions, smelting trials, or fights between sects.

"Next, there are consulting jobs. They mostly have to do with appraisals or miscellaneous advice. Lastly, there are custom jobs. Typically, these are either requests for specific magic-grade talismans or the customer has a need to fill, and they aren't exactly sure if talismans are the way to go. Let me give you an example. Let's say the mayor's son wants to go on an expedition, and the mayor wants a life-saving treasure. He isn't too sure what he wants, but he's sure that he wants an item that gives his son unparalleled speed for at least an incense time so that he has time to reach his Dao protectors[6]. Or perhaps he believes that running away is cowardly and wants a powerful offensive talisman that can slay his enemies. We let him know which talismans are available and at what cost and effect. He will then decide whether to proceed with an order."

---

[6] Dao protectors are effectively bodyguards.

"Are we reimbursed for the consulting time involved for these postings?" Cha Ming asked.

"If only," Huoshan grunted. "It's just a cost of doing business, but it's often the only way we can sell our higher-end products. Those on display might sit there for a long time before getting sold. Magic talismans are sold on consignment. A custom job, however, has a guaranteed sale if you win the contract."

"Then do you compete internally for each contract?" Cha Ming asked.

Feng Huoshan shook his head. "We all have our strengths. For example, my offensive earth and fire talismans are the best in our group. Luo Ming's defensive talismans are unparalleled. Hua Dong's healing talismans are the best. Granted, it's difficult for him to get work because medicinal pills are so much more effective. The only advantage talismans hold over pills is a complete lack of side effects and the potential for healing multiple targets."

"I think I get the general picture," Cha Ming said. Over the course of their conversation, he saw several qi-condensation cultivators move back and forth from the four jade slabs and using their medallions to authenticate and accept missions. "One last question. What if someone fails in delivering their mission?"

Feng Huoshan's expression darkened. "It's rare, but the consequences are quite severe. For mortal-grade missions, there is a large point penalty for failing to meet a deadline, as well as a warning. Every year, a member is allowed one warning. After a second offense, they may not accept missions for three years. These types of situations cost the guild greatly. Every time, the guild must hire a higher-ranking member to make up the difference so that the end delivery is not delayed.

"For master artists on the other hand, there is no penalty. The master artist's reputation suffers, and that is punishment enough. There are so few of us that a bad reputation will get noticed very quickly. This will directly affect his ability to sell high-level talismans. Therefore, master artists who fail to meet deadlines or fail to produce a product will usually perform remedial work for their client to smooth things over. Free of charge."

Huoshan led him to the next department, the storeroom. It was filled with bottles of ink, many types of which he had never heard of. "Is there really a point to having so many types of ink?" Cha Ming asked.

"There is," Huoshan replied. "You are a skilled artist, so you use liquified elemental essence because you value your time. However, some people are far less skilled and can't afford good brushes. They make do and use inks that, while terrible for any other talisman, increase either the efficiency or the success rate of that specific one. Some materials conform better to certain characters. In fact, I'll bet that if you used different ink, you could increase the quality of several talismans you crafted in your examination all the way to one hundred percent." While Cha Ming agreed this might be a possibility, it simply wasn't worth his time.

"There are also premium inks," Huoshan continued as they reached the back counter. The attendant there opened a cupboard in the back. It contained seven small flasks that emanated vibrant colors. "May I have the flask of fire evanescence?" he asked the attendant, who glared at him.

"You break it, you pay for it," the attendant said, scowling. He handed him a glowing red flask.

Feng Huoshan quickly opened the stopper. With a wave of his hand, a blazing hot river shot out from the flask. It floated around for a moment before Feng Huoshan waved it back. The flask was graduated, allowing Cha Ming to see that the amount returned equaled the amount withdrawn.

"By using elemental evanescence to create talismans, there is a one in three chance of forcibly upgrading it upon completion. A least-grade talisman would become a lesser-grade talisman, and so on. However, this ink is prohibitively expensive."

Cha Ming gulped. "How expensive?"

"One hundred times more expensive," Huoshan replied, causing Cha Ming to hiss between his teeth. "Assuming someone had a ten out of ten chance of succeeding in his crafting, a magic talisman would grant a tenfold return on investment. If elemental evanescence was used, the maker would break even. The success rate for most people is between one in three and one in two, making it a financial loss. Most people wouldn't bother unless they were crafting a life-saving talisman. I personally do not recommend trying it. You can't use pure elemental evanescence for your examination."

After exploring the remainder of the storeroom, they proceeded to the last location before the library—the brush maker's room. Before they headed into the quiet room, however, Feng Huoshan pulled Cha Ming over to warn him. "You must, in all cases, be extremely respectful to the brush maker. Brush making is a very rare craft, and we are lucky to have him. Please indulge any reasonable questions he might have of you. In terms of standing, the brush maker stands only below the branch leader."

With Cha Ming's nod of confirmation, they entered.

The room was nothing like Cha Ming expected. He thought the walls would be built of marble or stone. Instead, they were made of plain wood. Rather than having rack upon rack of brushes, he saw sixty white brushes near a desk on the side. On the desk sat a pile of paper and pot of normal ink.

In the center of the room was a clear wheel filled with various runic patterns. It seemed to be made from the purest glass. Upon further inspection, however, Cha Ming could see that it was made of a metal that resonated with his soul—soul steel. Soul steel was one material grade higher than soul alloy.

The remaining side of the room was a wall full of closets with unknown contents. Before he had a chance to ask Huoshan, a short balding man walked out from a room in the back.

"Greetings, Master Brush Maker," Huoshan said, bowing. Cha Ming followed his lead and greeted him in a similar fashion.

"Enough with the honorifics, they bore me," the older man said.

"Nonsense, Master Li, these are the honorifics you deserve," Huoshan said courteously. Seeing the smirk on the older man's face, Cha Ming realized that this was exactly what the man liked—to be complimented, but to reject the compliments and have them insist on them. However, flattery was an art, and Cha Ming wasn't sure how to join in.

"Who have we here, Huoshan?" the brush maker said. "Seems like a new face. Young, too."

"Cha Ming has recently passed his ninth-grade examination," Huoshan explained. "If I'm not mistaken, he will either pass this master examination or the next one."

"Very good, very good," Master Li said. "And at such a young age too. Crouch down now and let me look at you."

Cha Ming awkwardly got down on one knee to lower himself down to the man's four-foot height. The man didn't hold on ceremony and grasped his face with both hands, looking him straight in the eyes. Cha Ming averted his gaze, as staring into someone's eyes was considered disrespectful.

"Look at me straight ahead," the man said in a commanding voice.

To Cha Ming's surprise, he unconsciously listened to the command and peered into the man's nondescript black eyes.

"You practice an eye technique," the man said. "Your irises are special, and you weren't born with them. They resemble plates of pure green jade, inlaid with runes. What do you see that others can't see?"

Cha Ming's eyes flicked awkwardly toward Feng Huoshan.

What do you see that others can't see? the brush maker asked again mentally.

Shades of yellow, Cha Ming said hesitantly. *And auras of malevolent ochre,* he added.

What do you think they are? the man asked curiously.

Hesitating again, Cha Ming opted to respond with the truth. *Devils,* he replied.

Right. A useful ability, for some more than others. The older man nodded and released his head. "A fine young boy," he said. "I suppose you've come to beg me to make him a brush. What a coincidence; I happen to be free."

"You are? Wonderful!" Feng Huoshan said joyfully.

"I don't know if that's nece—" Cha Ming started.

"He would love for you to craft him a brush," Feng Huoshan cut in. Then he spoke mentally to Cha Ming. *Don't you dare refuse him. Not many people catch him in such a good mood. You have no idea how many times the other masters and I had to beg him to make our brushes.*

Cha Ming could only swallow down his words. Then he noticed the old brush maker's gaze fixed on him. "You know my rules," Master Li said. "Only the customer and I are allowed in the room."

"Of course," Feng Huoshan said. On his way out, he flipped the sign to mark the shop as closed and shut the door behind him. Cha Ming was left with the older man. He wasn't sure what to say. He didn't speak, but neither did the old man. Instead Master Li walked around Cha Ming with his hand to his chin, looking him up and down. Finally, he stood in front of Cha Ming.

"Now, why exactly is it that you don't wish for me to craft you a brush?" Master Li asked. He didn't seem the slightest bit upset, only curious. "It's always better to have a superior partner when crafting talismans. That means that you either already have a very good brush or you have one you are so attached to that you don't wish to part with. Which one is it?" Cha Ming noted that Master Li used the word "partner." He didn't see a brush as merely a tool.

"With all due respect, sir, it's both," Cha Ming said. He was very confident in the prowess of the Clear Sky Brush. Besides, how could he bear to part with it? It had accompanied him since before he began cultivating.

Instead of seeming offended, the older man chuckled. "Let's see it, then. Let me see this treasured partner that's so important to you."

Once again, Cha Ming hesitated. The Clear Sky Brush was a precious soul-bound treasure. Would he incur jealousy from the brush maker if he realized the truth? But he had come this far, so he ultimately decided to show him. The Clear Sky Brush, a perfectly cylindrical white brush with a white tip, appeared on the palm of his hand.

"Don't you worry, my boy, I won't hurt it," Master Li said. Then he waved at the brush like someone might do to get the attention of a dog. To Cha Ming's surprise, the brush shivered and flew up toward the man, curiously floating around his outstretched palm. Then it floated above it but didn't land. Master Li reached out to pet it, but it playfully avoided him.

"Curious," Master Li said. "A brush that refuses to be touched by anyone but its owner. How very curious. I can sense the presence of five elements on it. And something I can't quite put my finger on. Something ever changing, all encompassing."

"It's creation qi," Cha Ming explained.

"That would do it," Master Li said. "I'm not sure what I find more exciting—the fact that you can use creation qi or the fact that this brush can accommodate it. It is certainly not something I'm capable of. Five elements, not a problem. Creation qi, well, that's something you might only see in a transcendent realm." As he spoke, the brush continued dancing around his hand as though it were a game. And the man continued to observe it just the same.

"I'm not sure how to break this to you, but I'm afraid that your brush is incomplete," Master Li said.

"Incomplete?" Cha Ming asked. "I'm not sure how that's possible." As far as Cha Ming was concerned, the brush was a divine item. How could it possibly be incomplete?

"You don't believe me?" The old man chuckled. "Not to worry. I'll prove it to you. But first, do me a favor and pour your qi, every last drop, into the qi-sensing plate in the middle of the room."

Cha Ming obeyed his commands and moved over to the clear glass plate. He grasped it with both hands as he poured forth his foundation qi into the plate. As soon as it entered, it split off into seven different directions. Upon closer inspection, his qi wasn't a dense liquid like he was used to seeing in his dantian. Instead it took the shape of the sigils he crafted to establish his foundation.

"A sigil foundation, very impressive," the old man said. "I've only seen that once before. The man told me he took inspiration from the sigils he'd studied. However, he only made them with a single type of sigil, a frost sigil. And his foundation was very incomplete, only five pillars. A pity." He shook his head but continued observing the plate. All five points began glowing with increased intensity, while the white and the black runes floated in the center, forming a yin-yang symbol.

Soon the brightness reached its peak, and Cha Ming's qi was totally exhausted. As soon as the last of his qi poured in, a change occurred in the center of the plate. The white floated to the edges, forming a circle, while the black migrated to the center and formed a black star.

"Curious…" Master Li said. He left Cha Ming in front of the plate and went into the back, leaving the Clear Sky Brush floating playfully around Cha Ming.

Moments later, Master Li returned with a black box. He opened it, revealing a pile of clear dust. "This is the first test," the brush maker explained. "In order to accommodate so many elements, the brush should have a clear foundation, untainted by other elements. I predict it will consume about ten percent of this soul steel."

"Consume?" Cha Ming asked.

"Just watch," the man said, shushing him. He brought the chest up to the floating brush, which, as though finding its favorite snack, dove into the clear pile. Ten percent of the pile immediately disappeared.

The old man nodded. It was as he predicted. But after a moment, his expression paled. The brush continued to devour another tenth. He looked on nervously as one-tenth after another was absorbed by the brush until finally, only a single tenth remained in the chest.

Master Li looked at the pitiful pile remaining. "Why don't you just eat it all, you glutton," he said in an aggrieved tone. The brush, clearly energized by his words, ate up the remaining tenth.

Cha Ming was supremely embarrassed, but he didn't say anything because he was distracted by the huge difference he observed in the brush. Its body was now crystal clear, a stark contrast to its previous milky-white color. Further, he could sense the Clear Sky Staff had also strengthened. Its main body was no longer made of pure soul alloy but rather reinforced with soul steel.

The transformation seemed to invigorate the brush maker, who disappeared in the back once more and brought out five more boxes. One held a red lotus, another a blue lily. There was an emerald succulent, a bunch of golden grass, and something that resembled a yellow, daisy-shaped diamond. Each of these flowers seemed less botanical and more like precious gems. Cha Ming could sense high concentrations of heaven and earth qi stored within these treasures.

"Go ahead," the man said. The brush, sensing his approval, dove in without restraint. It crashed into the yellow diamond daisy, absorbing the fragments within itself, causing yellow-brown runes to appear on its clear surface. It crashed into the red lotus, drinking in concentrated fire that appeared in the form of red runic lines. The same happened for the blue lily, the bunch of golden grass, and the green succulent. Soon, all five colors were dancing around the brush. After finishing its feast, the brush floated around lethargically, as though trying to show that it was full.

"That should do for the main course," Master Li said. "Let's see if it takes a liking to any of the bristle materials." The master motioned for the brush and Cha Ming to follow. The latter could only helplessly tag along as the Clear Sky Brush followed its new best friend.

As they walked past closets, the man seemed to ask with his body language, "Do you want something here?" The brush vibrated intensely once they reached the third closet. The brush maker opened the closet and pulled out a long rack with fur, hair, and plants hanging from it.

The Clear Sky Brush wandered through the many items before finally resting its "gaze" on a pure white strand.

"You've got to be kidding me!" Master Li shouted, startling Cha Ming. "The hair of a qilin? Why don't you just kill me now!"

The brush shook indignantly. Cha Ming could sense its frustration, as if it were saying, *You're the one who told me to look for something I liked. How dare you say what I like is too expensive?*

"Fine!" Master Li said, his face red with rage. "Just take it! Go on!" The brush floated and attacked the entire group of white hair. Its bristle color transformed to a glowing white reminiscent of creation qi. "Are you full now?" the brush maker asked.

The brush shook. Cha Ming understood that as a no.

With an aggrieved expression, the brush maker continued to show it various closets, and to his relief, the brush sniffed in disdain at all of them. The brush maker was elated. "It seems that it's not full, but it doesn't want anything else," Master Li said.

"What is it doing floating over there?" Cha Ming asked, pointing. The brush had floated a little farther to what seemed less like a closet and more like a drawer.

"No, you will not!" the brush maker yelled. The Clear Sky Brush, aggrieved, floated in front of the drawer in protest. It refused to budge. After a brief struggle, the brush maker asked it, "Is this going to be the last thing?" The brush nodded. "Do you promise?" It nodded again. "Fine."

Master Li pulled opened the drawer and revealed a small bunch of long hairs that looked similar to the qilin hair, except these gave off a destructive sensation. As it ate a hair, half the brush turned black as the deepest night.

"It's the hair of a nightmare," Master Li explained. "Very difficult to find, and typically not used to make brushes. Brushes are used to create, not destroy."

After a few moments, the brush finished its feast and retreated back to Cha Ming. If it had a stomach, he was sure it would have let out a satisfied burp.

"Spoiled," Cha Ming scolded. The brush disappeared into the Clear Sky World. "How much do I owe you for all of this?" Cha Ming asked.

"Don't bother; it's a gift," the man said glumly.

Normally Cha Ming would have taken this at face value. However, he had seen the man's interaction with Feng Huoshan before.

"I insist. It's only right to compensate you," Cha Ming said. "At least let me make up your losses."

Master Li relented. "Fine. You can make up my losses. My profits will be the novel experience of dealing with a sentient brush. However, the cost of these materials is considered astronomical to most."

"Try me," Cha Ming said, feeling fairly confident. He couldn't imagine a brush costing more than five hundred or so high-grade spirit stones. And that would be for a peak-foundation-establishment treasure.

"The cost of the raw materials is ten thousand and eight high-grade spirit stones," the man said. "Let's make it a round ten thousand. How does that sound?"

For the first time since their fated encounter, Cha Ming lost his temper and began yelling mentally at the Clear Sky Brush.

Why don't you just kill me and take everything I own? he yelled at it while simultaneously handing the man a full crystal card. He suddenly empathized with the brush maker. It had been reasonable for him to get angry.

Chapter 12: Colleague

Cha Ming returned to the guild the next day, both exhausted and depressed. He forced on a smile as he met Feng Huoshan once more.

"So," Feng Huoshan asked, "how did it go?"

Seeing the man's expectant look, Cha Ming could only sigh and summon the brush. It was now clear and inlaid with multicolored runes. The bristles were now black and white.

"Isn't that the same brush as before?" Huoshan asked.

"It is," Cha Ming admitted. "But seeing how attached to it I was, Master Brush Maker improved it for me. His skill is far greater than I ever imagined." He was careful to conceal its nature as an upgradeable, seemingly sentient treasure. He was sure the brush maker wouldn't disclose such crucial information.

"It's good that you followed my advice and met with him," Huoshan said. "Now that you've seen everything else, it's time for me to show you the library."

Cha Ming followed him excitedly. He could do without the other departments, but not the library. Huoshan quickly led him to a large room that seemed to encompass a quarter of the building. It only had a single floor, but the shelves were extremely tall.

"Guardian Treasure, I need you for a moment," Feng Huoshan yelled. A golden blur shot out from between two bookshelves and ran straight up to the middle-aged man's face.

"Master Feng," the object said. It was a golden ruler that positively gushed over with spiritual force. "As much as I respect you for your attainments, you would do well to remember that THIS IS MY LIBRARY, AND YOU WILL BE QUIET IN IT!" This sentence was twice as loud as Feng Huoshan's original words.

What a hypocrite, Cha Ming thought. As though seeing the doubt in his eyes, the ruler floated up to his face.

"Do you have a problem?" the ruler asked.

"No, sir," Cha Ming replied respectfully.

"That's good," the ruler said. "Seeing as you're new here, I will issue you a library card. How much credit do you wish to purchase?" Cha Ming looked askance at Feng Huoshan. The man sent him a mental reply.

"Can I please have ten thousand credits to start off with?" Cha Ming asked, placing a high-grade spirit stone in front of the golden ruler.

"Certainly," the ruler said. It used its spiritual force to move the crystal to a box behind the desk and withdrew a card with ten golden marks. "Access to the outer library costs five hundred credits per month, and it will be deducted from your card automatically. Access to the inner library costs five thousand credits per month; access to the outer library is included. Now, before you proceed, are you aware of the rules of the library?"

Cha Ming fished through his mind before giving a tentative reply. "Don't eat, drink, or speak loudly?"

"Close, close," the ruler said approvingly. "There is only one rule, the golden rule: Don't damage my books, or I will burn you to ashes! The acceptable noise levels just depend on my mood and the person talking."

Cha Ming shivered as the ruler floated away. *Perhaps it's best to communicate mentally here,* Cha Ming said to Feng Huoshan.

That is indeed the case, Feng Huoshan replied. *Now that you have access to the library, feel free to browse around. Come see me if you run into any issues. I do some tutoring in my spare time.*

Master Feng left, and Cha Ming began browsing through the

outer library. He heard a mental chime as five hundred points were automatically deducted from his card. In this library, there was a large collection of jade slips, tomes, and scrolls, grouped together by theme or character. For example, there were two full shelves containing over five thousand scrolls with titles like "Calligraphy Exercises for Beginner Talisman Artists" and "Circle Drills—Using the Perfect Shape to Perfect Your Characters."

A little further on, he saw many hundreds of books for one of the simplest talismans, the Blaze Talisman. There were fifty or so how-to books and a few dozen books on increasing success rates. Some books were about specific ink usage. And this was only for a first-grade talisman.

Cha Ming moved on to the next row of shelves. This time, the shelves were occupied by materials on second-grade talismans. It contained double the information for every talisman compared to the first row. Seeing nothing useful, he continued to the third row, where the content doubled once more. In fact, it continued doubling until the seventh grade, where the number of books for each character dropped by a factor of four.

The shelf for the eighth and ninth grades similarly dropped in volume. In fact, the ninth row only contained information on thirty different talismans. Each talisman only had ten books or slips accompanying it.

After having recognized each talisman and being proficient in them, Cha Ming proceeded to a short wall with an open entrance. He could faintly feel a force field permeating the air. After bracing himself, he pushed himself through the intangible wall, and a mental chime informed him that another 4,500 credits had been deducted from his library card. He could also tell that if he had not had sufficient credits, the force field would have rejected him and denied him entry.

The room he entered was not physically isolated from the other library. Rather, it was incorporated into the middle of its circular design. The circular inner wall had four entrances, and like the one he entered, neither of them had doors. The short walls extended up to an invisible force field which both isolated the inner library and kept them joined in such a way that they shared the same roof. The roof was filled with beautiful frescos. In them, he could sense profound meaning represented in the paintings, resonating with his knowledge of runes.

As he wandered farther into the central library, he saw a green pillar in the center. It was covered in myriad runes, some of which he could understand, some of which he could not. This could only mean one thing: They were transcendent runes, runes he wasn't yet qualified to understand, though he could understand some key characters. On all four sides, a plaque was affixed, which translated these characters into the common language.

Library Rules:

1. *Willful destruction of library property will result in destruction of the guilty cultivator. To be verified by Inquisitor.*

2. *Willful damage of library property will result in crippling of the guilty cultivator. To be verified by Inquisitor.*

3. *Books can be signed out for one week's duration at most. All books must be signed out under oath, with a penalty of 1 high-grade spirit stone per additional day's absence.*

The list continued. There was also a waiting list for books that were in short supply. Given his low skill level, Cha Ming proceeded to one of the four shelves where information on least-level talismans was located. To his surprise, there were only fifty or so different books for each element, albeit with several copies each. Three dozen of them outlined least-grade talismans, while a dozen were introductory manuals to magic talismans of a specific element. The five elements as well as wind, lightning, light, and darkness were represented.

He also saw one book entitled *Five-Element Talisman Artistry—A Primer.* However, he noticed that there were no other books on multiple-element talismans. Each one was for a singular element.

Seeing that this book suited his cultivation technique, Cha Ming opened the book and read the opening lines.

Talisman artistry seeks to encompass the nature of the universe itself, imbue it into ink, and bind it with paper. As such, it is reasonable that the five elements, which compose all matter and energy, are best suited to approximating this nature.

The following text hopes to make complex matters simple and draw inspiration from nature to describe the perfect talisman-creation technique.

The lofty introduction was imbued with the presence of an expert, so even reading these short two paragraphs put immense strain on Cha Ming's mind and soul. Even with his superior memory as a high-level cultivator, he could barely remember the sentences he'd just read.

So powerful, so profound, Cha Ming thought before putting the book away. After a quick browse through the book, he saw that it did not contain any talisman formulas, so he continued to search. After looking through several categories, he remembered his confrontation with the golden devil on the way to Quicksilver. He currently lacked offensive fire techniques, so he settled on the simplest least-grade fire talisman, Five-Fire Cremation Talisman.

The talisman joined five different fire runes into a matrix that amplified them and focused them on a single animate target. It was much weaker than its sister talisman, Five-Fire Conflagration Talisman, which focused on collateral and structural damage. To Cha Ming, this was a good thing. It was also a much simpler talisman to paint. The book was annotated with a sheet of paper that marked it as suggested for the master examination.

After obtaining the book, he continued browsing but saw nothing of interest. He took two items to the central pillar: *Five-Fire Cremation, A Detailed Guide for Beginners,* and *Five-Element Talisman Artistry—A Primer.*

To sign them out, he followed the instructions and imbued a trace of his incandescent force into two drops of blood, one for each book, and sent them toward the jade obelisk. It glowed slightly after contacting both books, but as soon as the glow receded, Cha Ming felt an invisible binding on the books loosen while a different binding constricted around his soul. It didn't damage him. It bound him firmly to an oath to protect the books and to pay a penalty for late return.

The consequences of failing to adhere to these oaths were quite dire.

Three days later, Cha Ming was painting a talisman in a guild practice room. Sweat accumulated on his brow as he painted the intricate red lines that connected the five runic characters that he had previously painted on the talisman paper. He followed the method described in *Five-Element Talisman Artistry—A Primer*, drawing inspiration from the nature of fire. He incorporated flickering motions as he painted. As a reference, he kept a small, ever-burning fire beside him in the practice room.

The line he drew was much more than a line. It contained meaning, depth, thickness, and power. And like the many times before, the line was trembling as he painted it. Before long, the first line connected. But the second line he drew immediately afterward began to collapse. Cha Ming focused every fiber of his being on controlling the wild energy. But like the many times before, he ultimately lost control.

The ink did not return to his brush like it used to. Rather, it spiraled out of control, igniting the five flames that were imprinted on the talisman paper and enveloping him in a five-colored wreath of flames.

Cha Ming didn't panic. He threw up a water-based qi shield with practiced ease, dousing the five fires before they consumed him. His lightly burned skin healed in a few breaths, leaving behind only the smell of roast pork to assault his nostrils. His clothes were fine. The gifts he had received from Fuxi's Library were both powerful and durable. Half his hair had burned away, but it regrew in mere moments.

"Why can't I make this work?" he said out loud. He had less than two months to prepare for the examination, and he had barely made any progress. A single line out of fifty was hardly anything to be proud of. The most he had accomplished was setting himself on fire.

As he cleaned the soot and ash off his face, he heard a soft knock on the door. He frowned, wondering what anyone could need him for. It was considered rude to bother someone in seclusion. He opened the door and saw Feng Huoshan.

"That's the fiftieth explosion in three days," Huoshan said with a smile on his face. "Care to take me up on that offer?"

Cha Ming sighed but nodded, letting the man in. "What did you have in mind? I've been trying for days but with no progress."

The most frustrating part was that all the theoretical knowledge on geometric relations from Fuxi's Library wasn't helping him in the slightest. They were theory, and he was dealing with real-world applications. It reminded him of why construction workers mocked engineers, who in turn mocked scientists, who then mocked mathematicians. Each step down the chain was one step further removed from reality.

Feng Huoshan pulled a chair up and sat down beside Cha Ming. "This is quite normal in the beginning. Fortunately, you chose to start with fire, so I will be able to help you."

"What's the price for your tutoring lessons?" Cha Ming asked.

"Price?" Huoshan said, surprised. "I had something rather different in mind. You see, I might be superior to you in some ways, but in other ways I'm lacking. Therefore, I was thinking we could have more of a collegial relationship."

"I excel more than you in some ways?" Cha Ming questioned. "You mean…"

"Runes," Huoshan stated. "Your knowledge of runes far exceeds mine. I confess, during your ninth-grade examination, I couldn't comprehend a single character. Therefore, I propose to help you with this first fire-based talisman in exchange for tutoring on the earth characters you drew that day. To be clear, we will tutor each other until our comprehensions have reached sixty-percent efficiency, the requirements for the examination. What are your thoughts?"

Cha Ming considered for a while before nodding. After all, Feng Huoshan seemed like a nice enough person. He saw no issue in sharing knowledge with him. Of course, he wouldn't teach him the entire knowledge of Fuxi's Library. That was something reserved for fated individuals with merit halos.

"All right, since I offered, let's start by fulfilling my end of the bargain," Huoshan said. "Start painting the Five-Fire Cremation Talisman without worrying for my safety. I can take care of myself."

At his insistence, Cha Ming began crafting the talisman once more. His brush moved swiftly as he imbued the five characters into the paper, just like before. Then he began tracing the first line, which trembled as he painted. He was concentrating far too hard to notice Feng Huoshan's frown over his shoulder.

After the first line was completed, he continued on to the second, which immediately began collapsing. Cha Ming focused his qi and spiritual force to restrain the explosion, only to notice that Feng Huoshan did the same. Together, they suppressed the fire, saving Cha Ming the trouble of dousing himself and regrowing burnt flesh and hair.

Seeing Feng Huoshan's brooding expression, Cha Ming explained. "I fail at this step every time. Believe it or not, this is an improvement over yesterday."

The man sat in silence for a while before speaking up. "I have no idea where you learned what you did," Huoshan said, "but I suggest you unlearn it as quickly as possible."

Chapter 13: State of Mind

W hat?" Cha Ming asked, perplexed.

"The quivering, the flickering. It's unnecessary and destabilizes everything. Your brush strokes should be smooth, like gentle burning flames. You're adding too much wildness into the character. I confess, if you could ever condense the talisman, its destructive might would far exceed that of anything I could draw up. However, I have never seen anyone succeed with this method. Now that I think about it, where is your copy of *Elementary Fire-Element Magic Talismans: The Burning Brush Method*?"

Cha Ming frowned. "I didn't take it out. I took the book on five-element crafting instead."

Feng Huoshan's expression darkened. "I suggest you stop reading it. It is a flawed text, and you won't gain anything good from it."

"But I sensed great power from it," Cha Ming protested. "How could it possibly be flawed with such an overbearing presence?"

Feng Huoshan shook his head. "You don't understand. The one who wrote it, Mei Guo, was quite eccentric. He was a senior master here when I began my apprenticeship. Obsessed with creating his own path. Every day, countless explosions would happen in his workshop. Everyone had doubts, but given his rank, he was given much leeway.

"Unfortunately, things did not end well for him. You see, he died at seventy-five years of age, which is quite young for a foundation-establishment elder, whose lifespans can reach two hundred years. He died in an explosion in his laboratory while crafting a talisman. This book is the sole record of his research, but it is very frowned upon to learn from it. Fortunately, those who've stumbled upon it simply make no progress, and no major explosions occur. Therefore, it hasn't been taken off the shelves."

"Then what do you suggest I do, Brother Huoshan?" Cha Ming asked.

"For starters, return the book and take out the introductory book I mentioned," Huoshan said. "While I do not suggest studying it, if you are truly curious, wait until you gain more experience. I once heard our guild master say that there are many paths to success, and that everything converges upon a single point. Perhaps there is merit to his research, but it is better to read this book as an informed individual."

Cha Ming had a fair bit to digest, so he decided to first instruct Huoshan on a single fire rune and a single earth rune to start. He painted them in midair at a slow, deliberate pace, letting him absorb the essence of each rune as he painted it. After each rune was completed, he imprinted it on a sheet of talisman paper, which Huoshan could use for future study.

Huoshan attempted to paint each talisman three times before Cha Ming stopped him. "Technically you are performing every motion correctly," Cha Ming said. "But you're lacking the meaning and intent behind the character."

"Meaning and intent?" Huoshan asked in a confused tone.

"Don't you infuse meaning and intent into your talismans?" Cha Ming asked.

"No," Huoshan confessed, "the orthodox school of thought is that as long as one's technical skill is correct, the talisman will be successfully created."

"Then what is the highest level of efficiency you have ever achieved?" Cha Ming questioned.

"Perhaps eighty percent?" Huoshan replied.

"Then this is likely your problem," Cha Ming said. "It is less of an issue for the least complex characters. However, powerful characters require deep comprehension. According to what I have been taught, each character represents a truth of the universe. It is a name that holds power, and the name means something."

Seeing the man's confused look, he decided to try another approach. He took out his brush and began drawing a different rune, a basic rune at the fifth level. A glimmer of recognition flickered across Feng Huoshan's eyes.

"Look on as I draw the rune and reach out with your incandescent force. Try to *feel* the rune. Try to understand it." Cha Ming continued to draw slowly while Huoshan tried to perceive it from every angle. Once the talisman was completed, Huoshan looked even more confused.

"I didn't feel anything like what you just said," Huoshan said. "That felt like pure technical skill."

"That's because it was," Cha Ming said. "Now take a look at this one and observe it just the same." Cha Ming drew the rune once more. This time, he poured in his entire comprehension of the character, his feelings about it, and his knowledge of its purpose. Every stroke had depth. As he drew, he saw Huoshan's initial confused look begin to fade, slowly being replaced with a pensive one. "Do you understand now?"

"Only somewhat," Huoshan admitted.

"I would be surprised if you fully understood the first time," Cha Ming said. "I have never taught this subject before. You are the first. I learned this character under very different circumstances."

When Cha Ming had learned, the character had been presented on a different material, a material that made it easy for Cha Ming to isolate the intent and study it. It wasn't surprising that he couldn't mimic it exactly. Those same conditions would only be present for those who studied the jade slips he had been given. "Now, take a look at the power of these two talismans."

Cha Ming threw the first purely technical talisman at the dummy in the room. It was engulfed in mild flames, and the dummy reported its rating.

Fifth-Grade Mortal Talisman, Efficiency—72%.

Huoshan nodded appreciatively. Cha Ming then threw out the second one. The flame was noticeably more intense and burned much longer.

Half Sixth-Grade Mortal Talisman, Efficiency—98%.

Huoshan's eyes widened. "You mean to say that not only can you increase the efficiency to the high nineties, but you can increase the grade by a half step?"

"I'm not exactly sure of the specifics," Cha Ming admitted. "To be honest, I've never performed this type of testing before I came here. The half-step ratings during my exam surprised me as well, and I had assumed it was due to the power of the rune alone. Now that I think about it, I was indeed mistaken.

"I speculate that there are two components that are contributing. First, I have already explained that your understanding of the character impacts the character drawn. However, there is another component."

"Which is…?" Huoshan said.

"Intent," Cha Ming replied. "Your intent and feelings toward the talisman contribute to its power. Unfortunately, it is very difficult to separate your feelings and your comprehension. I'll hazard a guess that one-hundred-percent efficiency pertains purely to comprehension of the runic character, while the upgrade in quality is due to the intent projected. Unfortunately, I have no way to verify this."

Huoshan was silent for a moment, after which he picked up his brush and ink to go practice on his own. "Do come find me if you have any questions about magic talismans," Huoshan said. "I'll have to trouble you as I study."

"Naturally," Cha Ming said.

Weeks flew by as Cha Ming continued studying talismans under Feng Huoshan's guidance. In return, he taught the man many new characters. While they weren't immensely useful for higher-level talismans on their own, they gave him a foundation with which to research new magic talismans. They were both quite pleased with the arrangement.

Unfortunately, Huoshan's tutoring had its limits. With his help, Cha Ming progressed very quickly in fire and earth talismans, but that was his limit. Cha Ming eventually had to find different teachers for different elements. Feng Huoshan was happy to arrange such meetings. With Huoshan's help, he learned the Five-Fire Cremation Talisman.

He also took advantage of the man's proficiency in the earth element to learn the Lone Mountain Suppression Talisman. The center of this talisman was naturally a single mountain character. It was linked to several other characters—people, land, structures, and weapons. The link expressed a suppressive relationship.

Through Luo Ming, he learned the Myriad Ice Shield Talisman. From Hua Dong, he surprisingly learned two talismans. The first was the Eight Treasures Healing Talisman, while the second was of much darker origins. It was named the Five Poisons Talisman, and it contained six characters. The central character was that of a man, while the five surrounding characters represented the five poisons— snake, scorpion, centipede, toad, and spider. The relationship between these six characters was self-explanatory.

Unfortunately, Huoshan was unable to find Cha Ming a teacher for metal-type talismans. Moreover, the other least-grade talismans they had knowledge of would take Cha Ming longer to master due to their high count of runic lines. Therefore, in the three weeks he had remaining, Cha Ming focused on two things.

Firstly, he independently studied a metal talisman, the Nine Blades, One Dao Talisman. It was an offensive single-target talisman. In addition, he continued to frantically study the four poetic talismans. Unfortunately, out of fifty attempts, he only succeeded in creating a single Crumbling Talisman. This only made matters worse, as the emotional backlash made him feel as though the sky was falling.

Despite his poor chances of success, he decided he would still participate in the examination. It didn't hurt to gain experience on the proceedings. There was also little cost to the examination. He would only need to supply his own ink and pay a nominal fee. With this relaxed attitude, he rested on the last day. On Feng Huoshan's advice, he went to admire a famous tourist attraction, the Quicksilver Art Gallery.

Cha Ming had always admired artwork in any form, whether it be music, calligraphy, or paintings. He appreciated the construction of beautiful buildings and even well-done flower arrangements. This applied to both his previous life and his current life. After all, people only had one life. Why not enjoy the beautiful things while they lasted?

Like everyone else, he lined up to enter the museum bright and early in the morning. It was a national holiday, so many people were taking advantage of the free admission. He smiled as he saw kids bouncing in and out of the line, impatient and wondering what their parents wanted to see. They wouldn't appreciate moments like these until they were older.

Like everyone else, he walked around the art gallery as he pleased. He saw the works of many local artists. There were also guest pieces. They rotated between the art galleries in several kingdoms and empires.

Like everyone else, he saw things superficially with just a glimmer of understanding. That didn't take away from his enjoyment; quite the opposite—it made him realize the true level of skill involved in portraying things in such a thought-provoking way. No one would ever truly understand these famous pieces of art.

And for Cha Ming, that was half the pleasure.

The art gallery was large, so it took him the whole day to file through the building at a leisurely pace. It was near the exit that he spotted an intriguing exhibit. It was a closed-door exhibit, meaning that an additional fee was required to enter the separate room. He entered despite the extravagant price of five mid-grade spirit stones, and that made all the difference.

As soon as he entered the room, he felt incomparably relaxed. The scent of fresh roses gently kissed his nostrils. The humidity in the air peaked, as though there was a pool of hot water in his surroundings constantly giving off steam. To his surprise, that was indeed the case. In the center of the room there sat a large copper basin filled to the brim with hot water and rose petals. Four gorgeous maidens took turns filling the tub, but as they poured, the water level never changed.

There were also four large trees that dropped cherry blossoms on the floor of the room. This was all despite it being the middle of winter. The entire scene struck Cha Ming as surreal. His eyes flickered to the plaque beside a tree. It read, *Relaxing Spring of Youth by Jun Xiezi*. It was then that he realized that the tub, the maidens, and the trees weren't real. They were only part of the painting. Even the vivid scent of roses and the humid air he felt were also part of the painting.

"You seem troubled, young man," an aged voice said from behind. A silver-haired man walked up beside him.

"A little," Cha Ming said. "I have a troublesome examination tomorrow. To pass it, I need to make things that have eluded me for months. I made them once, my masterpieces. But I have never been able to replicate them."

This wasn't the only thing weighing down on him. He had visited the Alchemists Association a month prior and obtained less-than-consoling news. His status wasn't high enough to catch the senior alchemists' attention. Meanwhile, the junior alchemists were helpless to provide the pills he needed due to his unique cultivation method. As a result, his cultivation had practically halted in its tracks.

"Ah," the man said understandingly. "This happens to me

as well from time to time. I'm a painter, you see. Before I paint a masterpiece, not only do I need inspiration, but my mind and soul must be relaxed and at peace. I cannot create a masterpiece without pouring everything I am into it. But how can I do that if my soul and my emotions aren't in tip-top shape?

"In addition, I've noticed that I can never truly replicate a masterpiece. Even if I try to paint the same thing, it will always be slightly different. That is because I've changed as a person. I see it through a different lens than before, so my inspiration has changed.

"I often come to the art gallery, both for inspiration and for relaxation. Or I go to music concerts. On occasion, I play *Angels and Devils*. Meditation is too dry and dull, and even though it *seems* like my mind is relaxing, it isn't. It's working hard at calming down, which is ironic given my intent."

The man said nothing more, and both he and Cha Ming took a seat in front of the painting. Cha Ming let everything go as he immersed himself in the image. He imagined himself bathing in that hot tub. He let the smell of cherry blossoms permeate and purify him. And out of the corner of his eye, he could barely see an intricate component of the painting he had never seen before. Yet as he focused on it, it disappeared.

Was I mistaken? Cha Ming thought, only to see the flicker once more. After the second time, he was convinced: This was no mere painting. It was that and so much more. It was a runic diagram that drew on the energy of heaven and earth and gave it that surreal, calming quality. But the painting wasn't made of runes. The painting gave birth to them.

An hour passed before Cha Ming stood up and prepared to leave. "Many thanks, senior," he said, bowing. The old man simply smiled at him and continued relaxing. Cha Ming returned to his residence near the guild that night and didn't practice his talismans. He was free of care and tension and filled with the realization that tomorrow would either work out for him or it wouldn't. It truly didn't matter.

For the first night in three years, he had a good night's sleep.

Chapter 14: Examination

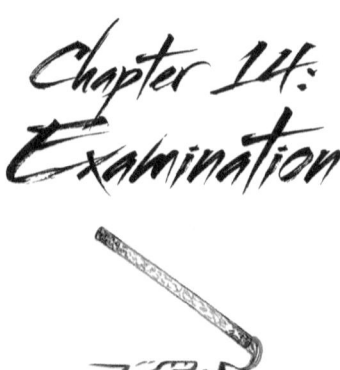

Cha Ming woke up feeling relaxed and refreshed. His mixed emotions, the ones he didn't know existed, had sorted themselves out subconsciously. Strangely, despite his repeated failures over the past few months, he felt quite confident in being able to pass the upcoming examination.

After washing his face, Cha Ming ate a large breakfast of rice porridge, vegetables, and pickles—one of the reasons he had picked this hotel in the first place. He especially enjoyed the hotel's bamboo dish. It was difficult to combine its texture and taste in just the right proportions; the chef here had done it by adding a complementary mushroom.

A brief walk followed breakfast. He took in the city's sights and enjoyed watching the people's routine walk to work. The examination's start time coincided with the standard work start time, one hour after dawn. He arrived just five minutes before the cut-off time.

"Cha Ming, you made it," Feng Huoshan said as he walked to the registration desk.

"Wouldn't miss it for the world," Cha Ming replied in a cheerful tone, a stark contrast to his stressed disposition the day prior. He signed up at the registration desk by presenting his bronze ninth-grade emblem. It contained all the pertinent information required. "Brother Huoshan, who will be conducting the examination?"

"A grand master artist," Feng Huoshan said, shaking his head. "He is sent by headquarters to ensure impartiality."

Cha Ming nodded and waited with the other thirteen examination candidates. Judging by their expressions, they were not confident in their abilities in the slightest. Many were pale and sweaty, unable to contain their anxiety. This was all despite having cultivations in the foundation-establishment realm, a minimum requirement to even attempt creating magic talismans in the first place.

There was one lone exception to this general trend. A girl stood apart from the rest. She wore a blank expression, and her eyes were closed. And despite her gorgeous looks, no one made a move to speak to her. She had silver hair that sunk down to her waist, and her skin was pale as fresh winter snow.

"Are you not nervous about the examination?" Cha Ming asked, hoping to liven the atmosphere.

"No need," she said softly. She didn't bother explaining herself, so Cha Ming could only shrug helplessly. He wasn't sure whether it was arrogance or general unfriendliness.

"So you've practiced sufficiently, then?" Cha Ming prodded. The woman frowned, and suddenly he felt like he had just plunged into a murderously frigid pool. His strong soul allowed him to recover quickly. By reflex, he activated Eyes of Pure Jade and peered at her figure. What he saw surprised him.

Instead of the yellow tinge or ochre coloring he had expected when exposed to her murderous aura, he instead saw a halo of resplendent jade light. It hugged her body, spreading out two inches from her skin and hair. The color felt kindly and pure.

Is this a merit halo? he thought. He immediately reevaluated the young woman.

"Oh?" she said, looking toward him. Her eyes still hadn't opened, but he felt a piercing gaze examining his very soul. "My apologies, kind sir, I just don't take kindly to casual conversation. I find it flippant and irrelevant. But I feel comfortable around you, so I will make an exception."

Cha Ming shot her a nervous smile. "I take it that your reputation precedes you. Were you standing alone on purpose?"

"Yes," the girl said, blushing. "My name is Luo Xuehua[7]. Like the snowflake."

"Mine is Du Cha Ming. The same Cha Ming as investigating[8]," Cha Ming said.

"How accurate," Xuehua said. "What did you discover with your investigation?" Cha Ming was caught off guard by the question but immediately recovered. After all, her disposition had changed after he observed her with Eyes of Pure Jade. It shouldn't be surprising that she had noticed his probing.

"I discovered that you are surely a righteous person," Cha Ming replied. "That you have done much good in this world."

The girl smiled bitterly. "If you could see what I see, you would not feel the same way."

Seeing that Xuehua had not opened her eyes yet, Cha Ming's curiosity got the better of him. "What *do* you see?"

"Darkness and shadows," she replied softly. "And blood, fire, and gold. Families torn apart and kingdoms crumbling. An hourglass with not much time remaining."

Cha Ming shivered. Not knowing how to react to these dark words, he could only remain silent and focus on the upcoming exam.

A middle-aged figure in gray robes appeared a half hour later. He looked over the fourteen candidates and motioned for them to follow. To Cha Ming's surprise, his body moved without his consent. He continued moving along in this fashion until they arrived at a large stone room where fourteen mannequins and fourteen desks stood ready. Each desk and mannequin were separated from the others by intricate formations that Cha Ming assumed would prevent explosions from spreading. They would only need to concentrate on the examination candidate.

"Well?" the man barked. "What are you all waiting for? Take a seat."

Cha Ming and the thirteen others scrambled to find a desk. Cha

---

[7] Xuehua means snowflake in Mandarin Chinese—雪花
[8] Chaming means to investigate or ascertain in Mandarin Chinese – 查明

Ming ended up second from the end, right beside Luo Xuehua. She still hadn't opened her eyes. He wondered whether it had to do with a special technique she cultivated.

"Here are the rules," the examiner said abruptly. "Firstly, you will have seventy-two hours to draw ten unique magic-grade talismans. Their efficiencies must exceed sixty percent. You will use your own ink, brush, and paper. Using pure elemental evanescence is forbidden for the purposes of achieving a higher rank via augmentation. However, although it is rather wasteful, you can use it as you would normal ink or as a blend.

"Do not worry about the safety of the other examination candidates, as they will be shielded from any ill effects of your talismans. However, your eyes will not be shielded, so it is your responsibility not to lose concentration in the case of a distracting explosion. Any and all attempts to willfully distract other examinees is strictly forbidden. It will not only disqualify you from the exam, but your current qualifications will be revoked, and you will be banned from the association. Any questions?" Cha Ming and the others shook their heads. "Good. Begin!"

Cha Ming immediately began painting his first talisman, the Five-Fire Cremation Talisman. He began by expertly drawing the five fires and embedding them into the paper. He then proceeded to draw the first, the second, and the third line in expert fashion.

As he drew, each line required increasing amounts of focus and control, greatly slowing down his progress. The five symbols and ten lines took him a mere ten minutes, but the next thirty took him the remainder of an hour. The next ten lines, the most difficult and least stable of the set, would take him an entire hour to paint.

Time ticked by, and soon he only had five lines remaining. Sweat dripped from his brow as he struggled to contain the liquified elemental essence with his qi and incandescent force. The line trembled, wanting to rampage and break free, incinerating not only himself but his entire surroundings.

Suddenly he saw a flicker of light from a failed talisman nearby.

His concentration broke, and the talisman unraveled and began the inevitable explosion.

"Damn, it looks like he failed his first attempt," Feng Huoshan said from an observation balcony.

"That's normal," another master artist said beside him. "Though I still don't know why you pay so much attention to the boy."

"He's young, and he knows things," Huoshan replied. "And he's a fair bit kinder than some old geezers I know. In short, he's worth befriending. Someone like you wouldn't understand."

The fat man beside him shrugged. "That may be. Let's see how he deals with this disastrous failure. It takes a lot of qi and spiritual force to stop an explosion. That will mean more recovery time and fewer chances to paint talismans in the long run."

"Who knows," Huoshan said. "But I have faith in my little friend. Eh? *What* is he doing?" Feng Huoshan looked on in amazement as Cha Ming did nothing to prevent the explosion. He didn't even raise a simple qi shield to defend himself. "Is he suicidal?"

A fierce explosion, much larger than the previous failures, expanded and threatened to break the formations surrounding Cha Ming. Huoshan was surprised to see the examiner flash across the room to reinforce the formation. As the cloud of smoke dissipated, they saw the semblance of a man sitting cross-legged with unharmed blue robes. The desk had been smashed to smithereens, but the dummy itself had recovered. Cha Ming now looked more like a burned corpse than anything else.

"Cha Ming!" Feng Huoshan yelled and jumped out toward the young man's examination enclosure. However, as he drew nearer, the examiner looked at him coldly and motioned for him to stop.

"Watch," the middle-aged man said, releasing his intangible grasp on Feng Huoshan. Taking in a deep breath, Huoshan realized that the burned skin and hair on Cha Ming's "corpse" was rapidly regenerating. It only took a few minutes for his hair and skin to regrow. Only ashes remained of his previously burned skin. After recovering physically, Cha Ming only took an incense time to recover his incandescent force and qi before starting once more. This time, he painted from the floor, not bothering to ask for another desk and chair.

"A body cultivator?" Feng Huoshan asked.

"Obviously," the examiner said, his voice thick with disdain. "Now get back upstairs and don't utter a peep. He obviously let the explosion hit him to conserve his qi and mental strength, bearing with the pain to gain additional chances for success."

Having been thoroughly reprimanded, Feng Huoshan flew back up to the observation deck.

"What a freak," the fat man said. "How can he stand to get hurt like that, and *on purpose* to boot. One's body is a temple, and one shouldn't let it be harmed for any reason.

"And this is why your defensive talismans are the best, Brother Luo Ming," Feng Huoshan said. "And it is also why you have the *largest* temple among the masters. By the way, shouldn't you at least show a modicum of support? He will be painting the talisman you taught him. It's a pity you don't value him more. I'm sure he could help you out in the future."

"What's the point?" Luo Ming said, pulling out a bucket of fried chicken. "I have no patience for research, so what's a few extra runes? My curiosity was piqued. Nothing more."

Cha Ming's confidence wasn't shaken in the slightest as he painted the talisman a second time. He simply continued as if nothing had happened. What *did* shake him was the glimpse he caught of Luo Xuehua. She had been calmly painting her talisman with her eyes closed. He began to wonder whether she could open them in the first place.

He pushed this thought out of his mind and pondered it no further. After ten lines, he'd gotten to the difficult part. He kept focused as he painted red line after red line. This time, there was no quivering until he got to the third to the last line. It was his best attempt at creating this talisman yet. With a look of joy on his face, he finished the least-grade magic talisman. The paper turned five shades of red as it resonated with the energy of heaven and earth.

Your completion is noted, a voice spoke to him mentally. He looked toward the examiner, who nodded. *Throw your talisman at the dummy for evaluation.* Cha Ming didn't hesitate and threw it at the fragile-looking wooden dummy. Five fires burst out and raged around it, concentrating their efforts in cremating its wooden body until nothing remained. Naturally, they failed miserably in their attempts. The only remaining trace of its power was a sign on the dummy.

Least-Grade Talisman, 71% efficiency.

Cha Ming had succeeded, but he was a long way from finishing the examination. This happened to be his most proficient talisman, and the next five wouldn't be a walk in the park. Not to mention the final four he would need to complete. Since he had finished a fire-based talisman, he proceeded to begin drawing an earth-based talisman. Fire fed earth, so his previous actions would interfere the least with the Lone Mountain Suppression Talisman.

Contrary to the burning brush motions from before, his pose was stoic and sturdy, his brush strokes stable and certain. He was a living mountain. This talisman had ten characters but still only fifty connecting lines. It was only slightly more complicated than the Five-Fire Cremation Talisman. However, he had much less practice with it and could only trust in luck for success.

As Cha Ming and Xuehua painted, the other examinees struggled to produce anything of substance. It took a full ten hours for the first to produce something passable. It was a simple wood healing talisman with an efficiency of six tenths—a bare pass. Other successful products trickled in soon after, but it was clear that this rate of completion wouldn't bring them a passing mark. On average, each talisman could only take seven hours. They would be hard-pressed to complete the examination and could only trust their fates to chance.

On the fourteen-hour mark, Cha Ming successfully created a talisman that summoned an illusory mountain, which bore down on the practice mannequin and crushed it with impunity. After recovering, a score of 73% efficiency was recorded, and Cha Ming moved on to the next one. Shortly after, Luo Xuehua finished her third talisman, once again an ice-element talisman. It summoned a thousand silver snowflakes to strike various vital points on the mannequin. Its efficiency was frightening—93%! This was the highest recorded efficiency yet during the examination. In fact, it seemed like an insurmountable record. Cha Ming suspected that the ice element resonated with her icy demeanor.

Another sixteen hours passed, and by the thirty-hour mark, Cha Ming finally managed to produce the Nine Blades, One Dao Talisman, the self-taught talisman which gave him the most difficult time. He barely passed with a mark of sixty percent. Unfortunately, almost half of his time had elapsed. It would be difficult to make up the lost time. He maintained his calm composure and proceeded to the Myriad Ice Shield Talisman.

"There it is, the Myriad Ice Shield Talisman!" Luo Ming exclaimed.

"Aren't you a little too excited?" Feng Huoshan teased. He had remained seated the entire time, unlike a certain slovenly friend who left periodically for meals.

"I can't help it, it's truly my favorite talisman," Luo Ming said, licking the grease from his fingers. "It captures the very essence of cultivation. Evolution, strength, and absolute defense. It has no undesirable qualities. With enough Myriad Ice Shield Talismans, one would never get injured."

Feng Huoshan rolled his eyes at his friend's usual banter. Fortunately, Cha Ming didn't disappoint. After two tries and four hours, he managed to complete the talisman. However, only thirty-eight hours remained for the final six talismans, so Huoshan couldn't help but feel nervous for his young friend.

"Hua Dong, how proficient is he in the Eight Treasures Healing Talisman and the Five Poisons Talisman?" Huoshan asked. The man had just joined them in the spectator stands.

"He's terrible," Hua Dong replied. "Cha Ming's success rate doesn't exceed 25% for both. It will be difficult for him to finish. Speaking of which, does anyone know which other four talismans he has under his belt?" The other two shook their heads and looked on with rapt attention.

Condense! Cha Ming yelled mentally, forcing the Eight Treasures Healing Talisman into submission. Then, after receiving his instructions, he threw it at the mannequin. It glowed green, and a value of sixty-five percent floated up. Unfortunately, generating the talisman had taken him six hours. This was better than average but left him with very little time. Forty hours out of seventy-two had elapsed. Painting talismans was getting increasingly difficult. Recovering mental energy became more strenuous as time passed.

With hands shaking from unpleasant memories, he began painting the Five Poisons Talisman. The backlash on the Five Poisons Talisman was much more brutal than the others, but he didn't have the qi or mental energy to divert in the case of a failure.

Two hours passed before he failed his first attempt. The runic lines collapsed, and a five-colored fog invaded his body. Excruciating pain shot through his limbs as he exerted the power of bone forging to force the poison out of his pores while simultaneously recovering his mental energy and qi. This process alone took another two hours to complete.

The next three attempts resulted in failure as well. Fifty-six out of seventy-two hours had passed. Gritting his teeth, he attempted once more. After so many consecutive failures, he noticed that the poison had a sensitizing effect. Each subsequent poisoning made the pain increasingly unbearable. To have any chance in completing the examination, he *needed* to finish this next one. Therefore, he took extra care and painted at half pace. Before long, four hours had passed. It was the sixtieth hour, and only three lines remained.

It was then that a blinding flash of light emanated from the shield next to his. The man had been attempting a dangerous lightning-based talisman, and the recoil of the failure was especially intense. The examiner was forced to disperse the shield and save him, but not before his right hand was scorched black. While it wasn't impossible to heal it via expensive spirit medicines, his ability to paint might be impaired for the rest of his life.

This shocking sight caused Cha Ming's poison talisman to destabilize ever so slightly. Unfortunately, he knew full well that it was the beginning of the end. After painting two more lines, the talisman began to shake uncontrollably.

I can't fail here, Cha Ming thought. The poisonous thread unraveled before his eyes, threatening to destroy the talisman. *I can't fail here,* he repeated. He sent out his incandescent force and qi, firmly grasping the shuddering thread. Its wild nature made Cha Ming cough up blood. Fortunately, he avoided spraying it all over the talisman and ruining it.

Submit! he yelled mentally. That was when he heard a snap. It wasn't the string that broke, but the invisible bindings on his soul. As soon as the binding was broken, he felt an even purer incandescent force pouring toward the talisman and preventing it from collapsing. His soul had advanced to the peak of the incandescent soul realm. Without hesitating, he used his qi and soul to guide the ink and draw the remaining lines. They fell into place, and the talisman shimmered after completion.

Cha Ming let out a sigh of relief as he threw the Five Poisons Talisman at the dummy, and its external coating dissolved while assessing it.

Least-Grade Magic Talisman. Efficiency—61%. A bare pass.

Chapter 15: The Final Hurdle

Cha Ming sat down and healed his wounds. He didn't open his eyes until four hours had passed. There were now only eight hours remaining to complete the examination. Four talismans in eight hours might seem like an impossible feat for most, but for Cha Ming it could happen. He just needed the stars to align.

Cha Ming did not immediately proceed to drawing the next talisman. Instead he withdrew a piece of paper and began adjusting his mental state. Due to his realization the night before, he knew that this period of adjustment was critical before drawing a poetic talisman. He needed to reinvent his original realizations.

This time, Cha Ming thought not only of his experience in the mines, but of his subsequent recovery. It was a story of breaking and healing. He relived this journey in vivid detail and lost track of time. After experiencing his previous epiphany, he remembered his struggles to get this far, his feeling of helplessness before the examination. Then he recalled the advice he'd received from the mysterious painter and the subsequent feeling of calmness and comfort.

Cha Ming alternated between desperation and comfort, emulating these emotions over and over. It was a tiring process, a time-consuming one. Three and a half hours passed before he regained his lucidity, and to the surprise of the master artists, he went straight to work. His brush flowed with a trembling hand as he poured out his emotions into the Crumbling Talisman. It took only an incense time before the words were fully written.

The weight of the world crumbles countless dreams;
Man's foundation is ever brittle.

He didn't stop there, immediately proceeding to the next talisman, the Hardening Talisman. His pose firmed up as he painted it with a steady hand.

Hardening through countless ages;
Never questioning his resolve.

As soon as he finished this second talisman, he felt his emotions destabilize ever so slightly. He would need to recover before painting these two talismans again. But that was a problem for another time.

Cha Ming immediately began attuning his emotions once more while simultaneously recovering his mental energy and qi. He didn't test the talismans for now, as this would only distract him. Testing them could wait. After all, the examination only required him to *craft* the talismans within the time limit.

Once more, Cha Ming remembered floating through life and his lack of ambition. He focused on the feelings of resistance and helplessness to fight against the current. At the same time, he recalled the feeling of momentum he'd been feeling since Fuxi's Library. One success leading to another. Even his current success as a talisman artist was due to this unstoppable momentum. Resistance and momentum were opposites, and they were both separated by a calm and relaxed disposition, the same one he had experienced in the art gallery.

Time continued to pass by, and before he knew it, only a quarter hour remained. His eyes opened. They were somehow simultaneously filled with both apathy and relentless momentum.

The ocean cares not for drowning children;
Man is a slave to the sea of fate.

He only took a brief pause before beginning the next talisman.

Flowing down from high to low;
Never questioning his direction.

It only took him two-thirds of his remaining time to paint both talismans, but it took him the remainder of the allotment to organize his turbulent emotions enough to control them. He was sure that any attempts to paint these four talismans would fail immediately and disastrously, and it would take a long time to recover his mental state like it had the previous day.

"The examination has ended," the examiner's voice called out. The shields immediately dispersed. "Luo Xuehua, Lin Dongming, congratulations on passing this examination. Xuehua will be awarded a lesser-grade master medal, while Dongming will be awarded a least-grade medal. The rest of you, don't forget to practice hard. Cha Ming, please go ahead and throw your talismans at the dummy. Your test results will be determined by their ratings."

Cha Ming nodded and stood up to throw them. He held the first talisman, the Crumbling Talisman, between two fingers, but just as he was about to fling it, an intangible force stopped his arm mid-throw. He looked over to the examiner with a perplexed look on his face.

"My apologies, everyone," the examiner said calmly. "The branch leader has requested that these talismans be tested via emulation formation. Everyone please take a seat while I set this up. It won't take more than a half hour." The man immediately proceeded to the center of the room, sweeping away the mannequins and formations as he walked. He then threw out several flags with written characters and began painting thick runic lines on the floor with a giant paintbrush.

"Brother Cha Ming, what an impressive display," a voice said from above. Feng Huoshan and his two friends flew down from the seats above. "Four talismans in a little more than five hours. We would be hard-pressed to do the same."

Cha Ming shook his head. "Brother Huoshan overpraises. The three hours of preparation beforehand were very important. It took me eight hours in reality. Besides, the talismans aren't yet evaluated."

"It's still an impressive feat," Huoshan said. "And the evaluation is just a formality. Setting up this formation comes at great expense. One only uses such a formation to appraise talismans without destroying them. The formation's value isn't less than a mid-grade talisman. Do you think they would waste so much effort on a failed product? At their realm, they already know the result but need proof to placate the audience."

True to his words, the examiner finished the formation in exactly half an hour. It was built with water and earth element components, many of which Cha Ming didn't recognize. He handed the talismans to the examiner while bowing courteously. The examiner proceeded to place the first talisman, the Crumbling Talisman, in the center of the formation.

As soon as the man stepped out, the crystals and lines in formation began to dim, and a projection lit up the room. Cha Ming saw two earth golems appear and begin fighting. They fought for an incense time with no result, showing that they were evenly matched. They continued fighting with increasing intensity and increasingly powerful blows until rocks began to fall off their freshly constructed bodies. A light flashed, and a brown talisman suddenly struck one of the golems. He let out a loud roar. To the audience's surprise, the next fist strike from the opposing golem shattered its chest. The next blow shattered its hip. A final strike demolished the golem's head. It was a clean victory.

Crumbling Talisman (Poetic Talisman—Du Cha Ming) Lesser-Grade Magic Talisman. Efficiency—100%. The display appeared briefly before fading.

The examiner then walked up once more, retrieving the used talisman and replacing it with the Hardening Talisman. Fist strikes rained down from both golems until they became powerful enough to damage each other. This time, a light flashed and struck the same golem. But instead of shattering, its rocky skin glistened like a freshly polished gem. It struck the other golem without fear, breaking off small pieces one at a time. After thirty breaths, the effects wore off, and the other golem's blows began taking their toll, and the lead he had developed granted an easy victory.

Hardening Talisman (Poetic Talisman—Du Cha Ming) Lesser-Grade Magic Talisman. Efficiency—100%.

Its effects weren't as surprising as the first, but plenty of talk ensued. The examiner ignored them and tested both remaining talismans sequentially. This time, the results were a lot closer. The Resistance Talisman caused the reaction speed of one golem to slow, but its attacks were difficult to interrupt. Ultimately, the affected golem succumbed.

The Momentum Talisman, on the other hand, caused the golem to deal much more damage, but its motions became awkward and difficult to control. Despite this handicap, it still won the exchange.

Resistance Talisman (Poetic Talisman—Du Cha Ming) Lesser-Grade Magic Talisman. Efficiency—100%.

Momentum Talisman (Poetic Talisman—Du Cha Ming) Lesser-Grade Magic Talisman. Efficiency—100%.

Four talismans at one-hundred-percent efficiency appeared simultaneously, and they were all original creations. Cha Ming was quite curious as to how the formation was able to determine he was the original creator. It also knew the original name he'd given it.

"Congratulations, Cha Ming, on achieving the rank of lesser-grade master artist," the examiner said, flicking his sleeve. A silver medal was quickly engraved with Cha Ming's credentials, and the examiner pinned it directly to his robes. "Do make sure to visit the guild leader once these formalities are over. And bring those talismans." The man's cold demeanor had softened considerably after Cha Ming's success.

"Congratulations, Brother Cha Ming," Feng Huoshan, Luo Ming, and Hua Dong said while clasping their fists and bowing.

"You are too kind, seniors," Cha Ming replied and returned the gesture. The master artists then made various excuses to depart.

"Congratulations to you, Brother Cha Ming," Luo Xuehua said sweetly. "It's impressive that you were able to not only pass but obtain your lesser-master qualification."

"The same goes to you, Sister Xuehua," Cha Ming said. "I just barely passed. You, however, did so with your eyes closed." He instantly regretted his poor choice of words, as the young lady with silver hair smiled bitterly.

"You should go ahead and see the branch leader," Xuehua said, walking away. Once again, she was surrounded by an aura of unapproachable loneliness.

Cha Ming proceeded to the branch leader's office immediately after the examination ended. He quickly used his water qi to freshen up, removing most of the dirt, blood, and grime that had accumulated over the course of the test. He then dried himself off using fire qi.

It was a short walk to the branch leader's office. He needed no one to guide him, as this was the only place in the guild that his incandescent force couldn't invade. As far as he knew, there were only two possible reasons for this. The first involved a large quantity of very expensive spirit-repelling materials to perfectly insulate the room. The second and most likely reason was that the branch leader was a core-formation cultivator. A core-formation cultivator's soul was qualitatively different compared to his incandescent soul.

Cha Ming soon arrived at a luxurious waiting room. The door to the branch leader's office was shut, so Cha Ming could only wait. He had no doubt that the branch leader already knew he had arrived; therefore he took his time admiring the four exquisite paintings situated on each of the four walls. They each represented a season, and by looking at them, Cha Ming could feel the temperature in the room change to match the season he looked at. The paintings felt familiar, so he looked for a signature. He soon found it hidden in a corner—Jun Xiezi. All four were Jun Xiezi's works.

An hour passed before the door opened and the examiner, after bowing toward the inside of the room, flew out of a side window without glancing at him. "Come in," a pleasant but strangely familiar voice called out.

Cha Ming walked into a room illuminated by a large window. The sun happened to be shining in his eyes and obscuring the man's figure. He could only look toward the side as he walked forward.

The room smelled of rose petals and morning dew, and to his surprise, the moment he entered, the residual blood and soot that he'd missed in his hasty cleaning had disappeared. In addition, he felt hidden wounds that hadn't yet regenerated heal instantly.

This room also had paintings on all four walls, but instead of four separate paintings, a continuous fresco traveled just below the ceiling. The two-foot-wide painting displayed scenes and people frolicking in a spring. The rose petals were being spread out by servants who waited on the young lords and ladies. He recognized the style, of course. It was Jun Xiezi's style.

"Art is a wonderful thing," a soft voice said. "Without it, life is emotionless and stale, a race for survival. A competition. People become so entangled in everyday life that they forget to appreciate what is around them, to sit down and smell the roses."

The speaker was a silver-haired old man. He was unfathomable, both in cultivation and soul. Considering the man's cultivation and apparent age, Cha Ming wouldn't be surprised if he had lived over four hundred years. Moreover, his identity was surprising. It was the man from the art gallery.

"Greetings, senior," Cha Ming said, bowing deeply. "Never could I have imagined that the branch leader was enjoying the paintings in the gallery like everyone else."

The man smiled. "Why shouldn't I? Not only do I get to enjoy the paintings, but I get a constant flow of appreciative company. Like yourself, for example."

"I see that you're very enamored with Jun Xiezi's paintings," Cha Ming said, observing the intricate artwork on the walls with appreciation.

"I should be," the man said. "A man should always enjoy his own work."

"You mean... *you* are Jun Xiezi?" Cha Ming asked, his eyes wide.

"Naturally," Jun Xiezi said. "How else would I have more of Jun Xiezi's artwork in my office than the rest of the city combined? Now tell me, what do you think of art?"

The question caught Cha Ming by surprise. It was an especially meaningful question, given that it came from such a prestigious painter.

Cha Ming hesitated. "Branch Leader, my knowledge of art is very shallow. Therefore, I believe my answer might lack depth."

"Entertain me," the man said, smiling. "And do away with the honorifics, as I really can't stand them. Please call me Jun Xiezi. Senior, if you must."

"Of course, Senior Xiezi," Cha Ming said. "Since you would like to hear it, I will share my meager thoughts on the matter. But for that, I will need to start at the beginning."

"Oh?" Jun Xiezi said. "Please go ahead, I'm curious to hear it. Meanwhile, let us have some of this herbal tea. I was brewing it before you came in, so I hope you enjoy it."

A clear teapot was sitting on the man's wooden desk, revealing a beautiful flower arrangement floating within its heated waters. Jun Xiezi's bony and wrinkled hand firmly grasped the teapot, pouring it into two small transparent cups. The tea was light and aromatic, as many herbal teas were. Cha Ming tapped both his fingers on the table after sitting down, then smelled the tea for a while before taking a sip.

"I can't say I've ever tasted anything quite like this," Cha Ming said. The tea tasted both hot and refreshing at the same time. If he were to describe its nature, it would be "pure," just like the sensation he felt as he walked into the room.

"I would be surprised if you had," the man said, smiling again. "These flowers come from a transcendent realm, and they are difficult for most people to procure. Fortunately I've taken to growing them in my garden." He motioned to a painting beside him depicting thorny rose bushes. "Please continue with your explanation."

"Right," Cha Ming said. "In the beginning, people were concerned with survival. They struggled every day. Their lives were full of suffering but full of purpose. They lived in caves. Despite this hard life, they still discovered that one could leave marks on a wall with coal, and they began recording stories. They did this both to remember and to facilitate the telling of stories orally. These stories were a respite from the monotony, something they *chose* to do, despite their struggle for survival.

"With time, society evolved. People gained additional free time, and their choices grew exponentially. Their stories grew, and their styles evolved. So too did the styles, the quality, and the quantity of paintings. The same applied to clothing. Art evolved with mankind and evolved with their prosperity.

"I dare to speculate that eventually, everyone will become so completely secure that their lives will seem meaningless and without purpose. This world has not yet reached that point, but I believe it will. Yet regardless of how meaningless life seems, people will never fail to appreciate the art they resonate with.

"Art is both a distraction from reality and an extension of it. During times of war, people wish they could be at home singing songs, telling stories, or participating in various art forms. During times of peace, people flock to art in droves.

"Art is wonderful because it's an expression of choice, something people historically have very little of. People can choose to make it, choose to enjoy it. It is an expression of the most powerful emotions mankind can produce. As such, humans will make art for as long as humanity exists."

Xiezi looked at him pensively, his eyes piercing into his soul. "It is very interesting for someone of this plane to have such a point of view," he said, sighing. "It is indeed as you say. Society will flourish to the point that people will lose motivation. This is what my teacher has told me. He is from a transcendent plane, you see; his perspective much vaster than you can imagine.

"Since you have been kind enough to give me an answer, I will now give you mine. Art, my friend, is the ultimate expression of emotions," the man said. "To the point that *nature itself* will resonate with art once it reaches a certain level. Moreover, art at a high enough level will birth runes intrinsically. Take a closer look at the painting you were just looking at."

Curious, Cha Ming gazed at the fresco. He didn't blink, lest he miss something.

"You are focusing too hard," the man said. "Don't focus."

Cha Ming blinked his eyes, letting them wander as they chose. Before long, his eyesight blurred, but *something* he saw became clearer. Shifting, glowing lines began to appear. They floated around the painting, dancing with joy. He could vaguely perceive them as runes, but he didn't have sufficient insight to truly see them.

"Only those who have gained inspiration on the true meaning of the painting will be able to see them," the man said, chuckling. "However, you have experienced their effect. As soon as you entered the room, they freshened and revitalized you. This is my understanding and my manifestation of art. The proof is in what you see around you.

"My paintings are infused with my desire to relax, travel, and appreciate the world's beauty. Every painting I make is infused with a wonderful scene that I've personally witnessed. This specific moment was decades ago, when I visited the decadent Sui Kingdom. This was one of their famous parties, one held by a royal prince. It was one of the most relaxing and invigorating experiences in my life."

They sat for a few moments, contemplating each other's answers while sipping tea. After a while, Cha Ming recalled where he was and looked up to see the man peering at him from his chair. "Senior Xiezi, the examiner told me you wanted to see me. I presume it has something to do with the talismans I painted?"

The man nodded. "Indeed. I had them test them differently because I would like to trade for your talismans."

Cha Ming had expected this answer, but he was quite reluctant. These talismans were a very personal production, with much emotional investment. No one else in the world could make them.

"I understand your reluctance," the man said, sighing. Then he motioned to the various paintings and the fresco in the room. "These paintings are my life's work, and it would pain me to part with any of them. In fact, the only reason some of my art is in the gallery is because I owed a friend a favor. I have never sold a painting, only gifted them. And while I like traveling, I owed another favor to the Northern Talisman Artist Guild's leader, who happens to be a master sculptor and gifted me one of his famous works. So here I am, shackled to this desk for ten more years.

"I propose a trade," Jun Xiezi said, his eyes glittering. "After you painted the first two talismans, I had an epiphany. I've created a polarized painting that I believe could be very useful to you. I hope you'll consider trading your talismans for it." The silver-haired man waved his sleeve. A six-foot-by-six-foot painting appeared in the room.

Cha Ming inhaled sharply as he stared at the painting, which looked a lot more like two individual creations. On the lower-right corner was vivid greenery, flowers, and vitality. He felt his emotions recover just by looking at it, and he could faintly sense that if he looked at it long enough, his emotional state would recover enough to be able to paint his four poetic talismans once more. However, looking at the upper-left corner, he saw dried-out trunks devoid of life and a poisonous miasma. It eroded at his soul and worsened his emotions.

Looking at the middle of the painting, this destruction and nurturing reached an equilibrium. He felt that during this cycle, his soul was slowly strengthening, wearing away at the bottleneck into the next realm.

"I was inspired by the polarized nature of your talismans," Jun Xiezi said. "When you came to the art gallery yesterday, you seemed confused and distraught. However, I noticed that my painting stabilized you and your emotions. This painting was made for you and is my gift to you, should you choose to accept it. It will help refine your soul, and perhaps in the long term, you can gain inspiration from it."

Cha Ming gulped as he inspected the painting a little more closely. It emanated a substantial pressure that far exceeded his Clear Sky Staff or Stormchaser Boots. "This is a core-formation treasure?"

"That's right, it's a core treasure," the man said. "But it's the least of core treasures, so don't bother yourself with that."

"This is much too valuable," Cha Ming said, shaking his head.

"Then trade me a promise as well," the man said. "When you make new poetic talismans, I want one of each of them. That way you don't have to feel guilty, and I can study your four talismans and look for inspiration with a clear conscience."

Cha Ming nodded. "Very well, it's a deal." Cha Ming took out his four talismans and placed them on the desk, and at Jun Xiezi's insistence, he stowed away the painting in his Clear Sky World.

"Fascinating," Xiezi said, examining one of the talismans. "You made your talismans using runic poetry. If I am not mistaken, you've infused emotions of resistance and momentum into the water talismans, while infusing crumbling and hardening into the earth talismans. How very interesting. My master once told me of a sect in the transcendent realm closest to this mortal plane called the Inky Sea Sect. They do something similar there."

Cha Ming chuckled. "You are certainly very well educated. I was taught talisman arts by a member of the Inky Sea Sect." Of course, Cha Ming had not known this at the time. It was only after he read Elder Ling's letter that he knew this.

"As I suspected," the man said, nodding. "Thank you very much for sharing these insights with me. "

Seeing that Xiezi's gaze lingered on the talismans on the table, Cha Ming took the hint and stood up. "It's been a pleasure, senior. I'm very tired and should be heading back to my accommodations."

The silver-haired man nodded slightly, and Cha Ming left him to his contemplation.

Interlude
A Meeting on the Mountain

Huxian was deep in thought over the issue of Silverwing, whom he hadn't seen since their adventure. He was resting on the jade plate at the peak of the mountain, enjoying its cool, mystical feeling. Its surface, which was covered in runes he couldn't understand, had a mystical charm to it. It mesmerized him and helped him focus. Just like it did in his dreams, where he painted talismans.

He was also thinking about Lei Jiang. The guilt he felt every time he saw the small mouse was unbearable. He knew he'd done wrong, but he wasn't sure what to do about it.

The sound of flapping wings awoke him from his stupor. *Is it Silverwing?* he thought. *No. Silverwing flaps much faster than that.*

The sound came every few breaths. And as the sound drew closer, the wind generated became increasingly difficult to bear.

A large brown owl landed near the jade plate where Huxian lay. It looked at him with its head twisted sideways. Huxian could tell at a glance that he would be unable to resist if it decided to eat him. "Are you the monarch?" he asked fearfully.

"Correct," the owl said. It hopped over and took a few sniffs at Huxian, who was too petrified to move. "You smell of humans," the monarch said. "Do you have a relationship with the humans? This is a very important matter, so answer truthfully."

Shit, he's caught me, Huxian thought. "So what if I do?" he cried. "It's not like I'd be the first beast to have a human as a friend." He held his ground against the overwhelming pressure, using every fiber of his Godbeast being to fight against it.

The owl snorted coldly. "How dare you talk to your superior this way." The monarch's pressure intensified, forcing Huxian down to his belly. Huxian bared his teeth but could do nothing to fight it.

"If you're going to eat me, just do it already," Huxian said through gritted teeth.

"Eat you?" the monarch asked. The pressure that had borne down on Huxian suddenly vanished. "Yes, eating you would be a very good course of action. Your delicious Godbeast blood would provide me the greatest nourishment."

Huxian gulped. He saw the owl walking toward him with its two large talons. He felt their sharpness despite their distance. He closed his eyes and awaited his inevitable demise. Instead, a fresh breeze buffeted his body.

Huxian opened his eyes and realized the owl was no longer there. The monarch had left as quickly as he had come. He left Huxian with his guilt and sorrow on the mountaintop.

He also left him with a new emotion: fear.

Chapter 16: Competition

Wang Jun yawned. An entire day's worth of proceedings had worn him down once more with nothing to show for it. They were at an impasse, and there was little he could do to resolve it.

"I just don't see why the third prince should have the right to extract such a valuable resource," an old advisor, Sima Liang, said toward the throne. The king was seated, as usual. If he had been in any reasonable shape, the dispute would have ended quickly. Unfortunately, time had taken its toll on the old king. He was on his last legs, and everyone knew it.

"The crown prince might be the designated successor, but does this give him a right to everything under the sun?" another advisor said. "If he wanted your wife, old Sima, would you wrap her up and deliver her for his pleasure?" He was Prince Lei's mentor, Hao Bodong. While he wasn't the most powerful man, his incisive tongue was an extremely valuable asset in the court.

Sure as rain, Sima Liang seethed with rage. "How dare a miscreant like you bring my wife into this! I recommend that he be suspended for his insolence."

"Then I am to suppose that you highly value your wife?" Hao Bodong continued. "Many people would pay a lot less for her than an immortal jade mine. Yet she is out of the question because you feel so strongly. Well, that's how it is with most things, isn't it? People feel strongly about the jade mine, so that is why we are meeting to discuss. And just like the crown prince can't take your wife whenever he pleases, neither can he take this jade mine just because he fancies it."

Sima Liang didn't know how to retort.

Such meetings had gone on for weeks with little progress. Yet progress was necessary. Otherwise the crown prince's advantage would continue unimpeded and his rule uncontested.

Contest, he thought. *Not a bad idea. Perhaps...*

The wheels in Wang Jun's mind began turning. While the older men bickered, he calculated. It wasn't long before he stood up swiftly, looking at the throne for permission to speak. Master Bei, the king's long-time servant and most loyal supporter, waved his hand for Wang Jun to speak.

"It seems to me that this court is at an unresolvable impasse," Wang Jun said. "Yet I'm sure that everyone agrees that a resource in the ground is of no benefit to the country. A resource is best utilized, and its taxes are better in the coffers sooner rather than later. Is this a correct assumption?"

The various voices in the royal court murmured in assent.

"Then I propose the following motion," Wang Jun continued. "A competition, whose winner will decide the mining rights."

"That's irresponsible," a minister yelled. "How can such an important matter be decided with an irrelevant contest?" Many other voices agreed, but surprisingly, neither faction applying for the rights voiced their opposition.

"The contest I am speaking of is extremely relevant, gracious minister," Wang Jun said. "Will you allow me to elaborate?"

"Very well," the minister said. "But let it be known that I will not support any decision that is not beneficial to the kingdom. I don't give a damn about politics or political maneuverings."

"Thank you, minister," Wang Jun said, bowing deeply. Then, looking around the room, he began explaining his idea. "The competition that I propose will, in fact, take us closer to securing the jade mine. This will happen regardless of who gains the mining rights. The Silverwing Mountain Range is far too dangerous for either the third prince's or the crown prince's forces to take individually. The cost would be too great. This means that the kingdom would need to bear the burden of clearing the beasts to secure its tax revenue, greatly reducing the kingdom's return on investment.

"I propose that each party send over forces below core formation, with each party bearing their respective expenses. The party with the most substantial contributions to securing the mountain range will gain the mining rights, while the one with the least substantial contributions will gain nothing."

The minister, Rong Bai, looked pensive. "This is indeed a good proposition. However, I do have some concerns that must be addressed. For one, it is not beneficial for the kingdom if the competing forces fight each other. This must be prevented at all costs. That aside, how are we to decide the results of the competition?"

"I have given this a great deal of thought, Prime Minister Rong," Wang Jun said. "And I fully agree with you that our forces must not fight each other and should direct their attention on the demonic beasts within the mountain range. To mitigate the chances of such treachery, I propose that a core-formation arbiter be sent to oversee the competition. Should one side willfully cause damage to the other, the offending party would be disqualified from the competition.

"At the same time, the supervisor shall keep a tally of accomplishments. I understand that it is difficult to be exact when judging contributions. If one side kills three-quarters of the beasts but loses nine-tenths of their forces, while the other kills one quarter of the beasts but loses one-tenth, it is clear which side has achieved an excellent result and which one has suffered disastrous losses.

"Further, killing beasts may not be the only way of resolving this issue. There are countless stratagems that can achieve a similar result, and I do not dare claim to be all-knowing. That is why I suggest the supervisor also be the judge of the competition, responsible for choosing the winner. If the result is a tie, we can only see this as the heavens themselves being undecided, and at that point we can simply decide the result by drawing lots. What are your thoughts, Prime Minister Rong?"

The older man pondered for a moment before nodding. "This is a good suggestion. But who do you propose be the judge? Among all present, I daresay that I would only trust the king's judgment. However, he is much needed in the kingdom at this time…"

This was a diplomatic way of addressing the king's current ill health without degrading his dignity. The man was impeccable to a fault, and practically an embodiment of justice. As a result, he had maintained his post as the prime minister for the past twenty years.

"Why, I am surprised that you should ask," Wang Jun said, raising his eyebrow. "After all, I think the only man aside from the king whose judgment all ministers trust unconditionally is your esteemed self. In fact, I believe both the crown prince and the third prince would testify to this point. Isn't that right, my princes?"

The third prince nodded in assent, forcing the crown prince to do the same.

"Very well, I accept this proposition," Prime Minister Rong said. "Who is in favor?"

One by one, the ministers forming the king's government stood up in unanimous support. The two princes, the only others with any authority on the matter, stood up as well. Wang Jun's eyes flickered when he also saw the king's hand tremble and lift ever so slightly.

"The matter is finalized. The competition will start in one week's time at the outskirts of the Silverwing Mountain Range. Spend your time wisely."

"How could you propose such a competition without at least warning me?" Prince Lei said angrily. Wang Jun smiled wryly at the uncharacteristic outburst from the usually calm man.

"Your Highness, you trust me, don't you?" Wang Jun said deferentially. The prince's agitation lessened somewhat. Wang Jun sat down and began brewing tea, giving the man more time to calm his rage.

"A stalemate was not advantageous to us," Wang Jun explained. "If the situation had continued, we would have been at a disadvantage in the eventual power struggle.

"My actions today used the practical nature of our prime minister to our advantage, breaking the stalemate. Make no mistake, it comes at great risk. Not only are we competing for the mining rights, but we risk severe casualties in the process. However, I still believe that such a competition is to our advantage."

"And why would that be?" Prince Lei asked.

"Prince Lei, let us examine our respective advantages," Wang Jun said. "Firstly, we have superior weaponry. We control the majority of weaponsmithing in the kingdom, and we have ample resources with which to arm our forces. Speaking of forces, most of ours are private forces while the crown prince controls much of the military. However, the military also belongs to the country…"

"Therefore, the crown prince cannot use them in this struggle," Prince Lei said, nodding. "I understand now. We have more investors on our side with which to hire more private forces. Meanwhile, the crown prince will need to beg and exchange favors with the nobility, a much more difficult task. However, they do have their advantages."

"Nothing is perfect, my prince," Wang Jun said. "They have an advantage in life-savings pills. They also have better relationships with veterans and retired generals, courageous people with iron veins. Also, the nobility's forces tend to be one step stronger and more loyal than hired hands. Still, I believe our odds of prevailing in this conflict are greater than eighty percent. That is, unless…"

Prince Lei frowned. "Unless what?"

"Your Highness, there may be some external interference in this competition," Wang Jun said. "If other kingdoms meddle and contribute forces or funds in secret, our advantage will be reduced. Therefore we must muster our forces and end this conflict quickly. The longer it drags out, the less advantageous the situation becomes."

Wang Jun returned to the Jade Bamboo Auction House after his conversation with the third prince. After giving several instructions to Elder Bai and Protector Ren, he retreated to his room and retrieved his core-transmission jade.

Ring. Ring. Ring.

One hundred breaths passed before Cha Ming's image appeared. "My friend, it's been a few weeks since we last spoke," Cha Ming said with a smile.

"I'll admit, I've been busy," Wang Jun said. "How did it go?"

"Passed with flying colors, of course," Cha Ming said. "You're looking at a genuine lesser-grade talisman master."

"Skipped over least-grade, I see," Wang Jun said, relaxing a little. With his status, Cha Ming would be able to lend him a hand in the upcoming conflict. "That's wonderful news. What do you plan to do next?"

Cha Ming pondered for a moment before answering. "There are two things I must do. First, I must secure medicinal pills and break through to at least mid-foundation establishment. Unfortunately, I am greatly lacking in battle techniques. In addition, I am concerned with the large amount of formations that appeared in the Song Kingdom during the Fairweather incident. I wish to find a formation master and learn to break formations. Otherwise we may be at a great disadvantage."

"You've matured," Wang Jun said with a smile. "In the past, you would always ask me for direction and advice. Now you know how to make your own decisions."

Cha Ming shrugged. "What can I say, I've been through a lot."

"Fair enough," Wang Jun said. "If you're going to study formations, you'll need to find yourself a teacher. Unfortunately, the occupation is rather rare. There is no formation master guild in

Quicksilver, so I can only recommend you try and join the Alabaster Group or the Obsidian Syndicate. Coincidentally, I have a matter there that requires your aid."

"Do tell," Cha Ming said.

"It's like this," Wang Jun said. "Do you remember the jade mine I mentioned? It's located in the Silverwing Mountain Range."

"Silverwing?" A perplexed look appeared on Cha Ming's apparition. "Does it have nine mountain peaks, each with a mysterious jade plate? One of the mountains has a tall spire that rises up above the others?"

"You're familiar with it, then?" Wang Jun asked, surprised.

Cha Ming shook his head. "I had a dream about it. I saw a bird called Silverwing and a mouse that devoured purple lightning. I saw a lion with brown scales overseeing an unnatural plain."

"You mean the silver creature that no one can identify? And the Reptilian Lion Sovereign?" Wang Jun said, shocked. "If I didn't know you better, I would guess you were a seer. But no, there must be a reason for your dreams." Wang Jun then explained the details of the competition.

"I need your help in securing superior cultivators for the expedition," Wang Jun concluded. "And to do that, you need to join either of the groups I mentioned. This will give you the ability to issue missions and more easily recruit their upper-tier forces if needed. I'm not sure if we'll need them in the end, but I need options."

"I heard these organizations are only open to those who receive invitations," Cha Ming said.

"You should receive an invitation from the Obsidian Syndicate shortly," Wang Jun said. "They have very loose rules and sell their services to the highest bidder. They believe in making money over anything. However, they aren't exactly a savory bunch. If possible, it would be best if you can join the Alabaster Group. Their members are of higher quality and of better moral standing. Hiring the Obsidian Syndicate would have me walking on eggshells."

Cha Ming nodded. "Not a problem. I've heard of both organizations, of course. I intended to pay them both a visit. I heard it's possible to purchase advanced techniques there. The only problem is securing an invitation to the Alabaster Group."

Wang Jun nodded. "Only the Obsidian Syndicate would sell its techniques. The Alabaster Group is much stricter, and money doesn't get you far in their organization. I must warn you that you probably won't like the Obsidian Syndicate. I finally finished my research on the man named Xiao Heilong."

Cha Ming frowned.

"He is a member their organization, though they don't really care if their members kill each other. Regardless, I discovered that he paid a member of his organization to divine your location and lock it into a compass. He has been absent for many months on an unknown assignment. He could return at any time."

"How did you obtain this news?" Cha Ming asked.

"I bought it from the Obsidian Syndicate, of course," Wang Jun replied dryly.

Cha Ming wrinkled his nose. "I hate them already."

Chapter 17: Obstruction

Wang Jun's projection winked out, leaving Cha Ming in his personal residence at the Talisman Artist Guild. The large apartment, one of the many perks of being a master member, was filled with various pieces of spirit-wood furniture. Each piece contributed to the ambiance in the room and increased Cha Ming's energy and revitalized his mental strength, albeit slowly.

Since the call was over, Cha Ming turned his attention to his previous activity, pondering the mysteries of the painting. It was unnamed when he received it, so Cha Ming decided to call it *Samsara*[9]. It was a fitting name, given that the painting embodied life and death as well as the mysterious realm in between.

As Cha Ming observed the painting, his soul was continually broken down by the poisonous energy and revitalized by the ample life energy. Even though his soul was at the peak of incandescence, it was becoming more tangible and stable. The process also allowed him to sort out the various confused emotions in his psyche. The painting was essentially an automated psychologist, a sounding board to help propel and reorganize his thoughts. He estimated that in one week's time he would be calm enough to paint his four poetic talismans once more.

Half an hour passed before Cha Ming ended his meditation session. He returned the painting into his Clear Sky World, instantly

---

9 The cycle of reincarnation.

eliminating the chaotic vitality in the room. Various plants had withered while others had grown significantly, due to the painting's energy.

I'll need to get rid of all these plants at some point, he thought. *Wait. I'll just replace them with succulents. Those things take forever to grow and are practically impossible to kill.*

Cha Ming exited the guild premises, nodding slightly to everyone he passed. Now that he was a master artist, those of lower rank were expected to bow in greeting. Not that he cared much for this sort of formality, but he accepted their gestures nonetheless. Doing otherwise would have been disrespectful and boastful.

It was the second day of the week, a busy day in Quicksilver. The first day of the week was quiet and reserved, usually due to the vast number of meetings that took place. Today was when people *did* work instead of just talking about it. Delivery carts traveled from business to business, restocking and resupplying them. Various temporary stalls had been erected with people hawking various wares. Cleaners cleaned, and craftsmen crafted.

Naturally, it wasn't the best day to visit the alchemists. They would have already booked orders for the week. However, this was beyond Cha Ming's ability to control. The test had occupied him until today, and he could hardly visit the Alchemists Association again without a better bargaining position.

Cha Ming only had to walk for an incense time before reaching the large yet plain building. He walked through those familiar doors before arriving at the secretary's desk. She was the gatekeeper, the person who decided whether one could meet with the alchemists in the first place. They had chosen the right person for the role. She scorned gifts and bribes and was known as an iron lady. Fortunately for Cha Ming, this meant she would respect his status and at least provide the opportunity for a meeting.

"Hello, my dear," Cha Ming said in a flattering voice. The secretary, used to this fawning treatment, grunted and looked at Cha Ming from top to bottom.

"You're back," she said. "And with a shiny silver badge. I suppose you'd like to meet those alchemists I said you couldn't meet before?"

"You've read my mind, of course," Cha Ming said. "By the way, you're looking particularly beautiful today."

It was a bald-faced lie of course. The secretary was hideous by any person's standards. However, this didn't stop the lady from blushing slightly before regaining her composure.

"I only obey the rules, you know," the woman said. "Please wait here while I go ask them. There are six master alchemists you are now qualified to meet with."

Cha Ming sat and prepared tea for himself by using a complimentary teapot and boiling water from a limitless pitcher. He had his own tea leaves, obtained from a fine merchant stall in Central Square. Wang Jun's tea habit had rubbed off on him, and he now had great difficulty drinking lower-quality teas.

Half an hour passed, and the secretary returned with an awkward expression. "My apologies, but they have all stated that they are otherwise preoccupied this week."

Cha Ming frowned. "Could you please ask them what their availability is in the next month?"

"Of course," the secretary said. "Please wait, and I'll be right back." This time, she returned in less than fifteen minutes with a flustered expression. "My apologies, but they have said that they are otherwise occupied for the next half year. They said that you are welcome to come back at that time to discuss."

Cha Ming sighed. He suspected the Wang family had a lot to do with it. Unfortunately, he wasn't sure where else in the city he could find an alchemist. While Cha Ming thought hard to find a solution, the secretary fumed.

"Those good-for-nothing geezers," she muttered under her breath. "Give me a moment. I'll get to the bottom of this. Do they really think they can keep something from me, the guild leader's sister?" Stomping sounds ensued as she traveled upstairs toward the guild leader's office.

"How frightening," he said, whistling through his teeth. "If anyone upset her, they would basically have to accept a life without medicinal pills." He was suddenly very glad for his not-so-subtle but effective flattery. As far as he knew, no person was completely immune to it.

An hour passed. The secretary had been gone the entire time, leaving Cha Ming to drink tea in peace. The silence was only broken when a client came to pick up orders. A small number of people also lined up at the secretary's desk, patiently waiting their turn with not a hint of anger. Clearly the fact that she was the guild leader's sister wasn't a well hidden one.

An incense time passed again before the door behind the secretary's desk creaked open. The ugly secretary crawled out with a smile plastered on her face. "The guild leader will see you now," she said.

Cha Ming raised his eyebrow and followed obediently. Apparently, flattery went very far with this particular woman.

He followed her up a plain flight of stairs built from a reddish wood. She led him down a plain wooden hallway made from the same material. "This red wood is from our hometown," she said proudly. "Everyone in the city fancies stone and metal, but that's just too cold for my taste. A proper building is made of wood." A little further down, Cha Ming saw a modestly sized painting. He immediately recognized the work as Jun Xiezi's work.

"Did Grandmaster Xiezi visit your hometown as well?" Cha Ming asked. The painting contained a multitude of trees whose colors were the same shade of red as the hallway.

"Naturally," she said. "He painted this after visiting Redwood Forest. Redwood Forest in the summer is ranked the third most beautiful natural attraction by the Gold Leaf Association. It's not uncommon for well-known artists to visit. My brother once made Grandmaster Xiezi a pill to help him break through to the peak of core formation. He created this painting of our hometown in return."

"This is a town?" Cha Ming asked, looking at the painting more closely. To him, it looked like nothing more than a forest with gigantic trees. Naturally, the painting contained chirping birds and fluttering leaves. He even saw tiny people wandering at the bases of the massive trees.

"You won't be able to see it in this painting," she said. "There are stairs at the roots that travel within the tree trunks. They lead all the way to the canopy, where the village is built."

Cha Ming whistled in amazement. One day he would travel the continent, and Redwood Forest was definitely a must-see location.

After walking a little further, they passed through two large wooden doors the width of the hallway. It led to a waiting room, which the secretary bypassed directly to take him to a much smaller door that led to the guild leader's office.

"Thank you for everything," Cha Ming said. "However, I don't even know your name."

"Yao Ling," she said shyly. "Do make sure to visit often."

Seeing her blushing expression, Cha Ming was forced to suppress a shudder. He had been friendly and charming, but surely she didn't think he had been hitting on her. His emotions suppressed, he steeled himself and entered the office. It was far different than what he imagined.

It didn't have the cozy feeling of an office. Instead it was filled with marble benches and glassware as well as various herbs and concoctions. It was an accident waiting to happen.

"Come in, come in," a voice yelled near the back. A short, balding man was busy performing what looked like a titration. The stirred flask below the titration apparatus was bubbling and hissing as the liquid dripped down.

Cha Ming's curiosity was piqued. As the clear liquid dripped one drop at a time, the bubbling liquid below began to turn purple for a fraction of a second. With each drop, the duration increased. It wasn't long before the solution stayed purple and the titration was completed.

"What can I do for you today?" the guild leader said, taking off his gloves and goggles. Afterward, he grabbed a clear bottle and took a draw from it. Cha Ming's face twitched when he saw the unlabeled bottle.

"Are you sure it's wise for you to be drinking in the lab?" he blurted reflexively.

The guild leader scowled and took another drink in protest. "My lab, my rules. You sound just like Ling Er." He then put the beaker down and motioned for Cha Ming to take a seat in one of the two chairs in the lab.

"Naturally I have a good reason to come see you," Cha Ming said. "But before that, I have a question for you. Why are you performing a titration? Doesn't alchemy specialize in using flames to manipulate herbs and their properties?"

The guild leader's eyes lit up. "It's because of the Royal Proclamation of Science and Engineering," the guild leader said. "There are physical principles in this world that can be measured and evaluated. Alchemy is not the only way to obtain results—chemistry is one such method that doesn't use qi. What I'm trying to do is incorporate chemistry into alchemy in order to reduce the amount of low-level labor. I mean, why should we waste half our time doing something just anyone could do?"

"Quite right," Cha Ming said. "Though it seems that not everyone agrees with this approach."

"Backwards people with no vision," the guild leader said. "Take the Spirit Doctor Association, for example. They don't even treat the common people, but every year they prevent countless commoners from practicing a lesser version of their craft. All in the interest of the 'common good.'" The guild leader basically spat these words. "Fortunately, the blacksmiths and alchemists are fairly reasonable. And so are the geomancers. The blacksmiths, despite their reputation, aren't very fond of pounding iron and other metals all day. The alchemists hate processing herbs they don't have to, and the geomancers are just sick and tired of arguing with the architects. With more engineers among the commoners to argue on their behalf, their life has become much less stressful."

Cha Ming nodded. "Fair enough. It's great to see progress. The reason I am here is because I'm looking for people to craft medicinal pills for me. I cultivate five elements with traces of creation and destruction qi. The last time I came, the lower-tier alchemists said they couldn't help me. Even though I've obtained my talisman-master qualification, the upper-tier alchemists still refuse to help. They say they are otherwise preoccupied for the next half year. Forgive me for being blunt, but that seems very unlikely."

The guild leader shook his head and fished out a letter from a messy pile on his desk. "Here. Read this," he said. Cha Ming scanned through the contents of the letter written by the Jade Bamboo Conglomerate. It was signed by the branch leader and stated that if a member of the Alchemists Association sold alchemical products to a man called Du Cha Ming, there would be severe consequences. It then reminded the association that eighty-five percent of all their business was conducted through the Jade Bamboo Conglomerate.

"There you have it," the guild leader said. "There's someone in their group who hates you, and I'm helpless against them. Not just that, they've threatened the individual alchemists. If they don't obey, it will be very difficult for them to sell their products regardless of whether they do so through the association or individually."

"Is there any other way for me to obtain the pills I need?" Cha Ming asked.

"There are three options," the guild leader said. "The first option, but the least likely, is to have a royal alchemist make something for you. They are beyond reproach by the Jade Bamboo Conglomerate. Unfortunately, many of these alchemists are in their pocket as well. It is also difficult to secure their services, as you would need a royal sponsor to make it happen.

"The second and third options are to contact the Obsidian Syndicate or the Alabaster Group respectively. Both organizations have transcendent cultivators as senior partners, so they don't care what the Jade Bamboo Conglomerate wants. The Obsidian Syndicate has two alchemists of sufficient tier, and they will help anyone with money. Unfortunately, this also means that you must be wary of their products. There is a chance that the Wang family has paid them to poison you if you purchase their pills. The price for guaranteeing no poison may be prohibitive.

"The Alabaster Group, on the other hand, only has one alchemist who can help you. As long as you are vetted as a well-meaning person, you can request his services. Unfortunately, he is always very busy with his research. He is the revered alchemist, Mo Tianshen, and he is constantly researching low-tier pills for the good of the common people. To secure a meeting, you would need to be a member of their organization. Even then it might be difficult. I should know; I am his student. I only get to see him every three years or so."

Cha Ming's head began to ache. "I don't suppose it's easy to get into the Alabaster Group?"

"It's very difficult," the guild leader said. "It's by invitation only, but they do gather evidence in the form of introductory letters. I can write you a letter of recommendation, but I must warn you—if the Wang family has gone through all this trouble, they have likely secured letters of scorn, which will make it very difficult for you to be selected. The Wang family definitely has members in the Alabaster Group who will try to keep you out."

"Thank you very much for telling me this," Cha Ming said. "I would be in your debt if you wrote me a letter of recommendation."

"No problem at all," the guild leader said, shrugging. "This is a partial apology at best."

Despite not having achieved his goals, the day wasn't a complete loss. Cha Ming was able to secure a letter of recommendation and further evidence of the Wang family's interference. After returning to the Talisman Artist Guild, he immediately asked the branch leader to write a letter of recommendation. Afterward, he continued producing least-grade talismans, both to improve his success rate and to arm himself in the event of a battle.

The sun set quietly that night, and just as quietly, an envelope was slipped beneath Cha Ming's door. It was pitch black, and when he opened it, he was greeted with polite words.

Dear Du Cha Ming,

You are hereby invited to join the Obsidian Syndicate as a junior member. Your skills in talisman crafting are highly valued. In the Obsidian Syndicate, we believe in capitalizing on value above all else.

As I understand it, you are currently looking for medicinal pills. Should you join us, we would be happy to arrange such transactions with a guarantee on quality. You will find that no other organization is as far-reaching as ours in the continent. Our vision is mighty, and our resources are limitless.

This is naturally an important decision in a cultivator's life. Therefore, I invite you to come to our association for a tour two hours after dawn. I am certain that you will find our facilities to your liking.

Sincerely,

Yang Mubai, Senior Partner

Chapter 18:
A Familiar Face

It was a cloudy day in Quicksilver. The sun was completely obscured by the thick cloud cover, causing the city's appearance to change drastically. The colors, which were usually accentuated by the persistent sunshine, were now drab and faded. Metallic decorations lost their luster, and the public fountains no longer glittered with iridescent tones.

Cha Ming normally wouldn't have noticed this, if not for his destination. The Obsidian Syndicate's building was black as sin—no, that wasn't accurate. Cha Ming knew now that sin was yellow, and evil was ochre. However, he couldn't help but shiver when he saw the obsidian building and its black spires. In the sunlight, it would have been glasslike in appearance. But beneath the cloud-covered sky, it was blacker than the deepest shadows. An oppressive feeling of unease washed over him as he walked to the doors.

"May I help you?" a beautiful attendant in a black dress asked in a suggestive manner. Her tone implied that she would help him in any way he wished. Not wanting to get caught up in anything unnecessary, he presented his invitation. The woman looked it over while huffing in disappointment.

"Right this way, Master Du," she said, walking through the ebony doors. Her hips swayed as they entered an entrance hall as massive as the exterior suggested. A mosaic of black and white granite covered the walls. The white was there to accentuate the black—after all, the existence of light is what made the darkness so frightening.

They passed a dozen black-marble desks, each accompanied by an equally beautiful attendant. Each desk had a different symbol adorning it. One had an alchemical cauldron and another a talisman. One had a formation and another a hammer. These were clearly for requesting services from professions. There were many other symbols like pills, herbs, and ores. One was in the shape of a sword, likely for hiring mercenaries. The last one had a question mark.

Is it for miscellaneous services or for more questionable services? Cha Ming felt an itch, so he rubbed his eyes. *Is there such a thing as allergies for cultivators?*

They left the entrance hall through a pair of ebony doors. There, Cha Ming saw what looked like many storefronts. Various attendants waited on customers and fetched goods as requested. Others operated more like workshops, proudly displaying men forging weapons, painting talismans, or preparing pills. Of course, these things took place behind thick panes of protective glass. Any disruptions could ruin a creation. They sought to strike a balance between displaying skill and exercising practicality. His vision blurred as he looked on, which was curious given he had entered the bone-forging realm.

"Is everything all right?" the guide asked.

"It's nothing," Cha Ming said. "I finished my examination yesterday, and I'm likely just tired." He couldn't focus. It was as though he'd spent weeks awake and couldn't make out finer details.

"Very well," the guide said. "Each craftsman is provided with a storefront and assistants. They may also hire others to assist them, but naturally our businesses thrive on premium services. We have very few customers, but they are all very rich. Only those with sufficient means are allowed inside."

Cha Ming noticed that she didn't say status. As far as they were concerned, money equaled status.

"Right this way," she said once more, curling her finger for him to follow.

The thick feeling of unease from outside the building returned. As he passed a smith who was beating away recklessly at a sword, his eyes itched more than ever. It was as though they were closed and wanted to open. So open them he did. His Eyes of Pure Jade activated on reflex, revealing a much different scenery than he was used to. The blacksmith he had been looking at shone deep yellow, even deeper than other cultivators he had seen before. The woman who accompanied him, however, was not tainted with any specific hue.

Perhaps this is an outlier? Cha Ming thought. He had wandered the city quite extensively over the past two months, and this was the first time he had felt such an intense reaction from his Eyes of Pure Jade. His eyes darted back to the other shops, verifying their employees. Everyone was normal, save for a few customers with light yellow coloring.

"Is everything all right?" the guide asked once more.

Seeing Cha Ming nod, they proceeded to the next room. It was filled with various small courtyards. Cha Ming's incandescent force could not penetrate their doors. "This is our information center. You can purchase almost any kind of information there."

"What if I wanted information on one of your customers?" Cha Ming asked.

She looked at him quizzically. "That depends on a few factors. We will never report on matters of senior members, but junior members are fair game. For regular customers, it depends if they've purchased anonymity. Contracts are very important to us, so we will respect purchased anonymity. But you must understand that information is worth quite a bit of money. Purchasing anonymity comes at a cost that often exceeds the revenue we can generate from the information. Surely you understand this principle."

Cha Ming only vaguely listened. He spent his time looking for unusual signs. He found none, but the ominous feeling was still increasing.

"Here is Sigil Master Guo Jia's office," she continued. "He is in high demand; therefore, he is often out of office."

Cha Ming's attention snapped back to reality.

"What did you say the sigil master's name was?" he asked, trying his utmost to mask his facial expression.

"Guo Jia," she said. "Are you already acquaintances?"

"No," Cha Ming said, shaking his head. "I misheard." He rubbed a spot on his forehead that still stung from his enslavement. "Please continue."

They proceeded through the residential quarter where many members stayed. The décor was top notch, a few tiers higher than Cha Ming's accommodations at the Talisman Artist Guild. The guide continued to explain the several benefits he would receive should he choose to join the Obsidian Syndicate. Cha Ming had to ask her to repeat herself more than once, as he was distracted by the eerie yellow-and-ochre glow peeking out from many of the residence doors. He decided that this was likely the cause of his agitation. This place had at least a dozen devils and devil cultivators.

"Is there anything else I should see?" Cha Ming asked.

"Of course," she replied. "If you ever need hired muscle, you can always come to the Mercenary Pavilion for top-tier fighters." She led him to a stone building with a sign at the entrance. The sign only had a single sword drawn in bloody ink. It gave Cha Ming the willies.

"After you, sir," she said, holding the door open.

Cha Ming walked in cautiously. He heard raucous laughter and breaking glass. He smelled iron and blood. He saw a sea of orange, at least fifty foundation-establishment devils biding their time. He finally realized the Obsidian Syndicate's true colors, and the reason why his eyes itched so badly. His eyes had tried to warn him, but he hadn't listened.

The Obsidian Syndicate was a den of devils, and he had walked right into it.

"You seem uncomfortable," a grave voice said. Cha Ming looked up at the somber silhouette in black cultivator's robes.

"Not at all, Senior Partner Yang," Cha Ming said.

"You're lying," the man stated with a deadpan expression. "I hate it when people lie to me."

Cha Ming gulped. His incandescent force was useless in evaluating the man before him. Which made sense given that he was a transcendent cultivator. "I admit that I am uncomfortable. Not only have I never seen a transcendent cultivator before, but it's my first time seeing so many foundation-establishment and core-formation cultivators in one location. I confess myself impressed at the Obsidian Syndicate's foundation."

The answer seemed to satisfy the man, who leaned forward and spoke in a gentler voice. "It's natural that you feel this way. After all, you are young and inexperienced. But you are a talented man, and we greatly value talent. I promise you that if you join us, you will have substantial freedom, and your monthly stipend will be exorbitant. This has nothing to do with your current accomplishments but my estimate of your future achievements.

"Cultivation techniques, battle techniques, talisman formulas… these can all be yours at the snap of my finger. You will grow stronger at an unimaginable pace. And as a member, you will enjoy access to many of our restricted goods and services."

While it did sound tempting, Cha Ming was nervous for several other reasons. His greatest worry was the man before him. He knew that his true shape was much different than what the naked eye could see. Behind the mask of skin and bones was a monster through and through, an ochre giant with deadly horns that could crush him at any moment.

"I need some time to consider," Cha Ming said. "I imagine that these benefits come with obligations?

"Naturally," the man said. "Nothing in this world is free of charge."

"May I have a copy of the contract to review?" Cha Ming asked. "This is a very important decision."

The man chuckled. "Of course you can. But be warned that the document is cursed. It is linked to your presence, and should other eyes see it, we will know. If you choose to accept, sign it in blood. If you choose to reject it, burn it and we will be informed accordingly. However, if you should wish to lose your life… then by all means, let others see it. Do you understand?"

Cha Ming paled. "I understand."

"Great," the man said. "I like straightforward people. You have great talent. Make sure to take advantage of this important growth period, when your ambition is at its fullest. Don't be foolish and squander it like many idealists out there."

Cha Ming stored the contract inside a normal bag of holding. He didn't dare show off the Clear Sky World in front of a transcendent cultivator. Then he hid his agitation and proceeded outside the building under the supervision of his eye-catching guide. It was only once he left through those ebony doors that he dared breathe normally.

Using his incandescent force, he hid away from the throng of people on the streets and disappeared. A half hour later, he reappeared inside his residence at the Talisman Artist Guild. Then, locking himself away, he withdrew the black package containing the employment contract. He burned it without looking. There was no sense in dealing with devils. He would rather die a thousand deaths than chance corrupting his soul.

A week passed, and Cha Ming entered a period of seclusion. He took full advantage of Jun Xiezi's painting, *Samsara*, to practice the talismans he had already learned. By the end of the week, his success rate in painting these talismans exceeded fifty percent. He knew that it would be impossible to improve them without substantially improving his crafting skills, so he decided to diversify his attention to other least-grade talismans. It didn't take long for him to master a wind talisman, Void Rend Talisman, and a lightning talisman, Nine Heavens Lightning Talisman.

Eventually, Cha Ming's emotional stability recovered, and he created another batch of poetic talismans. These were his trump cards, key items that would preserve his life in times of danger.

Talisman crafting aside, Cha Ming continued his usual efforts at cultivation. He advanced slowly but surely, gaining steady ground at a rate that would make many envious. Still, he knew it wasn't enough. A storm was brewing in the Song Kingdom, and it was only a matter of time until it erupted.

A storm raged in the Silverwing Mountain Range. The thunder woke Huxian from a deep and pleasant dream. In this dream, he was a master talisman artist. Many people respected him, and he developed his craft at a frightening pace. In fact, his works had gained the attention of the branch guild leader, a powerful figure who could kill mostly anyone in the city without fear of repercussions.

Why do I keep dreaming I'm human? he thought. *Isn't it best to be a demon beast? Besides, when I transcend, I'll be able to take on human form. There will be no disadvantages and only advantages to being a demon beast then.*

"Master, you've awakened," Lei Jiang said dutifully. His surroundings were filled with static that caused Huxian's fur to stand on end. Which he was fine with him. Spiked hair was in fashion nowadays.

"Have you seen Silverwing?" Huxian asked the purple mouse. As usual, the tiny mouse shook its tiny head. "He'll come and see us when he's ready. There's no rushing someone when they're upset."

Who's upset? a voice yelled out to them mentally. The proud Silverwing was flying overhead, clearly showing off his glittering wings under the sunlight.

"You look different today," Huxian said.

The falcon swooped down toward the ground in an exaggerated fashion, stopping mere inches from the rocky peak of the mountain. As Huxian looked him over, he felt a faint presence that hadn't been there before. He also noticed Silverwing's silver feathers had doubled in number.

"You've made a breakthrough in the blood-concentrating technique?" Huxian said with a bewildered expression.

"That's right," Silverwing said. "This elder brother is a talent among talents. Naturally, a silly blood-concentration technique is nothing for me. It's only a matter of time until I break through the second, third, and fourth stages."

"You have no idea how talented you are," Huxian said. By all rights, it should have been impossible. He'd specifically chosen the least effective technique to gift the bird in the hopes of having it surrender to his will. But Silverwing had defied all expectations and succeeded where tens of thousands had failed. "Will you be breaking through to core formation soon, then?"

The bird shook his head. "I'm in no rush. Besides, I can vaguely feel that concentrating my bloodline before forming my core will give me many advantages later on. Also, I want to find out what these tasty inherited memories are."

"That's easier said than done," Huxian said, shaking his head. "You'll need to concentrate your blood to the fifth stage of your current technique to stand a chance. However, if you had a stronger technique…"

Huxian's voice trailed off when he saw the bird's angry glare. This was unfortunate, because he had been about to offer a stronger one with no strings attached. He'd lost far too much face, it seemed. How would his friend react if he knew that he'd been tricked the entire time? "…but it shouldn't be necessary. With your natural talent, it's not impossible. You need to make sure that you concentrate your bloodline to the point where you gain inherited memories before forming your core. Otherwise you'll never gain them in your entire life."

The bird snorted. "This bird naturally knows what's best. Just watch and learn. Either way, that's not the reason I came here. How could I possibly be so bored as to come show off to you guys?"

"Did something happen?" Huxian asked.

"The humans have come," the bird whispered.

Huxian's expression became somber. "How many, and how strong?

"A hundred in each of two groups, all foundation-establishment cultivators," Silverwing replied. "Some are the lowest of the low, while others are peak-foundation-establishment cultivators. There is also an existence at core formation. I'm too weak to evaluate him."

Huxian clicked his tongue. "How troublesome. Between our two peaks, we only have two hundred or so demon beasts. However, the humans are crafty. They have weapons, formations, talismans, and medicinal pills. We only have our claws and our bloodlines to rely on." He looked at Silverwing. "Would any of the sovereigns help us?"

"Unlikely," the falcon said. "Perhaps I can convince one or two if worse comes to worst. Fortunately, we have the advantage in terrain, especially with your mountain's geomantic boa."

"What about the monarch?" Huxian asked. The mystical owl was the mountain range's true hidden reserve. Sadly, he was unlikely to act just to save one mountain and some immortal jade.

"You know as well as I that he loves honor and face entirely too much," Silverwing said. "Unless a core-formation cultivator participates, he'll just shut himself away and watch us die."

"A pity," Huxian said. "What did their leaders look like?"

The falcon sniffed. "They are both disgusting characters. They make me shiver. One of them has black hair and red pupils. He looked at me once, and it *burned* me. The other one is a young man dressed in green who loves drinking tea. His hair is gold like the sun, with a few stripes of white. But even with my keen eyesight I had trouble seeing him. He's constantly surrounded in shadows."

Hearing this familiar description, Huxian's foxy muzzle opened into a grin. "Blond hair with white stripes, you say? What a coincidence, a friend of a friend of mine looks exactly like that."

Chapter 19: Blowing off Steam

Cha Ming was restless. He had spent the past two weeks practicing his talismans and cultivating, but unfortunately, increasing his strength in this method would take time, time he didn't have. After mastering the most basic least-grade talismans, he knew that the limitations in his qi cultivation would make mastering others an arduous process that would take months or years.

Cultivation, Cha Ming thought. *It's all about increasing my cultivation base. If I don't increase it, I can't progress in talisman crafting, and my fighting prowess won't grow.* Typically, cultivators would temper themselves with endless fighting. But he didn't have a cause to fight for; he wasn't one to fight for no reason.

This was why Cha Ming was currently walking down a seedy street. It was a fine spring day, but he barely noticed the chilly wind. His resistance to the elements had skyrocketed with his cultivation realm. He was now immune to normal weather temperatures and day-to-day fatigue. As he walked, he saw several shivering figures—beggars. The type that couldn't support themselves.

I should really do something about this, he thought. He had given money away money to beggars in the past, only to see it stolen away by organized crime within minutes. *If I want to help these people, I first need to protect them.*

He entered a run-down restaurant that was suffering from lack of business, the type that most people wouldn't want to frequent. The moment he entered, the owner was fawning over him like no one ever had—this was the discrepancy in their status. After a quarter hour of negotiations, his bag of holding became a few spirit stones lighter.

Their arrangement was simple: He would feed the homeless people outside for the next month. The funds Cha Ming provided included enough to hire extra staff and mercenaries to keep the peace. Cha Ming would return in one month, and if he saw that the money was being wisely spent, he would keep the restaurant perpetually occupied. The only cost was that the inn had to cast away what little reputation it had. The inn's owner was in dire financial straits and couldn't help but agree to his proposal. And while Cha Ming knew that a certain amount would be embezzled, his status as a master artist would limit this expenditure through fear.

This small business settled, he entered the Mercenary Guild beside it. It was filled with honorable and unsavory characters alike, most of which were huddled around tables over drinks. They were discussing their upcoming missions.

"May I help you?" a large mountain of a man asked Cha Ming as he approached the wooden desk.

"Where can I find mission postings?" Cha Ming asked.

The man pointed him to a large jade tablet that contained various shifting lines of text. "Just project your incandescent force into the mission wall, and you will be able to view all available postings," the man said.

Cha Ming nodded and did just that, quickly browsing through the hundreds of missions.

There were many types available. Some involved killing beasts that had been causing issues; others involved clearing out bandit dens or bringing murderers and thieves to justice. Other postings requested guards for merchant caravans or temporary guards for businesses. Virtually any type of posting was available.

But what Cha Ming was looking for was rather specific. In his limited experience, it seemed that the devils were unlikely to be handled by the army, which meant that such cases could only be handled by the Mercenary Guild.

Mission #4950671: Eliminate the Silver Mountain Thieves. One early-foundation-establishment cultivator, eight ninth-grade qi-condensation cultivators, and other miscellaneous troops. Robbed a merchant caravan carrying important medicinal herbs. Reward: 1,000 mid-grade spirit stones. Will pay for recovered medicinal herbs at wholesale price.

Mission #4950679: Rescue Baron Ling's Daughter. Baron Ling's daughter was abducted shortly after her engagement ceremony. Reward: 20,000 mid-grade spirit stones for successful rescue. Additional reward of 10,000 mid-grade spirit stones if culprits are captured.

He sifted through these various missions. Most of them seemed like virtuous outings, but his eyes couldn't help but flicker toward the small percentage of yellow-stained cultivators in the room. There were also cultivators who emanated a light jade glow.

Mission #4950684: Eliminate the Swiftwind Bandits. These bandits have been plaguing Goldbar County, plundering farmers in unprotected areas. Strength is unknown. Reward: Can only offer either 10,000 mid-grade spirits stones or equivalent wholesale value in local ore production.

Note: While strength has not been determined, these cultivators are unusual. They have extremely strong bodies, some of which shine like jewelry-grade gold.

It was no mystery to Cha Ming what these bandits were. He had fought with gold-based devil cultivators on two occasions now. Reward or not, this was exactly the type of mission he was looking for. It was an opportunity to strengthen himself while fighting for a just cause.

"I'll take Mission #4950684," Cha Ming said to the man at the mission desk. The man nodded and retrieved the mission jade Cha Ming would return to the issuer upon completion of the mission.

"Are you sure you want to accept this mission?" the man asked. "Two early-foundation-establishment cultivators accepted this mission as a team. They have a very high completion rate, so I'm not certain if the mission will still be open by the time you arrive."

"I'm sure," Cha Ming replied. The man shrugged and passed him the jade. The Mercenary Guild did not require membership and made its money by taking a commission for completed missions.

Cha Ming exited the Mercenary Guild. On his way to the city gates he passed the restaurant where he'd left funds. It was packed full of local homeless people enjoying their first hot meal in who knew how long. While there wasn't much Cha Ming could do to help them, these meals would present them hope and an opportunity.

As for how many would grasp it, he hadn't the slightest idea.

Cha Ming's fleeting form dashed across fields of melting snow. Every footstep he took left cloudlike runes instead of footprints, which vanished after only a few breaths. He only traveled for one day before reaching the destination indicated on the map—a small mountain with caves where the bandits resided. His incandescent force constantly probed his surroundings. It wasn't long before he located two other strong souls, one of which noticed him and probed back. Feeling a familiar sensation, he approached the two souls, who kept together in one group, hidden away in the woods nearby.

His figure flew into a cluster of trees. He made no effort to conceal his presence, revealing himself to the two souls, and they stepped out of the shadows to meet him. One figure was a foot taller than Cha Ming and wore a six-foot blade on his back. The other cultivator, who bore a familiar aura, had a much smaller frame. Both were wrapped in black cloth as though fearing their identities might be exposed.

"Fancy seeing you here, Xuehua," he said to the smaller figure.

"We meet again, Brother Cha Ming," she said with a gentle laugh. "I take it that you've somehow accepted the same mission as us?"

Her companion was expressionless, but Cha Ming could sense

hostility in his eyes. The man's aura was not unlike Xuehua's. In fact, the layer of green jade that enveloped him was three inches thick, a whole inch thicker than his fellow talisman master.

"I have," Cha Ming said. "After seeing the details of the mission, I couldn't feel at ease leaving it alone."

"Don't you know common etiquette?" the man interjected. "One should typically accept missions that have not been claimed already. Besides, you don't know what you're getting yourself into. I suggest you leave, lest you get injured." His voice was harsh but laced with concern, as though the talk of etiquette was just to chase him away.

He might be harsh, but he means well, Luo Xuehua said. *Besides, I agree it would be best if you left. Things will get very dangerous here shortly.*

"I know something about this situation," Cha Ming said to the tall man. "You need not worry about my safety. But I understand your wanting to complete the mission without interference. How about this: I will tag along, but I won't interfere unless you need help. We can worry about the division of the reward after the fact."

"This…" The tall mercenary hesitated. Cha Ming naturally knew the source of his hesitation. How could one trust their back to a stranger?

"No need to worry, Senior Brother Hao," Xuehua said. "I trust his character. You trust my instincts, don't you?" She kept her eyes closed the entire time, just as she had during her talisman-master exam.

The larger man sighed. "In that case, you can call me Dongfang Hao. Pleasure to meet you." Luo Xuehua's words had mollified his attitude substantially.

The two cultivators didn't wait for night, approaching the caves through the shadows in the daylight. Cha Ming followed them from behind and observed their professional approach. Unlike what he expected, it wasn't the senior brother that led the way but Xuehua. The reason soon became apparent.

Every few dozen steps she would throw out a talisman that disintegrated on impact. The talisman revealed green lines and symbols that surrounded the area and subsequently disabled them. Cha Ming took note of their steps as he wandered through the disabled formations.

Talismans can be used in this way as well? he wondered.

Before long the trees parted, revealing a cave that was only a few hundred feet deep. It smelled a bit like smoke, and a faint light spilled out from the otherwise nondescript entrance. They had obviously intended to disguise it as an unused cavern, and they had done an impeccable job.

As Cha Ming spread his incandescent force inside the cave, he detected several hundred souls. Most of them were crammed inside a cage, but inside he saw two early bone-forging cultivators. A few half-step bone-forging cultivators, and a mixed bag of eighth- and ninth-level body cultivators were busy roasting food, sharpening blades, and doing physical-training exercises.

They should be able to handle these forces, he thought. He hid inside a shadow at the entrance.

Under the supervision of his soul force, the duo barged in. Luo Xuehua's talismans struck the walls, disabling their protective formation. Then her bulky companion charged at them, lashing out with his gigantic blade. He cleaved apart a half-step bone-forging cultivator in a single strike.

The two bone-forging cultivators transformed upon seeing the duo. Their skins hardened, and they charged toward the two cultivators separately. One of them blocked the massive blade with his bare hands, barely taking any damage. However, Xuehua's senior brother chuckled and broke his blade into hundreds of tiny swords that all began attacking the golden man ferociously. He could only fend off some of the various blades while defending against Dongfang Hao's knuckles, which were now coated with a silvery film. Cha Ming's eyes widened in surprise when he saw that the man was a dual bone-forging, foundation-establishment cultivator. It was this strength that granted him the confidence to face one of the bone-forging cultivators alone.

Meanwhile, Xuehua danced lithely amongst the dozens of

other body cultivators. Talismans flew out from her hands at a steady pace, each of them striking and disabling one of the weaker cultivators. Once all the lesser cultivators were frozen solid by her icy talismans—which Cha Ming recognized as the least-grade Ice Cage Talisman—she threw three other talismans at the bone-forging cultivator assigned to her. The instant they struck him, his golden skin corroded. This was a lesser-grade talisman called Instant Rust Talisman. It transformed the man's skin into a powdery white substance that shed away as he moved.

It seems like they truly don't need my help, he thought. *It looks like they really don't care about the reward. Xuehua used about 40,000 mid-grade spirit stones' worth of talismans to take care of all these opponents. Are they like me, people who can't stand these devil cultivators?*

As Cha Ming was deep in thought, he barely noticed as a fierce, brawny figure darted into the cave. He was twice as large as a normal man, and his ochre aura was overwhelming.

Middle-foundation establishment!

"It's a trap!" Cha Ming heard Xuehua shout as he automatically moved to intercept the creature. It didn't take long for him to arrive inside the cave. Xuehua and her senior brother were currently being beaten back by the middle-foundation-establishment creature. Xuehua tried her best to fight back using a silver sword to complement her talismans. However, each talisman that she sent disappeared as it struck the abomination's enormous body. Its skin seemed to be covered in a layer of bark, which easily absorbed the water and frost energy that the talisman delivered to it.

Cha Ming, run! The mental projection came from two voices simultaneously.

No need, Cha Ming sent back. *I can hold back this strange devil for thirty breaths. Can you eliminate the others in this time?*

They nodded in response. They were in dire straits, and if nothing changed, this place would be their grave.

Cha Ming used his enhanced Seven Cloud Steps and his Stormchaser Boots to dart across the open chamber. He slapped a

Hardening Talisman on his chest as he drew his staff out and used it to block a meaty fist. Ligaments tore as his muscles fought to hold on to his Clear Sky Staff.

So powerful.

He threw a Resistance Talisman at the abomination, slowing it down barely enough for him to avoid the next block and interrupt its movements. Unfortunately, the effect lasted only for two breaths.

Is it an elemental-restraining effect? he wondered. Then, looking at the place where the creature's fist struck him, he noticed the shield covering his skin in this area had disappeared.

The golden men are aligned with the gold element, Cha Ming thought. *This wooden man, for lack of a better word, is aligned with wood. In that case…*

Cha Ming's eyes gleamed as he threw a Five-Fire Cremation Talisman at the monstrosity. It roared as its skin, which Xuehua's saber couldn't pierce, began burning layer after layer.

Furious, it glared at Cha Ming, spreading out a green aura from where it stood. The aura turned into a maelstrom, which instantly began weakening Cha Ming. As he weakened, he felt his opponent grow stronger.

Dongfang Hao, this creature has a wood-based affinity. Use your sword, and we'll attack it together!

The large man, who had been attacking the others in conjunction with Xuehua, threw out his sword and began attacking the large creature. Countless blades ripped apart the creature's skin and muscles, directing the creature's ire to the much larger opponent.

"Your opponent is me!" Cha Ming yelled. He threw out two talismans. The first was another Five-Fire Cremation Talisman, which covered the creature in five layers of flames, while the other was the Nine Blades, One Dao Talisman. It pierced deep into the creature's body at nine different points as Cha Ming willed.

He didn't stop there. In an effort to further split the monstrosity's attention, Cha Ming lashed out with his Sword Staff Art. It wasn't as incisive as Dongfang Hao's hundreds of blades, but it added to the constant sapping of the monster's vitality.

"Now you've done it!" the monster roared in a voice that seemed entirely too human. "I hate giving up my food more than anything!"

Cha Ming stared in horror as a giant mouth appeared on the creature's stomach and began spewing out a corrosive dark green liquid. Dongfang Hao seemed to see this coming and darted out while maintaining his assault with the hundreds of flying swords. Cha Ming jumped away as well, using his Stormchaser Boots to hover off the ground. As a result, he was only affected by the corrosive fumes that fled from the acid pool.

Unfortunately, the pool was directed at Xuehua, who had been systematically destroying the wood devil's golden allies. Cha Ming swiftly used Seven Cloud Steps to jump around the wood devil and produced two Five-Fire Cremation Talismans, throwing them into the rapidly expanding acid pool. They weren't as effective as when attacking its body, but the two talismans set the acid pool ablaze, causing it to halt its advance.

Xuehua, seeing that the threat was nullified, used her flying sword to swiftly decapitate the two remaining gold devils. Their heads and bodies shattered with her icy strike and crumbled into piles of gold dust.

Can you buy me a two-breath opening? Cha Ming shouted mentally.

Dongfang Hao, who now had much greater respect for Cha Ming's capabilities, nodded in acknowledgment and threw out eight golden pillars. They crashed into the ground, forming a barrier around the wood devil.

"Eight Sealing Pillars," Dongfang Hao shouted. "First seal, silver!" One of the pillars glowed with silver runes. "Second seal, copper!" Reddish lines covered the next pillar. "Third seal, cobalt!" Blue runes activated. With every additional pillar activation, Cha Ming saw the wood devil shivering under their suppressive powers.

Looks like it's my turn, Cha Ming thought. He quickly used his boots to push off into the air above the wood devil. He threw out his remaining three Nine Swords, One Dao Talismans. Twenty-seven blades transformed into three, plunging quickly toward the wood devil. Cha Ming simultaneously threw a Crumbling Talisman at the devil. He knew that, as a wood element being, it would naturally suppress the earth-based poetic talisman.

Cha Ming didn't pause as the talismans traveled. He quickly pushed himself back to the ground. Using his powerful body strength to swing the Clear Sky Staff, which was now twenty feet long and a foot thick, he executed the largest Sword Staff Art he had ever attempted. The large staff was coated in a silver sheen as it bore down on the wood devil, whose pupils narrowed.

"Fourth seal, iron! Fifth seal, aluminum!" Dongfang Hao shouted. Two more pillars lit up, forcing the wood devil's arms to remain still rather than defend its vulnerable head.

Cha Ming exerted all his strength to take advantage of the opening. As his staff traveled, three swords struck the wood devil's thick skin consecutively, shattering eleven barky layers.

His five-thousand-jin staff bent as it struck the monster's head. Its edge was sharp and thick. It used the momentum generated by its wide arc and its absurd weight to lodge itself into the monster's thick skull. Then it proceeded through the skull and through the chest until it hit something hard in its stomach. Despite not having reacted when struck on the head, it howled in pain as its stomach was breached.

Dongfang Hao, attack its stomach! Cha Ming sent, abandoning his staff and jumping into the air. He threw his last Five-Fire Cremation Talisman into the gaping wound.

Simultaneously, Dongfang Hao gathered the hundreds of blade pieces into one and charged with all his strength. His blade turned golden as he stabbed toward the singular point that Cha Ming had indicated.

With one last howl, the monstrosity collapsed, leaving the three cultivators alone with piles of gold dust, sawdust, and over a hundred prisoners.

Chapter 20: A Devil's Alignment

The prisoners shivered as they looked at the powdery remains of their captors. If the bandits had been human, only enslavement awaited them. But what would such monstrosities have done with them? Fortunately, these were questions that would never be answered.

Cha Ming ignored his wounds and fatigue as he opened the cages, allowing the prisoners to wander around as they pleased. Then, seeing that they were extremely malnourished, he used his creation qi to make over a hundred food pellets. This naturally depleted all his creation qi, but to him it was well worth it. His actions naturally caused the duo to reevaluate him.

"Thank you, sir," a small child said. "You're so powerful! Can you teach me?"

Cha Ming looked at the small child strangely. "I'm not sure if it's possible to teach you. How about we discuss this later?"

The child cast his eyes down in disappointment. Cha Ming shook his head. He was helpless in this matter.

"Not only is your skill in talisman crafting amazing, but your battle prowess is as well," the mountain of a man said, approaching him. "Allow me reintroduce myself. I would be proud if you called me Brother Hao."

"Please call me Brother Cha Ming," he responded, bowing slightly.

"Brother Cha Ming, without your timely help, we would have fallen for their trap," Dongfang Hao said. "It's clear that they were baiting us, which isn't surprising given how many of their kind that we've killed."

"Oh?" Cha Ming said. "What's your count so far?"

"We've killed twenty-one devils and hundreds of devil cultivators," the man said proudly.

"As you may have noticed, we hunt them regardless of cost," Luo Xuehua added. She had been tending to the prisoners they had just freed.

"Including these three, I'm on five myself," Cha Ming said. "These devils, can you tell me about them?"

"Certainly," Dongfang Hao replied. "We encountered two types of devils today, two greed devils and one gluttony devil."

"Greed and gluttony?" Cha Ming said. "I thought they were based on the five elements, so I called them gold and wood devils. I've encountered a water devil as well."

"Oh?" Dongfang Hao said. "What characteristics did it have?"

"Illusions," Cha Ming replied. "It underwent no physical transformations but had a powerful mental attack that could devour souls."

Dongfang Hao nodded. "We call them lust devils. I personally have a very hard time dealing with them, so Sister Xuehua must do it. Only those with a strong soul can resist them, and I have nothing but brute strength.

"Greed devils cultivate using gold to strengthen their bodies. They also have an ability called Spending, where they willingly sacrifice a piece of their body in exchange for strength, but this is an ability used in desperation, and their greedy nature despises using it. Likewise, a gluttony devil can 'regurgitate' their food. They cultivate using life force, and their ability drains the life and vitality of nearby living beings. For example, these prisoners would have been its food."

Gasps ensued.

"Elder Brother, stop scaring them!" Xuehua scolded.

The large man shrugged. "Regardless, I haven't seen many other types of devils, so I'm not familiar with their abilities. Lust devils devour souls and emotions, but I'm not too familiar with wrath devils and sloth devils. I only know that they are fire- and earth-based beings."

"Are there other types?" Cha Ming asked, his eyes flickering.

"Yes, the more mysterious ones are pride devils and envy devils," Dongfang Hao replied. "Pride devils are lightning based, while envy devils are wind based. I'm not too familiar with their abilities, but all I know is that they are immensely difficult to kill using physical means."

"What is most effective against them?" Cha Ming asked.

"It seems energy-based attacks work best," Dongfang Hao said. Lightning, fire, and wind work best. Ice to some extent. Earth, metal, and wood attacks are useless against them, as are physical blows."

"Many thanks," Cha Ming said. Then, without any warning, he used his movement technique to strike at a small figure in the room. It was the child who had asked Cha Ming if he could become a cultivator. He struck quickly, leaving no time for Dongfang Hao and Xuehua to react. As his staff struck down, the figure of the small child vanished into the wind.

"You are certainly cunning, envy devil," Cha Ming said aloud.

"How impressive that you spotted me," a voice said from inside the cave. "May I ask how you did it?"

Cha Ming chuckled. "I see no reason to share this secret with a devil that's about to die."

Swift as the wind, he darted toward an empty spot in the room. It was empty to everyone but him, whose Eyes of Pure Jade could detect the invisible devil. It resembled an ochre mist. It wasn't surprising that it couldn't be harmed with physical damage. Fortunately, Cha Ming had a plan.

He threw a Nine Heavens Lightning Talisman at the seemingly invulnerable figure. Nine colored bolts shot out and caused the ochre figure to wail in pain.

"How is it that you thought to bring lightning talismans?" the figure shouted.

Cha Ming, seeing that it could still hold out, threw another. He only had three of these talismans left, and after them, none of his techniques would have any effect.

"Lightning is the bane of devils and evil spirits," Cha Ming said. "It was naturally important that I create these." Then, seeing that the lightning was losing its potency, he threw yet another talisman.

The nine colors of lightning grew in quantity and intensity. As the envy devil tried to escape, Cha Ming used his powerful incandescent force to form a cage around it. The disparity in their souls was quite large, and the devil was injured. Cha Ming wasn't worried about it escaping in the short term.

"You have no idea what you're dealing with!" the devil said in desperation.

Cha Ming, seeing that three talismans weren't enough, threw out yet another Nine Heavens Lightning Talisman. This time the ochre mist started to shrink.

Almost there, he thought.

"How about I teach you how to make a contract?" the devil implored. "You're a kind soul, and I can tell that the power you would gain is unimaginable. In fact, I don't see why you couldn't devilize more than once! You could become a greater devil beyond compare!"

What useful information, Cha Ming thought. *However, I can't leave him any breathing space. I need to eliminate him for good.* "I'll consider it," Cha Ming said.

"Truly?" the devil asked.

"Yes, I've considered it," Cha Ming said. "You can go back to hell where you belong." He threw out his remaining Nine Heavens Lightning Talisman.

The devil, of whom only a tiny wisp remained, evaporated into nothingness. The last vestiges of its ochre glow vanished. Unknowingly, two additional runes had now appeared in Cha Ming's eyes, one green and one azure.

"Impressive," Luo Xuehua said. "I never would have thought that an envy devil was hidden among the captives. How did you discover him?"

"I have an eye technique that can see devils," Cha Ming said. "Devils appear ochre while devil cultivators appear yellow. As an added benefit, I can also see that you both have jade merit halos. Therefore, I was able to trust you immediately."

"What a useful technique," Dongfang Hao said. "If I might be so bold, is this something you can share with us? I can see that you are one who abhors these creatures."

"If only I could," Cha Ming said, shaking his head. "I once gained an inheritance called the Devil Sealing Scripture. Unfortunately, the jade slip I learned it from has already lost its power."

"A pity," the man said. "Well, we should find a way to return these people right away. Now that they are fed, it's only right that we return them to their homes."

Cha Ming agreed, and they got to work right away.

It took three days to migrate everyone to Goldbar City for processing. They were greeted at the city gates by the city lord and the family members of those who had disappeared. They were invited to a congratulatory feast, which Cha Ming accepted, but the other two rejected graciously. They did, however, accept their portion of the reward to recover some of their losses.

The feast was extravagant, but Cha Ming was more concerned about networking with the local lord. It never hurt to have more connections. Once his status as a talisman master was revealed, the lord opened up and discussed their local mining business.

"This city is called Goldbar due to the presence of a gold mine," the city lord said while eating a large piece of chicken. The decorations in the dining hall were heavily laden with gold. This reflected their pride in their mining business. "But few people know that it was named for other reasons."

"Are there other gold-related resources here?" Cha Ming asked.

"Naturally," the city lord replied. "A thousand years ago, immortal gold jade was our primary export. Unfortunately, this has all been exhausted. Now we mostly extract varieties of gold and liquified elemental essence. However, there is one product that has been kept secret. We mostly sell it to the royal family and to the Talisman Artist Guild." The man approached a wall in the dining room, and after prodding certain locations, it opened a secret compartment. He entered some sort of combination before withdrawing a tiny vial. It contained perhaps a jin of a golden liquid.

"Gold evanescence," Cha Ming whispered.

"Exactly," the city lord said. "It's a precious resource that is generated deep in the mines using an extraction formation. This is also where we gather liquified elemental essence. As an additional token of our thanks, and as a selfish gift to forge better ties between us, I would like to offer you this small vial."

It was a heavy gift, one which Cha Ming would normally reject. But at that instant, he felt the Clear Sky Brush vibrate, indicating it wanted him to accept it. "This… I won't deny that I need this vial," Cha Ming said. "However, the value is far too great. Could I perhaps purchase it from you?"

The city lord frowned at the refusal. "It is meant as a gift, and I insist that you accept it."

"How about I purchase it from you at the same price that you would sell it to the royal family or the Talisman Artist Guild?" Cha Ming suggested.

"Fine, we can do that," the city lord said. "We sell it to them at half the retail value. This small bottle would sell for ten high-grade spirit stones."

Though it caused his heart to ache, Cha Ming took out ten spirit stones in exchange for the vial. The favor was still worth ten high-grade spirit stones, which was ten times the value of the reward they had received.

"I owe you a favor, then," Cha Ming said.

The city lord shrugged. "Just come by whenever you are free in the future. I always need talismans, but the city would benefit the most if you could offer pointers to our talented youths."

"Then it's settled," Cha Ming said. "I am not free now, but I will return in the future."

Their conversation continued for a short while before Cha Ming finally left for Quicksilver City.

The wind fluttered through Cha Ming's loose hair as he ran above the ground.

Traveling is much more convenient as a foundation-establishment cultivator, Cha Ming thought. It was a moonless night with not a cloud in the sky, a night with an overbearing silence that forbade even the nightly creatures from coming out to announce their presence.

Cha Ming's mind shook as his core-transmission jade vibrated. He established a link with the jade to allow for audible communication only. "Brother Jun, what's bothering you so late at night?"

"Where are you?" Wang Jun asked. "Are you in the city yet?"

Cha Ming frowned. "No, not yet. Should I be?"

"Get to the city as soon as possible!" Wang Jun said. "Xiao Heilong has returned from his mission, and his cultivation has increased to upper foundation establishment. My sources say he just left the city."

"So fast?" Cha Ming increased his pace. "But he's got a compass to track me. What do I do?"

"You need to somehow evade him and get inside the city," Wang Jun said. "He wouldn't dare cause trouble within city limits. There are dozens of core-formation cultivators in the city that won't tolerate a ruckus."

"Many thanks," Cha Ming said. "How are things—"

His sixth sense alerted him to a sharp dagger flying toward him. He swiftly cut off the connection and used Seven Cloud Steps to evade, but three more daggers had already arrived at his destination, and he was forced to summon his Clear Sky Staff to bat them away. The daggers burned with a crimson glow.

"Why does it have to be this way?" Cha Ming shouted. "Can't we discuss?"

A large figure appeared in front of him. He wielded two daggers and wore obsidian-colored armor. "What is there to discuss?" he said. "You killed my subordinate, and I will kill you in revenge. Even better, you rejected the Obsidian Syndicate's invitation. There's no one who can save you." The man was surrounded by an ochre flame.

Wrath devil.

Cha Ming quickly used his core-transmission jade to send a brief message. He couldn't stay distracted for long. The man seemed to notice his intent and quickly appeared in front of him, his curved daggers slashing down at his chest.

So fast! Cha Ming thought. He pushed himself away in midair and used his Flaming Wheel Defense to guard. His staff deflected a dozen blows, but one managed to sneak past his guard. Intense pain shot through his shoulder, and skin, muscles, and nerves melted away like butter. Fortunately, his bones were hard like magic treasures and didn't shatter.

"There's no use running," the man said. "How about you save us both some trouble and give up. Then I won't have to use your friends and family to quench my anger."

Cha Ming ignored his taunting and activated a Myriad Ice Shield Talisman. A shifting crystalline shield enveloped him, absorbing another two blows that threatened to pierce his heart. He used this moment of respite to dash away at his fastest speed, forsaking defense in favor of distance.

"You think your pathetic speed and defenses can stop me?" Xiao Heilong said. His figure transformed into a blur, appearing in front of Cha Ming and threatening to decapitate him.

Cha Ming quickly zigzagged around him, using his Gentle Staff Art to deflect the six blows that threatened to kill him. Only one came through, but it was absorbed by the myriad ice shield.

I need to get to the city quickly, he thought.

The city was only twenty miles away, which was nothing for a foundation-establishment cultivator. But under the threat of Xiao Heilong's vicious blades, he could only take the least efficient route. Blow after blow weakened his shield, which finally shattered a quarter of the way in. Cha Ming promptly activated yet another talisman. Then a second, a third, and a fourth. They were still five miles away when Cha Ming heard a cold voice whisper in his ears.

"I hate it when I lose my temper," it said. A cold shudder ran through Cha Ming's body as Xiao Heilong appeared in front of him.

Contrary to what his words hinted at, his devilish figure wasn't bursting with anger. Instead he was cold and calm like the night. His flaming daggers had changed as well. They no longer raged with blazing flames but burned coldly with icy black flames.

Along with this transformation, the surrounding temperature dipped to that of a cold winter day. The little humidity in the air changed to frost on the grassy ground, and Cha Ming felt his limbs numbing and slowing.

Just five more miles, he thought. He didn't notice the dagger approaching him from behind until his ice shield began cracking. Xiao Heilong's presence was now undetectable, as though the dissipation of his anger was shielding him.

Cha Ming could only dash away in a straight line was quickly as possible. Two stabs. Four miles. Three stabs. Three miles. Two stabs. His shield broke at the two-mile mark.

This is bad! Cha Ming thought. He was forced to slow down, taking his staff out to probe his surroundings as he moved. There. A slight shudder in the air. Cha Ming struck out in its direction with his Hard Staff Art. Unfortunately, this left his arms numb.

Are you almost here? he sent via core-transmission jade.

No one answered. The surrounding temperature dipped even further. A blue light shot out and struck an inconspicuous area, which burst into a blue ice lotus. It broke immediately, revealing Xiao Heilong.

Quick, we need to run to the city, Xuehua's voice said. *He's much stronger than us.*

Luo Xuehua and Dongfang Hao appeared beside him. Fortunately, Xuehua had water-based Daoist spells that surrounded them, keeping them from being surprised by Xiao Heilong. As a result, they were able to advance while defending. What didn't get detected by her spells was discovered by Dongfang Hao. His hundreds of swords orbited around them, and they detected Xiao Heilong's presence whenever one of them disintegrated or shattered.

As they approached, the city gates became visible. Surprisingly, they were wide open and waiting to welcome them.

We used our connections to have them open the gates, Xuehua explained as they dove into them.

Xiao Heilong naturally didn't follow. Since he had come out in the middle of the night, he clearly had his own connections to let him in and out of the city.

It didn't take long for them to arrive at the Talisman Artist Guild.

"I'm in both your debts," Cha Ming said, thanking them profusely.

"Not at all," Dongfang Hao said. "You saved us previously. Besides, when fighting devils, we're always willing to go the extra mile."

"Regardless, feel free to come by the guild anytime," Cha Ming said.

"We won't hold back," Dongfang Hao said. "Those lightning talismans are awfully handy, and so are additional elemental talismans for different opponents."

"If that's the case, I'll give you a discount," Cha Ming said.

"Then I'll be impolite," Dongfang Hao said. Then he and Xuehua took off to a different part of the city. After briefly contacting Wang Jun, Cha Ming collapsed on his bed.

He was far too exhausted for cultivation.

Interlude
Filial Piety

A large fire illuminated the night sky above a small army encampment. It only held fifty or so men, but anyone who knew anything about their recent military exploits would rather face an army of a thousand than these elite troops. Ten thousand, even.

Ten soldiers in fifty kept careful guard as their companions slept. They did this even though no unlucky encounters had happened for years under their colonel's watch. "Prepared men make their own luck," the man had once said. And these soldiers listened to his words like they would a royal decree. They were always prepared.

In the distance, a white figure grew larger as it approached. It was a white-clothed messenger riding a white horse. If it were war times, such clothing would be frowned upon. However, in the current peaceful times, it was customary for a messenger to wear white to alert allies before arriving.

"Greetings, messenger," one of the soldiers said.

The young man riding the horsed hurriedly hopped off and bowed as he delivered the letter.

"For Colonel Feng," the man said. The soldier that received him summoned his partner and sent him off with the letter. He invited the young man to sit by the fire.

"Will you be leaving shortly?" he asked, serving the man a bowl of stew. He looked exhausted, as though he'd been riding for days on end.

The young man shook his head. "I must return with Colonel Feng's reply as soon as possible. A meal and a bed for the night would be nice."

"We'll take care of that, don't you worry," the soldier said. "Corporal Liu!" he barked.

One of the patrol members ran over and stood at attention. "Set up a tent for this fellow."

The soldier bowed and went straight to work, quickly setting up the tent with military precision. It only took him a quarter hour.

Just as the tent was completed, a tall figure in black armor could be seen walking from across the camp.

"Colonel Feng!" the soldiers and the messenger said, standing at attention.

"At ease," Feng Ming said. His men relaxed but didn't reduce their vigilance against the things that might be lurking in the darkness. With these men, he could brave hell or high water. They protected him, and he protected them in return.

"Have you prepared a reply, Colonel Feng?" the young messenger asked expectantly.

Feng Ming shook his head. "No need. Please tell my father that I won't be returning. I am accomplishing many important things, and I won't get involved in political squabbles."

The messenger paled. "Could you please write something short for my sake?" he implored. "I have a pen and paper ready for you to use."

"Fine," Feng Ming said. "For your sake." He wrote a short hundred-character message and sealed it with wax and the ring on his finger. "Stay the night before you leave," he said. "This message isn't so urgent that you shouldn't rest." The messenger hesitated but nodded, visibly relaxing. "As for all of you, I don't want to hear any rumors about this conversation. Is that clear?"

"Yes, Colonel!" they shouted.

Feng Ming didn't join them by the fire. Instead, he sat in his tent and pondered. His father had sent him a letter, asking him to return home due to the current political instability. For the sake of the family, he said. But to Feng Ming, filial piety only went so far. While he was out here leading his men, he prevented much suffering and chaos in the kingdom. Could he really abandon these people just to please his father?

He only hoped his decision wouldn't affect too many things in his family. As the only son, his input and contributions were important.

They should be all right, he thought. *Father never listens to me anyway. I just hope he stays neutral and doesn't get involved in petty squabbles for the throne.*

The night passed quickly, and before he knew it, dawn had arrived. Fortunately, sleep didn't matter much for someone in his realm. Eight golden runes floated in his mental space. They embodied all the merit he had accumulated through his daring deeds. To condense them, he had slaughtered countless bandits, rebels, and vicious monsters. Now, he was only missing a little more.

In just a few more months, he would condense the next rune and cultivate the next stage of the Good Fortune Scripture—Lucky General.

Chapter 21: Invitation

A man walked through the forest at a tranquil pace. All around him, spirit beasts either prowled or slept, depending on their roles in the blackness of the night. They didn't see him. Not many could see this man who was wreathed in shadows.

He walked calmly and without fear. With every footstep, twigs almost broke and leaves almost bent. Shadows merged with his own, covering his body like a cloak, warding him from the most damaging element: light.

It wasn't long before he reached the peak of the mountain where the sovereign was located. He sent his incandescent force into a small cave situated near a jade plate. It was there because of the abundance of demonic qi, and it was a perfect place for a beast sovereign to cultivate. To his surprise, however, he found nothing.

"You came," a voice said behind him. He turned around in time to see a large black-and-white fox. He was surrounded by an aura of light and shadows that emanated from his two tails.

"Sovereign Two Tails, I presume?" the man asked.

"That's right," he said. "You do know the consequences of infringing on a beast sovereign's territory, don't you?"

"I suppose you'll want to fight me to assert your dominance," the man said nonchalantly. "If so, you may as well get it out of the way."

The two-tailed fox growled and split into two clones, one black and one white. The white clone sent out an aura of suppression as it attacked. The man made not a sound, choosing to immediately form hand seals. His shadow elongated, taking advantage of the purifying aura of light to lengthen itself. Then it split into a thousand hands that reached out and grabbed the black fox. The black fox would have none of it, however. It plunged into the black hands and began absorbing them.

"Shadows of fate, heed my call," the man said. "My shadow is yours, your shadow is mine." Instantly, black threads of karma shot out from the shadow hands and bound themselves to the black fox. It continued to try absorbing the hands that gripped it, but the hands absorbed back whatever they lost. The shadow could only remain trapped.

"You like to play dirty, huh?" the fox said. "*Light in the darkness!*" Its shadowy form spread out to cover the entire area. The clone of light transformed into a shining sphere and shot toward the man. The man grunted and simply walked forward, *through* the ball of light, distorting as though he didn't truly exist.

"You can't hurt me, Huxian," the man said. "Perhaps if you broke through to peak purification, it would be a different story, but for now you're helpless."

"Isn't it the same with you, Wang Jun?" Huxian replied. "You couldn't hurt me even if you wanted to. You can *stall* me, but that hardly counts as a victory."

"Fair enough," Wang Jun said. "You've grown up. Cha Ming will be quite happy to see you're safe and sound."

"You spoke to Cha Ming?" Huxian said, instantly shrinking to his baby form.

Wang Jun smiled. "Regrettably, only recently. He disappeared for years and was only able to contact me a few months ago. He's making quite a name for himself in the north."

Huxian remained silent for a few moments. "What have you come here for?"

"I'm sure you know what I came here for," Wang Jun replied. "I'm hoping we can negotiate something peaceful that's advantageous to the both of us. The others won't give you that. Besides, do you know the name of the leader of the other group?" Huxian didn't reply. "His name is Zhou Li."

Huxian pulled his ears back and bared his teeth. "Do you know what he did?" the fox said in a hoarse voice.

"I do," Wang Jun said. "And I intend to get revenge. But for that, I need your help. I need the immortal jade to gain an economic advantage over him in the Song Kingdom."

"I suppose you can't back out from this joint attack?" Huxian asked.

"You're very clever for a baby fox," Wang Jun said. "Yes, we're financially invested in the attack. Not just that, but if we give up, the kingdom will support Zhou Li's faction. Core-formation cultivators will come. You and I both know that while the outcome would be bloody, it's a price they are willing to pay. And once they obtain the jade, Zhou Li's faction will gain the economic advantage."

"And what do you propose?" Huxian asked.

"I propose that we trade," Wang Jun said. "The immortal jade is useless to you but very valuable to us. Fortunately, our mission here is not to decimate the beasts on the mountain. That's just one possible solution. I believe that it's most reasonable for us to trade resources that you beasts require most."

Huxian looked pensive. "I want resources, seeds, and something else. I want a peace treaty with the Silverwing Mountain Range. We will not send beast tides to human lands to the south or to the northern pass so long as the humans do not invade our lands. We will expand north and east, into other beast territories. In exchange, we will trade with you."

"That's a little beyond my ability to negotiate," Wang Jun said.

"It isn't, and I'll tell you why," Huxian said. "The formation contains immortal jade core. And it's in a well-hidden area. You wouldn't be able to find it without a competent earth-aligned beast."

"Such as a geomantic boa…" Wang Jun said softly. "How much are we talking? We only have estimates."

"The original formation has three thousand jin of elemental

immortal jade," Huxian replied. "But the hidden formation has six hundred jin of immortal jade core."

Wang Jun's eyes widened when he heard the number. The immortal jade was already double what they had originally expected, with a value of about 450,000 high-grade spirit stones. However, the immortal jade core was worth twice that much, even with such a small quantity.

"What do you want, exactly?" Wang Jun asked. Huxian sent him a list mentally that almost caused Wang Jun to cough up blood. "Trying to rob me into an early grave? You know I'm desperate, but this is extortion."

Huxian shrugged. "Think about the military cost savings alone. If the Song Kingdom doesn't have to defend against the beast tides at the mountain range, not only will military costs be reduced, but the villages will be able to grow crops and mine in peace."

"And how will we guarantee this treaty?" Wang Jun said. It was a tolerable deal. Not only did the materials he requested cost less than 100,000 high-grade spirit stones, he would avoid serious losses in human life, which would increase the third prince's reputation. Meanwhile, the Song Kingdom would take thirty percent of the jade as a tax, nearly three times as much as the beasts would net. This advantage would enable them to grow troops faster than the beasts could. In fact, they could hire many masters to improve the local professions and start a virtuous cycle.

"That part is easy," Huxian said. "If you can guarantee me the resources, I can convince all the other sovereigns and the monarch. However, we will have to perform these trades in installments. I can exchange for twenty percent in the first month and ten percent every six months thereafter."

Wang Jun frowned. "Thirty percent up front, and ten percent every three months thereafter. This concerns my own family matters, so I can't budge on this. But there's still the problem of guaranteeing the peace treaty."

"Look at the top ten items on the list," Huxian said.

"What about them?" Wang Jun said, raising an eyebrow.

"With these, every beast sovereign will be able to break through to core formation," Huxian said. "Beasts rely only to the carrot and the stick. What beast doesn't want to improve their strength?

"Besides, I won't be staying around the mountain for very long. To guarantee the contract, we will form a blood pact with the sovereigns of each mountain and with… hm, let's say that nice minister down there. The one with the core-formation cultivation base. He seems like a loyal enough fellow. I'll also take a blood oath from this third prince you support. And yourself."

Wang Jun raised an eyebrow at this condition. "I can't sign blood oaths," Wang Jun said.

"You and I both know that this restriction doesn't apply when you willingly sign with source blood," Huxian said.

"I need to consider," Wang Jun said, shaking his head. "There are too many parties, and I doubt they or you would sign an agreement without the initial trade materials. I need to see when I can secure them. Also, we need to start attacking you to keep up appearances. I'm sure that we can work something out that minimizes casualties…"

"That can be arranged," Huxian said. "I'll instruct my subordinates to play gently with yours, and I trust you'll do the same. This way, I can divert more forces to Zhou Li's side and minimize our casualties by killing more of his." Huxian looked toward the bottom of the mountain with a murderous expression.

"Oh, one more thing," Wang Jun said. "While core-formation experts won't come due to the presence of the owl monarch, I expect reinforcements to trickle in on Zhou Li's end. You need to convince the other beasts as soon as possible."

"Fair enough," Huxian said. "I do need one last thing from you before you leave. I want to talk to Cha Ming."

"Of course," Wang Jun said before taking out his core-transmission jade.

The next morning, Cha Ming woke to the delivery of a white envelope beneath his door. The sun had just risen. He donned his blue robes and tore open the letter. It was written with exquisite penmanship. Cha Ming had no doubt that the writer was very experienced in the runic arts.

Dear Cha Ming,

It is my great pleasure to invite you for an interview for admission into the Alabaster Group. We believe that you possess qualities that will be of great benefit to our organization.

Should you choose to accept this interview, please report to our office in Quicksilver City within the next three days. I won't lie—the examination will be difficult. We take the recruitment of members very seriously, and we do not extend an invitation to just anyone.

I look forward to your kind response.

Sincerely,

Lu Tianhao

Cha Ming was overjoyed at the unexpected invitation. To his knowledge, securing an invitation was very difficult, and he'd expected it to take an astronomical amount of time.

The timing was wonderful. He was trapped in the city until his strength increased enough to fight Xiao Heilong, an insurmountable task without medicinal pills and foundation-establishment battle techniques. Not only was his qi cultivation stalled, his body cultivation was as well. Immortal jade was impossible to purchase due to its small quantities and wondrous effects. There were many buyers but no supply.

He was about to walk straight to the Alabaster Group when his core-transmission jade vibrated. He activated the voice-only function. "Brother Wang, it's only been a short while. What's the occasion?"

"Can you activate the video function?" Wang Jun's voice asked.

"Sure," Cha Ming said. He sat cross-legged on his bed before activating a green hologram.

"Brother!" a voice shouted. Cha Ming broke into a grin when he saw the tiny fox beside Wang Jun.

"Huxian, I've missed you greatly," Cha Ming said warmly. "I'm glad to see you're doing well. Did Brother Jun just find you?"

"We talked business for a bit first," Huxian said. "That aside, what realm have you reached?"

Cha Ming shook his head. "I haven't advanced much. I reached initial foundation establishment and initial bone forging a short while ago. Many experiences... delayed my advancement."

"Oh," Huxian said. "Well, it shouldn't be a problem for me to delay advancement now. "I'm a late-purification demon beast, so you need to work hard to catch up."

"I promise I will," Cha Ming said. "What have you been doing?"

"Small things," Huxian said. "I conquered a mountain and befriended the boss of another mountain. Oh, and let me show you my soul slave, Lei Jiang!" A small purple mouse appeared.

Cha Ming's eyes narrowed when Huxian mentioned the words "soul slave."

"He'll do anything I want him to, even if I tell him to kill himself," Huxian said. "Look. Lei Jiang, run in a circle." The little mouse only ran a half circle before Cha Ming couldn't take it anymore and cut the transmission.

A single tear ran down his reddened eyes. He clenched and opened his fists for an incense time before finally calming down.

He's only a kid and doesn't know any better, Cha Ming thought. *He's only a kid and doesn't know any better.* Cha Ming repeated this mantra many times. *I can tell him that slavery is wrong, but will he listen to me?*

Wang Jun looked at Huxian awkwardly as the transmission cut out.

"What happened?" Huxian asked. "Is this thing broken?" He sniffed at the core-transmission jade.

"It's not broken," Wang Jun said, sighing. "He's just very disappointed in you. So much so that he couldn't continue the conversation."

Huxian was hurt and confused. "What did I do? I just showed him all the awesome things I did."

"That's the problem," Wang Jun said. "Cha Ming has been through much these past few years, and it is why he's only just stepped into initial foundation establishment and initial bone forging." Wang Jun's eyes darted to Lei Jiang. "Send him away first, just seeing him makes me angry."

Huxian scrunched his foxy eyebrows but did as he was told. He wanted to get to the bottom of this.

"You see, Cha Ming just barely survived the tribulation. He was crippled. He slowly recovered his cultivation, only to…"

As Wang Jun recited Cha Ming's story step by step, realization dawned on Huxian. He was saddened when he heard of Cha Ming's injury and recovery, but his anger flared when he heard of Cha Ming's enslavement and the one year he spent in the mines.

"We need to kill that man Wei Chen!" he shouted.

"Why should we kill him?" Wang Jun said. "Is slavery a big deal?"

"Well, no," Huxian replied, clearly having missed Wang Jun's sarcasm. "But this is Cha Ming we're talking about. We need to get revenge."

"The perpetrator is already dead," Wang Jun said. "But the concept of slavery hurts Cha Ming greatly. He can't bear to see that you have a soul slave. You need to understand that Cha Ming feels sad for anyone who is enslaved. He may even feel ashamed to call you brother. The act of enslavement is heartless, and Cha Ming has a big heart."

Huxian remained silent, thinking of everything he knew about Cha Ming. "Is this kind of like the not-eating-meat thing?"

Wang Jun nodded. "It's exactly like the not-eating-meat thing. In fact, he feels hurt every time he sees you eating meat because he feels for the animals. But he doesn't say anything because he knows you need to eat. Likewise, he feels very strongly about slavery. He doesn't feel slavery is justified in any situation. He will feel upset whenever he sees a creature like Lei Jiang. In his eyes, what you are doing is very wrong. He probably hung up because he was angry but didn't want to yell at you and hurt you."

Huxian wasn't sure how to react to this information. It had never occurred to him that the things he enjoyed doing could upset his brother. Then, thinking back, he also thought of Silverwing's reaction when he almost sacrificed Lei Jiang. Silverwing had been very upset when Huxian didn't treat Lei Jiang as a friend. Was it possible that both man and beast saw things this way?

"I'm upset as well," Wang Jun said. "I'm upset that you hurt my brother. If you don't change your ways, you'll soon find yourself without friends."

Wang Jun left as silently as he had arrived. Huxian whined softly at the peak of the mountain. And for the second time in his life, the baby fox felt guilt. The feeling had a bitter taste. A taste he would never be able to wash away.

Chapter 22: Interview

Cha Ming pushed his way through waves of people in Central Square. Today was the one day in seven when people rested, and the city's residents especially liked enjoying Central Square's decorative fountains. He saw children playing in the waters. It was against the rules, but it was a rule that was hardly enforced by the easygoing guards. There were much worse crimes for them to prevent, like pickpocketing and rabble-rousing.

Cha Ming eventually found his way to the large white building that stood opposite the Obsidian Syndicate. Instead of feeling uneasy beneath its shadow, he felt reassured.

Perhaps my speculation on the two organizations is correct. Perhaps there are also angels in this city full of devils.

As he walked into the large building, he noticed substantially fewer desks than in the Obsidian Syndicate. Instead of gorgeous ladies manning the desks, there were three middle-aged men. The desks were made of white stone that he was sure was alabaster.

"Greetings, fellow Daoist," one of the men said warmly. "What brings you here today?"

Cha Ming handed them the white envelope. "I've come to see Lu Tianhao."

The man nodded. "You may call this servant Kang Zexi," the man said, stepping out from behind the desk. "Please follow me. I will lead you to Senior Partner Lu." As Kang Zexi led Cha Ming through the white wooden doors, he was amazed at the similarity between this building and the Obsidian Syndicate. They had a similar layout and organizational structure. The various workshops and storefronts appeared much the same, albeit with fewer artisans than the former.

"Honesty is a pillar of business," the man explained. "And so is reputation. Our customers may observe our artisans crafting their wares whenever they wish."

"Aren't you worried about espionage?" Cha Ming asked.

"Not so much," Kang Zexi said. "For one, our members are at the pinnacle of their craft, so it is difficult to steal their secrets through imitation. Second, the honesty brings us extra business. *Another* organization has storefronts to put up a show, but we do not. It's a quality check. We recruit craftsmen, not actors and prostitutes. At the same time, we do not welcome everyone to be our clients. We refuse to do business with unsavory individuals and with those who have unverified reputations. The customers we approve are very unlikely to do things like espionage."

As they continued, Cha Ming was led through wonderful gardens and accommodations. "These are the standard accommodations for our members," he said simply. He didn't elaborate, didn't embellish. As they traveled, they passed several other offices and residences. Cha Ming could faintly see a jade glow beneath the crack of each door.

When they passed the library, Kang Zexi explained that members could study certain books depending on price and achievements. He was ambiguous on what these achievements or prices were. When Cha Ming asked if spirit stones were required, the man simply shook his head and laughed.

It wasn't long before they arrived at one of the many offices. "Senior Partner Lu will see you now," he said before leaving Cha Ming outside the door.

Remembering his previous experience with a transcendent devil at the Obsidian Syndicate, Cha Ming gulped and pushed the door open.

He was greeted with a large, simply built office. The floor tiles were made of marble, but they were inscribed with various formations he didn't recognize. On the walls were several bookshelves made of mortal oak, also reinforced with formations. In fact, as Cha Ming looked around, he didn't see any extravagant materials. Everything was plain but reinforced with a formation of some kind.

Peering inside the room, he saw no one. The office contained an empty desk. On the desk was a small turtle shell inscribed with a talisman beyond his comprehension. There was also a stack of paper, various crystals, and a small doll. The doll, like the many other things in the room, was made from ordinary materials. But unlike the others, it wasn't inscribed with any protective formations.

Cha Ming was very curious about the contents of the shelves but kept his hands to himself. Instead, he sat down in front of the desk and waited. Time passed slowly as he sat, but still he waited in silence, for fear of offending a transcendent existence. It wasn't until half an hour passed that he heard soft footsteps walking through the entrance.

"What a patient young man," a voice said. Cha Ming turned around and saw a man with long white hair. He wore plain white robes, the type that one would wear in mourning at a funeral. Cha Ming couldn't see his realm, but neither could he feel a stifling pressure from the man. There was a vivid green jade aura surrounding him. It was nine inches thick but unlike the ones he had seen before, converging at the man's back, where it shaped itself into wings.

"An angel," Cha Ming whispered.

The man chuckled softly. "Only of the lowest tier, young friend. No need to pay attention to these wings of mine. My name is Lu Tianhao. Please call me Senior Lu for now."

Cha Ming clasped his hands and bowed. "Senior Lu, please call this junior Cha Ming."

"Very well," Lu Tianhao said. "Now then, let me review this trusty checklist my administrator provided." He took out a creased sheet of regular paper.

"Soul Level: Peak Incandescent Realm—Superior compared to cultivation level.

"Cultivation Technique: Perfect Five Elements Cultivation Technique—Superior.

"Cultivation Level: Initial Foundation Establishment—Unsatisfactory.

"Body Cultivation Technique: Unknown, suspected to be a five-element technique.—Above average until confirmed.

"Body Cultivation Level: Initial Bone Forging—Unsatisfactory.

"Combat Prowess: Low-Tier Mid-Foundation Establishment—Superior. Verified by members Luo Xuehua and Dongfang Hao."

The mystery behind the sudden letter of invitation was now solved. He had received two internal recommendations from members he'd fought with.

"Profession: Talisman Master, Lesser Grade. Capable of poetic talismans. Verified by Luo Xuehua.

"Verified Special Abilities: Eye technique that identifies devils and devil cultivators, verified by Luo Xuehua and Dongfang Hao. Technique also identifies merit halos and angelic endowment, verified by Lu Tianhao. Evaluated as a superior-grade ability due to its ability to transcend cultivation realms.

"Now then," the kindly man said. "Are there any special abilities you would like to add?"

Cha Ming thought for a while before nodding. Revealing personal information to a literal angel probably wouldn't backfire on him.

"One more," Cha Ming replied. "Minor shapeshifting. I can transform my appearance into any other human's that I have seen, as well as an amalgamation of their features." To elaborate, he transformed his appearance to mimic Lu Tianhao's, then immediately reverted.

"A very useful ability," Lu Tianhao said cheerfully. "Now that the useless paperwork is done, we can start the real interview." He crumpled the sheet of paper and tossed it into a nearby wastebin. "Are you relaxed yet?"

Cha Ming felt the bit of the tension that had accumulated dissipate with this question. "I suppose I am," he replied, chuckling.

Going through the motions of a regular interview had stressed him a little, but he realized the familiar process had helped ground him.

"Excellent," Lu Tianhao said. "Why do you wish to join the Alabaster Group?"

Cha Ming was surprised by the question. He had not been asked such things when offered a position at the Obsidian Syndicate. "I wish to ask Mo Tianshen to concoct pills for me. I realize this is difficult, but I am currently embargoed by the Wang family's Jade Bamboo Conglomerate in Quicksilver."

"Why is that?" the man asked.

"Due to their family politics," Cha Ming said helplessly. "Their second young master is my friend, so I have been blacklisted by association."

"No, not that," Lu Tianhao said gently. "I don't care about the reason for your embargo. What I'm asking for is your reason for wanting alchemical pills."

Cha Ming answered in a confused voice, "To increase my realm quickly, I need alchemical pills. It is very difficult to find someone able to craft pills for my unique constitution."

"Once again, that's not what I meant," Lu Tianshen said. "Let me rephrase: Why do you wish to improve your strength quickly?"

"Does it matter?" Cha Ming asked.

"It makes all the difference," the man replied seriously.

"There is trouble in the Song Kingdom where I come from," Cha Ming said. "I need to gain strength quickly to help them."

"What kind of trouble is it?" the man probed again.

Cha Ming stayed silent for a moment before responding. "There have been devil attacks, attacks which involve the royal family. I have seen the consequences of their actions, and I need to help the people in my country."

The man nodded understandingly. "That wasn't so difficult, was it? Now that you know what I'm looking for, please answer my next question. Why did you reject the Obsidian Syndicate?"

"Because it's a den of evil," Cha Ming said curtly.

"Explain," Lu Tianhao said.

"When I was introduced to their facility, I saw no less than fifty devils within their barracks," Cha Ming said. "In addition, I have been under the effects of a slave sigil before, which was inscribed on me by their sigil master, Guo Jia. Finally, when I met their transcendent senior partner, he too was a devil. Isn't that a good enough reason on its own?"

The man nodded. "That's a very good reason! Most people don't know that the Obsidian Syndicate originated from the Alabaster Group. One of our senior partners fell into depravity and became a devil. However, I never imagined that they would blatantly recruit devils in such large numbers." He looked down at his feet wistfully. The silence that followed seemed inappropriate to interrupt. "Are there any other reasons you want to join the Alabaster Group?"

Since Cha Ming had already divulged so much information, he decided to stick to the complete truth. "I have two more reasons. Firstly, I may need to recruit forces at the request of my friend Wang Jun if a conflict in the Song Kingdom escalates."

Lu Tianhao frowned a little but remained silent. He clearly wasn't pleased with this reason.

"As for the second one, I'm looking to learn battle techniques and formation arts. If I could pick one, I would pick formation arts. My opponents in the Song Kingdom used formations extensively." Cha Ming quickly described the sequence of events in Fairweather.

"Guo Jia," Lu Tianhao said.

"Pardon?" Cha Ming replied.

"Guo Jia is one of the three mortal formation masters in the city," Lu Tianhao said. "We hold one of them as well, and the royal family has the last one. The Quicksilver Kingdom is nearest to the Song Kingdom, so the probability of Guo Jia laying those formations is rather high. In addition, the Obsidian Syndicate is the only group that would accept such a mission."

Cha Ming frowned. "But isn't Guo Jia's skill level too high to lay down those basic formations?"

"Not at all," Lu Tianhao said, chuckling. "He was likely there for a larger formation and laid the others down in passing. He is a very frugal individual and will never make something of higher quality unless he is asked to do it. As for what that other formation was… who knows?"

Cha Ming sensed an impending headache coming. "What's the next question?" he asked.

"That's it," Lu Tianhao said nonchalantly. "You're in."

"Just like that?" Cha Ming asked incredulously.

"Just like that," Lu Tianhao said. "Now for proper business. I can help you out with battle techniques and formations simultaneously. However, there is a price to pay for everything."

"What's the price?" Cha Ming asked nervously. What could a transcendent being possibly want?

"All I want is confirmed devil kills," the man in white said. "I'll give you twenty-four hours of instruction per confirmed devil kill. For now, I'll credit you seventy-two hours. In addition, I can lend you books."

"That's it?" Cha Ming asked.

"That's it," the older man said. "I'm a rich man, but unfortunately I am a transcendent being. I can't directly harm all the mortal devils on this plane due to karmic restrictions. All I can do now is recruit likeminded people and teach them."

"Why isn't hiring people to kill devils restricted by karma?" Cha Ming asked, curious.

"It's due to the plane's interference," Lu Tianhao explained. "Basically, my power is too great for this world, and it wants me out. It doesn't want me acting directly, because every move I make can potentially destabilize the plane. Therefore direct hostile actions by me are strictly forbidden. If I dare kill a mortal directly, the heavenly tribulation resulting from it could damn near kill me."

"What about fighting other transcendent beings?" Cha Ming asked.

"Still forbidden," Lu Tianhao said. "And very deadly if a tribulation strikes us in mid-combat. We wouldn't dare to do such things. In any case, I know that you are still weak, but I see great potential in you. If you sign a contract with us, I can secure you a meeting with Mo Tianshen. No guarantees on whether he will help you, though. If he can't, your only alternative will be to cultivate using energy-gathering formations. I can teach you those as well. You'll burn through money like it's going out of style, but there's nothing that can be done. As a member, you will not be allowed to frequent the Obsidian Syndicate and their pill-making resources."

Cha Ming though for a moment. "I can't leave the city currently. Xiao Heilong has me locked in. He is tracking me with a fengxue compass locked on to me using karma."

"That *is* troublesome," Lu Tianhao said. "I don't have anyone available to deal with him quite yet, but I do hope that you can kill him eventually. For now, all I can do is help you learn a movement technique with which to outrun him once you get to early foundation establishment. Is that fair?"

"Very fair," Cha Ming said. "Where do I sign?"

Chapter 23: Formations

The formalities were completed a short while later, and Lu Tianhao immediately dove into a mini lecture on formations. "Cha Ming, what do you know of formations?"

Cha Ming hesitated before responding. "They are like talismans in that they incorporate runes and runic lines?"

Lu Tianhao nodded. "That is correct, but not completely correct." Lu Tianhao waved his hand, and twelve blue stones appeared on his desk. With a second wave, the stones organized themselves in a peculiar pattern. With a third wave, qi poured into the twelve stones. Simple runes that Cha Ming immediately recognized lit up, and roughly fifty lines appeared. They were immediately followed by a shifting ice shield. The room's temperature immediately plunged.

"When you were outside the city, I noticed that you used the Myriad Ice Shield Talisman," Lu Tianhao said. "This uses the same base but different methods. What differences have you noticed?"

Cha Ming, who had been observing it with his incandescent force the entire time, replied in an uncertain tone. "From what I can gather, the runes have been prepared into these stones. However, they are not finalized and require soul energy and qi to activate. The second difference is that the lines have not been predrawn; they are drawn with qi and regulated with soul force. A talisman is static, and a formation is dynamic. However, a talisman is built to expend itself on use. But from what I can see, this formation will continue indefinitely."

"That's right," the old man said. "Not only can I supply it energy, but it plunders energy from its surroundings. That is why larger formations are so effective—they use their large size to draw on a greater amount of energy. In fact, many formations use auxiliary energy-gathering formations that have no other effects than to support the original."

Cha Ming thought of the blood-gathering formation and the gold-gathering formation he had seen in Fairweather City. He nodded solemnly once he understood the implications. *Any* energy could be used.

"The disadvantages are also obvious," Lu Tianhao continued. "They take more time to prepare. Also, since it's a dynamic process, it can be interrupted and countered after activation. A talisman cannot." Lu Tianhao threw out five brown stones from his sleeve. They fell into position outside the shield, and five brown runes and ten brown lines simultaneously shot out. They shattered the blue shield and its lines, stopping the process entirely.

"What are some other advantages and disadvantages you can think of?" Lu Tianhao asked.

"It seems that the capital cost of setting up a formation is higher," Cha Ming answered. "But at the same time, the components can be reused. Another advantage is that you can supply external energy. I am extrapolating here, but I assume spirit stones and liquified elemental essence and the like can be used. But the energy consumption is far greater than the one-time effect of a talisman."

"All these claims are accurate," Lu Tianhao said. "Another advantage is that, after initial setup, the formation self-regulates because it is in harmony with heaven and earth. Therefore, less precise control is required over a greater quantity of energy. Formations are more tolerant of mistakes, leading to a higher success rate."

"How does one break formations?" Cha Ming asked.

"Through knowledge, power, and preparation," Lu Tianhao

answered. "Let me ask you, how many runes do you know, and to what efficiency?"

"Ten thousand," Cha Ming replied. "To above ninety-five percent."

"What do you know of runic lines and logic?" Lu Tianhao asked.

"I know the basics of addition, subtraction, and grammar, but not perfectly," Cha Ming said. "If I were to give myself a score, it would be eighty-two out of a hundred."

"And what of sigils?" Lu Tianhao continued.

"A smattering," Cha Ming said. "I know the very minimal core of the five elements, thunder, and lightning, but my knowledge is far from complete."

"Great, great," Lu Tianhao said, eyes shining. "You've been to Fuxi's Library."

Cha Ming was shocked at the man's inference.

"No need to be surprised. I come from a transcendent plane and have been to many mortal planes. While I have never been to a library, I know that they are closely guarded resources by major sects. They send their heaven-chosen there every year in the hopes of perfecting their Dao foundations. Although I would appreciate knowing the location, I would never force you."

Cha Ming relaxed after this explanation.

The man then stood up and grabbed a thick book, laying it on the desk. "This book summarizes the creation of formation stones and formation flags. Before you come back, I want you to create twelve formation stones for each rune you know." He continued along the bookshelf and picked out twelve or so thick books. "Before you come back, you need to have memorized and successfully formed all first-through ninth-grade formations. We won't bother with any exams, as I have the authority to grant you a formation-master certification of the appropriate grade."

While the books were being laid out in front of him, Cha Ming was performing quick mental arithmetic.

"Relax, you'll find that time flies once you get started," Lu Tianhao said. "I also suggest that you continue studying talismans, as your experiences in creating formations will benefit you. Truth be told, ninth-grade formations are equivalent to least-grade talismans in terms of complexity."

Cha Ming took up residence at the Alabaster Group in order to use the formation practice room at his leisure. For identification purposes, he was supplied with an Alabaster medallion that displayed his rank—junior member.

Later, he found Luo Xuehua and Dongfang Hao in the communal courtyard. They congratulated Cha Ming on his admittance and decided to collaborate on further devil hunting missions. Apparently, they had a similar arrangement with Luo Tianhao. Despite the split in credit from collaborating, Cha Ming's ability to identify devils and see them even when invisible was invaluable, and his combat prowess was nothing to sneeze at.

The next day, Cha Ming procured 120,000 elemental stones. They were priced like mid-grade spirit stones and could be used to cultivate at greater efficiencies for specific elements. The stones were called Vital Emeralds, Fiery Rubies, Foundation Granite, Gold Essence, and Eternal Ice Rock for the five elements. The two other elements Cha Ming was proficient in, wind and lightning, used more expensive stones as focuses. Azure Wind Stones and Iridescent Lightning Stones were the gems of choice. Given the large quantities, Cha Ming acquired them at the commodity exchange. He didn't change his identity like last time, so the creation of a different account was necessary.

Finally, Cha Ming began an arduous one-month seclusion. The process of programing a rune into an elemental stone was extremely straightforward—he needed only to paint it like a talisman onto the stone and watch it sink inside. Still, at fifteen breaths per rune, painting twelve each of the ten thousand runes he required for the first through ninth-grade formations took roughly twenty-five days of his seclusion.

The rest of his time was spent practicing formations. He also continued tempering his soul and mental state, successfully completing several sets of his poetic talismans.

Katcha!

Cha Ming's awareness spiked as his soul broke through a part of its invisible shackles. Instead of a transparent white-colored soul, his soul began to show traces of a transparent green-jade-colored vestment. He knew intuitively that he had achieved half-step resplendent soul realm. His soul force was still incandescent in nature, but his spiritual awareness and control had increased by a factor of five.

He faintly became aware of a tether that connected him to someone in the distance. It was a black-and-white dot he immediately recognized as Huxian.

Huxian, can you hear me?

Only a faint reply returned. It resembled a message: affirmative.

I take it that your soul isn't strong enough to converse with me? Affirmative.

I'm sorry for getting angry at you the other day, Cha Ming said. *I don't know if you know this, but I was a slave only a short time ago. It pains me to see anyone enslaved. It's just wrong, and I can't accept it, Huxian. No matter how much power it gets you, it's not worth it if you need to destroy someone's will. I hope you can understand that.* Grief and sadness came back.

In any case, let's talk about this when we can have a proper discussion. Agreement.

Having finished this important discussion, Cha Ming expanded his incandescent force until he covered the entire city. Based on his prior experience, he assumed it had a range of twenty miles. There was no way to be sure, as the city walls isolated soul force. Transmission jades were required to communicate outside the city. After flexing his proverbial soul muscles, he retracted his incandescent force, dusted off his clothes, and headed toward Lu Tianhao's office.

He knocked softly, and the door opened invitingly. Lu Tianhao was at his desk, holding on to an ordinary doll. Cha Ming sat down respectfully and allowed him to finish what he was doing.

"Do you know why I have this doll?" Lu Tianhao asked.

Cha Ming shook his head.

"It was my daughter's. My daughter and my wife were killed by devils while I was out tempering myself. It's ironic that I never deigned to take care of their menacing presence before then. And by the time I started caring, it was too late. I had already lost everything." The older man sighed. "That's why I spend my life fighting against devils and doing all I can against them." He put the doll down gently, then focused on Cha Ming. "Have you accomplished everything?"

Cha Ming nodded. "I've infused twelve of each rune I know into elemental stones, and I've memorized every formation in these books."

"Very well," the man said. "Show me." The office suddenly disappeared. It was as though they were in a different dimension. "This is my domain," Lu Tianhao's voice said, echoing in the darkness. "I am in complete control here. You don't need to care about damaging things."

The man waved his hand, forming one of the most elementary first-grade formations with twelve brown stones. Twelve stones were usually the minimum requirement for a formation, and there were few exceptions. "Break it."

Cha Ming thought for ten breaths before thinking of the optimal counter formation. He laid it down and poured a minutia of energy required to activate it.

"Too slow!" Lu Tianhao yelled. He threw out yet another twelve brown stones in a different arrangement. "Break it!"

Cha Ming thought once more before taking out the optimal counter. "Too slow again!"

They continued the process for six hours, shifting between various formations. Every time, Cha Ming was berated for being too slow.

"Let's take a break," Lu Tianhao said. "We'll start again shortly, but this time I want you to use the first formation you think of that could possibly counter my formation, even if it's not optimal. In a battle of formations, breaths matter. Think about it: I wasn't reacting at all while you were breaking my formation. How many more formations could I lay down? Ten? Twenty? Any response that takes more than one breath is garbage unless you have a huge advantage."

A few minutes later, Cha Ming stood up once more to resume. Twelve blue stones flew out. They made a completely different formation than the ones he was familiar with. However, it looked like one of them. Without thinking, he threw out twelve brown stones and activated a formation. The blue formation broke in less than a second.

"Good. Next."

Twelve green stones flew out, forming another unknown formation. Cha Ming threw out his first guess. It didn't break the formation, but this time Cha Ming was prepared for such a result. He threw out his next best guess, which shattered the formation.

"Good response. Keep it up," Lu Tianhao yelled.

Whenever he threw a formation out, Cha Ming would break it in one or two attempts. Some would take three. As time passed, the number of attempts required shrank. Cha Ming gained an understanding of what generally worked and what didn't. Some formations were effective at breaking dozens of others, while some failed repeatedly or only broke one or two formations. He was quick to discard these as useless for breaking formations, and instead focused on the more effective ones.

Before long, one thousand formations became two hundred, and two hundred became fifty. Out of these fifty, he used thirty or so the most but used the remainder in a variety of special cases. It dawned on Cha Ming that breaking formations was not as difficult as laying them down, and that precision wasn't as important. Instead, power and general effectiveness were the key. The flexibility of specific runes was another key component. For example, out of the thirty-six formations, many of the runes were transferable. Out of the remaining fifty, all the runes were recycled. Cha Ming quickly became aware of the core-breaking runes.

"We'll stop here for the day," Lu Tianhao said.

The last minute of Cha Ming's first twenty-four hours of instruction had passed. Lu Tianhao waved his hand, and four thick books flew from the shelf and landed in front of Cha Ming.

"Learn as many of these least-grade formations as you can before returning," he instructed. Then he retrieved another book. "To form them, you'll need to either condense sigil focuses or infuse formations into formation flags, depending on your preference. As for the stones you just produced, you can just use them to cultivate or something. They are garbage now."

Cha Ming's face twitched, but Lu Tianhao ignored him. "It's your choice whether to condense sigils or produce flags. Sigils are more flexible but less effective. They rely on your comprehension to substitute for prepared formations. Flags, however, are more precise but far less flexible."

Another book landed in front of Cha Ming. "Since you will likely try to condense at least a few sigils, here are some elementary combat formations. This will fulfill my first promise to you about a movement technique. There are a few combat formations in this book that you can use to greatly increase your movement speed."

Cha Ming bowed respectfully before exiting Lu Tianhao's office. He didn't return to his residence right away but proceeded to a different part of the residence courtyard.

It was time to meet Mo Tianshen, the reason that Cha Ming had come to the Alabaster Group in the first place.

Chapter 24: Mo Tianshen

The sun was shining brightly through a large open window in the Alabaster Group's residential quarters. This was also where the Grandmaster Alchemist Mo Tianshen spent most of his time, as the sunlit area was the only convenient place for him to grow most medicinal herbs. A good twenty-five percent of the courtyard was off-limits for just this reason. It wasn't a physical demarcation, but rather an understanding that cultivation could cause the medicinal herbs to wither. Angering a core-formation alchemist was considered a career-limiting move.

Cha Ming was seated outside the alchemist's office, waiting for him to finish whatever work he was doing. There was a convenient button just outside the door that allowed Cha Ming to leave a message without causing any noise or disruption. The alchemist would let him in once he read it.

He waited for an hour before an explosion echoed across the courtyard. Black smoke puffed out from the office, which doubled up as a workshop. After a few breaths' time, an alchemist walked out, coughing and wheezing. He was a graying man with long hair tied in a topknot. His green alchemist robes were covered in thick soot.

Cha Ming looked down awkwardly, avoiding any eye contact with the obviously embarrassed alchemist. Patting sounds ensued, and so did the sound of a bucket of water being poured. A roaring flame indicated that it was safe. Cha Ming finally looked up to see the grandmaster alchemist in tip-top shape.

"I presume you are Cha Ming?" Mo Tianshen asked. Cha Ming nodded. "Come on in then."

They walked into a workshop, which was filled with various beakers, vials, powders, and tiny balls Cha Ming could only assume were medicinal pills. Some medicinal herbs were growing on a shelf, while others were either drying or soaking. The place smelled like a cross between a botanical garden and a funeral home.

"What can I do for you today?" the alchemist said, picking up a tiny brown sphere from the table. He also picked up a green vial and a dropper, which he used to douse the small sphere with varying amounts of the green liquid. With every drop, the brown sphere glowed brighter. A glistening secondary coating appeared, but it ultimately crumbled. The alchemist shook his head in dismay and moved on to the next sphere. "Well? I don't have all day."

"Grandmaster, I'm looking for someone to make me medicinal pills to advance my cultivation," Cha Ming said. "I've been embargoed by the Alchemists Guild due to my participation in the internal politics of the Jade Bamboo Conglomerate. In addition, my element configuration is special, making it difficult to find a sufficiently skilled freelance alchemist."

"I see," the alchemist said, proceeding to the next batch of spheres. "Why don't you go to the Obsidian Syndicate?"

Cha Ming frowned. "Not only is it against the rules, but I don't think it's worth it to do business with them."

"Excellent," the alchemist said. "So, you agree that some things are more important than advancing your cultivation." Various drops of a red viscous liquid fell on some metallic spheres. "Do you know what I'm doing with these experiments?" he asked.

Cha Ming shook his head.

"I'm creating hope," the alchemist continued. "These pills are all extremely low-leveled pills. Quite frankly, I could be making a fortune making core pills. However, I've determined that the worth of what I'm doing here is far greater than anything I could accomplish in the upper echelons of society.

"My current talent-infusion pill is at its eighth iteration. It costs me ninety silvers to produce it, yet it only gives a ten-percent chance to infuse one with first-grade cultivation talent. Many people think this is already pretty good, but I know for a fact that this price point is too high for ninety-eight percent of the population. If that's the case, no amount of time will make it so that cultivation talent is widespread enough for the mass-scale projects envisioned by the king.

"For that, I need at least twenty-percent success and a material cost of only ten silvers. To do this, I need to be very selective about using low-grade medicinal herbs. I need to involve mortal chemists in the eventual mass production, and it needs to have very minimal involvement with traditional professions. No one with a qualification of third-grade alchemist or higher will ever want to produce this pill, because it simply doesn't pay enough."

The alchemist then looked Cha Ming in the eyes. "Which leads me to my next question. Is your cultivation speed more important, or is the improved livelihood and prosperity of fifty million citizens in this empire more important?"

Cha Ming wasn't sure how to answer this question. He knew that his struggle was important, but it implicated five million people at most. "There are people dying," Cha Ming said. "I need to get stronger to help them."

"That is admirable," the alchemist said gently. "Therefore, you can understand why I don't want to divert time away from my experiments. No one else wants to do what must be done, and only my apprentice and I bother with it. Without widescale prosperity, the citizens are helpless against the upcoming turbulent times. Even if they survive, the empire will take centuries to recover." Mo Tianshen continued to perform his experiments as Cha Ming sat down, brooding. It was quite difficult to make a selfish case in the face of that reasoning.

After thinking hard and not finding a solution, Cha Ming decided to observe Mo Tianshen's experiments. He had always been a problem solver, and this puzzle could potentially change the fate of an entire nation. He felt an itch that he needed to scratch.

"Are you trying to solidify a coating atop an existing pill?" Cha Ming asked casually.

"Something like that," the alchemist said while dripping another solution. "These aren't exactly pills; they're compressed powder pellets that are easily generated by apprentice alchemists or apothecaries. It contains all the active ingredients required in an effective medicine, but these ingredients are not available enough for human absorption. In addition, there are various pill toxins that make it so that one cannot take it more than three times. With this coating, I am hoping to provide a compound that can dissolve the active ingredient while also destroying the pill toxins."

As he said this, the last batch of pills was coated. The alchemist took out a press and began manually pressing batches of various powders.

"Why does it need to be a coating?" Cha Ming asked.

The alchemist continued to work while patiently answering his question. "It needs to be a coating because both the activating ingredient and the counter ingredient to the toxins will ruin the pill if exposed for too long. In fact, the ingredients were originally part of version three, which had four-percent efficiency and could be used four times. I speculate that if the pellet, the activating ingredient, and the counter ingredient are introduced at exactly the same time, the efficacy will be much higher."

"Why can't the liquid be taken separately?" Cha Ming asked.

"You really like to ask questions, don't you..." the alchemist said, not slowing his pace in the slightest. "Well, I could perform these experiments with my eyes closed, so no harm in explaining. You see, if the liquid is taken at the same time, it will react quickly, but the solid pill will dissolve slowly in the stomach. Thus, only three percent or so of the pill is enhanced by drinking the liquid, and the rest is not. I need a coating that dissolves at the same rate as the pill."

Tricky problem, Cha Ming thought. *Would a textured coating work? No, it seems that it's a stability problem. The coating reacts with the pill. It needs to be applied in a dissolvable, stable way. However, this would also affect the chemical makeup. Is there a way to affect the physical properties without affecting the chemical makeup?*

A half hour passed as Cha Ming thought through various scenarios. During this time, Mo Tianshen was able to complete his next batch of pellets. He also continued the process of applying different drops from different vials.

"May I try something?" Cha Ming said after a sudden epiphany.

"What do you wish to try?" the alchemist asked.

"I wish to try applying the coating in the shape of a rune," Cha Ming said.

The alchemist's hands paused. "I tried one hundred first-grade runes in the past," the alchemist said, sighing. "It didn't work."

"Then it's convenient that there are another nine hundred runes of the same level remaining," Cha Ming stated.

Frowning, the alchemist placed a vial in front of Cha Ming. "How many runes could you form that are compatible with this liquid?"

Cha Ming sifted through the thousand runes in his mind. "Without experiments, I can think of sixty-four that *could* be compatible. Seventeen would have characteristics of stability. In fact, it could also be possible to paint several different runes simultaneously to obtain a combined effect."

"Hm…" the alchemist said, stroking his beard. "Let's try it, then. Do you have everything you need?"

"Yes," Cha Ming said, taking out the Clear Sky Brush. At the alchemist's direction, he tried all seventeen runes with varying dosages and concentrations of medicinal "ink." He performed two hundred and forty-six trials, of which forty-two formed a stable runic coating, conveniently leaving most of the surface area of the pill exposed for simultaneous dissolution.

"How many elements can you paint?" Mo Tianshen asked, looking at the forty-two potential successes.

"Wood, fire, earth, metal, water, wind, lightning, creation, destruction," Cha Ming said. Mo Tianshen raised an eyebrow.

"Strictly speaking, I can't paint in pure creation or destruction," Cha Ming added.

"Well, regardless of your skill, that's the perfect mix for experimentation," Mo Tianshen said. He returned his gaze to the forty-two stabilized pills. "I don't dare divert too much time away from my experiments, but I'll tell you what. How about you help me make nine more duplicates of these forty-two. Then I'll perform trials in the upcoming week. If the results look promising, I'll make pills for you. At cost. However, you must continue to help me with my experiments in the future."

Cha Ming stayed for another two hours before finally returning to practice formations. His future cultivation speed would depend on the success of the upcoming experiments.

Cha Ming walked down a deserted street in the wee hours of the night. He wore white robes and sported long black hair. His face was pale and skinny but had an overall cheerful disposition. He was also six inches taller than normal due to the size-manipulating abilities of the Seventy-Two Transformations Technique.

As he walked, various beggars, thieves, and prostitutes made way for him. The city guards watched him with suspicion but didn't dare say anything. Cha Ming constantly emanated the pressure of his half-step resplendent soul. Such a pressure was suffocating to anyone under middle-foundation establishment.

The reason he walked in the middle of the night was to procure sigil focuses. Sigil focuses were made of soul steel and other expensive ingredients. They were always made to order, as the cost of each set was astronomical. Unfortunately, the only spiritual blacksmith in the Alabaster Group didn't have enough skill to craft them. This left only one blacksmith in the city capable of crafting them, and he belonged to a shop that was under the influence of the Wang family.

Cha Ming walked slowly for a full hour before arriving at the blacksmith in question. The main storefront's lights were off, but Cha Ming could hear a beating hammer and a roaring furnace in the back of the shop.

Cha Ming didn't knock. Instead he gently reached out with his incandescent force, making the blacksmith instantly aware of his presence. The spiritual blacksmith didn't acknowledge him but continued hammering away at a searing-hot, sword-shaped chunk of metal. The strange material glowed white as he beat it hundreds of times. Sparks showered onto the heat-resistant surroundings. The smith wore no shirt, but his skin was hard like steel and yet also supple like copper. The white-hot sparks didn't leave a single mark.

You can let yourself in, the man sent as he worked. Cha Ming did as he was told and walked through the unlocked front door. He headed to the back of the store where the forge was located and sat on a small wooden bench. He watched in rapt attention as the smith worked. The man's skin glistened in the firelight.

The smith's pounding hammer was music to Cha Ming's ears. Every strike seemed in tune with heaven and earth. The symphony of metal and flame eventually ended with a sharp quenching sound, accompanied by a sharp rise in heaven and earth qi. He had no idea what the quenching medium was, but it wasn't water.

"How can I help you this fine evening?" the smith said as he walked over. His eyes flickered briefly to the white medallion pinned on Cha Ming's white robes.

"I require a full set of sigil focuses," Cha Ming said. "One hundred and eight in total."

"What kind?" the smith asked, grabbing a towel to wipe off the sweat and grime.

"Unaligned," Cha Ming specified.

The smith nodded. "And you're aware that unaligned sigil focuses are twice as expensive as normal ones?"

"Of course," Cha Ming replied. Unaligned focuses were versatile and could be changed from one alignment to another on demand. It was an uncommon choice, but not unheard of. He was wary of revealing his five-element alignment in a place owned by the Wang family.

"I have work lined up for the week," the spiritual blacksmith said. "Please come back then."

"I need these within forty-eight hours," Cha Ming said. "Will this be possible?"

The blacksmith shrugged. "The base price is four thousand high-grade spirit stones. If you can give me five thousand, I can push off my other projects for a couple of days."

"Then it's settled," Cha Ming said, placing a crystal card on the table. "Do you mind if I wait here until it's complete?"

"Not at all," the blacksmith said. "What can I call you?"

"Lin Mu," Cha Ming said.

The blacksmith nodded before sitting down to recuperate his energy.

Chapter 25: Sigilcraft

Lao Mo, the grandmaster smith, exhaled deeply, removing the remaining tension from his taut muscles. He was tired due to having forged all day. In his youth, he could have forged for weeks without fatiguing. But hundreds of years had taken their toll on the aging blacksmith. Now, he constantly struggled to make enough money for his arthritis medication.

Fortunately, a rich customer had requested a rush job. The nice thing about rush jobs for non-contracted customers was that he didn't need to sell below market price. An item like a set of sigil focuses normally sold at a market price of four thousand high-grade spirit stones. This specific transaction would net him two thousand spirit stones.

Heavens, I hate arthritis, he thought, flexing his strong but stiff fingers. By all rights, a marrow-refining cultivator like himself shouldn't be affected by such a base affliction. The entire situation had baffled the local medical community, and his special treatment required a small fortune every month.

Lao Mo retrieved a heavy box from under his workbench. It was chock full of thick standardized rods made of pure soul steel, the only material that could be used for making unaligned focuses. He had used the same material to make his magic-grade hammer focus many centuries ago. He had only worked with the material five times since then.

The aged blacksmith took the heavy rods and brought them over to the workbench for pretreatment. He then took out a vat of universal solvent, an alchemical substance that dissolved just about anything given enough time. Anything but soul steel. He isolated his mouth and nose as he dumped a bundle of rods into the vat. It hissed and sizzled, a clear indication of the impurities remaining on the outside of the rods. These impurities were the result of the imperfect manufacturing process. Lao Mo had always wondered how they could be so thoughtless as to leave impurities on such an expensive metal.

The pretreatment was quick, lasting only a single hour, after which Lao Mo removed the rods and drip-dried them. He then evaporated the remainder of the solvent with a burst of fire qi and placed the purified rods on a tray made of refractory, a stone material that was extremely resistant to high temperatures. They quickly heated up to the melting point of steel. Once they were cooking nicely, he doubled the temperature of the furnace using his core qi, then doubled it again for good measure.

Soul steel was undoubtedly one of the most difficult materials to work with. Fortunately, he didn't need to hammer it. Hammering didn't create very nice sigil focuses, whose base forms were polished spheres. No, they needed an entirely different process. While he didn't need to melt the metal, he still needed to soften it until it was as malleable as stainless steel.

After properly heating them, he carefully placed one of the rods through a hole in a black device he'd taken out while they heated. It was made from the purest void steel, an unaligned material that was unfathomably hard and resistant to heat. Lao Mo materialized his spiritual hammer and smashed down onto the rod, forcing it through a smaller opening on the other side. To make the sigil focuses the proper size, he needed to extrude the rod and make it thinner. This was the very reason why he said it was too big in the first place.

After completely extruding one rod, he processed the remaining eight. One rod made twelve focuses, and the rods were reheated after extrusion. He increased the temperature by another fifty percent to further increase the malleability of the material. He then took out two more pieces of void steel as they heated. One was a cylindrical base meant to hold the rod in place, while the other was an interlocking piece with a sharp void-steel blade. Lao Mo grasped a clear rod with a pair of black tongs and placed it between both pieces. Then, with a loud smack of his spiritual hammer, he cut a twelfth of the rod off. He repeated the process ninety-nine times to produce a hundred and eight bits, which were kept in the hot furnace after being severed.

Once again, he increased the heat by fifty percent. The rod pieces began glowing with a soft white light, standing in sharp contrast to the dark-blue flames used to heat them to this temperature. Blue flames were something only a master smith could produce. Green flames came next, and he had no idea what came after. Not that he would live to see the next grade. He blamed arthritis.

Another black box was placed on the bench. This time, it contained two spherical halves. He placed a bit of soul steel, flat tip downward, into the spherical template. After placing the other half over the top of the rod bit, he smacked his hammer onto the top plate. This resulted in a ball of soul steel with a circular ring called a "flash," which he would remove in the next step. He kept the newly formed sphere in the furnace as he finished making the others.

After completing all hundred and eight preliminary spheres, Lao Mo retrieved the first one with a pair of short tongs and gloved hands and took out a sharp void-steel carving knife. He used it to expertly shave off the unnecessary layer of flash. Only a small amount of residual soul steel was left on the otherwise perfect sphere. He processed them one at a time, carefully removing as much flash as possible. Too much excess flash would make the next step extremely difficult. Hours passed as Lao Mo methodically scraped. Every time the temperature dipped too low, he exchanged the cool sphere with a hot one and continued shaving away.

Lao Mo soon finished removing the flash from the last sphere. After carefully removing all of them from the furnace, he formed one hundred and eight hand seals, and a black cloud made from void-steel dust formed in front of him. He threw the spheres inside it and tediously controlled the black dust, using it to wear away at the tiny imperfections remaining on each clear ball. This step alone took half a day. Had he left any more flash, the processing time would have doubled or tripled.

He was halfway done. Stoking the flames of the furnace, he brought the spheres to an extreme temperature where the balls burned with a blinding white color. Lao Mo took out a small barrel of liquified elemental essence and a small case. From the case, he withdrew five vials of elemental evanescence, which he used to carefully dope the liquified elemental essence.

Truth be told, all the previous steps were cosmetic. The spherical shape somewhat helped when forming the sigils, but the reason that soul steel could be shaped in the first place was due to this imbuement with elemental essence and evanescence. Lao Mo carefully gathered all hundred and eight spheres in a black basket and immersed them in the quenching bath all at once. It boiled, but he used his careful control over heat to drive excess energy into a black box in a corner of the room. The item was called a heat sink, and he could store heat in it as he pleased.

An hour later, the spheres were fully quenched. The quenching was necessary for imbuing them, but it had made them hard and brittle. One additional step was required to complete the sigil focus: tempering. Lao Mo placed the balls into a red fire, which he carefully supervised for six hours. The properties of the soul steel slowly changed over this period of time. The hardness created by the quenching process slowly melted away. He continued until he saw a qualitative change in the metal. Then he withdrew the crystal spheres from the fire and let them cool down to room temperature.

Now for the final test, he thought. He carefully guided a wisp of his resplendent force into each of the metal orbs. They squirmed like blobs of quicksilver as he willed them to take whatever shape he desired. This property was what allowed a sigil to be imbued and runic lines to be drawn using nothing but qi.

His task completed, he placed the quarter-inch balls of malleable metal into a low-level bag of holding and handed it to his client, who hadn't moved the entire time. Then he retrieved the man's change from the cash register. "Thank you for your swift services," the man said before leaving the premises.

"What a mysterious fellow," the blacksmith muttered. He wanted to lie down and rest, but he had a huge backlog of paperwork to take care of since his assistant had resigned. With a sigh, he retreated to his office to tackle anything important that might have come up. His desk was piled with letters and reports. Most of them were bills.

He started with the topmost letter, the one delivered most recently. It contained various orders, the same as always. A few of the next ones were junk mail, which he burnt to a crisp without looking. He sifted through the long pile before reaching a red letter. Red letters were urgent, so he opened it right away.

The letter spoke of the current embargo list. Several criminals and competitors were listed, but most of them had been on the list for decades. Soon, he saw the picture of a young man. Foundation establishment, five-element cultivation, bone-forging cultivator. Recently joined the Alabaster Group and was studying formations. Penalty for procuring goods was one thousand high-grade spirit stones. Due to his presence, the entire Alabaster Group was also on the embargo list.

"God dammit," Lao Mo yelled, smashing his fist onto the desk. He winced as pain ran through his joints.

Well, what's done is done, he thought. *I never liked those embargos anyway.* After thinking for a short while, he decided on a viable course of action.

How do I explain the theft of my valuable stock of soul steel? Perhaps a vacation was in order. People got robbed while on vacation all the time. He figured the insurance should cover it.

Cha Ming reverted to his original form after arriving at the Alabaster

Group residence. His long black hair changed to wavy brown, and his black eyes turned jade. He also shrank six inches, making his movements considerably more comfortable. The world was built for short people. He'd lost count of the times he'd hit his head on low-hanging objects.

His bones crunched as his frame transformed, becoming slightly more compact and a bit more heavyset. His gaunt face filled out, and his skin returned to its usual light-bronze coloring.

"I didn't know you had a shape-changing technique," a gentle voice said from behind him.

Cha Ming turned around, smiling. "I usually keep it a secret, but you're a trustworthy person."

Luo Xuehua was once again wearing blue. Under the morning sunlight he could see a faint coloring around her eyes that seemed out of place.

"Then it's fair that I also share a secret with you," she said, leading Cha Ming to a nearby bench. They watched rainbow-colored fish as they swam through a lily-laden pond. There was an artificial breeze in the residence that caused the water to ripple.

"I lost my eyes when I was three years old," Xuehua said, fiddling with a white lotus she had picked from the lake. "My town was attacked by devil cultivators, and many of us were killed in the process. Thankfully, we were lucky enough to have a formidable expert in the village that fought them off.

"It was Master Lu who took me in when I was seven. I was begging on the streets of Quicksilver when he found me. It was a hard life, and there was no lack of lascivious people trying to take advantage of me. I was helpless. He took me in and trained me to use my soul to see instead of my eyes. He calls it the "mind's eye." Cultivators cannot cultivate qi until they are sixteen, but there is no such restriction on the soul.

"Ever since then, I have dedicated my life to following Master and hunting devils. Master teaches me without reservation, and in turn, I go out and hunt whenever I've improved."

Luo Xuehua said nothing more, so they sat in silence, looking at the fish and feeling the morning breeze.

"Thank you for sharing," Cha Ming said quietly. Then he took out the bag of sigil focuses and began using his qi to shape the clear, malleable spheres.

"Sigil focuses?" Xuehua asked.

"Yes, unaligned ones," Cha Ming replied.

"They must have cost you a fortune," Xuehua said. "To this date, I have only accumulated twenty-four. They are all water-aligned focuses based on ice." She swept out her sleeve, revealing twenty-four light-blue sigils. There were many multiples among them, but for the most part, they incorporated features of ice. He saw them change shapes into characters like black ice, blue ice, heavy ice. It was this mutable feature that made sigils so valuable. They were much more flexible than formation flags.

"It seems like I have a lot of work to do to catch up, then," Cha Ming said, chuckling. He retrieved his sigil focuses and stood up to leave.

"I heard a rumor," Xuehua said. "Mo Tianshen has been performing some experiments. The results have been promising. Expect good news in a few days."

The corner of Cha Ming's mouth curved into a smile as he walked back to his residence.

A clear, mutable sphere floated before Cha Ming as he contemplated the sigil he was about to draw. It only took the most miniscule amount of soul energy to manipulate it, but he found the motions comforting. He had only pondered for a short time before deciding to procure these focuses.

Magic formations, as a rule, had at least twelve major elements that composed their runic structures, and these elements were reuseable. The supporting formations could be inscribed on formation flags or other items like formation stones. They also required a large amount of liquified elemental essence and spirit stones to supply the required energy in the case of larger formations. This did not apply to combat formations, which were quick, economical formations that relied purely on prepared sigils and the user's qi.

There were far fewer combat formations than normal formations. Looking at the manufacturing process, he had also observed similarities between combat formations and his previous soul-pearl manifestations. Sigil focuses needed to be imbued with sigils like soul pearls needed to be imbued with runes. The major difference between the two techniques, however, was that combat formations were real formations while the manifestations were just pale imitations. Combat formations were very flexible in their effects.

The first step involved painting the base sigil. Cha Ming poured his foundation qi and liquified elemental essence into the Clear Sky Brush and produced a green thread. Green threads piled together into a three-dimensional rune that encompassed all of life and death, growth and decay. It was the same wood sigil he had used to form his foundation. As he painted, he faintly saw shapes that somewhat resembled the least-grade talismans he had created thus far.

Are talismans just derivatives of the original sigil? he wondered. He finished the last three strokes, causing the sigil to snap together due to its balanced nature. It was like a formation in a sense that it supported itself dynamically and was intrinsically stable.

The next step was fusion. Cha Ming gently brought the clear sigil focus and merged it gradually with the green sigil he had just painted. The process was much like encapsulating an object in a drop of water. Too fast, and it would cause the drop to split. It needed to be done slowly to allow the sigil focus time to adapt to the sigil's shape.

The fusion progressed quickly, imbuing the clear sphere with a dark shade of green. The next part was supplementation. Cha Ming quickly painted over a thousand runes onto the sphere. Every time, it glowed with a different shade of green as it "memorized" the rune and incorporated it into the sphere. The sigil could now replicate the rune and combine it with others by using the core sigil as a template.

This ability to utilize different runes enabled the sigil focus to form different formations on demand. However, the derivative characters that could be absorbed depended on their compatibility with the focus. Luo Xuehua's base sigil was ice. As a result, she could only incorporate the different derivatives of ice in her sigil focuses. Cha Ming, on the other hand, could incorporate all wood-related characters into this sigil, which gave him far more options.

The resulting sigil was a small emerald pearl. Not wanting to waste any time, Cha Ming repeated the process with eleven more pearls. He followed up with twelve ruby-colored pearls, twelve brown pearls, twelve gold pearls, and twelve light-blue pearls. Then he created twenty-four purple lightning pearls and twenty-four azure wind pearls, for a total of 108 pearls, which he joined together in a rosary that he wrapped around his right wrist.

The process took three days. Once he finished, he noticed a soft blue light at the door of his residence. He walked over to the blue light and touched it.

"Come see me when you have time," Mo Tianshen's recorded voice said.

Chapter 26: Stormchaser

The scent of medicinal powders and fragrant herbs assaulted Cha Ming's nostrils, and the floorboards creaked as he walked into Mo Tianshen's laboratory. The man in question was standing at a workbench, pressing out what must have been the hundredth pill pellet of the batch.

"The results of the experiment were interesting," Mo Tianshen said as he pressed the powder. "The medicinal efficacy was only five percent, a far cry from the current ten percent."

Cha Ming didn't bat an eye. He would have been very surprised if so few experiments would produce an optimal result.

"However, these pills could be used *five* times instead of the original three times for the current version."

"I'm sorry, but I'm a little confused about something," Cha Ming said. "How exactly did you obtain such accurate statistics with only ten of every pill?" It should have been impossible to obtain anything more than a pass or fail, and that was being generous.

"I used an Illusory Pill-Testing Formation supplied by Partner Lu," he said. "This way, it was possible to test the effects roughly a hundred times for every pill. However, the pills slightly degraded in quality with successive repetitions of the trial, something which must be adjusted for when tabulating the data. Besides, what did you expect me to do? Conduct live trials with untested medicine? Animal trials that don't relate to our body chemistry in the slightest?"

Cha Ming did, in fact, consider that the man may have tried these unsavory methods. He just hadn't expected the man to spend so much wealth on a high-level formation to test low-level pills. He had underestimated his dedication.

"Human life is precious," the alchemist said. "Even animal life is, to a lesser extent. It is best to spend more money to avoid such suffering if possible."

"Will we be continuing with experiments, then?" Cha Ming asked.

"Of course," Mo Tianshen said. "However, it won't be easy. This successful research has sparked many new ideas with many element combinations. As such, I've already generated one thousand powder formulas with which we'll need to test ten thousand liquids. At ten samples apiece, I can't see us getting by without at least ten million pill combination tests."

Cha Ming nearly puked blood. *How can he be so advanced in some subjects but so backward in others? Hasn't he heard of experimental design? Where am I to find time to practice formations, create talismans, and cultivate? Where will he find time to make me pills?*

"It's very important to remember that this work will establish the foundation of an empire—no, the foundation of the continent," Mo Tianshen said. "It could take a decade or so to sort everything out. And that's being optimistic."

Who has a decade to waste on this? Cha Ming thought. *More to the point, it's completely unnecessary.*

Recalling that he was in the presence of a core-formation cultivator, Cha Ming composed himself before edging his seat forward. "Grandmaster Mo?" Cha Ming asked. "Have you ever heard of designing experiments to reduce experimental effort?"

The grandmaster alchemist paused his mechanical movements. "What's that?"

"Well, let's take this as an example," Cha Ming explained. "Let's say you have one thousand trials. Nine hundred of them simply use various doses of different medicinal ingredients, correct?"

"This is so," Mo Tianshen admitted.

"And with the liquids, could you possibly be thinking of trying out ten or so dosages for each liquid?" Cha Ming pressed.

"Twelve, to be exact," Mo Tianshen replied.

"Now, for all of these, you must have some sort of best guess on what dosages work best," Cha Ming continued. "For example, you must have a low and a high dosage in mind that might obtain optimal effects. In fact, somewhere in the middle of those two doses might be best. Is that right?" The alchemist nodded. "Then I will suggest a different approach to these experiments," Cha Ming continued. "Can you please write down which medicinal ingredients you will be trialing, which liquids, and at what dosage ranges?"

"I can, but certain ingredients interact too strongly," the alchemist said. "That's why it's so important to do so many experiments." He started writing down the list regardless of his argument.

"Don't worry about that," Cha Ming said. "It's not like you're using live subjects to begin with. Besides, the first step is reducing the ten million experiments to one thousand. By using them to evaluate various effects, we'll notice trends. We'll then take the best results and study them in detail. This way, we can get preliminary results in one month and much more detailed results one month later."

He then began creating an optimization plan. He also wrote down his reasoning in terms that could be understood by the senior alchemist. After all, mathematics and statistics weren't unknown in this world; only their practical application was lacking.

Soon enough, the alchemist's eyes brightened as he came to understand the logic behind the method. "Brilliant!" he shouted. "Let's give it a try on my most optimistic variations, then." He immediately summoned a few dozen powders, and his soul force mixed them in midair with great precision. In his excitement, he didn't waste time with the manual press but directly formed pellets. Then he motioned with his hands, drawing out dozens of different liquids. They were mixed in various doses and poured into vials. The man was a quick study, so this new experiment had been designed exactly as it should be.

Seeing that the experiments had all been laid in front of him, Cha Ming got to work. He only used the best guess rune for each mixture. Determining more specific runes would happen later in the process. He spent the entire afternoon like this, painting alchemical runes, and he didn't stop until the initial batch of experiments was completed.

As Cha Ming worked, Mo Tianshen was quite idle, secluding himself to the back and using his alchemical flame and various medicinal ingredients to forge pills for Cha Ming.

Cha Ming slumped down in his chair once he'd completed his work. His qi and mental energy were exhausted due to the exaggerated work pace.

"Good timing," Mo Tianshen said while walking out from the back. "I just finished the first batch of pills. This first bottle contains ten least-grade Pillar Expanding Pills, while the second bottle contains three least-grade Pillar Eruption Pills."

Cha Ming's face twitched a little when he heard the pill's names, but it couldn't be helped. *This guy's naming sense is something else. You'd think he was giving me aphrodisiac pills with names like those.*

"Take the pills in the first vial one at a time until you reach a bottleneck. When charging through the bottleneck, consume the three Pillar Eruption Pills simultaneously. You need that extra boost since, for some reason, you have three times as much qi as a cultivator should have at your cultivation realm."

"Many thanks," Cha Ming said while receiving the vials.

"No, it is you I must thank," Mo Tianshen said. "You've saved me decades of effort. This is the least I can do."

Cha Ming shook his head. "It's still too early to judge the results. One mustn't be too biased while conducting experiments."

Mo Tianshen snorted. "If one didn't expect results, why would they waste their time on experimenting?"

Cha Ming didn't disagree. He didn't stay long and quickly left the laboratory to cultivate.

Cha Ming allowed his mental energy and qi to fully recover before ingesting one of the Pillar Expanding Pills. The pill immediately dissolved upon entering his mouth, feeding concentrated five-element qi and creation and destruction qi into his dantian. The destruction qi didn't harm him; neither did the others, for that matter. They directly bypassed any obstructions and proceeded to their ultimate destination: his qi pillars.

Cha Ming felt his sigil-shaped pillars expand at a noticeable pace. In fact, the first pill alone increased the volume of each of his pillars and their supporting black-and-white grid by twenty percent. He estimated that this one pill had saved him an entire month of arduous cultivation. It had taken him only one hour to fully dissolve its energy.

Seeing such a great effect encouraged Cha Ming, who proceeded to ingest them one after another. With every pill, the effectiveness shrank. The second grew his pillars as much as ninety-nine percent of the first one, then ninety-eight percent, and so on. The last pill only increased the length of his pillars a tiny bit before abruptly stopping as though they had hit a wall.

Cha Ming didn't immediately try to break through. Instead, he cultivated to expand the volume of foundation qi inside the foundation seas surrounding his qi pillars. It didn't take long for the calm qi seas to reach the same heights as the pillars in question, threatening to flood over them at any moment.

It was at this moment that Cha Ming ate the three Pillar Eruption Pills simultaneously. A surge of potent energy rushed into his five pillars. There were also traces of something else—a corroding power that affected the stability of each sigil. Each pillar creaked, ready to burst from the massive influx of energy. It only took one final push from Cha Ming's soul to crack through an invisible barrier, causing the pillars to abruptly expand. As they did, the foundation seas drained to supply the energy needed for the transformation.

The process continued until his seas were completely empty, and the growth abruptly stopped. Cha Ming then spent hours refilling the empty qi reservoirs. As he did, he noticed that not only had the quantity of his qi increased, but the purity had as well. The seas contained foundation qi that was much more viscous than normal.

I always thought the difference between realms in foundation establishment was a matter of accumulation, he thought. *It seems that I was wrong.*

His breakthrough complete, Cha Ming focused his attention on the next important matter—combat sigils. Formations were generally very complicated, much more so than single-use talismans, but that didn't mean that all formations were this way. Combat formations were a specialized set. They only used sigils for execution, and they were streamlined in such a way that greatly increased personal qi consumption and eliminated other ways of compensating, like supplying energy through spirit stones. They were also considerably weaker than other formations of the same tier, and their rankings were based on their difficulty and their required cultivation realm. He opened one of the many books Lu Tianhao had lent him.

Combat Formations

Introduction

Congratulations on condensing the necessary sigils to practice combat formations. Combat formations are an essential part of a formation master's strength. Not only do they provide unsurpassed flexibility, but when used correctly, they are superior in quality to combat techniques.

Warning: Before proceeding to the next page, it is strongly recommended that you practice condensing formations from first grade through ninth with your condensed sigils. One's foundation is very important. If it takes longer than a single breath for the reader to condense a ninth-grade formation using a single sigil, the remainder of this book will be a waste of time. Combat formations are useless if the user is slain before activating them.

This was the reason behind Lu Tianhao's drills. He had been preparing Cha Ming for combat formations all along. To test his hypothesis, Cha Ming recalled the first-grade blaze formation. A ruby sigil shot out, and using his qi and incandescent force, he expanded it into twelve runes joined by various runic lines. A small blaze took shape above the formation. It was the simplest formation he knew, and it had taken him less than a breath. The uniform nature of the sigil made the formation he conjured stable throughout the process.

Cha Ming felt a sense of nostalgia as he thought of the soul-pearl manifestations once more. He withdrew his qi from the sigil, and the formation collapsed. Nine-tenths of the qi originally used returned to his foundation sea, while one-tenth of it vanished.

What a huge advantage, Cha Ming thought. While it seemed like the formations summoned used a lot of energy, the energy was recycled.

As a test, he summoned the blaze formation again. This time, however, he substituted a few runes and changed some lines, transforming it into a burning formation. Only a little additional qi was required, and it wasn't until he needed to retract the energy that he noticed a ten-percent loss in qi.

The second advantage of sigil formations was very clear—components were interchangeable, so formations were mutable and interchangeable so long as certain rules were followed.

A week passed quietly as he tried out different combinations, quickly familiarizing himself with the sigils. At the end of the week, he could easily summon a ninth-grade formation on a whim. He then moved on to combat formations proper. He had his eyes on a lesser-grade combat formation, which was the fusion of two least-grade combat formations.

Ten percent of Cha Ming's creation qi left his body as he used twelve wind-element sigils to form twelve different ninth-grade formations simultaneously. He used his qi to expand connecting lines between the sigils in order to join them into an organic whole. The process was considerably easier than drawing a least-grade talisman, but he still failed on his first attempt, losing thirty percent of the energy he had invested. Still, he didn't despair. Practice made perfect, and he refused to give up until he could summon the combat formation without any problems in less than a breath ten times out of ten.

One day later, he finally completed the Heavenly Cloud Steps combat formation. He summoned it under his Stormchaser Boots, making his feet feel especially light. To test the new technique, he rushed out of his residence and began running in the air and along the walls. His feet didn't touch anything solid, simply walking on the air itself.

Twice as fast as before, he thought. *And my ability to walk in the air has greatly improved. I can now walk a hundred feet above any surface.* Satisfied, he retracted the formation and resummoned it continuously until he could do it ten times out of ten.

The second combat formation he mastered was the Heavenly Lightning Steps Formation. It was composed of twelve iridescent lightning runes joined in a seemingly haphazard manner. Given his previous experience with the Heavenly Cloud Steps Formation, condensing this least-grade formation didn't take long. He continuously practiced it until mastery. Not only did it boost his movement speed by a half time more than the Heavenly Cloud Steps Formation, but its ability to instantaneously change directions was also much better.

Now comes the difficult part, he thought, calming his breath. He summoned twenty-four sigils at once. *It takes wind and lightning to form a storm. Thunder and clouds strike quickly and mightily.*

Twelve lightning sigils floated out, forming the framework of Heavenly Lightning Steps, while twelve wind sigils formed the framework for Heavenly Cloud Steps. They meshed together with additional formation lines that completely changed the energy flow.

Sweat beaded on Cha Ming's forehead as he used his strong soul to guide the formation lines. Fifty lines became sixty, and sixty became seventy. Before he knew it, ninety-five lines had been formed. The last lines were the most difficult.

Ninety-six… Ninety-seven… Ninety-eight… Ninety-nine… One hundred!

On his first attempt, the lesser-grade combat formation Stormchaser Steps fell into place beneath his feet. He felt the lightning crackle beneath him and the wind blow around his legs. The Stormchaser Boots pulsed after he summoned the formation, and they instantly transformed into gray clouds that complemented the wind and lightning, as though they were made for each other.

Did Fuxi predict this? Cha Ming wondered.

He ran through the courtyard, his feet bare covered in crackling clouds. His speed was five times what it had been when he first modified the Seven Cloud Steps technique.

Enough to completely outrank Xiao Heilong if I encounter him again, Cha Ming thought.

"Have you had enough fun yet?" a cold voice asked behind him.

Cha Ming looked back at Lu Tianhao's figure. His eyes were red and covered in dark circles.

"What might be the problem?" Cha Ming asked, gulping.

"Oh, I don't know," Lu Tianhao said. "It's just that I like coming to my quarters to catch some sleep every decade or so, and some inconsiderate bastard decided to use the courtyard instead of his training room to practice. Not just that, but he's woken me *three times*. You wouldn't happen to know where I can find this miscreant, would you?"

Not only had Lu Tianhao exited his chambers, but dozens of other members were glaring at him from below. The oppressive sensation forced him to the ground, where his technique instantly dissipated.

"It won't happen again, I swear," Cha Ming said weakly.

"Damn right it won't!" Lu Tianhao yelled.

The dozens of cultivators all came at him together and beat him black and blue. Despite his bone-forging body cultivation and some newly learned healing formations, it took him an entire day to recover.

Chapter 27: Hidden Agenda

Huxian was in pain. Not physical pain, but mental pain. For starters, he had nasty dream where he was beaten half to death by a few dozen cultivators. He now realized it was the result of his connection with Cha Ming. Thankfully, the cultivators didn't seem to have any ill intent. It only resulted in temporary pain on his part.

It was only superficial mental pain. His true anguish stemmed from his feelings of guilt, which had left him bedridden. He felt pain in his heart whenever he saw Lei Jiang, who was constantly out on patrols near the cultivator encampment.

The thought of the mouse seemed to summon him. Purple lightning crackled across the sky before the small mouse appeared in front of Huxian.

"Permission to speak freely, Master," the mouse yelled.

Huxian sighed. "Granted."

"Two skirmishes have occurred in the past week, one with the blond-haired one and one with the dark-haired devil. Our losses were greatest against the devil, exchanging two of our purification demons with two of their foundation-establishment cultivators. Our beasts fought valiantly with the terrain advantage, but their tactics were cunning and vicious. On the other hand, not much happened when we fought the blond-haired tea drinker. A few bones were broken, and a few cultivators were grievously injured, but nothing worth mentioning."

"Is that all?" Huxian asked dispassionately.

"Yes, Master," the mouse replied.

"Lei Jiang, do you hate me?" Huxian asked.

The small mouse stared at him with wide eyes as though incapable of understanding the question. "How could I possibly hate the master? Master is most benevolent, most magnificent. The stars would lose their luster without Mast—"

"What I mean," Huxian said, cutting him off, "is would you hate me if you didn't have a slave mark and weren't my general."

Lei Jiang stared at him blankly. "I can't imagine such an existence. I can only think that it would be a very lowly existence, not worth living at all."

Huxian knew he wouldn't get anywhere. He had asked these questions many times and had gained no ground. No matter how he tried, whether it was ordering him to act normally or using a bunch of qualifying statements, he couldn't pry a single bit of personality out of the mouse. He wasn't like Silverwing, who would get mad at him or speak what was on his mind. It was like Lei Jiang's entire world revolved around Huxian.

Huxian sighed once more. "Come here, Lei Jiang," he said. The mouse swiftly ran in front of Huxian. "Closer," Huxian said. The mouse approached until he was just before the fox's head. Huxian began to glow brightly, surrounding them both with a black-and-white bagua. The bagua symbol on Huxian's head glowed, and so did one of trigrams on his tail, the trigram for lightning.

Simultaneously, the "general" character on Lei Jiang's head also glowed a soft purple color that faded into the mouse's tough fur.

"Lei Jiang," Huxian barked authoritatively, "I pronounce you free!" The instant he spoke these words, the character on Lei Jiang's forehead shattered. The normal expression of adoration slowly turned to that of fear and panic. "Go!" Huxian barked, exerting his Godbeast presence on the pitiful creature at peak purification. The bagua faded, and the mouse disappeared in a flash of purple.

"I hope you do well," Huxian whispered, a tear trickling from his jade eyes. He lay there for an entire day and spoke to no one. No, that wasn't it. Rather, no one dared to come speak to him. It wasn't until noon the next day that he heard a familiar fluttering sound. Depressed, he forced himself to exit his cave.

"I'm proud of you," Silverwing said. He was perched on a tree just outside the cave.

"How is he?" Huxian asked.

"Scared out of his wits," Silverwing replied. "He doesn't know who he is. But one thing is certain—he's not the Lei Jiang you once knew."

"I could tell the moment his eyes changed," Huxian said. "By the way, I have something for you, Silverwing." The black and white colors on Huxian's fur suddenly faded to gray, converging into a black-and-white ball. The fox looked exhausted, but his black and white coloring returned shortly.

"What's this?" the falcon asked, pecking at the small ball.

"Just eat it," Huxian said in irritation. The falcon didn't think twice before gulping it down. Enlightenment flashed through his eyes.

"This is…" the falcon said unbelievingly.

"I lied to you," Huxian said. "I'm a terrible friend, and I regret it. I've been keeping this peak-level-purification technique from you. What's worse is that it's specifically suited for those with roc bloodlines. It's useless to me, but it means the world to you. Yet I kept it away from you, wanting to trick you into becoming my general.

"I'm a failure as a friend, and I don't deserve to know someone like you." Huxian turned around and headed back into the darkness of his cave and continued to mope. He was alone now, with no one to rely on. Except perhaps Cha Ming, if they met again one day and he wasn't mad at him.

An incense time passed before he heard Silverwing's familiar flapping. It was likely the last time he would hear it. After all, it wouldn't take much time for him to gain his ancestral memories and break through to core formation. Why would he bother sticking around these desolate mountains once he advanced? He would be free to fly through the skies, a single flap of his wings enough to take him across the whole continent.

He wished for nothing more than a good life for him.

"You really don't like battle achievements, do you?" Zhou Li said mockingly. "It's no wonder you're the second young master and not the first. I wouldn't pin the hopes of my family on a turtle like you either."

Wang Jun shrugged. He was seated in front of an ornate tent, sipping tea as usual. There was no flicker in his expression, no anger or irritation. Just like he practiced day in and day out. "I am very calculative in my actions," he said. "And I don't like to kill off good men when there simply isn't a reason to."

"No reason?" Zhou Li said incredulously. Smirking, he added, "Yes, that's true. There isn't any reason for you to compete with me. After all, how could you possibly compete with an oracle in strategy?"

"Quite right," Wang Jun said. "I suppose you've divined the outcome of our battle?"

Zhou Li's expression darkened at these words. Wang Jun knew full well that the only thing Zhou Li could divine was darkness. He divined the same thing every day. The future was shrouded to him, which was why Wang Jun dared to engaged in subterfuge with him in the first place.

"Tell me," Wang Jun continued. "How many more sin flames must you accumulate to break through to core formation? You mustn't need much more, considering the chaos you've been causing outside the cities. Perhaps a few thousand more dead children and tens of thousands of innocent virgins will do the trick?"

Zhou Li's eyes narrowed. "I don't see why you would accuse me of all these things," he said. "The black flames I cultivate do not require sin. In fact, they require the opposite—preventing national disasters, preventing war. It's quite tiring to prop up a nation when there is chaos everywhere.

"Meanwhile I need to deal with entitled brats who don't know their place. There is one I have to deal with on a daily basis that is particularly annoying. He's useless even amongst useless men. In fact, I received a juicy bit of information the other day about him. I heard that when he was young, he let his sister die." The sounds of a shattering porcelain attracted glances from the minister's camp. Zhou Li smirked. "What I spent to find that out wasn't wasted in the slightest."

Wang Jun regained his composure swiftly and chuckled before taking out a second teacup and continuing his lounging. "If you paid money for that information, I can only shake my head at your idiocy. There are many people who would have happily told you for free."

At that moment, the tent flap opened beside them. "Are you two bantering again?" a voice said.

"Esteemed minister, we wouldn't dare," Zhou Li said.

"It was innocent verbal jousting, Your Grace," Wang Jun replied.

"I can tell," Minister Rong said. "If the broken porcelain is any indication, you both have razor blades for tongues and the cunning of a fox. Now then, what's the tally for the day?"

Zhou Li was the first to reply. "Reporting to Minister Rong, this week we killed one mid-purification demon beast and one early-purification beast. However, we lost two foundation-establishment experts in the process due to a disadvantage in terrain."

"And you?" Minister Rong asked Wang Jun.

"A few broken bones and a few serious injuries," Wang Jun replied. "No kills, but no significant losses."

"Sometimes you must risk a little to gain a little," Minister Rong said, looking at Wang Jun meaningfully.

"Naturally," Wang Jun said. "On that note, I wonder if we might meet in private after this report?"

"We can," the minister said. "But if any attempts to sway me personally are made, I can assure you that this competition will be over before the hour is up."

"I understand," Wang Jun said. He waited with clasped hands for Zhou Li to finish. The latter smirked at him before bowing and leaving them behind.

"This way," the minister said, opening his tent flap. They entered a space much larger than its external appearance would suggest. "Speak. No sound can travel inside or outside this tent."

"Very well," Wang Jun said. "Do you mind if I make you tea while we chat?"

"That is... acceptable," Minister Rong said. This was the only luxury he afforded himself. Good tea relaxed the mind and strengthened the soul, enabling him to do his utmost for the country. Wang Jun didn't take long to set up a tea table, boil water, and begin pouring tea for two with a practiced hand. Each cup only contained only a single draught, but this was the best way to enjoy this particular blend.

"Before we begin, I wish to confirm something with Minister Rong," Wang Jun said. "It was agreed previously that the one with the most merit in obtaining the immortal jade would be given the rights to the jade. What would you define as merit?"

"As I explained before, it is a balance between cost and results toward obtaining the jade," Minister Rong said.

"And if we stole it with minimal loss, this would be considered a positive result and count as merit?" Wang Jun asked.

"*Any* result," the minister reiterated.

"Excellent," Wang Jun said. "Some time ago, I met secretly with the sovereign of a nearby peak, who happens to be contracted to a friend of mine. I asked for access to the jade, and he agreed that the beasts of all nine peaks would agree to trading it."

"They would simply trade it?" the minister asked incredulously.

"It's useless to them, and it's a hot potato in their hands. *However*, what they want isn't limited to a trade. The goods they require for trade only amount to a hundred thousand high-grade spirit stones, and I've already determined that they can be made available in a few months. What they really want is a peace treaty for the next five hundred years."

Minister Rong frowned. "How could we sign a peace treaty so easily? The lords of the forest rotate every few decades. The only stable existences are the sovereigns on each mountain, as well as their reclusive monarch, and he would never let himself be beholden to such a contract."

"I've confirmed that the sovereigns of the forest are all willing to sign a blood oath on it," Wang Jun replied. "They would limit their expansion efforts to the north and east, other beast territories that we are not concerned with. It's a win-win. Not only would they get resources to develop, but they could use the peace to expand their territories. Meanwhile, we wouldn't have to spend so much on military expenditures."

Minister Rong seemed deep in thought. "Who do they want as signatories on our end?"

"They want you, the third prince, and me, the second young master of the Wang family," Wang Jun said.

"That's all?" Minister Rong asked. Seeing Wang Jun nod, the minister's silence continued. "What do you know about the southern border?" he asked after an incense time. It was an unexpected question. The southern border seemed completely unrelated to the current conflict.

"Nothing much," Wang Jun answered honestly. "I come from a merchant family, and we are most concerned with profit. I can somewhat understand how a nation works, but only as a business."

"Well, then," Minister Rong said, "as you might know, we do not have any kingdoms on our western border due to the mountains. We only have a great wall that separates us from the beasts, which has proven to be strangely effective in containing them. There are opposing kingdoms to the north, the east, and the south. We are on very friendly terms with the north and the east. The north doesn't mind us because there is a mountain pass we can defend with ease and vice-versa. To the east, we have an alliance through marriage that has lasted generations. To the south, however, we are always waging war. And for many years, we have been losing ground.

"Regrettably, we haven't been able to redirect troops due to the ample number of beast tides to the north and the west. Both are important, and if we allowed the beasts into our territory, it would be very difficult to reclaim it. The fertile plains would grow over with forests, and the qi would turn demonic.

"Therefore, we have lost ground many times over the past decade."

"I assume this is relevant to the potential peace treaty?" Wang Jun asked.

"Of course," Minister Rong said enthusiastically. "If we can secure a peace treaty, we could use our freed-up troops to reclaim lost land and resources. There's no telling how much we could expand toward the south in five hundred years. In fact, it may be possible to retake South Hope Fortress. In that case, we wouldn't have to worry about attacks from the south for centuries!" Minister Rong frowned. "Though, you said they wanted one hundred thousand high-grade spirit stones' worth of trade goods. What is their estimate on the jade reserves?"

"There's good news on this front as well, Minister," Wang Jun said. "Not only is there three thousand jin of immortal jade, but there is also a hundred jin of immortal-jade core."

The minister's eyes widened at these numbers. "If you can close this deal, I will sign the blood oath and appoint you as the winner," the minister said. "However, you must get Prince Lei's agreement. In addition, we need forty percent of the resources traded on signing of the contract."

"I negotiated thirty," Wang Jun said. "I can't go any higher than that."

There was a slight paused. "Fine," Minister Rong said at last. "How long will this trade take to execute?"

"Three months," Wang Jun replied.

Minister Rong nodded. "Then you'd better hope that Zhou Li doesn't take over the mountain in the next three months. And I don't want to be seeing any *funny* business."

"Yes, sir," Wang Jun said with a solemn face. He was laughing inwardly. After all, no one else needed to know about the additional five hundred jin of immortal-jade core.

"You did *what*?" Prince Lei was fuming. Wang Jun understood why, of course. This entire time he had been telling the prince to be patient while his opponent's forces claimed battle merit. Now he was suggesting the riskiest play of all.

"Calm yourself, Your Highness," Wang Jun said. "I've already discussed it with the minister. In three months, if everything goes well, we'll be the ones in control of the mountain range while the crown prince's forces will have weakened. It's a double win."

"But what if things *don't* go well?" Prince Lei said through gritted teeth.

"May I be brutally honest?" Wang Jun said. The prince waved his hand to grant permission. "We grossly underestimated the crown prince's forces. By a factor of three. They hired people from outside the kingdom to grant them an advantage by using foreign money. They've been trickling them into the kingdom this entire time. How can we possibly win against them using conventional means?"

The third prince massaged his brow. "Can we sign right now?"

"We can't, because we need the initial trade to kick off the contract," Wang Jun replied. "The prime minister is too much of a stickler for the rules to bend on this. The beasts won't bend because they need the resources to strengthen themselves. And if they lose a few demons, so what? They will simply split the resources amongst a much smaller population. It's the way demon beasts operate."

"Can we sign before they take the mountain range?" Prince Lei asked.

"Yes," Wang Jun said. "We have an eighty-percent chance, assuming they don't get additional reinforcements. Plus, we can increase those odds with a bit of subterfuge."

Prince Lei shook his head. "The minister will be watching for that."

"My dear prince," Wang Jun said, walking up to him. His figure shimmered slightly before blending into the shadows. His body disappeared entirely. "There is no one in this camp who can stop me from walking where I please. No one."

Chapter 28: Formation Battles

Cha Ming dodged using Stormchaser Steps, barely avoiding a literal inferno that had materialized beneath him. Least-Grade Conflagration Formation, he determined. Fortunately, it was much easier to take down such a formation than to set it up. He rapidly threw out twelve water sigils around two key nodes, pouring qi into them to sprout a combat formation. The formation condensed in half a breath, forming a vortex of water that doused the two formation eyes. The fiery formation flickered before destabilizing and collapsing. Cha Ming wasted no time in collecting his hasty combat formation and recovering his precious water qi.

He didn't linger. Staying in one location was a bad idea in a formation battle. Gold lights flashed as twelve formation flags flew into the ground, and the white-haired, white-robed Lu Tianhao took out a gray brush. Cha Ming recognized the placements of these formation flags and the formations spreading out from them. A combat formation wouldn't be enough. Therefore, he quickly decided on a counter formation, the Least-Grade Smelting Formation. It was especially good at destroying metals, metallic techniques, and weapons. And it was obviously a lethal formation given its high temperatures.

Cha Ming quickly threw out seven ruby sigils and five formation flags with specialized formations. He used combat sigils whenever possible to save time and energy, but he had accumulated many specialized formation flags over the last month of practice. With but a thought, his Clear Sky Brush expanded into a large formation brush. He quickly painted the most key connections while using the sigils to set up the lesser ones. It was a slightly lower-tier formation than the one Lu Tianhao used, but it countered his perfectly. They finished their formations at the exact same time. Cha Ming's red elemental essence clashed with the gold elemental essence from Lu Tianhao's brush. They began collapsing simultaneously.

Cha Ming didn't relax, however. Instead he quickly formed another combat formation. This one was small, but it was the fastest one he knew. It was a metal-based formation, Least-Grade Spike Bomb. Meanwhile, he spread out his incandescent force to detect the next formation being laid. This one was an Ice Lotus Garden Formation, a formation with tiers ranging from least grade to top grade.

This formation also couldn't be countered with a combat formation, so Cha Ming threw out eight earth sigils, transforming them into eight Mount Tai Formations of the ninth grade. He linked them together with another four unique formation flags that revolved around absorption. Twelve swift brushstrokes with brown ink complemented the tendrils from the eight Mount Tai Formations. His formation completed slightly before the Ice Lotus Garden Formation, so he quickly used Stormchaser Steps to dart through the disrupted formation nodes toward his teacher.

The man grunted as he immediately laid down a Lightning Dragon combat formation. Cha Ming responded with a Wind Blades combat formation. It was hardly a proper counter, as both formations would bypass each other and aim for mutual destruction.

Lu Tianhao, unconcerned, forged ahead with the Lightning Dragon. Cha Ming, on the other hand, quickly dodged it and threw his formation to the opposite side of Lu Tianhao. He avoided the lightning dragon by a hair's breadth, but it swiftly turned around to chase him as though smelling blood. That was when Cha Ming revealed his Least-Grade Spike Bomb. He threw it past the lightning dragon, activating it. The lightning dragon reacted to it as though it was the most delectable snack. The current followed the spikes all the way to the ground.

Meanwhile, Cha Ming activated the Wind Bladed combat formation, buffeting his teacher with seven sharp blades of wind. He gathered back the formation and threw out twelve flags. It was his most powerful least-grade formation, Blistering Inferno. Unfortunately, he couldn't use sigils to make it, as it was too complex. Lu Tianhao, who had just been pushed back, took out his paintbrush to counterattack Cha Ming. But Cha Ming knew he wouldn't be successful. The man had fallen into his trap.

While Cha Ming's movements were swift and graceful like an artist's, Lu Tianhao's were heavy. This was normal, given that he was fighting the pressure of the full Larger Than Mount Tai Formation that Cha Ming had laid to counter the previous ice formation. Cha Ming's formation was powerful and accurately placed, ensuring the formation's survival at the end of their conflict.

Cha Ming finished his Blistering Inferno formation a half breath before Lu Tianhao could finish his counter. Roaring flame dragons rotated and attacked Lu Tianhao, making it impossible for him to complete the formation.

"Your win this time," Lu Tianhao said. "Good job. Now try this one."

Twenty-four blue lights shot out instantly, outlining a formation with over a hundred lines. One hundred lines was a demarcation, the hundredth line being much more difficult to draw than the previous ones. It was also the threshold which separated lesser-grade and least-grade formations.

Cha Ming did not recognize the lesser-grade combat formation. But he didn't hesitate. He encapsulated three of the nodes with an earthen formation, which served no other purpose but to disrupt. Meanwhile, he sent another wood-based combat formation to disrupt four other nodes.

The blue combat formation trembled under the combined assault. Unfortunately, Cha Ming knew full well that it wouldn't stop at that. He looked up to see a golden light flashing. A sharp sword tore through the air toward his heart. It stopped a bare millimeter away from his chest.

Clap. Clap. Clap.

"Congratulations," Lu Tianhao said. "You're a fast study, and I can't teach you anything more about least-grade formations. To beat me, you'll need to learn lesser-grade ones."

Cha Ming clasped his fists together and bowed. "Thank you for your guidance."

"Not a problem," the white-haired man said. "If my calculations are correct, you've run out of credit and need to go hunting devils again if you want another lesson."

He tossed a spatial ring to Cha Ming. "I went through the trouble of retrieving books on lesser-grade formations," he said. "Don't lose them. Also, you can keep the spatial ring. I noticed that you don't have a suitable disguise for your spatial artifact. Some higher-tier core-formation experts may be able to detect it. We don't want you attracting unwanted trouble, do we?"

In the blink of an eye, Cha Ming appeared outside the man's office. He bowed to the closed door in thanks.

After returning, he cultivated normally for a half day. His qi was no longer turbulent like it was when he first broke through to early foundation establishment. The day after he broke through, he was told not to use medicinal pills until his foundation stabilized into clear qi seas without ripples. Only a few ripples formed when he cultivated now. According to Lu Tianhao, the only way to stabilize one's foundation was to constantly deplete and replenish qi, effectively scrubbing away any residual, lower-quality qi from the last level. Most people did this by practicing a profession or through combat. Cultivating in silence wouldn't be as effective as these two options.

I really should go out and hunt devils, he thought. *Time to contact Luo Xuehua and see what they are up to.* He took out his core-transmission jade and activated their imprints. Two jade projections appeared in front of him a few breaths later.

"Look who decided to finally call us," Dongfang Hao said in a cheerful voice.

"I was learning," Cha Ming said, shrugging. "Formations are hard work, and I'm not very useful in combat unless I learn more combat formations. Which is why I called you guys. I'm planning on going on another hunting mission. Are you interested?"

The duo looked at each other awkwardly. "I'm afraid we can't," Luo Xuehua said. "We're on a mission one week away. You won't arrive before we finish it, so you're on your own for now."

"Fair enough," Cha Ming said. "Do let me know when you're back." The call disconnected, leaving Cha Ming to his own devices. His first stop was the Alabaster mission board, where a middle-aged lady tended to the postings.

"Hi, Yueming," Cha Ming said in greeting as he looked over the postings. "Are there any postings for Senior Partner Lu here?" All postings where devils were confirmed were automatically assigned to Lu Tianhao.

"Nothing," she said, shaking her head. "The last mission was taken by Senior Member Xuehua and Junior Member Hao."

Cha Ming nodded as he continued looking through each individual posting for suspicious signs. There were many cases of villains, murders, and nobles looking for protection. But nothing stood out among them.

I can only look elsewhere. He thanked Yueming and walked outside.

Cha Ming flew on a flying sword outside the Alabaster building. On his chest, he wore two silver medallions. One was his lesser-grade talisman-master medallion, while the other was a least-grade formation-master medallion. One qualification was uncommon but not unheard of. People with two qualifications were extremely rare.

On his way to the Mercenary Guild, he checked in with the restaurant he had commissioned to feed people. One month had passed, and he reviewed the ledgers to see how many homeless people were served. He also looked at the people frequenting the establishment. He noticed they were less gaunt, a little less miserable, and more importantly, he saw something that wasn't there before: hope. He concluded that it was money well spent and decided to continue a one-year contract. The restaurant's owner was overjoyed.

He then headed straight for the Mercenary Guild and reviewed various mission postings. These weren't organized in the same way as the Alabaster Group's were, so it was like sifting through sand to find gold. There wasn't any gold to be found that day. Cha Ming left after having gained nothing.

Curious. From what I know, there have been devil-cultivator attacks everywhere, Cha Ming thought. *I might be catching the stupid ones by looking for mission postings, but what about the smart and careful ones? And what about the ones that leave no survivors?*

Realization dawned on him that devil sightings likely wouldn't land on his lap. Fortunately, he had the perfect skill to find them—his Eyes of Pure Jade. Even a whiff of a yellow aura could detect the presence of a devil cultivator.

Having made his decision, Cha Ming directed his flying sword to the west entrance of the city. He passed by many people on his way out. They looked up as they rode on the light rail the same way he had when he first arrived in the city. It was a new rail line, and due to the proper management of cultivators and mortals, the rail line had been installed in two short months. Each additional line increased the prosperity of the outer city by making it possible to operate businesses in cheaper locations.

How long before it becomes too expensive for the common person to live inside the city? he wondered.

Cha Ming dismounted his flying sword at the gate. The guard waved him through without an inspection, which he gathered was due to his two qualification badges. Then, hopping onto his flying sword, he traveled five miles out of the city. It wasn't long before he noticed a presence behind him.

"It took you long enough," Cha Ming said, looking back at Xiao Heilong.

The man looked at him coldly. "You only increased your qi cultivation by one sub-realm, and you're already back to court death?

Fine by me. Why don't you stick around this time instead of running with your tail between your legs? You could get lucky and win."

"Now why would I do that?" Cha Ming said, and twenty-four sigils flew out beneath his feet. Forty percent of his creation qi drained away as he activated Stormchaser Steps. The sudden appearance of wind and lightning beneath his feet caused his boots to dematerialize into black clouds. He flashed away from Xiao Heilong instantly, evading a dagger strike that was meant for his heart.

Xiao Heilong wasted no time and activated his consumption ability, rapidly dropping the temperature around him and increasing his speed substantially. However, Cha Ming chuckled when he saw this and increased his own pace. He was slightly faster, and there was nothing Xiao Heilong could do about it.

I wonder if I can kite him? Cha Ming thought. He threw a least-grade combat formation behind him. Xiao Heilong simply grunted and smashed through it using the force of his body and his daggers. Not one to give up easily, Cha Ming flew back toward him, evading the many slashes that came his way. With every dodge, he threw out one flag until twelve flags were in position. Then he threw out twelve sigils to create an overlaying formation. While he wasn't very fast at making them, he had a few lesser formations up his sleeve.

Cha Ming took out the Clear Sky Brush and continuously evaded while painting line after line, dancing with death. Blue brushstrokes covered the ground with frosty lines while dozens of lines shot out from the well-placed sigils.

Xiao Heilong's eyes narrowed as the final lines connected. Cha Ming felt the pressure on him dissipate as the man disappeared from the formation's limits, just in time for it to activate. Countless icy shards began to circulate as the formation drew from the energy of heaven and earth.

"It seems we're at an impasse," Cha Ming said calmly. Setting up the array had been exhausting, but it was now impossible for Xiao Heilong to attack him. He immediately began to circulate his cultivation to recover his qi. The formation would continue until it was interrupted or stopped.

"You might be quick, and you might be crafty," Xiao Heilong said, "but don't fall asleep. It might not be worth my time to hunt you down, but I know people who could make you disappear in the blink of an eye."

"If you could hire them, you already would have," Cha Ming shot back. "I know your kind. You would never do anything for free."

The man grunted before vanishing. Cha Ming's gamble had paid off. Unless someone else interfered, he didn't need to worry about Xiao Heilong for the time being. That is, until he decided to kill him.

Now where to go, Cha Ming thought. *There are dozens of small towns before the nearest city. I'll start there.*

A large man let out a loud burp after downing a mug of ale. "Now this is what I've been missing out on," the man said. "I'll take two more of those, innkeeper, and a nice bowl of stew."

"Can you pay?" the innkeeper said, looking at the man dubiously.

"Of course," the man said, slapping some silver on the table. "I don't stay out in the woods all year for nothing, you know. There's money to be made out there if you know what to look for. How else do you think I could come here every month to stock up on provisions?"

"Fair enough," the innkeeper grumbled. "Just don't cause a ruckus like you did last time."

"Sure, sure," the large man said. "Is Li'er still around?"

The innkeeper shook his head. "She's not into that line of work anymore. She's got a respectable job now at the tailor's, so I don't want you causing trouble for her."

"I was just asking..." the large man said, downing another mug. "I don't suppose anyone else took her place?"

"Xie'er is who you're looking for," the innkeeper said in a half contemptuous, half amused voice. "I can call for her if you like, but her price is a silver more an hour than Li'er was."

"A full silver?" the man exclaimed. "She'd better be worth it."

"Worth it or not, I don't want you bruising her up," the innkeeper cautioned. "If you do, I'll call the town watch on you." The innkeeper retired for a while, leaving the man to his drink and his stew.

"I heard you say there's good work in the woods?" a man in a black cloak said, pulling back his hood. He looked young, around seventeen. He had long black hair and normal features, save for a pair of piercing jade-green eyes. He wore a sword by his side, a peak-mortal-grade treasure. He also wore a large gold chain. The type that nobles would wear.

"There is, for those who are willing to work hard," the larger man said. Despite his pot belly, his muscles rippled with strength.

"That's not a problem," the young man said. "I'm at the sixth level of qi condensation and the sixth level of body cultivation. Whether it's killing spirit beasts or heavy lifting, I'm quite confident. By the way, my name is Li Hou."

"Man Tou," the man said, clasping his fists and bowing. Seeing the young man's smirk, he continued with a deadpan voice. "Yes, like the steamed bun. I didn't choose my name, but I can't very well change it now." Man Tou took a long draw of beer. "You're not from around here, are you?"

"Of course not," Li Hou said disdainfully. "The noble Li family would never have members in such a small town. But I'm still young and growing, so I've decided to go out for an adventure. If you can give me an experience worth remembering, I definitely won't forget our friendship."

Man Tou hesitated. "Fine, you can come into the woods with me. I'll introduce you to our team. If you want an unforgettable experience, I can definitely arrange that. However, I need a hundred gold up front."

"Gold?" Li Hou asked, clueless. "Does gold hold such value? I'll tell you what, I can give you ten high-grade spirit stones if you make it worth my while." Ten glittering stones appeared in his hand.

Man Tou gulped. "It's not wise to throw your wealth around like that. People might cause you trouble."

"And who would cause trouble for the Li family around here?" Li Hou said arrogantly.

"Fair enough," Man Tou said.

At that moment, the innkeeper arrived with a petite young lady. She looked well worth the additional silver for the extra-special experience. Man Tou licked his lips. "We'll take off in two hours then, young friend." Then he disappeared up the stairs with the young lady.

Chapter 29: Hunting

Cha Ming—or Li Hou, as he was currently called—walked alongside Man Tou with a serious expression. It wasn't so much the nature of their conversation that caused Cha Ming's stone-faced disposition. Rather, it was the act of constantly suppressing his soul, body, and qi cultivation. It had taken him days to find someone with a thick enough yellow aura. He had discovered on this trip that the yellow aura didn't necessarily mean the man was a devil cultivator. No, it represented sin, just like the jade aura represented merit.

Fortunately, these things usually came hand in hand. With a thick enough yellow aura, the probability of dealings with devils increased substantially. It wasn't long before they were joined by many other individuals in the qi-condensation realm. Each of them also had a thick yellow presence, largely increasing the possibility of a devil cult. Regardless, they were up to no good. His façade was a trap, and his attitude toward them would depend on their actions and behavior.

"I see that you've found us a new companion, old bun," a graying, skinny man said jovially. Cha Ming could sense that his cultivation was at half-step foundation establishment.

"Who are you calling an old bun?" Man Tou said. "I'm much younger than you. Call me a fresh bun at the very least."

Many of the men chuckled. Cha Ming would have chuckled too if he hadn't seen the murderous glints in their eyes.

"You all stay here in the woods?" Cha Ming asked.

"Yes, young lord Li," Man Tou replied. "We have a camp in a clearing. It's very safe, and no one can find it unless we bring them there."

"That secretive?" Cha Ming said. "What could make it unfindable?"

"We have a mystic formation," Man Tou said proudly. "Anyone who looks for it will simply see a normal forest. In fact, you'll experience it yourself just up ahead. It's only a mile away."

A gust of wind caused a bloody scent to assault Cha Ming's nostrils as they neared the clearing. He could see the runic lines of a formation. Three flags were visible from his viewpoint, and while he could easily break it, what fun would that be? The element of surprise was much too valuable to squander.

"Brace yourself," Man Tou said. "We'll be crossing the boundary shortly. I'll hold on to your shoulder so you don't lose your sense of direction." The man's large, meaty palm clapped down on his shoulder, and Cha Ming was forced to sag down in discomfort lest he expose himself.

Cha Ming's vision distorted, and his sense of direction became chaotic. It only lasted for the fraction of a breath before he became aware of his surroundings once more. But instead of the camp he expected, a large ritual formation painted with blood materialized. Desiccated husks that used to be living men were piled up beside it. Off to the side, Cha Ming saw cowering mortals awaiting their fates.

"Is it to your liking, young lord?" Man Tou said harshly.

"Yes, it's exactly what I was looking for," Cha Ming said, looking around calmly. His composure evidently startled the men who had accompanied them. They wouldn't be startled much longer. Cha Ming calculated their positions and threw out twelve ruby sigils. Fifty tendrils shot out as they formed a basic least-grade combat formation. The motley crew, who hadn't even reached foundation establishment, didn't stand a chance. Only ashes remained.

"Who dares?" a voice yelled. Instantly, five figures appeared in front of Cha Ming. Two were early-foundation-establishment experts, while the others had barely broken through. Invariably, they all possessed ochre phantoms.

Clouds and crackling lightning instantly appeared beneath Cha Ming's feet as he dashed over to the five cultivators. He swung out his staff, bashing against them with quaking power. Two of them backed away, coughing blood, while three others with stronger bodies transformed and grasped at his staff. They wrenched it out of his grip, but Cha Ming was unconcerned.

Three charged at him, while two others shrank back, sending waves of soul attacks at him. Cha Ming released the full pressure of his soul, refusing to get entrained into their illusory world. They coughed out blood once more due to backlash, but instead of red blood, it was blue.

"We're no match for him," the lust devil with the highest cultivation said. "Activate the defensive formations!"

Cha Ming's pupils constricted when he felt five terrifying formations activate around him.

Shit, he thought. *They may not have a formation master, but they had someone lay down so many defensive formations. Heavens damn you, Guo Jia.*

Each formation complemented the element of the user. The two lust devils activated two illusory formations, causing Cha Ming's eyesight to become useless. Even his Eyes of Pure Jade were obscured. Meanwhile, countless blades cut him and tongues of flame licked him. His body's vitality began to sap away.

Cha Ming wasted no time. He slapped out three talismans. They were shielding talismans in water, earth, and metal elements. He darted around randomly, hoping to distract them as he focused on the most important task—restoring his vision.

Cha Ming sent out twelve earth sigils, setting up a twenty-foot-wide absorption combat formation. He felt the illusory formation strain slightly as the local moisture was sucked into it. He also felt his outermost shield break and felt his body shift as three attacks landed on his temporarily stationary body.

Cha Ming clicked his tongue. He threw out a Nine Heavens

Lightning Talisman, a Five-Fire Cremation Talisman, and a Nine Blades, One Dao Talisman at the intruders. They instantly backed away, leaving him alone in his private space. At the same time, they continued raining attacks from afar. Ice shards, sapping vines, and tongues of flame impacted his shields one after another.

To buy himself time, he laid out twelve blue formation flags and twelve water sigils. They formed a mirrorlike shield around him, intercepting all of the incoming attacks.

First step accomplished. The defensive formation, while small, was just there to buy him time. He extended his soul outward, probing the limits of the illusory formation while his shield weakened little by little. *One... Five... Twelve... Seventeen... Twenty-four!* All twenty-four nodes appeared in his mind's eye, along with the formation lines. *Circulation of water energy between these eight points is vital... Now to make it circulate even more.*

He threw out twelve rarely used green flags, followed by twelve green sigils. His qi surged as he poured eight percent of his wood qi into the combat sigils. Meanwhile, he summoned his Clear Sky Brush from thin air and sent out brushstroke after brushstroke of green liquified elemental essence.

Three more breaths...

Unfortunately, it was then that he heard fierce roars as his opponents activated their consumption abilities. Their powers increased by an entire sub-realm. The shield began to crack and break before shattering into a thousand shards of blue qi.

"You're mine!" a voice yelled.

Cha Ming swiftly used Stormchaser Steps to move around them, turning lethal stabs and bashes into cuts only inches deep. Meanwhile, he continued painting the remaining formation lines.

Three... Two... One... Done. As the last green brushstroke landed, the formation consolidated. The moisture in the environment instantly disappeared, and the five devils finally appeared in plain sight as massive vines wriggled out of the forest floor.

"What have you done?" the most powerful lust devil yelled. Evidently she was distraught by the illusory formation's disappearance. Their energy had been drained to supplement the formation that Cha Ming had laid down, the Lesser Thousand Vines Formation.

It was peculiar in that it was a constricting formation that devoured energy. Often they were laid down with supportive water formations that were sacrificed to feed the vines. In this case, Cha Ming used the opponent's water formation as the sacrifice.

Cha Ming didn't bother to discuss it with them. He immediately set half the vines on the two lust devils, who could only cry out as their water-based vitality was sapped away. Meanwhile, the other vines intercepted the other three devils, who began fleeing.

Cha Ming darted out, abandoning the formation he had laid to catch the fastest of the devils, the wrath devil. He sent out an ice-based talisman to trap the devil in an icy prison and then laid down a combat formation to finish him off with deadly spikes.

Two more to go. The next fastest, the early-foundation-establishment greed devil, was already ten miles away. Cha Ming slapped out a talisman to further increase his speed by fifty percent. Soon, the greed devil appeared in his line of sight.

"Why do you bother with us?" the devil said in a panicked voice. "We clearly wouldn't have picked on you if you hadn't invited yourself in."

"I'm afraid that I don't need a reason to hunt creatures like you," Cha Ming said. He summoned a flaming combat formation around the devil, who could only wail in agony but couldn't escape. Cha Ming was simply too fast. He could move the formation and kite him at his leisure.

"You won't escape our master," the devil howled. "I'll be back, and we'll see who has the last laugh in the end."

The devil soon melted into a puddle of gold, which Cha Ming retrieved along with the devil's bag of holding. Then he disappeared in the direction of the gluttony devil. It was a creature of the forest, surrounded by living trees and animals. There was no way it could escape Cha Ming's twenty-mile detection radius.

Cha Ming rushed through the trees for a half hour before

finally catching up to the large creature with barklike skin. It was surrounded by an acidic pond.

"Just give up and accept your fate," Cha Ming said. "I'll grant you a quick death."

The devil hesitated. "Fine," it said, throwing up its arms. In response, Cha Ming summoned twelve gold sigils, covering the area around the monster with thousands of golden blades. It quickly hacked him apart until only a solid green core was left.

Suddenly, Cha Ming eyesight went blurry, then black. Pain overwhelmed him as power seared his eyes with the appearance of a ninth rune. An ancient voice sounded out within his mind, granting him inspiration on a new source of power.

Only those who share my will can understand my resolve.

Information surged into Cha Ming's mind. He quickly became aware of an intangible will that had been building up inside him as he slew devils one after another. It was the power of devil sealing, Devil-Sealing Intent. He instantly knew that from now on, whatever talismans he crafted and whatever formations or battle techniques he executed, would contain this special power. Even simple fist strikes would now be imbued with the power of devil sealing, naturally restraining the devils. And while the power was quite weak now, it would grow stronger with his increasing kill count.

Time to free those prisoners, Cha Ming thought. Unfortunately, a third of them had died due to the aftershocks of the battle. He fed and healed the ones that remained and escorted them to a nearby city, where they were sorted out by the local lord. There was no reward, but that didn't matter. He had tempered himself and steadied his cultivation, and he had developed Devil-Sealing Intent.

Besides, he had also earned five devil kills, enough to earn him more much-needed lessons from Lu Tianhao. There wasn't much time remaining, and Cha Ming had to make the best use of these quiet days.

"I wonder who leaked the information," Prince Lei grumbled.

"It's difficult to say," Wang Jun said. "Someone may have intercepted the minister's correspondence. They may have also connected the dots when they saw the vast amount of demon-beast materials being bought out by the Jade Bamboo Conglomerate and your residence. Either way, things aren't looking good."

"Do you think they'll be able to hold out until the materials arrive?" Prince Lei asked. They were both drinking tea in Wang Jun's tent, the most spy-proof tent in their camp.

Wang Jun shook his head. "Not with their current strength, even with the information I send. However, there is a way to make things happen. I'll need to sneak out again."

Prince Lei frowned. "What could possibly sway the odds in our favor?"

"You're better off not knowing," Wang Jun replied.

A figure appeared from the shadows in front of Huxian's cave. "Still feeling depressed?" he asked. There was silence for a few moments before the sound of dragging paws, followed by Huxian's pathetic figure appeared. He was both depressed and wounded.

"What do you want?" Huxian asked.

"You're losing this war," Wang Jun pointed out.

"You're not wrong, but it's not like I can't escape at the last minute," Huxian said. He was right of course, but Wang Jun could tell that he wouldn't. His character was too proud. But if things dragged on, he would die. And so would Cha Ming.

"I've come with a gift," Wang Jun explained, retrieving a jade box from his robes. He opened the box and revealed three treasures.

Huxian's eyes glittered. "One five-hundred-year-old flood-dragon heart fungus, one thousand-year-old silver jasmine root, and one earth-demon core crystal. What's the catch?"

"You remember those six hundred jin of immortal-jade core?" Wang Jun said. "I want five hundred of it to be handed off to me secretly when we conduct the initial trade. I don't want the others to know."

Huxian nodded. "Definitely worth it. You have yourself a deal."

Wang Jun placed the box on the ground without another word and walked back into the shadows.

Huxian left his mountain after handing the earth-demon core crystal to the geomantic boa. It wouldn't be an issue for her to break through to peak purification with it, greatly increasing their terrain advantage. He naturally had another candidate for the silver jasmine root. It was just a matter of whether he would accept it.

"Silverwing, do you have a bit?" Huxian yelled to the tall spire where Silverwing's cave was. He was greeted by an empty silence. Shaking his head, he tossed the jasmine root onto the ground. It emitted a smell that most demon beasts found irresistible.

"The war is going terribly down there," Huxian said. "I have a treasure here that will help you break through. It's strictly business, so no need to thank me." Then, seeing that Silverwing wouldn't come out easily, he ran back to his own mountain peak. He wasn't there when a silver bird swooped down and grabbed the root, taking it back to its cave at the peak of the spire.

Chapter 30: Parallel Arts

A complex combat formation lit up in front of Cha Ming, an array of green complementing an array of red. It conjured a living green flame that sought to consume and grow. This was a new type of formation to Cha Ming, one that he'd learned out of necessity. Learning formations was draining his ample coffers much more quickly than he found comfortable. He simply couldn't afford an extra set or two of sigil focuses, though this didn't really matter because no one would sell them to him. The only solution was to use two-element formations.

They had their advantages and disadvantages, of course. A Living Flame Combat Formation could not be countered with water or metal, since water fed the flame and metal was weakened by it. The downside was that it became somewhat vulnerable to flame, and its effectiveness against metal was decreased. Earth, however, could no longer absorb the heat that shattered through it using the wood element, so the flame was no longer at half strength but rather fifty percent more effective than a neutral formation. Everything was balanced.

Cha Ming withdrew the formation as quickly as he had formed it. In order to finance his increasing collection of formation flags and formation crystals, he had started painting talismans again. He was pleased to discover that the occupations were complementary. What would have taken a month before now took less than a week to learn, so Cha Ming was quickly able to paint lesser-grade talismans on a regular basis.

Meanwhile, the amount of emotional depth he could infuse into his talismans increased with his qi capacity. His poetic talismans were now mid-grade ones. In addition, he was surprised to discover that any he had created previously could be augmented a single grade. They were unlike any other talisman he had ever seen. They grew with him.

Cha Ming's soul developed as he studied Jun Xiezi's painting. His knowledge of dual-element combat formations and both single- and dual-element standard formations grew exponentially. He started to sell lesser-grade talismans through the Alabaster Group to vetted buyers, funding his increasingly large collection of formation flags and formation stones.

One day as he was meditating, he recalled his first excursion outside the city. A small vial appeared in his hand with but a thought. It contained the golden liquid that resonated with the Clear Sky Brush. The resonating feeling appeared once more as he withdrew the vial.

What use could you have? he thought. *People sometimes use evanescence to increase talisman grades, but the cost to benefit ratio is atrocious.*

Sighing, he uncorked the cap and sucked it into the Clear Sky Brush. The brush passed emotions on to Cha Ming—pleasure and satisfaction. He sent his awareness into the Clear Sky Space and noticed that one-tenth of a jin evaporated into nothing. One-ninth, however, was deposited into its own small pool beside the pool of liquified elemental essence.

Things didn't stop there. Out of nowhere, a small channel appeared in the liquified elemental essence lake, leading it to the small pool of gold evanescence. Cha Ming didn't stop it, figuring that there must be a reason for this behavior.

Cha Ming looked on as the pool of evanescence diluted again and again. A ninth of a jin of evanescence was diluted into one hundred, then a thousand, then nine thousand jin of liquified elemental essence. The normally blue liquid was now light gold in color.

Is it just normal ink? he thought, summoning the light gold liquid to his brush. He infused gold qi into it and guided it with spiritual force. He tried it on a least-grade talisman. Unfortunately, something went wrong, and the talisman crumbled into nothing.

The ink is very different, he thought. *It's like it has a completely different nature, and it's not compatible with my current painting technique.* Then it dawned on him. He recalled the book he had studied previously, *Five-Element Talisman Artistry—A Primer.*

That's right, he thought. *The light gold ink seems more aligned with nature. If that's the case, I should use a technique that's more in line with nature as well.*

Cha Ming tried again. This time, instead of light slashes, he made bold, incisive strokes. At the same time, they were soft and malleable. It was a mystical brush technique, one that Cha Ming had greatly admired when he first read about it.

One by one, the brushstrokes laid runes and lines down onto the sheet of paper. It wasn't long before the paper turned light gold. Amazed at the success, he tried ten more times. One success piled up after another. Intrigued by this result, he moved onto a lesser-grade talisman of gold alignment. Here too, he met with great success. He didn't fail a single time as long as he utilized the *Five-Element Talisman Artistry* method, but he would invariably fail miserably if he used his previous method.

In fact, this familiar feeling reminded Cha Ming of formations. Formations naturally stabilized together because they were in harmony, both with themselves and with heaven and earth. His previous talismans had not been made using proper materials and the proper form, so they felt unnatural. Now that he had corrected his mistake, his talismans were automatically coming together without much strain on his part.

This was great news for the current Cha Ming, since he was low on funds. One more day generated enough income to buy the next set of evanescence. He returned to the Talisman Artist Guild and sold the talismans at nine-tenths their face value, a privilege that only master artists enjoyed. After eight more days, he had completed the cycle and purchased one jin of each element. He had even made a small profit.

The only thing that concerned Cha Ming now was how to remedy his problem with combat formations since he couldn't purchase more sigil focuses. That and stabilizing his cultivation. He could get the pills whenever he wanted, since his regular work with Mo Tianshen was proceeding smoothly, and the experiments were promising. Over the course of the past month, they had narrowed down the number of powder compounds to five and the number of rune materials to ten. The remaining experiments revolved around optimizing rune structure, dosages, and powder balance.

How to optimize my base sigils, Cha Ming thought. Sigil focuses were reusable, but he had tried to stick two different elements into a single sigil focus in the past. The results had been disastrous.

All I can do is upgrade them for the time being.

Unlike his foundation-establishment pillars, which only contained the barest stable sigil for each element, he could continue building onto the foundation of his sigil focuses. In fact, he didn't even have to completely reprogram the focus. Withdrawing one from the rosary on his wrist, he made a gesture that ripped out the existing sigil base. The multiple characters imbued inside the malleable blob remained, and they were still linked to the base sigil. Cha Ming opened his mind's eye as he used his newfound comprehension in talisman artistry to imagine the remaining structure. The outline of the full sigil of water became clear to him.

Cha Ming breathed deeply and summoned the dark-blue ink that had appeared when he mixed water evanescence with liquified elemental essence. His strokes were fluid but turbulent, showing resistance and momentum simultaneously. It wasn't long before the perfect water sigil snapped into place. After sending it back into the sigil focus, its effectiveness had increased by thirty percent. Further, retracting energy from the sigil focus led to a very minor loss in qi. Only a single point out of one hundred was lost. Having met with success, he repeated the same process for all hundred and eight sigils.

All in all, it was a very eventful week and a half. He had made great progress in terms of talisman arts, sigils, and formations. All he was missing now was time. And a solution to his combat-formation problem.

Boom.

Cha Ming was thrown back into a wall. For the twentieth time today, he had lost his formation battles against Lu Tianhao. "Let's stop here," the white-haired man said. "Do you know why you keep losing?"

"Because of the combat sigils," Cha Ming said.

"That's right," Lu Tianhao said. "While the dual-element formations have their advantages, it's simply impossible to fight me adequately with them. They aren't strong enough to take advantages of those instances where double effectiveness is desired instead of fifty percent greater. You've capped the power of your formations."

Cha Ming knew he was right, but he was helpless. "If I could get additional sigil focuses, I would. However, the embargo by the Wang family caught me where I'm weakest. I can buy formation flags just fine, but procuring focuses would take a three-week journey to another kingdom."

"It's only three weeks," Lu Tianhao said.

"To you it's only three weeks, but I have less than six weeks left," Cha Ming said. "I just don't have the time or the funds. I'm better off cultivating and learning more lesser-grade formations. Maybe I'll be able to scrounge enough funds to make more formation flags at the mid-grade level."

Lu Tianhao sighed. "I have a spare set of combat sigils, but you can't even use them. And I can't send someone in the Alabaster Group to purchase them on your behalf, because all of us have been embargoed."

"Sorry," Cha Ming said sheepishly.

"They'll get what's coming to them, don't you worry about that," Lu Tianhao replied. A cold gleam appeared in his eyes. "If I hadn't transcended, this would already be resolved. I absolutely hate it when people make good men suffer for the sake of petty political squabbles."

"I'll figure something out," Cha Ming said.

That night, Cha Ming sat on the cold stone floor of a practice room. It was a durable one, as Cha Ming wasn't sure what would happen when he tried his crazy idea. It would stretch the very limits of his capabilities. He summoned a water sigil like before, separating the sigil from the focus. It was in its perfect, upgraded form.

Instead of painting directly on it, he started creating another sigil. This time, he painted the full form of the wood sigil. Once this was complete, he followed up with the fire sigil, the earth sigil, and the gold sigil. All five floated before him in a neat circle. After resting, he continued by drawing the outer ring and inner star. He did this with pure liquified elemental essence, untainted by any elements. He didn't even use creation or destruction qi, as neither could be imbued into the liquified elemental essence.

The sigils snapped together into a stable formation once the last line was drawn. The liquified elemental essence turned white and black.

"Excellent," Cha Ming whispered. "Now fuse!" He motioned for the mutable sigil focus to combine with the five-sigil ring. Its liquidlike form began encapsulating the symbols, incorporating a quarter, then one half of it. But that was all.

Cha Ming frowned. *Is it too large to fit into the sigil focus?* Using his half-step resplendent soul, he began compressing the sigil. It shrunk by twenty percent, allowing the blob to incorporate slightly more of the combined matrix. *A little more.*

The formation began to shiver slightly as he compressed it further. The instability grew significantly, but the volume integrated into the blob only increased slightly.

Just a little more, he thought. He pressed the formation further and heard a loud snap. Suddenly, great destructive power rampaged through the room. Even the five sigils that made the formation were disrupted, resulting in an explosion of all five elements. Cha Ming quickly slapped an ice shield talisman on himself and protected his vitals with his qi.

The smoke cleared, and Cha Ming discovered that, aside from slight damage to his body, nothing else had happened. The room was very durable. What left him most surprised was that the sigil focus was unharmed save for the loss of the many runes that swam within it. It was now pure and unaligned.

The result, while devastating, was quite encouraging to Cha Ming. Although he had lost some elemental essence and a bit of time, he had proven that it was possible to link the sigils together, much like the foundation-establishment matrix in his dantian. Whether or not he could compress them enough was a different matter.

Perhaps it's a matter of luck.

Over the next week, there were many explosions in that same practice room. But there were no successes, only failures.

The deadline was approaching, and Cha Ming was beyond stressed. He had wasted an entire week. He would have been better off traveling to another kingdom, politics be damned.

Naturally, he decided to visit the art gallery for inspiration. The last time he had visited, he met Jun Xiezi, who had resolved his problem.

Who knows, Cha Ming thought. *Maybe I'll meet another mystical character who can help me.*

Instead of looking through paintings, Cha Ming decided to look at sculptures. He had always admired sculptors. The precision and the visualization in their work was mind-boggling. He had always wondered how someone could lay eyes on a piece of marble and say: This is *definitely* a man and a woman frolicking in the wilderness.

There were nude statues and clothed statues, statues of landscapes and statues of cities. Like the art gallery before, he started by looking at amateur works and proceeded to look at the works of great artists. There was something to appreciate in every piece.

After spending the whole day in the main gallery, he stopped by the premium sculpture exhibition. He walked in, and to his surprise, he saw Jun Xiezi once more. No one else was there, so he cracked a joke. "I don't suppose you sculpted this one as well?"

"Cha Ming?" Jun Xiezi said. "Gods no. It's hard enough to push your limits as a painter. How could I possibly think of taking up another equally difficult art form?"

"Equally difficult?" Cha Ming said. "But in art, there is so much depth of color. It is something statues can't hope to achieve."

"But what they lose in color, sculptures make up in their three-dimensional shape," Jun Xiezi replied. "Just think about it. Could you possibly imagine creating such a vivid sculpture?" he said, motioning to the large exposition in front of them. It was a single giant sculpture made of marble. There were twelve characters in the sculpture, all equally flawless and expressive.

"The hardest thing about sculpting," Jun Xiezi said, "is that you need to work with the material you're given. You can't just take a big block of marble and do whatever you like with it. A single wrong move and you could shatter the piece in half. You need to work with its nature, drawing out its potential into a sort of compromise between your will and the stone's. When I paint, I don't need to worry about all this."

Cha Ming nodded. "You mentioned before that you go look at paintings to relax. Why do you come look at sculptures?"

"For inspiration," Jun Xiezi replied. "Sometimes when you paint, you imitate three dimensions using two dimensions, shading, and color. It's very difficult, and sometimes looking at something in the proper three dimensions can help. I mean, look at this." He waved at the sculpture. "You have twelve people, but they aren't standing beside each other. Some are leaning over each other, while others are sleeping on one another. That lady there is seated on her husband while holding a baby. It's not just a matter of fitting twelve people together; it's a matter of meshing them together in a way that works for everyone while still maintaining the nature of the marble. It's a fascinating piece of work."

"You see here," Jun Xiezi started as he looked behind him. But Cha Ming had already disappeared. He had gotten the inspiration he needed, and he didn't want to let it slip through his fingers.

Chapter 31: Tooth and Nail

Cha Ming was excited, a stark contrast to his stressed and fatigued demeanor less than an hour ago, rushing back after hearing Jun Xiezi's words. The sigils were like pieces of granite. They couldn't be forced together however he wanted. They needed to be placed in accordance with their nature.

He secluded himself in the stone room once more. Once again, he painted the five sigils he wished to join, along with the supporting black-and-white framework.

If I can't compress them together on the same plane, what if I twist them?

He carefully used his incandescent force to twist both the water sigil and the earth sigil clockwise. As they twisted, so did the framework. The sigils realigned themselves accordingly. To Cha Ming's surprise, however, they didn't simply move rigidly with the frame. Rather, the frame slid alongside the sigils to keep them facing outward.

It seems they have a preferred orientation, Cha Ming thought. *I need to work with this. At no point can I have them facing anywhere but outward.*

As he continued twisting, he pressed them toward each other. As expected, there was much less resistance to this movement. He continued to twist and compress, twist and compress. The white circle was now a white spiral, and the black star no longer looked so starlike. In fact, both the white spiral and the black "helix," for lack of a better word, got thicker as the length between each point reduced.

Cha Ming began to worry that it was going too well. The sigils had smoothly collapsed to half of their original volume, and it still continued. Since things were going so well, he was hesitant to try incorporating the twisting formation into the sigil focus.

I'll wait until I hit a barrier or limit. One half soon became four tenths, and four tenths became three. The sphere was an optimal three-dimensional shape. It minimized volume for any specific radius.

To Cha Ming's amazement, as he pressed them together, the sigils themselves began to change. It started with a subtle shifting in their runic structure. The inner side became thinner, and the outside became bulkier. The original black and white lines had also quadrupled in thickness. In fact, Cha Ming felt as though they were almost touching.

A little more, he thought. And then he heard a pop. The formation in his hands had stabilized in the three-dimensional shape. It was now in the form of a perfect sphere. And in between each gap of five colors and black and white, a cloudy gray substance had filled in. The same gray he had seen in his meridians.

He didn't hesitate to fuse the sigil with the sigil focus, merging them together like drops of water, and the sigil focus's color changed from clear to the same gray that filled the spaces. The same gray as Fuxi's brush. And the same gray as the qi seals connecting his qi pathways. At that moment, Cha Ming felt like he had discovered a universal truth.

He didn't notice as the qi of heaven and earth rushed into him, replenishing his dantian, his body, and his soul. He didn't notice as one after another, he summoned sigils into existence with a few swishes of his brush. He didn't notice as his whole rosary turned gray.

Nor did he notice when every stroke of his brush brought hundreds of runes into existence, which rushed into the gray sigil focuses. He was a heavenly painter, bringing something very natural into the world.

Lu Tianhao sat at his desk, gently holding his late daughter's doll. Oh, how he missed her. But there was no bringing her back. Even the few immortals he had asked were helpless. A person would always be reincarnated, but they wouldn't be the same person as before. By the time he had found his daughter, she was already living a happy life with her new family. His own daughter was dead, and someone else's daughter was born. How could he take her away from them?

That was how his hunt for devils began. Since his strength was feeble in a transcendent realm, he headed for the lower realms, where he would be at the peak of power. His actions would be limited, yes, but he could guide others onto the correct path. Like he did his brother for a time. It ended badly, but for hundreds of years they accomplished great deeds together.

Treachery, Lu Tianhao thought. *I have experienced treachery far too often in this life. First one, then the other.*

Suddenly, he felt all the energy in the city moving toward him.

No, he thought, *to somewhere else in the building.* It moved toward a remote corner in the Alabaster Group, the practice room that Cha Ming had rented. The disturbance was far too great for him to ignore. In a flash, he appeared beside Cha Ming. He watched as the young man painted with blank eyes and created sigils as though they were nothing. He fused them into forms Tianhao couldn't understand, and he painted runes by the hundreds.

Is this enlightenment on the Dao? Such an experience could never be sought, only found by chance. And as his teacher, it was his duty to be his Dao protector.

Lu Tianhao's eyes flickered as he sensed an approaching

transcendent. The man wore a black cloak and emanated a deadly baleful aura. Tianhao flashed in front of him, blocking his path. "What are you doing in my territory, pray tell? Do you think I'm afraid of you?"

The black-cloaked figure's eyes looked toward the practice room where Cha Ming was located. "Enlightenment on the Dao? Such a precious moment. Surely you don't think you can prevent me from disrupting him?"

"I'm afraid normal distractions won't cause him to bat an eyelash," Tianhao said calmly. "But if you actually harm him, I'm sure you know the consequences. Do you think it's worth it?"

The man swished his sleeve, sending howling winds toward the Alabaster Group's building. Everything shook, causing much noise to permeate the entire complex. This included Cha Ming's chamber. Naturally, he didn't wake.

The cloaked man shook his head. "Not worth it, then. Protect away." He disappeared in a puff of smoke.

"What about you all?" Tianhao said, projecting his voice across the city. Many figures in Daoist robes came out of hiding and bowed. They were all core-formation ants, and they knew better than to barge into the Alabaster Group's territory. After all, there was a bit of a workaround to transcendent interference. He had installed a Five-Element Purple Helios Formation in the building but had granted the control to others in the group. If they acted, using the formation and spirit stones, they could decimate anyone at core formation or below. It wouldn't incur too much karma for him either. It was all about intent, after all. Making a shield to defend someone didn't upset the plane's will so badly, but attacking could damn near kill you.

I wonder how long it will last, he thought before sitting cross-legged in meditation. A single glare of his was enough to frighten just about anyone away.

"Rise and shine," a gentle voice said, waking Cha Ming from his sleep. He felt the stone floor beneath him as well as a sticky puddle. It was blood.

"What happened?" Cha Ming asked, groaning.

"You gained enlightenment on the Dao, creating some very mysterious sigils in the process," the voice said. Cha Ming now recognized it as Lu Tianhao. "I was negligent. At the end of the enlightenment session, you collapsed while at your weakest. You bumped your head very hard, and you know how scalp wounds are. They bleed like an open faucet. Doubly so for someone with such powerful vitality, since you regenerate your blood faster than it bleeds out."

Cha Ming opened his eyes and saw his white-haired, white-robed teacher seated in front of him. Off to the side were the hundred and eight sigil focuses. He willed them to his wrist and finally noticed that they were gray.

"Gray..." Cha Ming said. "That's right. I found a way to fuse the five elemental sigils. I condensed them into an eight-colored sphere. Everything merged into gray."

"I should add that you somehow added around ten thousand runes to each sigil focus within twenty-four hours," Lu Tianhao said. "I'm not entirely sure which feat is most impressive. Regardless, you should probably come up with a name for these sigils. They are entirely new, and I can't promise you I won't copy them."

"The five elements came from destruction and creation," Cha Ming said while standing up, "and this gray feels like the fusion between creation and destruction. But the Dao created two, and two created many. Then is this gray the Dao?"

"A bold assumption to say the least," Lu Tianhao huffed.

"Then it's settled," Cha Ming said. "I'll be bold for once. I'll call these Dao sigils." He heard the older man chuckle. "Now then, let's have a rematch."

"Are you ready?" Tianhao asked. Cha Ming nodded and bowed. "Begin!"

The white-robed man cast out twenty-four flaming sigils that turned into twenty-four formations. One hundred and fifty thin threads shot out from the twenty-four sigils, threatening to form a Lesser-Grade Burning Dragon Combat Formation. In response, Cha Ming shot out twenty-four Dao sigils that morphed into blue formations. He laid them down so that they blocked the red lines being formed. Blue tendrils shot out to form a Lesser-Grade Ice Dragon Combat Formation.

To his surprise, however, Lu Tianhao retrieved these sigils and cast out twenty-four earth sigils. In turn, Cha Ming retrieved his and cast out twenty-four more Dao sigils. They continued this dance for many cycles as Cha Ming wondered as to the point of it all. The result of such a cycle was a draw. Or was it?

It got Cha Ming thinking. Why was he spending so much time retrieving the sigils? Why didn't he keep them out and exchange the qi after taking it back?

Cha Ming decided to try it. He changed his earth formation to a metal formation, then swiftly withdrew the wood qi and inserted fire qi. He also slightly changed their positions to accommodate a new combat formation as quickly as possible.

To his surprise, Lu Tianhao kept the pace. The speed he used was clearly not the fastest he was capable of. Despite Cha Ming's increased speed, the cycle continued. After many cycles, Cha Ming finally began to wonder—why was there a need to withdraw and insert qi in the first place? He could convert qi by two steps if he so chose. That is, his wood qi could either become fire qi or earth qi.

This was one of the wonders of his Perfect Five Elements cultivation technique.

Once again, Cha Ming's pace increased. He didn't withdraw his qi. Rather, he simply willed it to become the next element in sequence, and it was so. His gold formation became a water formation directly in response to Lu Tianhao's shift from a wood formation to a fire formation.

After a few more cycles, he didn't even withdraw the qi tendrils. Instead he shifted the sigil formations from one position to the next while changing the runes and the qi element in the formation lines simultaneously. Then when Tianhao's pace increased once more, he thought about how else he could save time. Why did he need to completely shift the formations? Could he perhaps shift to two-element formations? Then he would only need to change twelve runes out of twenty-four. The new runic lines would be substantially reduced as well.

As Tianhao's gold formation shifted to water to counter Cha Ming's shift from wood to fire, Cha Ming instead chose to transform half his formation. Instead of changing to an earth formation, the counter to water, he only shifted half of the fire to earth. He used his spare soul force to rapidly condense them, finally creating the first formation of their match, the Lesser Magma Formation. Tianhao could only grit his teeth and activate his combat formation, which could only show three-fourths of its prowess as opposed to Cha Ming's, which could show one and a half.

"Impressive," Lu Tianhao said. "But how will you deal with this?" He threw out another twelve sigils. Runic lines shot from these sigils and joined his existing formation. A mid-grade combat formation activated, and Cha Ming's magma formation was immediately overwhelmed by their difference in rank.

"I can't beat a mid-grade formation," Cha Ming said, shaking his head.

"Who knows," Lu Tianhao said, shrugging. "If you only use formations, you're completely correct. However, I've seen people break formations with their fists. This entire time, I've never prevented you from using all means at your disposal.

"In any case, let's stop here for the day. You're qualified as a lesser-grade formation master now. And now that your cultivation is stable, you should consider breaking through to the next level. You have nothing to gain by remaining in early foundation establishment."

Cha Ming inspected his qi seas and saw that they were now like still mirrors without any hint of turbidity. His teacher was right. It was time.

Interlude
Fanning the Flames

The soft spring dirt cushioned Hong Xin's footsteps as she and Hong Yinyue walked to their next destination. Wherever they went, they would stop at an inn to play. The room and board was free, and whatever tips they made over and above that was theirs to keep.

It took some time to get used to such favorable treatment. She barely remembered the days when she was a mistreated tavern wench. The only memories that remained were those of a burning man and running in the dead of night. But now she was focused on the road. She loved the road and loved music and loved dancing. She wouldn't trade them for the world.

"You have a little hop in your step today," Hong Yinyue said. "What has you so excited all of a sudden?"

"It will be my first time inside a big city," Hong Xin said. "I'm very excited. Tell me again how many residents Quicksilver has?"

"Around ten million," Hong Yinyue said calmly. "But that is a conservative estimate. Their domestic policies have greatly increased the wealth and livelihood of their residents. In fact, they have a saying in some political circles. 'Always Be Constructing.' Whenever they need to make some tough choices, they remind themselves to always choose growth over other minor matters."

"Ten million," Hong Xin whispered. "That's an awful lot of people. I could know a dozen people in the city and never see them.

Even our performances wouldn't change that fact."

It was hot out, so Hong Xin took out one of her red fans to cool down. They called their group the Hong Sisters. It wasn't her idea, of course. Hong Xin found this title very embarrassing due to Yinyue's age. She herself was just a woman in her early twenties, but Yinyue had lived for several centuries—or so she said, though she still maintained the appearance of a young woman in her midtwenties.

"You should focus on the road," Yinyue said, projecting her voice so that only she could hear. Hong Xin's eyes darted around as she maintained her calm demeanor. Her "elder sister" would only say such things if there was trouble. And trouble meant that Hong Xin would have to take care of it all by herself. Yinyue always refused to act.

"Could the gentlemen in the woods be so kind as to greet us in person?" Hong Xin asked in a sweet voice that pierced through the hearts of men. A dozen men stumbled out awkwardly, weapons in hand. They all looked at each other in confusion, which made sense, given that her suggestion had changed their original intent to catch them by surprise.

A person that seemed to be their leader stood forward. "You both know what we want," the man said. "These are hard times, so we need to spread the wealth. Understand?"

"But we're just innocent travelers," Hong Xin said, waving her fan in a way that caused the bandits' hearts to throb. "Surely you wouldn't harm beautiful ladies such as ourselves."

The man looked confused but quickly regained his composure. "We won't hurt you if you give us your money, your instruments, and your fans. We've heard the rumors. You Hong sisters get lords and kings begging for your favor and showering you with gifts."

"So you'll let us go if we give you our money?" Hong Xin asked with a flutter of her hand, a sway of her hips, and a voice that could compel any man to answer.

"Y-yes, of course," the man said nervously.

Lies. She had gotten very good at spotting them. It came from having to put up with all the flattery and the promises. It obviously didn't help the man's case that the dozens of men behind him were releasing enough murderous intent for a thousand men.

"Elder Sister Yinyue," Hong Xin said gently, "could I please get some music?"

"Of course," Yinyue replied, chuckling. Before anyone knew it, a jade zither had appeared before her. Her fingers plucked some introductory notes, setting the stage for Hong Xin. Hong Xin knew that Yinyue could decimate the group if she wanted to with those same notes, but she intentionally kept the music normal. It was an accompaniment, nothing more.

The temporary confusion subsided as the bandits realized what was happening. They began to organize themselves in a formation. Hong Xin would have none of that. Her body twirled as she made eye contact with them. Their hearts melted, and they couldn't help but let their weapons fall. A swish of her fan brought blazing flames to scorch them. It was only then that they realized they were completely helpless.

"Mercy!" the leader said. He tried to pick up his weapon, but the burning metal singed his hand. His arms were blistering under the intense whirlwind of flame conjured by the single fan.

"I don't show mercy to creatures such as you," Hong Xin whispered. Then, with a murderous look, she swung both her fans and intensified the flames fourfold. And inside the flames she saw three figures growing and mutating. One had gold skin, and another's was barky. Yet another had fiery eyes, but his fire was nothing in front of her flames. In fact, an inner fire could be seen burning out of control from inside him. His pent-up anger came to a head and cracked through his skin, destroying him from the inside out.

Soon, nothing remained but ashes. Hong Xin swept both her fans, and the ashes blew into the nearby woods. Then, the last note sounded.

"Your dance is getting better," Yinyue noted.

"It's because I get so much practice," Hong Xin replied. "Who would have thought that so many of these creatures were plaguing the countryside."

"It will only get worse," Yinyue said, sighing. She stowed away her zither, and they continued their journey.

That day, the Hong Sisters played in the northern side of Quicksilver. They passed by the Alabaster Group and proceeded without stopping. After all, the city was huge. Even if they knew a dozen people in the city, it wasn't likely they would spot each other.

And in this city, Hong Xin only knew one person.

Chapter 32: Beast Tamer

Huxian overlooked the battle at the base of the mountain with a worried expression. He was busy conserving his energy for his breakthrough and couldn't spare any to help the beasts getting slaughtered by the dozens. It didn't help that the geomantic boa was undergoing her breakthrough either. And Silverwing... well, he wasn't sure what Silverwing was up to. He hadn't seen Silverwing in a long while.

Down below, beasts from all nine peaks were clashing with cultivators sent by Zhou Li and the crown prince. Kings were mingled in with lords while mid-foundation-establishment cultivators were mixed in with initial- and early-foundation-establishment experts. The lesser beasts weren't qualified to mingle. It was a meat grinder.

The seven remaining sovereigns, on the other hand, held back. They were the reserve force that kept the late- and peak-foundation-establishment cultivators in check. The core-formation cultivator on the human side didn't participate at all, and neither did the owl monarch, but Huxian could constantly feel their senses assessing the situation, ready to jump in at any moment.

The natural defenses were breaking down. Trenches and walls that had been erected by the geomantic boa before her seclusion were collapsing. There were traps in random places throughout the mountain that the beasts used to their advantage. However, they were outnumbered and outclassed. The reinforcements brought over by the humans had greatly changed the tides, and their battles became increasingly savage. The last few days had been loss after loss for the Silverwing beasts.

Down below, a ferret lord summoned the power of earth to fight against a water cultivator, but he was firmly suppressed by a nearby wood cultivator. Wood cultivators that focused on battle were rare but not unheard of. It didn't take long for the ferret lord to be felled by the human tide as they rushed to take over Silverwing's mountain. They were like a knife cutting through the butterlike battle formation the beasts had erected. Tactics were never their strong suit, and the absence of the geomantic boa aggravated that weakness.

Huxian saw the sovereigns looking on nervously as the file of human cultivators began encircling them from the high ground. It was a turning point in the battle. Five of the seven launched into battle, intending to eliminate the threat, but they were quickly intercepted by five cultivators on flying swords.

"Are you sure you want to be interfering in the matters of juniors?" an old man said.

The Reptilian Lion Sovereign roared and pounced on that same cultivator. His strength was overbearing, to the point that three human cultivators were forced to step in to restrain him. Meanwhile, four other sovereigns joined the fray. There was a small pink bird, a massive wolf that blended in with the shadows, and a lanky monkey that controlled the nearby greenery. And surprisingly, a massive panda.

The cultivators were at the peak of foundation establishment but couldn't obtain any advantage from the beasts. It was a well-known fact that beasts on the same tier were invincible. The heavens, in their fairness, made their advancement incomparably difficult in exchange.

Seeing that the lesser beasts would be routed, the two other sovereigns dove toward the spear of cultivators, intending to decimate them. These were the sovereigns with the fiercest attack power, Mantis Sovereign and Eagle Sovereign. They were also the fastest.

Unfortunately, it seemed the humans were prepared for this. Six cultivators dove in to intercept them, rendering their efforts to join the battle useless.

"How could we possibly let you take away this victory from us?" one of the cultivators said while exerting himself to block the two incoming sovereigns. "This battle will end in a landslide victory!"

Huxian, who was overseeing the battle from his cave, was tempted to halt his breakthrough to interfere. With his help, the situation would easily be defused. But then he wouldn't be prepared for their last wave and the inevitable reinforcements.

But I can't just let them die like this, he thought. *They won't last much longer.*

It was then that he felt demonic energy pervading the mountain range, rushing toward a single point in the middle ranges of his mountain.

Great! he thought. *The geomantic boa broke through!*

It took no time at all for it to complete the absorption and erupt with sovereign-level power. The mountain ranged shuddered as the boa tunneled through the rocky ground. Then, the shuddering subsided. The humans didn't notice the commotion, but the beasts did and fought with increased fervor.

Suddenly a mile of earthen spikes shot out of the mountain, impaling several dozen cultivators at once. The nearby beasts took advantage of the opening and began slaughtering the cultivators with impunity. One spike after another appeared, completely negating the humans' advantageous combat formation.

"Come out, you silly snake," a human with an authoritative voice shouted. He wore brown robes that flapped in the wind as he flew north of the latest spike with his flying sword and plunged down to the ground. As he dove, he withdrew a much larger sword. The earthen qi that poured into it was blinding.

"Not you again," a feminine voice slithered. A giant wall of earth was summoned from the ground to intercept the man. His blade plunged through it, but his momentum was greatly weakened. Just as he was about to hit the ground, his eyes narrowed, and he retrieved his sword just in time to avoid a lashing tail.

The man snorted. "Don't think you can act up with me around," the man said.

"Oh?" the geomantic boa replied. "You think you can stop me?"

"Just try and do something," the man said solemnly, holding his sword in front of him. He seemed like an unmovable fortress, a single soldier to guard the mountain pass.

"But I already have," the snake said, flicking her tongue. She began attacking the confused man, but Huxian knew exactly what she was talking about.

The previous spear of cultivators had been completely cut off from their support due to the volley of spikes that had appeared earlier. A substantial portion of the human forces were decimated, and the humans were being forced to retreat. That and the landslide she had started devoured one human cultivator after another. Huxian chuckled. The cultivator who'd used the words "landslide victory" was probably puking blood by now in embarrassment.

The spear of human cultivators was now more like an arrow at the end of its flight, its momentum spent and unable to cause any further damage. The cultivators were mauled and bitten until they no longer moved.

"This isn't over," the man said coldly to the geomantic boa. "Retreat!"

The cultivators fled toward their camp at once. The beasts chased for a short while before also retreating. Huxian knew full well that this wasn't the end. There were more and more new arrivals every day, one of which worried Huxian greatly.

Thinking of that man, he turned his eyes hatefully toward another camp in the mountains. It was a secluded camp with many cages. He watched on as the pale, black-cloaked man worked his vicious magic.

The man stared curiously at his next victim. This one was some kind of cross between a bear and a cat. Beasts were so amazing, and their ability to create new species as though it was nothing intrigued him.

He liked amazing things. They made the best of projects.

"Open the cage," Guo Jia said. The burly man beside him went to work, lifting a heavy iron grate with the strength of his fleshly body. Guo Jia ducked under the small opening and entered the large cage containing the forty-foot beast. Its paws and neck were chained and anchored to the rocky ground below. "What a fantastic specimen," he whispered, causing the other few people in his camp to shudder.

Guo Jia withdrew a black pen and began tracing a complicated sigil with black ink. Truth be told, the money he gained by taming beasts or humans wasn't worth the time or effort. But it was an enjoyable hobby, so tame them he did. His brush painted with fluid motions, forming a complex black sigil. It was different than the slave sigil, as beasts were fundamentally different in nature. Human souls needed to be chained and restrained. With beasts, there was a much more effective method.

It didn't take long for him to complete the sigil. He didn't make any subsidiary master sigils. His own sigil was that of a monarch, while the recipient's sigil was that of a subject. It burned into the beast's forehead, and instead of penetrating its soul, it seeped into its blood. After a few breaths' time, it shuddered in fear as it saw Guo Jia's overwhelming pressure.

"Monarch," the beast said, bowing. Guo Jia knew that it recognized his monarch sigil as the bloodline pressure of a true monarch. This was what beasts were weakest to. It was the foundation of their society but a fatal flaw in their organizational structure.

"Release him," Guo Jia said. His attendants, who were used to these methods, unlatched the chains from their anchors and retrieved them. The bear-cat didn't dare move in the presence of its monarch. Guo Jia addressed his new servant. "You will now respond to Bear-Cat One."

"Yes, Master," Bear-Cat One said. He left the cage shortly after and joined the other tamed beasts. They were a growing reserve force that would play an important role at a critical moment.

Guo Jia looked toward a large cloaked man standing beside him. "Xiao Heilong, how have you been?"

"Not bad," the man replied. "Some small fry got a good movement technique and managed to give me the slip. Not a big deal."

Guo Jia snickered. "I always find it strange how calm you are given your nature."

"And I always find it strange that you don't frequent brothels, given your nature," Xiao Heilong said. "Instead you have these twisted, perverted pleasures."

"These are my sweet dreams," Guo Jia said. "Everyone has them. You dream of slaughter and hatred, despite your calm exterior."

The man grunted. "Whatever. In any case, I brought you a present. Take it as a favor and help me out with that brat later."

"A present?" Guo Jia said, excited. "For me?" He took a bag from the man. Inside was a slumbering, purple mouse. He used his incandescent force to probe it. To his surprise, it was a peak-purification demon beast.

"Deal," he said. He took his black brush out once more and started painting.

Lei Jiang? Huxian thought, trembling.

He had been observing Guo Jia's actions the entire time, but it was the first time he had acted on someone directly related to Huxian. Roaring, he leapt out of his cave and expanded to his forty-foot form. The pressure he emanated, the pressure of a peak-purification Godbeast, was dreadful. He had only used a small part of the herb to break through to this level, and the rest was directed toward his advancement to half-step core formation.

Huxian's eyes were murderous as he charged forward. But to his surprise, a shadow dashed in front of him. "Stop," Wang Jun said, materializing from the darkness.

"I won't," Huxian shouted. "He's taking Lei Jiang." He moved to bypass Wang Jun again but noticed that thick shadowy lines were currently entangling him.

"That's the same man who enslaved Cha Ming," Wang Jun noted.

"Then all the more reason to kill him," Huxian snarled, struggling against the tendrils.

"You'll die if you go there," Wang Jun said calmly. "Another one of Cha Ming's enemies is down there, Xiao Heilong. I also want them dead more than anything, but to do that, you need to break through. I'll let Cha Ming know about the situation and get him to recruit some help for us. It will be expensive, but it will work out for the best. I can spare one hundred thousand high-grade spirit stones. What can you contribute?"

Huxian hesitated for a moment before nodding. "Very well. I can contribute six stalks of core-stabilization grass. They are the most expensive component for core-formation pills."

"Good," Wang Jun said. "Those six alone should net us the help of six half-step core-formation cultivators. The other spirit stones should fetch us a few core-formation cultivators as a contingency and a small army of foundation-establishment experts."

Huxian relaxed substantially. "Fine. I'll be entering seclusion now. I assume that we still need to survive Zhou Li's attack before we even consider eliminating that Guo Jia bastard."

"That's right," Wang Jun said. "Right now, it's a national matter. I can't interfere. But once Zhou Li and the crown prince are gone, there will be nothing stopping us from crushing those from the Obsidian Syndicate and rescuing your pet mouse."

"He's not my pet," Huxian snapped.

He's my friend, he thought, sighing inwardly.

Ring, ring, ring.

Cha Ming had just finished recovering from his match against Lu Tianhao. He used his qi to activate Wang Jun's symbol on the core-transmission jade. Wang Jun's spectre and a giant Huxian appeared.

"You've grown quite a bit since we last spoke," Cha Ming said, raising his eyebrow. The fox immediately shrank in size.

"You have to help me, Brother," Huxian said.

Wang Jun raised his hand to cut him off.

"Brother Cha Ming, we'll need your help soon," Wang Jun said. "We'll need you in one month. Huxian and I have amassed a small fortune, and we need you to post a mission in the Alabaster Group."

Cha Ming hesitated. "What's the background of the enemies they'll be facing? I hate to be blunt, but the Alabaster Group is very selective in which missions they accept. Then they need to do background checks. Besides, it likely won't sit well amongst many of them to fight alongside demon beasts. Beasts have a reputation of slaughtering innocent mortals."

"That won't be a problem," Wang Jun replied. "We won't be attacking anyone from the Song Kingdom directly. This is an operation that will take place *after* the main battle."

"Can you elaborate?" Cha Ming asked.

"The Song Kingdom has been recruiting mercenaries from many organizations. One of these organizations is the Obsidian Syndicate," Wang Jun said. "In fact, your old friends, Xiao Heilong and Guo Jia, are already here. Guo Jia is here taming beasts, and he tamed Huxian's friend. That's why he's so incensed."

"By taming, you mean enslaving?" Cha Ming asked, his fury mounting.

"Quite right," Wang Jun said. "The mechanics are different, but the end result is the same."

"There are also a bunch of weird figures down there. Xiao Heilong and that Guo Jia are only two of them," Huxian cut in. Wang Jun was about to silence him, but Cha Ming thought of something.

"What did you see?" Cha Ming asked Huxian.

"Malevolent ochre auras, the sign of devils," Huxian said. "And yellow auras surrounding many cultivators. These mercenaries have spilled much blood and committed many sins."

"You also obtained the Eyes of Pure Jade?" Cha Ming asked, surprised.

"We share weal and woe, Brother," Huxian said. "In the future, I will also share such good fortune with you."

"Good, then it's decided," Cha Ming said. "Please deliver the funds to me as soon as possible and send me a list after our conversation. I know a senior partner who would be *very* interested in topping up the reward since devils and the Obsidian Syndicate are involved."

The call ended, and Cha Ming swiftly made his way to Lu Tianhao's office.

"Are you certain that devils are involved?" Lu Tianhao asked Cha Ming after reviewing the mission briefing.

"One hundred percent," Cha Ming said. "Not only were Xiao Heilong and Guo Jia from the Obsidian Syndicate spotted, but I know for a fact that Xiao Heilong is a devil. I saw it myself, and I fought against him. So did both of your apprentices, I might add."

"He is hardly enough of a reason for me to issue additional rewards," Lu Tianhao replied calmly. Cha Ming knew that the man was in a high position and needed to consider the overall situation.

"The total reward offered by the Wang family is 100,000 high-grade spirit stones," Cha Ming explained. "And the Silverwing Mountain Range offers six stalks of core-stabilizing grass. That aside, there is some information that I didn't disclose to you previously."

"Oh?" Lu Tianhao said, raising an eyebrow.

"When I was still in the qi-condensation realm, I had the good fortune of forming a contract of brotherhood with a talented many-tailed fox," Cha Ming explained. "He is currently one of the sovereigns of the Silverwing Mountain Range. We share weal and woe together, if you understand my implications."

Lu Tianhao paused for a moment before asking, "How many devils did he confirm are participating?"

"I'm glad you understand," Cha Ming said, smiling. "He has confirmed that thirty-seven devils have already arrived at the mountain range, with more coming every day."

Lu Tianhao tapped his fingers as he fiddled with his white hair. He was looking at the small doll on his desk. "Very well," he said. "I will personally sponsor this mission. This is a great opportunity to kill a large number of devils. And we can take a chunk out of the Obsidian Syndicate while we're at it. I'll give you a final roster twenty-five days from now."

Chapter 33: Fusion

Cha Ming opened the door to Mo Tianshen's laboratory. He was a regular now and had a pretty good idea of when it was safe to enter. Today was a scheduled powder-pressing day, which happened concurrently with symbol experiments. Cha Ming could enter at his leisure.

"Good timing," Mo Tianshen said from the back. As usual, he was pressing powders like a lowly apprentice alchemist. The goal wasn't speed; it was a matter of replication and whether a dummy could perform the many of the sub-steps to save costs. "The next batch is over there, and I have a good feeling about this one. With any luck, we'll have a ninth version that's almost twice as good as the eighth, and at half the price to boot.

"That's great news," Cha Ming replied. "However, I'm afraid I'll have to go abroad in one month's time. I'm not sure when I'll be back." He noticed the older man's expression droop. "How about I find you a bunch of low-leveled talisman artists and teach them the necessary talismans for producing this batch? I don't believe that even senior alchemists know a good half of these symbols."

The older man nodded. "Very well. But you need to come back and help me. By then, I'll have a rather large stockpile for you to process."

"Deal," Cha Ming said. He got to work immediately, painting one pressed pellet after another. They had gotten to the point where the runes painted no longer cracked. Each pill was effective to lesser or greater extent, and the pill poisons were neutralized to a lesser or greater extent. For this batch, however, he needed to produce one thousand of each pill, as they would be used for human trials.

The day passed swiftly. While Cha Ming was busy producing the prototype pills, Mo Tianshen was busy in the back. The man was likely producing the next batch of pills required for his breakthrough.

He finished at sunset. Mo Tianshen walked out from the back at the same time with a look of exhaustion on his face. "You'll kill me with these pills of yours," the man grumbled, handing two large bottles and two small ones to Cha Ming.

"These are…?" Cha Ming asked.

"Can't you read labels?" he said gruffly. "You said you'd be gone for a long time, so I made you both the lesser-grade and mid-grade pills." Cha Ming's heart warmed when he heard this. "You need to wait until your cultivation stabilizes before using the next batch. Take them the same way as before. And by the way, your pills are killing me. They're bleeding me dry. I'll need you to hunt for some materials for the next batch. I'll need a Nine-Petaled Creation Lotus, a Crimson Annihilation Fruit…." The list grew, and Cha Ming took note of each ingredient.

The alchemist waved his hand, and dozens of jade boxes appeared. So did a jade sickle. "Use the jade sickle to pick them and store them inside these jade boxes. Only pure jade can fight the world's corruption and impurities after harvesting, allowing them to maintain their freshness and vigor."

Cha Ming gave the alchemist a heartfelt bow. "I won't let you down."

"I don't actually care if you find the ingredients," the alchemist said nonchalantly. "You'll have to help me with my experiments regardless, pills or no pills. I'll beat you to death if you don't."

They smiled at each other with amusement.

After securing the pills, Cha Ming proceeded to the Talisman Artist Guild and went straight to Jun Xiezi's office. The man received him warmly. "Have you made another talisman for me yet?" he asked jokingly.

"Almost," Cha Ming replied. "I have some thoughts on the next one. It relates to 'sharpness.' I'll let you know soon. I leave in one month."

"For?" Jun Xiezi asked.

"I'm just going on a trip," Cha Ming said. "I'll be sure to return when it's done."

"Make sure you do," Jun Xiezi said sternly. "You owe me, and don't you forget it. Now then, what brings you to my office today?"

"Straight to the point, I see," Cha Ming said. "Can we at least chat business over tea?"

"Ah, so it's a business matter," Jun Xiezi replied. "I always brew tea over business, and I happen to have a flower tea that just finished growing." The man took out a green ball and threw it into a large pot of hot water. It unfurled into what looked like a rainbow peony. "It's such a beautiful flower. Simple, but sweet tasting."

They both merrily sipped tea in the branch leader's office. "So. Business," Jun Xiezi said.

"Yes," Cha Ming said. "I need to recruit assistants for Mo Tianshen's research and for pill production for the upcoming ninth iteration of the cultivation-instillation pill."

Jun Xiezi raised his eyebrow. "That hardly seems like something I can help you with. Have you tried the Alchemists Association?"

"You misunderstand me," Cha Ming said, smiling. He then took out his brush and painted dozens of characters in midair. For each character, he withdrew a vial of liquid. "I had an epiphany some time ago. Mo Tianshen and I have been cooperating on a concept called runic alchemy. By using runes, we can enhance medicinal efficacy and manipulate physical properties for application." He motioned to the runes floating in the air. "These runes are all first-grade runes. They can be made with this medicinal ink or with other normal inks."

"Amazing," Jun Xiezi said. "But I'm afraid that none of our talisman artists know these runes. Even I don't, somehow, and I'm a grandmaster talisman artist. The heritage I have is incomplete, and my master was unable to pass on more knowledge to me."

"Thus, my offer," Cha Ming said. "I want you to offer the services of low-level talisman artists, at cost, to Mo Tianshen's efforts on this project. In return, I will teach the knowledge of all first-grade runes I know to the Talisman Artist Guild."

Jun Xiezi licked his lips. "All the way up to fifth grade," he said.

"Come now, second grade is really the best I can do," Cha Ming said.

"This is an indefinite agreement," Jun Xiezi said, shrugging. "The cost is astronomical, and the benefit of these low-level runes is limited. Fourth grade."

"You know full well that this will greatly expand the capabilities of the guild as a whole," Cha Ming said. "But you are right that low-level runes won't have such a big effect. Let's meet halfway at third grade. I truly can't pass on much more than this. I'm already stretching the limits of my oath. My students, for the full heritage I possess, must have condensed merit halos. By the way, do keep an eye out for people with thick accumulation of merit. As a favor to me."

Jun Xiezi's eye twitched at the mention of merit halos. "Fine. But I want them imprinted on knowledge-transmission jades. That way I won't need to fetch you to teach students all the time."

"How does that work?" Cha Ming asked.

Jun Xiezi pulled out ten jade plates, which Cha Ming saw were similar teaching jades he already had.

"Pour your qi and incandescent force into these plates," Jun Xiezi said. "Then pour your whole knowledge of these characters and paint them with your mind. The jade slip will preserve the knowledge, and the ones learning will see you 'painting' them and hear your words as they study the slip."

"So, I'll be a teacher to most of the guild," Cha Ming mused.

"As much of a teacher as someone who writes a textbook," Jun Xiezi said dryly. He watched as Cha Ming poured his knowledge into the slips. "Anything else?" he asked after Cha Ming completed his task.

"I have one last thing," Cha Ming said. "I always repay kindness, and you've given me so much advice free of charge. I felt I should share a discovery I made. But to do that, I need to ask—do you have a bottle of evanescence? Any kind will do."

Jun Xiezi pulled out a small golden vial with barely ten drops in it. Cha Ming waved his hand, pulling the stopper from the bottle and retrieving a single drop. Then he waved his brush and sprinkled ten thousand drops of liquified elemental essence into the air. One by one, they fused with the liquified gold evanescence until only a pale golden blob remained.

"I call this gold essence," Cha Ming said. "Likewise, there exists fire essence, water essence, earth essence, and wood essence."

"And what is it used for?" Jun Xiezi asked.

"Well," Cha Ming said, drawing a small portion of the blob into his brush. "If you use the classical techniques for creating talismans, it's beyond useless. The nature of the talisman will be unstable, as though the ink and the technique were incompatible. In fact, the rune might explode due to the instability." He began to paint a lesser-grade talisman on a slip of paper. "But if the technique conforms with the nature of the ink, the talisman creation will proceed smoothly, almost as smoothly as laying a formation."

Jun Xiezi watched as Cha Ming painted the talisman from start to finish. A look of enlightenment appeared on his face as Cha Ming placed the last stroke. "This is the technique described in *Five-Element Talisman Artistry—A Primer*!"

"That's right," Cha Ming said, smiling. "By using gold essence to paint talismans, their nature is aligned with heaven and earth. By using a technique that is also aligned with heaven and earth, an artist's success rate when drawing talismans will increase greatly.

"I don't know the exact reason, but I have a theory. You see, gold evanescence and liquified elemental essence come from the same source. The same applies to other forms of evanescence. But this is seen as a valuable impurity. The two components are separated on extraction and sold separately. As a result, the liquified elemental essence becomes purer, but it is farther removed from nature. Therefore, the technique required to draw talismans must also be adjusted.

"Formations are more aligned with heaven and earth in the first place. Which means the effect of using liquified elemental essence is less pronounced and almost nonexistent. But for talismans, it has a huge impact. Senior Xiezi, my success rate for lesser-grade talismans is above nine out of ten since I changed my methods."

Nine out of ten was actually an understatement, but Cha Ming wasn't one hundred percent sure of the success rate with a normal talisman brush.

After a while, Jun Xiezi broke the silence. "I'll have to study this further. You need to account for the brush type in addition to those things you just mentioned. Your brush is quite expensive, from what I gather. The composition of the brushes used may need to be changed. But that's fine—the brush maker enjoys a challenge."

Cha Ming nodded. "I'll be off, then," Cha Ming said. "I have much to do before leaving."

Cha Ming's five qi pillars creaked and crackled as they broke past their limits with the help of the improved medicinal pills. Each pill contained double the energy they had previously, swiftly growing his pillars to the next bottleneck and subsequently crushing it.

As the pillars broke past their limitations, his qi seas drained to accommodate their growth. And once they dried up completely, Cha

Ming replenished them with a much thicker foundation qi. The seas were turbid and wavy, filled with impurities from his last sub-realm.

Immediately after recovering, Cha Ming summoned thirty-six Dao sigils and practiced many combat formations that he'd read about. He planned to take full advantage of the next three weeks. As he practiced, he also thought about his next poetic talisman. Over the past several months, he had come to a realization.

It wasn't long before he lit the gray candle and settled into a meditative trance. The talisman he produced, if any, would tell him whether his insights were correct.

Cha Ming was in a dream. This time, he saw two giant blades in the sky. They were wielded by two giant gladiators, gods if their sizes were any indication. As they fought, the heavens trembled. Each strike of their swords brought waves of destruction to the world down below.

As they fought, their swords were covered in nicks. They lost their effectiveness. But one of the gladiators was determined. With every strike of his sword, he improved. And as he improved, the sword grew sharper.

His speed quickened and began outpacing his opponent. Finally, he cut off the giant's head. Throngs of people came out to greet him, but he wasn't satisfied. Instead of celebrating, he returned home and focused on his mistakes. He practiced the sword for years before returning to the arena for his next challenge.

Giant after giant was felled by his blade. As his skilled improved, his sword grew increasingly overbearing. It soon reached the point where all he needed was a single strike to cleave through his opponent's sword and armor.

But many people began to grumble. They said his sword was too powerful, that his position as the number-one gladiator wasn't deserved. So they challenged him to fight the second-best gladiator with a normal iron sword. They told him they would only acknowledge him as the best if he won under these conditions.

Instead of the indignant reply they expected, the gladiator did something unthinkable. He threw his sharp sword at a nearby mountain, where it shattered into 10,008 pieces. Then he picked up a dull iron ruler, an ancient weapon that resembled an edgeless sword, built to incapacitate instead of wound.

The surrounding people laughed at his arrogance. How could one possibly beat an iron sword with an iron ruler? The second-ranked gladiator also laughed. He took up his own iron sword and charged forward, confident in his victory. Seeing this, the lead gladiator arrogantly lashed out with the iron ruler. His opponent slashed out to defend with his sword, aiming to cut the ruler in half. But to his surprise, it was his own sword that was cut in half. And his armor. And his body. And his soul.

The crowd gasped. The gladiator had relied on pure skill. His blade was sharp because his skill was high, and not the other way around.

Do you understand? the voice asked.

Cha Ming woke. He drew out the next talisman with a practiced hand.

Honing his worth through endless practice;
Never questioning his skill.

He called it the Sharp Talisman. The key defining characteristic of metal was shape, and humans shaped themselves through endless practice. That was the epiphany he had gained after practicing talismans and formations for so many months.

"So," Lu Tianhao said. He held his arms behind his back. "I suppose this will be your last lesson before you leave in three days?"

"I hope I won't disappoint you," Cha Ming said, bowing before they began their sparring match.

"Unlikely," the white-haired, white-clothed man said. "You're always full of surprises."

As usual, he made the first move. He sent out thirty-six blue sigils, creating a complex shape filled in with runic lines. Cha Ming countered with an earthen combat formation, soaking up some of the qi used to create them.

"Plundering my qi now, are you?" Lu Tianhao said, chuckling. He instantly summoned three lesser formations that struck Cha Ming's at key points in the creation process. Cha Ming's qi was in turn absorbed by these formations.

"Fair is fair," Cha Ming said, shrugging. He activated Stormchaser Steps and ran toward his opponent. As the man cast out another combat formation, Cha Ming threw out his own, but he also bashed with his staff, slightly disrupting some lines as they extended. They shivered, but the process was far from interrupted.

"You're learning," Lu Tianhao said. "You can't break my formations with your weak fist strength, but you can slow it ever so slightly with no disadvantage to yourself."

"You told me to use everything I have," Cha Ming said, throwing out a proper lesser-grade formation. He threw out twelve formation flags and twelve combat formations.

"Competing with speed against power?" Lu Tianhao said, summoning a thirty-six-symbol combat formation.

Cha Ming, seeing the element used, threw out twelve more formation flags. This second formation meshed perfectly with his existing formation, creating a bi-element mid-grade formation. Their formations were completed simultaneously. Cha Ming's formation was slightly superior, but ultimately, they were mutually destroyed.

Cha Ming didn't stop. Having just gained the initiative, he continued to throw out one combat formation after another, using his staff to disturb runic lines whenever he could. His advantage grew greater and greater, and finally he created a gold formation that cut down Lu Tianhao's incomplete wood formation and slammed toward him.

"Fine," Lu Tianhao said. "Try this!"

As expected, seventy-two water sigils shot out. The difficulty of this next level was a watershed, using twice the number of symbols and double the runic lines. Least-grade formations required up to ninety-nine runic lines, lesser-grade up to 199, and mid-grade up to 299. High-grade formations required up to six hundred runic lines. The power of heaven and earth rippled as the high-grade formation began to take shape.

I need to stop it! Cha Ming thought. He repeatedly hit the formation with his staff while summoning his own earthen formation. Lu Tianhao didn't stop his, clearly indicating that Cha Ming's own formation was insufficient.

If only I had more disruption, Cha Ming thought. *But have I really used everything?* His trained eyes could see several weaknesses and vulnerabilities in Lu Tianhao's arrangement, but he had no way to attack them. Or did he?

Cha Ming thought fast. He took out seven least-grade talismans from the Clear Sky Space. They were one of his favorites, Lesser Mount Tai talismans. The illusory mountains crushed down on seven of the key weaknesses. The rapidly growing formation shuddered before shattering. The seventy-two sigils flew outward.

"Well done," Lu Tianhao said in congratulations. "You're not a high-grade formation master by any stretch of the imagination, but now you know what to do if you need to break formations beyond your level. It's not always about matching a master's level against another, it's about using your knowledge of formations to break them and defeat your opponent."

Cha Ming bowed. "Thank you for your instruction, teacher," he said.

"It's nothing," Lu Tianhao said. "Now go and prepare yourself. Paint some talismans or something before you leave. And when you do, kill me some devils. And most importantly, don't forget to come back alive."

The scenery around Cha Ming faded, and he discovered that he was no longer in the man's office or inside his domain. He was back inside his own bedroom. And on his desk, he saw twelve thick books from Lu Tianshen's personal library on high-grade and peak-grade formations. And beside them was a ring. He used his incandescent force to probe the ring and discovered several large stacks of unmarked formation flags. It was the best gift Cha Ming could ask for.

Chapter 34: Friendship

Claws and teeth collided with swords and sabers. Daoist spells clashed with demonic abilities. It was an all-out fight, a battle for survival. The beasts on the mountain could only rely on themselves, as the shipment of resources had not yet arrived, and the contract could not be finalized. This was their final stand.

Even the weakest beasts took part in this struggle. The humans reaped them like wheat on harvest day, but it wasn't without impact. One by one they piled onto the cultivators, slowing down their blades and delivering potent poisons. They were glad to sacrifice their lives for their sovereigns. Such was the nature of beasts.

The geomantic boa helmed the beast forces, using its superior intelligence and terrain manipulation abilities to trap, surround, and stall enemies where required. Its children assisted on a smaller scale, using their weaker geomantic skills and their poisons to cripple mighty foes. Meanwhile, seven sovereigns were fighting tooth and nail. They held back nothing, and neither did Zhou Li's forces.

Zhou Li stood at the back and threw curses down on the beasts like they were nothing. Some were blinding curses, while others cursed their luck. Others still cursed the durability of their claws and hides, revealing fatal weaknesses for the humans to take advantage of.

Then there were the tamed beasts. Guo Jia, Xiao Heilong, and various others participated in the battle. Guo Jia controlled his tamed minions to take the Silverwing beasts by surprise. The humans rejoiced, but the beasts wept. They were losing.

But they were buying important time for the eighth sovereign, Sovereign Two Tails. His seclusion was set to end soon, and when he exited, he would martial them and turn the tides in their favor.

"Loose!" a cultivator yelled. His group unleashed Daoist spells in groups, pelting the massive army of beasts with deadly flaming dragons and earthen spikes.

"Hold!" the geomantic boa slithered. A giant earthen shield flew up, blocking over half of the incoming projectiles. Many kings of the forest used their massive bodies and innate abilities to tank the spells, freeing up the lesser creatures, which charged to the front lines.

"Collapse!" the geomantic boa roared. An entire ridge crumbled, a gravity trap dragging hundreds of cultivators down. Beasts jumped down as well, using their massive frames to their advantage as they dropped down to crush those cultivators.

"Flames!" Another squad of humans blew fire into the pit the beasts had dropped into.

"Wind!" A massive flock of birds flapped their wings in unison, blowing the flames back into the human cultivators, who used earthen shields to block this counter in turn.

Things changed fast on the battlefield, but the beasts were still getting pushed back little by little. Before long, their eastern flank collapsed, resulting in the rout of their sturdy ferret battalion, and the beasts were forced into disarray. In the middle of the chaotic group, thirty-six blue formation flags pressed down. The surrounding area was covered in a blooming lotus composed of thousands of icicles. They were bloody due to the thousands of beasts they crushed.

"It's over," the geomantic boa said, sighing. She was exhausted, and she had done all she could. If their sovereign didn't come out soon, their forces would collapse within the hour.

"Who said it's over?" a loud voice said. It projected across the whole battlefield, causing the humans to shudder and the beasts to tremble in excitement.

"Sovereign Two Tails!" the beasts roared in unison. They fought with renewed fervor, ignoring their fatal wounds to deliver one last blow for their sovereign. In the distance, a giant fox with two tails appeared. He was only one hundred feet long, but the mountain trembled as he ran.

"Slay the humans!" Huxian shouted, his eyes bloodshot. A white healing light shot out around him. It suppressed his enemies but healed and invigorated his own forces. Many beasts, who had been on their last legs, took comfort in that healing light. They managed to kill a few more humans before falling.

Meanwhile, a black clone shot out from Huxian's figure. It dove into the ground, merging with the countless beast shadows that littered the bloody forest floor. Whenever a beast approached a human, its shadow would also attack. Each blow it landed damaged the humans directly.

Huxian wasn't satisfied with these meager results, however. He looked toward Guo Jia and Xiao Heilong and charged at them with his white clone.

"You're courting death," Guo Jia snarled. He pulled back his ice formation and laid down thirty-six green flags in addition to thirty-six green sigils. Hundreds of lines spread throughout the area.

Huxian didn't care. Even if it was a high-grade formation, he would still tear it apart with impunity. He was a noble half-step core-formation Godbeast. Even initial core-formation experts would be hard-pressed to resist him.

"Xiao Heilong, head back here this instant," Guo Jia shouted. Xiao Heilong, who had been fighting a sovereign earlier, retreated toward the pale, black-robed man. In addition, a purple blur of lightning shot in front of Huxian.

"Lei Jiang!" Huxian shouted. He was infuriated. He tried to sidestep Lei Jiang, but the small critter was much faster than he was.

He couldn't avoid its attacks. Purple lightning rained down from the skies. Lei Jiang, his former subordinate, hissed wildly as he attacked his former master with wild abandon.

It's all that Guo Jia's fault, Huxian thought. *If I don't kill him, I don't deserve to be called a Godbeast.* Huxian recalled his purifying aura from the battlefield and directed it to the much smaller space in front of him, which was covered with a formation. Massive vines flew out toward Huxian, who was forced to bite and claw them away. Meanwhile, Xiao Heilong arrived.

He and Lei Jiang attacked in tandem, forcing Huxian to defend himself and take significant blows from both parties.

Didn't Cha Ming say he'd run away from that guy? How did he get so strong and so fast? That's when he noticed an additional mental attack from Guo Jia's direction. In his peak condition, it would have been like scratching an itch. However, in this heated battle, it forced him to make mistake after mistake. Cuts began to accumulate on his body, poisonous cuts that sapped away at his strength.

I can only buy time, Huxian thought. *Perhaps an opportunity will come.*

Meanwhile, the tides of battle had shifted in favor of the beasts. The fast infusion of energy and their soaring morale caused them to unleash far more of their potential than they thought possible. The geomantic boa, in turn, used this to her full advantage. She exhausted herself, abusing every opportunity, every crack in her opponent's strategy.

It was only a matter of time before they won the battle and the humans were forced to retreat.

If looks could kill, Zhou Li's would *slaughter*. He was so close to securing a victory. Unfortunately, he knew the trade goods would arrive today, and there was nothing he could do about it.

If only I hadn't gotten greedy, Zhou Li thought. *If only I'd given them a larger piece of the pie.*

It wasn't that he was incapable of mounting a larger force; it was that he had taken a calculated risk by bringing the right amount of forces. His calculations had shown that they had an eighty-percent chance of success. But to boost their chances by an additional ten percent, he would have needed to spend 100,000 high-grade spirit stones on additional forces.

Now he would have to spend 300,000 additional spirit stones to capture the mine. Not to mention all the forces he'd already lost in the struggle thus far. But on the bright side, they could extract the ore very quickly, and illegally. They wouldn't need to pay taxes. It just wouldn't count as merit for the crown prince, which was a shame but still a tolerable outcome.

Wars are fought with money, Zhou Li thought. *Money, money, always money. If I had as much wealth as the Wang family, this war would already be over.* Money bought weapons, medicines, and fighters. It bought political influence. Which was why he was hesitant to spend the extra 100,000 high-grade spirit stones in the first place.

He used his core-transmission jade to connect to a contact in another country.

Ring. Ring. Ring.

Young Master Zhou, I'm so pleased to hear back from you, a voice transmitted from the other side. *What can I do for you today?*

I need those forces we spoke of, Zhou Li transmitted. *I need them here as soon as possible.*

A pause ensued before the voice replied. *They can be there in three days, and not a moment sooner. I trust you'll have our payment delivered before the forces arrive?*

I will, Zhou Li said. *I always do.*

Zhou Li finally turned his attention back to the battlefield. They were losing, and it was time to cut his losses.

"Retreat!" he yelled. Failure had a bitter taste. Fortunately, the bitterness would soon be soothed by the sweetness of success.

Huxian was struggling. He was at the end of his rope, despite having retrieved his second clone. Both were fiercely struggling against the vines, against Xiao Heilong, and against Lei Jiang. It came as a huge relief when he suddenly heard the call for retreat from the human encampment.

We made it, he thought. The vines continued entangling him, but the three figures he had been fighting with previously began running away.

"Not so fast!" he yelled. He gathered the power of light to flash through the formation with ease. His target was Guo Jia. If he could kill him, Lei Jiang would be set free.

Unfortunately, a purple flash appeared in front of him, blocking off his approach to the dreadful sigil master. The very creature he was trying to save was giving his all to fight him.

Very well, Huxian thought. *If I can't kill him, I'll collect a consolation prize.* His jaws snapped on Lei Jiang's struggling body as Guo Jia and Xiao Heilong escaped. He used his powers of light and shadow to restrain the small creature.

First, I'll free you, he said. *Then we'll get your revenge.*

"Second Young Master," said voices from above. Two blond-haired men, core-formation experts, landed inside Wang Jun's encampment.

"Uncles," Wang Jun replied while traveling from his tent. "I trust everything is in order?"

"Of course," one of the two said. "We wouldn't dare neglect our duties. The funds have already been transferred from your account in Songjing." The other threw out a ring, which Wang Jun caught and placed on his finger.

"Everything is in order," Wang Jun said. "You may leave." Then he sped off toward the minister's tent.

"The goods have arrived," he yelled. Soon, Prime Minister Rong sped out and joined him. They went out to the battlefield, where only beasts remained.

"Huxian!" Wang Jun yelled out. A black-and-white fox immediately descended from the mountain. "We've come with the trade goods and the contract."

"About time," the fox grunted. "Sovereigns, to me!" he yelled. The mountain trembled as the seven sovereigns that had participated in the battle arrived.

"Here is the contract and peace treaty," Wang Jun said. "Pre-signed by myself, the third prince, and the prime minister." He then emptied out the storage ring. "The first delivery of goods, as promised."

Huxian looked them over before declaring that everything was in order. Then, a drop of his blood shot out from his glabella and imprinted itself onto the contract. The other seven sovereigns followed suit. Shortly after, the geomantic boa arrived, dragging a pile of glittering jade. She then spat out a tiny drop of blood, imprinting it on the contract.

"Silverwing!" Huxian bellowed. An incense time passed before a tiny drop of blood flew from the mountain, ratifying the contract.

"On behalf of the Song Kingdom, I welcome an era of peace between the beasts of Silverwing and our kingdom," the prime minister said joyfully.

"I also look forward to five hundred years of peace," Huxian said.

However, it was evident that he was less than pleased by the carnage that had ravaged his people.

"Prime Minister," Wang Jun said, "please excuse me while I discuss with Sovereign Two Tails. Meanwhile, can you please order the soldiers away? We have a peace treaty now, and it's important to show our good faith."

"They'll be gone by the end of the day," the prime minister promised.

Wang Jun followed Huxian's gloomy figure to the peak of the mountain.

"Speak. What is it you want?" Huxian asked. He was tired of this war, tired of all the death and carnage. When he was younger, he thought little of death and destruction. Now he was filled with regret. He could have simply excavated the jade and dumped it beside the mountain. Maybe that would have spared them much heartache.

"Two things," Wang Jun said. "First, I'd like to warn you. Don't let your guard down. I have a hunch that Zhou Li won't let this defeat lie, so I invited Cha Ming and some of his associates to come. They'll be here in three days.

"Second, I'd like to complete our private deal."

"Inside my cave," Huxian said dismissively. "That can wait, though. I won't give it to you unless you help me with something." He spat out a small, unconscious ball of fur. "I need your help breaking his slave sigil."

Wang Jun raised his eyebrow. "And what makes you think I'm capable of that?"

"My intuition," Huxian said. "Besides, I don't need you to break it. I can take care of that myself. What I need you to do is reveal the flaws in the sigil to me."

Wang Jun rubbed his chin. "Let me give it a try." He flicked his sleeve, revealing a large mural of shadowy text. Then he pulled out a particular piece of text. It closely resembled the sigil on the small mouse's forehead.

"This is the 'subject' portion of the monarch/subject sigil," Wang Jun said. "You have two options. You can either destroy it by attacking its weaknesses here, here, and here... Or I could obscure the formation, transforming it into something else."

"Transforming it into something else?" Huxian said. "What would it transform into?"

"It wouldn't be a big change," Wang Jun answered. "I know nothing of sigil arts, but I am confident I could obscure the perception of who the monarch is. If I make you the monarch, Lei Jiang would serve you as his monarch, a very normal behavior for a beast. It will be like nothing happened to him."

"Absolutely not," Huxian said without hesitation. "I'll take my chances on breaking the sigil."

"But you'll be risking his life," Wang Jun said. "Sure, it will influence his way of thinking, but it won't be that different from the normal beast hierarchy."

Huxian closed his eyes. "He's my friend. I saw him when I removed his soul seal. I saw the fear in his eyes. I can't let him remain a slave. He doesn't want such a fate."

When Huxian's eyes opened, a majestic aura burst out from him. Eight trigrams spread out from his fur, surrounding the small purple mouse. His fur lost its color and faded to gray. But he didn't care.

Bagua Fox Technique—Eight Trigrams Rune Extraction!

The eight trigrams spun around the small creature's forehead, peeling the sigil from it. Eight Trigrams Rune Extraction was a powerful formation-breaking technique developed by his ancestor. At its peak, it could pull millions of runes from their origin for him to devour.

Unfortunately, he was still weak. With his half-step core-formation cultivation, he could barely execute the technique. All he could do now was peel it off, but he couldn't eliminate the connection to Lei Jiang.

"The flaws," Huxian said in a weak voice.

"Here, here, then here," Wang Jun said confidently.

Huxian nodded and summoned three sharp gray needles. He coughed up blood as he summoned them, overdrawing his strength. This was the second part of the technique, Rune-Breaking Needles. Extracted runes could not be eaten directly. They often needed to be broken before consumption, like chewing food. Unfortunately, summoning these rune-breaking needles exceeded the limits of his purification-realm body.

"Break!" Huxian yelled. The runes pierced the sigil in these three locations in order, and the sigil crumbled. Huxian lost consciousness soon after.

"Boss, boss!" a high-pitched voice yelled. "Wake up, boss!"

"Who's your boss?" Huxian said groggily.

"Boss is boss of course," the high-pitched voice yelled.

"Lei Jiang?" Huxian muttered, opening his eyes. He was exhausted. His eyesight was blurry, but soon he was able to make out the small shape of a purple mouse.

"Of course it's me," the mouse said.

"Don't call me boss," Huxian said. "I'm not your boss."

The mouse looked hurt. "You're my boss if I say you are."

Huxian sighed. "How could I possibly be my friend's boss?" he said, smiling with his foxy muzzle.

The mouse looked at a loss. "Why can't you be both?" the mouse asked, confused.

"This…" Huxian wasn't sure how to answer that. He'd always taken their boss-minion relationship as a one-way street. But then he thought more about it and realized that he was slightly subservient to Cha Ming. Cha Ming and he were brothers, but Cha Ming was the elder brother.

"I suppose you're right," Huxian said. "You admit that I'm your friend, even if a bad one?"

"You're the best of friends," Lei Jiang said. "When you took away my soul seal, I was scared. My thoughts became confused. I had a lot of time to think before they finally caught me. That second time, I thought I would never escape." The little mouse sniffed. "But who would have thought that when I woke up, I would see the boss? Not only that, you were wounded. Your blond-haired friend said you spent a lot of strength to save me. How could anyone but the best of friends do that?"

"I guess we're friends," Huxian muttered. "Well, as the older brother in this relationship, you need to listen to what I say." The mouse nodded. "However, I promise to always protect you. I should protect my friends. You'll support me, and I'll protect you. Deal?"

"Deal!" Lei Jiang said.

Suddenly, the trigram on Huxian's tail lit up. It was the same lightning trigram as before, and a character appeared on it. On Lei Jiang, a symbol appeared on his forehead. It wasn't the character for "general." Rather, it was the character for "friend."

And to Huxian's surprise, they had the same abilities as when Lei Jiang was his thunder general. Except now, he had an obligation. But he also had a friend.

To Huxian, that made a world of difference.

Chapter 35: Alabaster Corps

Cha Ming's awareness returned to his surroundings after briefly cultivating. He retrieved a set of freshly painted talismans from his desk before heading out to the Alabaster Group courtyard. It was dark out. The first rays of sunshine had yet to illuminate the night sky. In the courtyard, several figures sat cross-legged in meditation, improving their conditions one last time before the upcoming battle. They all wore white, making the entire group seem like a funeral gathering.

I suppose it is a funeral gathering, Cha Ming thought. *Many of those who would accept the mission have lost family members and friends to devils. These people accept missions every day to defend the helpless and destroy those who persecute the innocent.*

After further reflection, he changed his clothes to the same alabaster white. He had lost acquaintances as well. The deaths of Han Jinlong, Bei Ling, and those many people near Fairweather were reason enough.

"You're finally here," a familiar voice called out to Cha Ming. It was Luo Xuehua. Her silver hair and permanently closed eyes did not take away from her smile.

"How many people are participating?" Cha Ming asked.

"Forty foundation-establishment cultivators, including us," Xuehua replied. "And six half-step foundation-establishment cultivators, as well as seven core-formation protectors."

Cha Ming raised an eyebrow.

Xuehua chuckled. "Surely you don't expect the Obsidian Syndicate to remain honest, do you? These core-formation cultivators are there both as insurance and to cash in on this chance to clash with the Obsidian Syndicate. It's not beneath them to kill a few foundation-establishment juniors if we are outnumbered, but this is also considered a tempering exercise to us juniors."

"Fair enough," Cha Ming said while surveying the blanket of cultivators. "Who is in charge?"

"As Lu Tianhao's apprentice, yours truly fills that role," Luo Xuehua replied. Now that Cha Ming looked around, he noticed many looks of admiration directed toward her.

Cha Ming faintly heard something in the distance. It was the sound of the wind. Xuehua clearly heard it as well. A white shadow flashed and landed before Xuehua, briefly bowing before reporting.

"I've been keeping watch on the Obsidian Syndicate," he said, panting. "However, everything was strangely quiet. To be certain, I checked the city gates, and sure enough, a large group of them left the city a few hours ago."

Xuehua's look hardened. "They want to play such tricks." Then, amplifying her voice, she spoke to everyone present. "The Obsidian Syndicate has already departed. We are leaving now." All white-clothed figures present stood in attention, while several people flew out of their residences. Then, turning to Cha Ming, she asked, "Did you learn the Wind Walk Formation?"

"Only to lesser grade," Cha Ming replied. "But I can do you one better. If I consume high-grade spirit stones to keep up the energy, that is."

Xuehua tossed him a few dozen high-grade spirit stones, which Cha Ming shamelessly accepted. He was far too broke to afford the steep transit cost.

Cha Ming breathed deeply before floating up above the courtyard. He threw out eighteen Dao sigils, nine purple crystals, and nine azure stones. He poured his personal qi into the gray sigils, transforming half into lightning sigils and half into wind sigils. Then he took out the Clear Sky Brush. It glowed light purple as he painted large connecting lines with the lightning essence he had recently prepared. Just like the five-element evanescence, wind and lightning evanescence could also be mixed in with liquified elemental essence. Unfortunately, it was much rarer and could only be harvested in the high mountains. The price was exorbitant.

The purple brush quickly changed color, and azure lines floated into place just above the ground, meshing with the complementary combat-formation lines. Azure and purple alternated until he finally threw out ten high-grade spirit stones, bringing the formation to life.

The formation was called Stormwalker Formation. The Stormchaser Steps he used was a simplified derivative of this large one. He discovered by accident that, while he couldn't improve his success rate by using wind and lightning essence when painting formations, he *could* increase their stability. As a result, he could increase the scope of the formation. This naturally applied to all formations he knew, increasing his formation abilities by a half step.

Purple lightning and azure winds billowed in the hundred-foot range of the formation. His Stormchaser Boots disappeared and became dark clouds that integrated with the formation.

"I need ten high-grade spirit stones per hour to maintain this formation," Cha Ming said. "But it increases the speed of our group by several times."

Xuehua nodded. "Everyone, step into the range of the formation. We're moving out!"

They left the city like the wind, and the guards didn't dare inspect them. When the Alabaster Group was out for blood, no one could prevent it.

Wang Jun sat at the peak of the mountain brewing tea. He very much enjoyed watching the jade platform there. It was very mysterious, to the extent that he couldn't read its story, though judging from the runes on it, it was surely a formation plate.

I need to get Cha Ming to look at this, he thought. *According to Huxian, there's a plate on each of the nine mountains.*

A yawn suddenly came from the cave. Huxian, who had just finished recovering from his wounds, walked out. The mouse, Lei Jiang, quickly darted to the peak of the mountain.

"Now that we're fully recovered, let's storm those humans remaining at the base of the mountain," Huxian said. "Over two-thirds of the humans left with that prime minister of yours, so we should be able to defeat them easily."

"About that," Wang Jun said with an awkward look on his face. "Some company arrived. I'm afraid it's not us who will be attacking, but the other way around."

Huxian's eyes narrowed as he looked at the previously tiny camp. It had grown to over double its previous size. In addition, he sensed a dozen terrifying auras.

Core-formation cultivators, he thought.

"Will the monarch help us if they meddle?" Wang Jun asked softly.

Huxian shook his head. "Although he will… I don't think he can handle those twelve on his own."

"Then let's hope they're here just to enjoy the show," Wang Jun said. "Cha Ming and the Alabaster Group are coming soon, but we need to hold out for a few hours."

Huxian nodded. "Geomantic boa!" he yelled. The mountain quaked before the gigantic snake poked out.

"I would appreciate it if you used my new title," she said arrogantly.

Huxian rolled his eyes. "Geomantic Sovereign, would you be so kind as to do something for me before I beat the venom out of you and have you begging to this father for mercy?" The giant snake's throat shivered. "I need you to lay down as many traps as possible to delay those cultivators down there."

"This…" Geomantic Sovereign looked at him awkwardly.

"What's the matter? Can't do it?" Huxian yelled aggressively.

"It's not that I can't do it…" Geomantic Sovereign said, frightened.

"Let me summarize," Wang Jun said, walking between them. "She thinks you're stupid and have no strategic sense, but she's too afraid to disobey your direct orders."

"How dare you!" Huxian said, looking wounded. *He's right, intelligence really isn't my strong suit,* Huxian thought. *I'll have to use all available resources.* "Fine. You and she can plan, just keep me posted."

"Thank you, Sovereign Two Tails," Wang Jun said mockingly. "For the sake of education, I'll summarize. During the last few battles, the traps you set were effective because all forces were evenly matched. The weak forces that couldn't help but fight near the ground were hampered by these weak walls of earth, spikes, etc. It was very effective.

"This situation is different entirely," he continued. "Their high-end forces outnumber ours four to one, but our low-level forces outnumber theirs. Therefore they will only use their lower-level forces to distract ours. What we really need to delay is them rushing in to slaughter our leaders. The previous formations won't be effective against top-tier forces, as they can just shatter these walls and traps at will.

"That's why the Geomantic Sovereign and I will collaborate to build illusory and concealment formations. She will set the base using terrain features as natural formation eyes, while I will supplement them with the power of shadow. The only downside is that we won't be able to fight in this battle. I will be the strategist, and the Geomantic Sovereign and I will constantly change and manipulate the formations to our greatest advantage."

"Is there anything I can do?" Huxian asked.

"Sure," Wang Jun said. "When the battle starts, look for their tactician and try to kill him. We will try to find him as well. Zhou Li will not participate in this battle because it will break the terms of the treaty, which will weaken the crown prince's grip on the throne.

"I speculate that he used his fate powers to manipulate karma, which is why he was able to hire these forces in the first place. He would have had to first do business through a variety of intermediaries using ambiguous promises. Then he would have needed to burn any remaining karmic threads using fire and fate. Fortunately, he must stay out of a direct confrontation, or the karma will be reestablished.

"Does this mean *they* don't have a strategist?" Huxian asked.

"I refuse to believe that Zhou Li won't find a replacement for himself," Wang Jun said. "There will be a tactician. The second priority target is Guo Jia. He will be well defended, as he is the key to dismantling our defensive formations. They won't be able to advance without breaking them, so your beasts will need to distract him as much as possible. In turn, I'll be able to use their movements to potentially determine the location of their strategist."

Huxian sighed. "Do you think we can hold out for three hours?"

"It will be one hour before both sides are ready," Wang Jun said. "Holding out for two hours against this lineup, however? We can only try."

Zhou Li walked toward a skinny, black-robed cultivator. He was one of the twelve core-formation cultivators that had just arrived. The ones he hadn't ordered. "I don't suppose you're here just for sightseeing?" he asked.

"We're here as insurance," the man said in a relaxed manner. "For an extra 200,000, we will participate in the battle. I'll note that our spies indicate that the Alabaster Group will be here in less than three hours. This information is free of charge."

Zhou Li gritted his teeth. "You're basically taking out all the profits from this operation."

"That's only because you've been so stingy," the man retorted coldly. "We do fair business. If you had paid us earlier, we could have helped you conquer the mountain range before the treaty took place.

I'll note that *we* are the ones who provided you the information on the treaty in the first place.

"Now I'll kindly warn you that if you that if you hire us now, we can end this battle quickly before they arrive. Ten of us will hold off the monarch while the others reap lives on the battlefield with impunity. What say you?"

Zhou Li hesitated. "What are your calculated odds of success?"

"Eighty percent," another man said. His realm was far below core formation. In fact, Zhou Li wouldn't be surprised if his cultivation was lower than early foundation establishment. "But only based on the information provided. External factors that you have not reported may significantly affect the odds."

"And who is this?" Zhou Li asked the core-formation expert.

"His name is Zhong Fa," he replied. "This is the master tactician you paid for. He's the best we have, and I will never question his judgment."

Zhou Li held his chin and pondered for a while before shaking his head. "I'll take eighty-percent odds for now. You and your men can enjoy the show."

Black-robed armies flooded the battlefield in unison.

"Kill!" they shouted, spreading their baleful aura toward the opposing beasts. Now that the Song Kingdom's forces had retreated, many of them revealed their true forms. A full half of them were devils with fighting prowess above their realms.

They advanced slowly up the mountain with Guo Jia at their center. According to Wang Jun, their directions were impaired and required formation eyes to be broken as they advanced. The concealment formations made it difficult for Guo Jia to break the formation eyes and prevented the humans from detecting the beasts in the first place.

The invaders halted. They stood by at attention as Guo Jia spread out sigils and flags. Huxian saw several formation eyes erupt one after another before their group packed up and advanced another hundred feet in their direction. It was impossible to replenish the broken formation eyes. The Geomantic Sovereign and Wang Jun could only divert their energies to prevent him breaking them in the first place.

One more stop, Wang Jun sent to Huxian mentally. Huxian had half the upper echelons of the beast forces with him. The lower-tier forces and the other half were on the opposite side, awaiting their signals. Guo Jia broke yet another few formation eyes and stopped again a hundred feet later. Just as they moved once more, Huxian signaled his beast forces to attack. They caught the human forces by surprise.

The beasts had activated their abilities before charging in, taking full advantage of the concealment formation. The first layer of humans fell to their attacks, but the upper-level human forces immediately adjusted and countered their battle formations.

Retreat, Wang Jun's voice sounded.

Huxian relayed the command, pulling everyone back. He glared hatefully at the ochre figures and the ochre mist spread across the black-robed group.

Did you find their tactician? Huxian asked.

Negative, Wang Jun replied. *None of their movements revealed any such weakness. However, we did obtain some information. They've slowly been edging toward Silverwing's mountain. If I'm not mistaken, they are heading toward the ore deposit. They will likely try to excavate it, which means they likely have a hidden geomancer in their midst. They are planning on excavating everything quickly, so they won't need to fight us under these circumstances. They want to force the issue, so we must face them at a disadvantage.*

What can we do? Huxian asked.

We can only delay as much as possible and chip away as many of their forces as we can, Wang Jun said. *That way we can study the opponent and weaken them before the final confrontation. If they were just wandering aimlessly, we would have the terrain advantage. They clearly have the intent of eliminating that advantage and forcing us to respond. What a great tactician. It's open intrigue at its finest.*

Suddenly, Huxian heard a voice transmission. *Huxian, we're getting closer,* a voice said. *How are things looking on your end?*

Cha Ming! Huxian replied. *You're in range. Things aren't looking good. Wang Jun said you'll be here in one and a half hours, but by then they'll already have won.*

Pass this information along to Wang Jun, Cha Ming instructed. *We intentionally delayed as we exited the city in case spies took note of us. We have kept this hidden for half the trip: We're speeding up now. We'll be there in a half hour.*

Huxian quickly passed on the information, and after a short while he heard Wang Jun's reply. *We'll begin a large-scale battle in a quarter hour. They shouldn't expect it, and by then it will be too late to adjust their plans.*

Huxian martialed his troops and brought the various sovereigns, kings, and lords into position.

We need to change plans, Zhou Li heard via voice transmission. *I just heard from our spies that the Alabaster Group is only a half hour away. I suspect a surprise attack from the beasts soon to take advantage of oncoming reinforcements. I now put our odds at fifty percent at best.*

How exactly were we informed so late of their impending arrival? Zhou Li asked.

It was deception, the voice replied. *They must have intentionally traveled slowly. Fortunately, we have spies in the Alabaster Group itself. I suggest that we hire the core-formation experts to try taking out priority targets in advance. But if and only if they attack us.*

They're bleeding me dry, Zhou Li thought. His heart ached. His precious war funds were falling through his fingers. *Very well. I authorize it, but if and only if we get attacked. Also, I want a fifty-percent discount.*

A moment of silence ensued, followed by a response. *Thirty percent.*

Fine, Zhou Li said.

Pleasure doing business with you, the voice answered.

Chapter 36: Monarch

The opposing forces suffered substantial damage as Huxian's group crashed into them. There was a quarter hour left before reinforcements were to arrive, and their job was to buy as much time as possible. He couldn't worry about the fates of the low-level soldiers. His job was to fight against six half-step core-formation cultivators. It wasn't going well. Every one of those that faced him specialized on restraining techniques and defense, effectively locking him out of the battle.

Meanwhile, the other sovereigns were suffering greatly. Each was confronted with multiple stronger opponents, unable to break free. It wasn't long before the first one fell. The Reptilian Lion Sovereign, with his iron-hard defense and poisonous claws, was subdued by three other cultivators just as strong as the ones restraining Huxian. Only one of the three cultivators perished in the process.

Things weren't going much better in the middle of the battlefield. Now that Guo Jia was no longer concerned with breaking formation eyes, he brought out the best out of his high-grade formations, incinerating low-level demon beasts by the score. Their advantage on that front was dwindling.

Two incense time left, Huxian thought. He didn't use his most powerful abilities, as they left large openings that could be exploited by his opponents. *Hurry up, Brother,* he sent mentally to Cha Ming.

The battlefield was a meat grinder, even considering the

Geomantic Sovereign and Wang Jun's efforts in erecting random walls, spike traps, and timely concealing formations. By the time an incense time remained, a quarter of the beast forces had been decimated.

Why did we have to intercept them again? Huxian asked Wang Jun.

Because we didn't want to allow them time to set up a defense, Wang Jun said. *Someone tipped them off on Cha Ming's arrival, so they had started setting up permanent defensive formations. Formation masters are especially frightening when given enough time to prepare, and the losses would have been staggering if we attacked them later. Once Cha Ming's forces arrive, we'll be able to fight them on even terms. Before then, however, we can only distract them and sacrifice forces.*

I get that, Huxian said. *But couldn't we have—*

Run! Wang Jun sent mentally. Huxian looked toward the sky and spotted the twelve core-formation cultivators, who had suddenly jumped into action.

They must be suicidal, Huxian thought. *Unless they know something that I don't.* He felt a massive pressure on his bloodline as a giant owl suddenly appeared on the battlefield. Despite his size, he was several times faster than Huxian was.

"You dare interfere in this battle between juniors?" the owl shouted, flying toward the core-formation cultivators and baring its talons. Ten of the cultivators attacked it with their weapons and various Daoist techniques, barely managing to hold it back. Two of the core-formations cultivators avoided its talons and dashed at unreasonable speeds. Straight toward the retreating Huxian.

Shit, he thought. He combined his two clones into one body and laid a bagua trap behind himself. Eight trigrams imprisoned the two pursuers, but only temporarily. The trap only bought him five breaths. *How in the nine heavens am I supposed to survive this?*

One the cultivators, a gray-haired old man, formed ten thousand hand seals in the blink of an eye. A giant two-hundred-foot-wide frost lotus sprouted beneath Huxian's paws. They tore through his fur as he struggled to dodge. From above, ten thousand swords rained down on him. His fur was tough, but not tough enough to completely negate techniques from core-formation cultivators. Over twenty of them cut deeply into his black and white fur, leaving patches of red.

Brother Cha Ming, Huxian sent. *It looks like I won't be able to hold out. I'm sorry.* As he darted between the forest of ice and steel blades, he saw Lei Jiang's familiar purple glow.

Run away! Huxian sent to him. *You can't fight them!* The purple mouse ignored his words, summoning nine purple lightning dragons to attack the two core-formation cultivators. They simply snorted, and with a wave of their sleeves, Lei Jiang was thrown onto the side of the mountain coughing blood. His lightning dragons dissipated into nothingness. This was a suppression of realms.

With Lei Jiang disposed of, the two stone-faced cultivators formed hand seals once more. This time, two giant spears appeared above Huxian. One was gold, the other was crystalline. He roared in defiance at the spears as they came plunging down toward him. His surroundings went dark, and he simultaneously transformed into a sphere of light that pushed back against the spears. Cracks appeared on that sphere as the core-formation cultivators exerted their powers.

This is the end, Huxian thought as the cracks expanded.

Suddenly, a sharp cry pierced the cool mountain air. The winds shifted suddenly, and a silver glint broke through the darkness that surrounded them. The streak of silver dove down from above the clouds and cut a sharp arc in its descent, suddenly smashing into the two spears that were attacking Huxian. The silver streak was like a sharp blade tearing through wet paper. The two core-formation cultivators coughed up blood as their techniques were destroyed.

Silverwing! Huxian shouted. He didn't waste the hard-won opportunity and continued fleeing. The core-formation cultivators struggled to chase after him, but they were pelted with swipe after swipe of deadly silver wings. *You came back, my friend.*

What else was I supposed to do? the falcon cooed.

You didn't lock yourself up because you were mad at me? Huxian asked.

How could this noble friend of yours be so selfish? he said indignantly. *I locked myself up to upgrade my bloodline and retrieve my inherited memories. Then when you dropped off that delicious silver root, I immediately used it to break through to core formation. I just didn't expect it to take so long. I could barely move, and sending out that drop of blood took more power than you can even imagine. It delayed my breakthrough by several days.*

Huxian's heart warmed. *Thank you for coming back, my friend,* he sent. The two core-formation experts had quit pursuing him. Instead, they took the opportunity to slay two more sovereigns before finally retreating. The other core-formation cultivators, Guo Jia, and the other foundation-establishment experts retreated as well, just in time for Huxian to see a large group of men in white cloaks on the horizon with the rising sun.

He looked at the battlefield mournfully. One-third of all the beasts and sovereigns had been slain in this crucial battle. Was it worth it?

The leaders of the beast and human forces stood at odds at the peak of Silverwing's mountain. Wang Jun, as the only human among the beasts, was in an awkward position. The owl monarch stood proudly, watching the newly arrived core-formation cultivators with a guarded expression. The sovereigns glared at them. They had suffered too much bloodshed at the hands of the humans lately.

The leader of the humans looked around awkwardly, obviously unsure of what to do.

"Huxian!" Cha Ming yelled, flying out toward the group of beasts. The black-and-white fox jumped out and shrank in size substantially.

"Brother!" the small fox yipped, jumping into his arms. Cha Ming pet his head, and Huxian licked Cha Ming's face. The awkward tension that had built up between both groups diminished substantially. Both humans and beasts watched on with incredulous expressions.

"I'm sorry for being late," Cha Ming said. "The Obsidian Syndicate snuck out of the city, so we had to rush to get here on time."

"As long as you're here," Huxian said.

Then, as if realizing that he was surrounded by what was essentially the royalty of the Silverwing Mountain Range, he coughed and reverted to his normal size. "This is my brother, Cha Ming," Huxian said in a much more authoritative voice. "I have signed a contract of brotherhood with him. You must treat him as you treat me." The expressions of the sovereigns and even the monarch softened substantially when they heard this. Likewise, the Alabaster Group's vigilance lessened as well. After all, all the beasts but the monarch seemed submissive to the black-and-white fox. If he was one of their members' contracted beasts, it wasn't impossible to work together.

After briefly discussing with Huxian, Cha Ming withdrew thirty-six formation flags. Using his Clear Sky Brush, he set up large-scale healing formation, the Mid-Grade Respite Formation. The beasts, who had been severely wounded in the battle, began recovering at a visible pace.

"I hate to interrupt this teary reunion, but we don't have much time," Wang Jun said suddenly, stepping toward Cha Ming and Huxian. "I'm not sure if you all realize that our forces are currently at a disadvantage should the Obsidian Syndicate attack."

"How are we at a disadvantage?" Flaming Eagle Sovereign questioned. "With the monarch on our side, we will surely defeat them."

"I'm afraid that he's right," the monarch said. "But I'm not comfortable talking about the reasons behind this in front of everyone. I would like Huxian, Cha Ming, Wang Jun, Silverwing, Flaming Eagle Sovereign, and two representatives from the Alabaster Group to follow me to discuss. I will tell you everything. Does that sound reasonable?"

After looking at the eldest and most powerful core-formation cultivator, Luo Xuehua nodded. "I, Luo Xuehua, and Protector Meng will represent those from the Alabaster Group."

"Excellent," the large gray owl said. "Follow me."

They followed the large owl down the mountain toward the valley below. The valley was known as Owl Monarch Gorge, and it was off-limits to man and beast alike, save those the monarch approved of. The nine mountains came together like an ellipse with the valley at its center. The mountains were prosperous and full of life, while the valley was full of death and decay. Wherever they looked, they saw withered trees that had long been broken apart by the wind.

"This is far enough," the owl said. Then, to everyone's surprise, it slumped to the ground. A large red stain trickled out from beneath its left wing for all to see. Looking closer, they saw three swords had pierced its side where its heart should be. "The reason we are at a disadvantage, as our very observant friend put it, is because I am dying. I am on my last legs, a lamp on its last few drops of oil."

The owl didn't react as Cha Ming threw out a healing combat formation near the wound, which refused to close. The owl shook its head. "It's no use. You would need a core-level formation to make any difference. The vitality of a core-formation spirit beast is far too high, and your formation is just a drop in the bucket. Now then, Wang Jun, how could you tell?"

"Everyone has a story," Wang Jun said wistfully. "Unfortunately, yours is far too easy for me to see. There is only one ending for you, and that is your death."

The owl sighed. "I have a few days at most, and that's if I don't fight. Therefore, our alliance against this band of devils is much weaker than you might think. If we fought against them, we would last at most a week."

Wang Jun shook his head. "Not even that. They clearly have a spy in the Alabaster Group." Luo Xuehua glared at him, but he continued. "They couldn't have known when we would be arriving and have arranged a counter ploy if they didn't. They clearly knew when we would attack them."

He looked at Cha Ming. "That means they also know that Cha Ming is a formation master. Given enough time and resources, Cha Ming could make this battle very difficult for them, despite Guo Jia's presence. After all, formation masters are best defensively. That means that they will attack within the hour to not give him that chance. We need to be ready to use everything we have at our disposal."

"Everyone from the Alabaster Group is ready to lay their lives down to kill devils," Luo Xuehua said. The elder beside her nodded. "I can also call the Alabaster Group to send additional forces. They won't stand by idly as we're slaughtered by those from the Obsidian Syndicate. Give us twenty-four hours, and we'll have more core-formation reinforcements."

"This the other reason they will attack sooner," Wang Jun said.

"We beasts always get the short end of the stick," the owl said weakly. "We do not care about these petty battles between angels and devils. We care not for karma. We have always been neutral. But why do we always get caught in the crossfire?"

"It's because demons always populate areas with natural riches," Wang Jun explained. "How could greedy humans possibly stay away from them?"

"You are right of course," the owl sovereign said. "Core-formation demon beasts can live five thousand years, which is ten times as long as a human. I have seen many wars and many struggles for riches. As such, our land has dwindled steadily. Now all that is left of my great-grandfather's domain is the Silverwing Mountain Range, named after his friend Silverwing. Your ancestor," he said, shooting a meaningful look to Silverwing.

"In any case, aside from discussing the reality of the situation, I came to bring you hope," the owl said. "I see things sometimes. Things that help us beasts navigate the difficult currents of each age. This time, I saw a man wielding a black and white brush, activating Silverwing's Pure Jade Defensive Formation."

The group looked to Cha Ming, the sole formation master. "What grade of formation is it?" Cha Ming asked.

"Throughout the mountain range, there are nine jade formation plates," the owl explained. "In the center, there is a control plate. The formation is a core-level formation, but the foundation is already set. In addition, the energy is supplied by the mountain."

Cha Ming shook his head. "I'm afraid that's far beyond my ability."

"It isn't," the owl said. "Not this one. I can *feel* it. But it will take you and your fox brother to accomplish it. Do you dare trust me?"

Then the owl's eyes changed. When Cha Ming looked at them, he felt as though he could see through the mysteries of the Dao, as though he were lost in a sea of mysteries.

You can see things that others can't, the owl said mentally. *It is in your destiny to activate the formation. The Dao will make everything possible.*

"Impossible," Zhou Li said. "We clearly have the advantage. Why should we rush and attack now?"

"Because they've just gained a substantial advantage," the voice whispered. "A formation master named Du Cha Ming."

Hearing this familiar name, Zhou Li grimaced.

"It is also very likely that the Alabaster Group will send reinforcements. Are you able to pay more for additional services? Besides, it's not like you are losing anything. We've already been paid, and you only stand to lose if you don't act now."

Zhou Li thought for a while before nodding. This was the last chance they would get, and if they didn't succeed, he would be up to his elbows in debt. He hated debt.

Cha Ming and Huxian followed the owl monarch as it hopped with small flaps of its wings. Each flap sprayed copious amounts of blood onto the dusty forest floor. The land here seemed to be dying. And according to what Huxian said, it was also absent of demonic qi, something unusual so far into beast territory.

"Why is the land so gray here?" Cha Ming asked.

"It is as it looks," the monarch replied. "It has been dying ever since the formation was put into place. It was set up as a potent defense, but the price was half the energy the land had to offer. It will never recover so long as the formation stays."

"But why set it up in the first place?" Cha Ming questioned.

"My ancestor had a dream," the owl said. "The True Seer bloodline is powerful, allowing its descendants to see what others can't. He saw the destruction of our people, and he knew that the only way to prevent it was through this formation."

They continued advancing through the broken, desolate forest. Even the waters seemed strange. They were clear like the purest streams, yet lifeless. Not even swamp creatures that feasted on death dared occupy them.

Before long, they reached a large clearing where Cha Ming and Huxian finally saw a large jade plate, much like the one he had seen on Huxian's mountain peak. This one was circular instead of rectangular, with lines heading in nine different directions. It too was covered in runes. Although he was able to read them, Cha Ming could tell what was required of him was far beyond his capacity.

"I can't do this," Cha Ming said, shaking his head. "I can't even grasp a tenth of this formation."

"You can," the owl said. "It's just that there are some things you still don't see. The formation was made to be easy to use, assuming one meets certain prerequisites."

"And what prerequisites are those?" Cha Ming wondered aloud.

"A key. And a technique," the owl replied. "If you have the key, the technique will appear."

"And what is this key you speak of? Where can we find it?" Cha Ming asked.

"I already mentioned it," the owl said. "My ancestor dreamed of a disaster and built this formation. He was inspired to build a testing stele, so that the destined one might gain us a slim chance for survival. I, on the other hand, had a different dream. I dreamed of a man who wielded a brush and a black-and-white fox with two tails. The brush was the same as you were wielding when you arrived."

It dawned on Cha Ming then. The key was the Clear Sky Brush.

Chapter 37: Between Light and Darkness

You will soon understand everything," the owl said. "Huxian, when I asked you if you had a close human friend, I was asking to confirm my dream. I heard your lie, so I've been keeping an eye on you. Otherwise, how could the Reptilian Lion Sovereign possibly give in to Silverwing's demands?"

Huxian transmitted a brief account of what had happened to Cha Ming.

Destiny is a strange thing, Cha Ming thought. *But this time, I wasn't pulled along helplessly. I chose to learn talisman and formation arts. And even if I was given the Eyes of Pure Jade, I chose to use them. And finally, I chose to learn formations and help Mo Tianshen with his pills. Is everything truly predestined? Or are there many potential destinies, and my choices have led me to this one? Are there other similar destinies out there that I have abandoned?*

He thought of the dual nature of the Clear Sky Brush. It didn't favor light over darkness. He could have easily chosen the devil path. It was a choice he'd made, regardless of what he might have thought at the time.

As Cha Ming thought this, the owl led them to a stone stele near the jade plate. It looked positively ancient, and it was covered in myriad runic lines. To Cha Ming's surprise, he did not understand a single character. At least with the jade plate he understood everything. This was why he was so certain he couldn't use it. These runes were completely different.

"I recognize those," Huxian suddenly said. He walked up to the stone stele, sniffing. "These are runes of light and darkness. I am no formation master or talisman artist, but I remember them. If you can master them, they will be very useful for me in the future."

Cha Ming shook his head. "How could I possibly learn them? I can't manipulate light or darkness qi, so I couldn't even begin to comprehend them. Learning runes starts with imitation. Without imitation there is no understanding." As he said these words, he traced the shallow grooves on the stone stele with his finger. They called to him.

"Don't you have that creation qi technique or whatnot?" Huxian asked, confused.

"It's not so simple," Cha Ming said, smiling. "The five elements, wind, and lightning are encompassed in creation. The same elements are a part of destruction, or so I understand thus far. But certain attributes cannot be created or destroyed. They are a resulting law, a consequence of everything else.

"Light and darkness are opposite forces of consequence. If I light a fire, I will create light. If I manipulate earth, I can block out light and create darkness. I can't manipulate them directly like you do. The same applies to the power of fate, merit, and sin, and their category, karma. It is the same for space and time."

"Then if you had access to light and darkness qi, it would solve your problems?" Huxian asked.

"Indeed, it would," Cha Ming answered. "If only gaining access to light and darkness qi were so easy."

"Not a problem," Huxian said joyfully, sitting on Cha Ming's lap. "With my help, you will be able to use light and darkness qi. Of course, it's demonic qi, but shouldn't that work just the same?"

Cha Ming felt the link between Huxian and himself deepen. He understood that, at least in a range of one hundred feet, he could draw on Huxian's qi. Meanwhile, Huxian could do the same to him.

"Nice!" the young fox said, summoning a ball of flame. "I've always wanted to summon flame. It's really cool, but every bagua fox only gets one contractor in their lifetime. That's why our knowledge on techniques for these elements are so limited. I can only adapt from the techniques meant for my beastly generals. Beastly friends. Whatever they are."

"Speaking of which," Cha Ming said awkwardly, "how come I haven't seen your minion, Lei Jiang?"

Huxian shook his head self-deprecatingly. "He's not my minion anymore. He's my friend. I released his soul seal, but he ran away..." Huxian narrated the sequence of events while looking away, not daring to meet Cha Ming's eyes. Cha Ming couldn't help but scratch his ears.

"You did well, my friend, you did well," Cha Ming said. "Now tell me, what do you know about the nature of light and darkness?" Cha Ming summoned two balls of qi, which he controlled using his incandescent force. One was pure white, one was pure black, just like his creation and destruction qi.

"Not much, I'm afraid," Huxian said. "We're in tune with nature from our birth. We don't need to understand its nature—we *are* its nature. Whatever element we cultivate, we are its embodiment. What I can tell you is this—light is inseparable from darkness. They only show their true nature when they are together."

Cha Ming pondered deeply as he summoned the Clear Sky Brush. He imbued liquified elemental essence and tried to guide it just like with any other qi. To his surprise, the liquified elemental essence and the demonic qi merged slightly. The liquified elemental essence began to glow, as though it was returning to its original nature. It reminded Cha Ming of the process of creating gold essence and the others.

He tried the same thing with the darkness qi. The liquified elemental essence took on a slightly obscure shade. "Light essence and dark essence," Cha Ming whispered. He couldn't help but think that, if demonic beasts had the capacity for learning that humans did, they would surely be the best talisman artists. And blacksmiths. And anything else he could think of.

After having confirmed the usage of the demonic light and darkness qi, he walked over to the ancient stone stele. He looked at one of the least complicated runes and sent his incandescent force into it.

This character reminds me of the dim illumination of an overcast morning, Cha Ming thought. He tried painting the character he sensed, only to have it dim immediately afterward. He frowned. *No, that's not it. It's the dim illumination on an overcast morning before dawn.*

On this second try, the character didn't fade; it stayed illuminated.

Cha Ming didn't switch to darkness characters right away. He continued painting character after character, knowing full well that on the mountain range, an intense war was being waged.

Luo Xuehua, Wang Jun sent mentally, *three hundred feet to the left, throw an Ice Grave Talisman and slow their pincer. Flaming Eagle Sovereign, fly overhead and intercept their supporting cultivators with flying swords. Boar lords one through seven, charge through the opening created and attack the three mid-foundation-establishment cultivators there.*

Wang Jun shouted orders incessantly while also manipulating a grand formation with the Geomantic Sovereign. Not only did he have to control the flow of battle, he had to counter whatever tricks Guo Jia was up to. Meanwhile, the opponent's commander was elusive. He could not find him anywhere, and whenever he thought he spotted him, he vanished like the wind.

Half of the Obsidian Syndicate has assumed a devilish form, Wang Jun thought. *Why wouldn't the commander?* He directed a message to Luo Xuehua. *Xuehua, do you know of any devilish creatures that have non-physical transformations? Ones that are good at hiding?*

There are two, in fact, she replied while fighting a burly, bark-covered man that was suppressing her. *Envy devils can disguise themselves as any person and can transform into wind, becoming immune to all physical attacks. I killed one once with Cha Ming, but that's only because his eye technique can see them in their unsubstantial form.*

The Eyes of Pure Jade? Wang Jun asked.

That's right, she said. *I also noticed that his fox friend has those very same eyes.*

Then it's very unfortunate that they're both gone, Wang Jun said. He turned his attention back to the battle. In this case, he wouldn't bother trying to find their commander. He would wait until Cha Ming and Huxian came back and destroy him in one fell swoop.

It looks like I've reached a bottleneck, Cha Ming thought. He had tried the remaining light characters many times, but he was unable to gain any further comprehension. Huxian was off to the side, playing with a blob of lightning. He was learning qi manipulation like a child learned languages.

"Any advice on how to proceed?" Cha Ming asked.

Huxian appeared beside him immediately. He looked at the lit-up characters.

"Hm…" Huxian said. "I suggest you start with darkness runes now. Light and darkness are not as far removed as you think. Maybe you'll gain inspirations as you paint." He then went off to the side and began summoning a small sphere of darkness.

Cha Ming's eyes narrowed, and he yelled out instinctively, "Huxian, stop playing with the destruction qi!" Huxian cast his eyes down and scampered off to the woods. Immediately after his disappearance, Cha Ming could feel his destruction qi being drained once more. He shook his head helplessly. *Kids.*

Two hours passed before Cha Ming once again got to another

bottleneck. He was left with an equal amount of uncompleted darkness characters.

Just what am I missing? he thought. He had been through dozens of descriptions on each side of the spectrum, and yet he couldn't understand any of these other runes.

One rune in particular baffled him. The feeling he got from it was one of light and darkness duality, but he knew it could only be drawn with one kind of ink.

I get the feeling that this is candlelight. But what am I missing? How many ways can you interpret candlelight?

As though he was trying to prove a point, he summoned a large sphere of darkness qi, which blotted out his surroundings. Then he summoned a small flame. It flickered, creating light as a consequence. And wherever it went, the darkness receded ever so slightly. It suddenly dawned on Cha Ming that he had been thinking about it backward.

Light is not just light, he thought. *Light is also receding darkness. Likewise, darkness is also receding light.*

He looked back to the light-based character and pictured something else in his mind entirely. He didn't focus on the candle, he focused on the area surrounding the candle where the darkness retreated. Then he infused his insights into the rune he'd painted with light essence. The completed character glowed and remained, not fading away.

Cha Ming, excited by his new epiphany, began interpreting the different characters in different ways. It wasn't long before every character on the stone stele glowed white or black. Once the last character was drawn, it immediately began to crumble. Huxian, having heard the commotion, appeared beside Cha Ming. The dust settled and revealed a small purple jade slip. It had a title: Demon-Subduing Eyes.

Cha Ming summoned the slip with his incandescent force and immersed his mind into the technique. Images, feelings, and scenes flooded his mind. He imagined he was a monarch, a sovereign. Thousands of beasts groveled before him. He was forced to abruptly cut the connection. He looked at the jade slip with a strange expression.

"How would anyone ever be able to cultivate this?" he thought.

"Let me try," Huxian said. He placed his paw on the jade slip. It glowed with an intense light. Three breaths later, the jade slip shattered into a small pile of gray dust. He then looked at Cha Ming, who shivered when he saw Huxian's eyes. They were the same jade color as his eyes, except for a conspicuous purple ring on the outside.

Cha Ming doubled over in pain as a similar ring etched itself into both his eyes. He immediately realized why he couldn't cultivate the Demon-Subduing Eyes it in the first place: It was a demonic technique. As such, only a demon could cultivate it. Cha Ming learned it only because Huxian did. The same applied to using light and darkness qi. He shivered as he recalled the owl saying it dreamt of a black-and-white fox and Cha Ming activating the formation. Had the owl predicted them using their link to make the impossible possible? Had the original owl monarch done the same?

When Cha Ming looked at Huxian, the fox appeared different than before. He saw a light green halo but also a purple one. Then Cha Ming looked around the clearing. He saw intense purple lines around the jade plate as well as many colored lines shooting off in different directions. Then, focusing on the mountains, he saw towering purple auras that blotted out the skies. The dead forest beside him was conspicuously empty of the purple qi that Cha Ming now recognized as demonic qi.

"Now do you believe you can activate the formation?" the owl monarch asked. He had been absent until this moment, but now he'd fluttering back over.

"I think I can," Cha Ming replied. "But it will take a few hours. Do we even have that much time?"

"I'll make us time," the owl monarch said. "Do you need Huxian? He's needed in the battlefield."

Cha Ming stared at the massive array of runic lines. "Please buy me as much time as you can."

Wang Jun, I'm back, Huxian sent mentally. *And so is the owl monarch.*

What about Cha Ming? Wang Jun asked.

He's busy activating the formation, Huxian replied. *We're here to help buy you time.*

I see, Wang Jun said. *What about the owl monarch?*

We're here to buy you time, Huxian replied. *Whatever the cost.*

Wang Jun stared out at the battlefield. It was ever changing, twisting according to both tacticians' desires. It was a dance, a very dangerous one at that. Any slight misstep would mean the loss of many lives. The allied beasts and humans were at a disadvantage. Fortunately, they were on the defensive, and they were able to keep their losses at a minimum. However, the losses they were sustaining were beginning to take their toll. It wouldn't be long before their forces crumbled.

How long does he need? Wang Jun asked.

A few hours, Huxian replied. *As much time as you can get him,* he added.

Wang Jun closed his eyes to think of various countermeasures. He opened them after a few moments, his eyes flashing with resolve. *To buy that much time, we need to take out their hidden tactician. Huxian, can you see anything unusual with your Eyes of Pure Jade? A hidden enemy that blends into the wind?*

A moment later, he received a reply. *There is an ochre mist pervading the whole battlefield. It's difficult to make out anything specific.*

Wang Jun nearly killed himself in shame. Of course he couldn't spot their commander. It was because he wasn't in any specific location, he was everywhere at once.

Does the orange mist retreat quickly whenever any fire, lightning, or wind techniques are used? The techniques were few and far between, with fire being the most prevalent, but they were still being used periodically.

Yes, now that you mention it, it does, Huxian said. After confirming his suspicions, Wang Jun formulated a bold and daring plan.

Geomantic Sovereign, Wang Jun sent, *I'll need you to...*

Cha Ming wasn't sure where to begin, so he started from the most distant line leading away from the plate. He hovered in the air and wielded his Clear Sky Brush, painting a wide blue line as he went. The amount of ink he used was staggering, but he didn't have much choice in the matter. Fortunately, a foundation had already been established. Each line stabilized immediately on completion.

As he approached the faraway mountain, he spotted several minor formations. He used his ink and brush to trace over their outlines, which appeared in either purple or elemental colors. The formations became more and more complex before finally arriving at the mountain. It split off into several lines that snaked up the mountain before finally merging into a jade plate at the peak.

Cha Ming carefully painted these lines, and as soon as he finished, the jade plate glowed with multicolored characters.

One formation plate down, he thought, wiping the sweat from his brow. *Eight to go.*

Chapter 38: Gambit

Wang Jun looked at the battlefield dispassionately. Ever since his instructions to the Geomantic Sovereign, the casualties had skyrocketed. She no longer focused on defense. Rather, she focused on setting up a small formation in the center of the battlefield. Meanwhile, Wang Jun could not divert as much attention to obscuring vulnerable parties as before. He focused on obscuring the formation being erected stealthily beneath the battlefield.

I still don't understand why you're doing this, the Geomantic Sovereign sent mentally. *People are dying up there in droves. Don't you care at all?*

Wang Jun remained stone-faced. Ironically, he was the only one not in danger during these encounters. He'd looked so hard to find the opposing tactician; conversely, the other tactician had given up on finding Wang Jun right away. Which wasn't surprising. Wang Jun was located in a remote location underground, and beside him was the True Seer Owl. He constantly displayed a video projection of the battlefield, zooming in and out as Wang Jun pleased.

I care very much, Wang Jun said sternly. *This is all a ploy to capture their commander, and these deaths are necessary. When you command a battlefield, you need to make difficult decisions. It's not just beast lives that I'm throwing away, it's human lives as well. All to save so many more. I'd sacrifice you just the same if it was worth it.* Silence ensued. *How long until the formation is complete?* he asked.

An incense time, the boa replied.

Good, Wang Jun said. *Now to start the most dangerous part.*

Huxian fought tooth and nail while constantly monitoring the ochre mist, ensuring it didn't escape. He didn't use many special abilities. Wang Jun had specifically requested that he conserve his energy. Everywhere around him, his fellow beasts died. Many humans were dying as well. Wang Jun did not differentiate between man and beast with his decisions. He was cold, mechanical, and ruthless.

He would make a great demon beast, Huxian thought.

Suddenly, instructions flooded into his mind. *You want me to do what?* He didn't hear a reply. He could only grit his teeth and execute. This was war, and second-guessing the commander was tantamount to suicide. Therefore, Huxian followed his instructions to a tee and dived straight into the melee, where it was least safe. At the same time, everyone else on their side pressed inward, pushing everyone further into a more confined space. Wounds and casualties mounted instantly. Huxian even felt a sharp blade leave a deep slash in his shoulder blade.

Huxian didn't question Wang Jun. He was Cha Ming's friend, and that was a good enough reason to trust him. He just hoped that he remembered their friendship and didn't sacrifice them both as well. Just like he had so many men and beasts.

Something's wrong, Guo Jia said, laying down formation after formation. He was exhausted. The only thing that kept him going was an ample supply of pills, but even that was dwindling rapidly.

Nothing's wrong, the voice said. *This commander is far too young to be facing off against me. He's finally made a mistake, thinking he can surprise me. Look at what they're doing—they're using larger amounts of area-of-effect attacks. But he forgot to account for your formations, which will show their greatest potency in a small area.*

It's best to be cautious, Guo Jia said. *There's a reason why we accepted coming here for such a low price. The Wang family subsidized this expedition, all to take out this Second Young Master. If the first young master of the Wang family feels threatened by him, should we not treat him with some level of caution?*

Fair enough, the voice replied. Suddenly, everything changed. Man and beast alike instantly charged out from the tight battlefield and began retreating instantly. *There, I told you he made a mistake. And now he realizes it. All we need to do now is butcher them as they retreat. What a— Oh. Oh dear. Guo Jia, defend me!*

That was when fire, lightning, and wind rained down from the heavens, blocking Guo Jia's line of sight. He quickly set up the best defensive combat formations he knew, hoping he would survive the assault.

Now! Wang Jun yelled. The many beasts that had rushed in before retreated all at once. In the confusion, the enemies chased after them in an expanding circle. All but one enemy. After all, they had painfully set up a restraining formation earlier at the cost of many lives. Rushing in seemed like a mistake, but it was a ploy used to set up this very moment.

On Wang Jun's cue, the large owl monarch floated up in the sky. He flapped his wings many times, flooding the area inside the formation with a devastating wind. It also pushed downward, keeping the wind devil's intangible form pressed to the ground.

Fire rained down from the heavens as dozens of cultivators unleashed techniques. Lei Jiang, who had been saving his power the entire time, burned his blood essence to unleash a lightning storm unlike any Wang Jun had ever seen. Meanwhile, Huxian sent out his aura of suppression into the formation. It was laced with the feeble Devil-Sealing Intent he had accumulated. Silverwing, who had also been holding back, unleashed thousands of windy blades into the formation.

It was just a bonus that Guo Jia and a few other cultivators were stuck in the area. They were the strongest and therefore the least watchful. This combined attack couldn't hurt them, but it could drain their energy.

The dust soon settled, and on the surface, the losses did not seem to outweigh the gains. But Wang Jun knew better. The roar of defiance yelled out by Guo Jia after the attacks faded confirmed the death of their tactician. So did Huxian's Eyes of Pure Jade.

Now they would have no problem holding out defensively until Cha Ming arrived.

"One more," Cha Ming muttered to himself in exhaustion. His brush felt heavy, his soul force overtaxed. He took a quick break to recover his soul's energy. The painting Jun Xiezi gave him filled and nourished his soul.

The dual life-and-death theme didn't seem so awkward to him this time. Life and death were much like light and darkness. Resistance and momentum. Crumbling and hardening. These opposites only existed relative to each other. Warmth suffused Cha Ming's soul as it greedily drank from his surroundings.

Kacha!

He felt a slight shattering sensation within his soul. The remainder of an invisible shackle crumbled away, and the incandescence in his soul reached a peak. But to his surprise, it didn't continue to another level of resplendence, as he had expected would happen with a resplendent soul. Instead the incandescence in his limbs concentrated onto the cloth on his torso. It became tangible and bright. The resplendent garment draped his soul. At that moment, he felt his soul sense expand five times to one hundred miles. The quality of his soul force—which was now called resplendent force— was far easier to manipulate and control than before.

His mental exhaustion immediately vanished. He picked up his painting and took out his brush once more and began completing the formation more rapidly than ever. The speed at which he painted doubled. And while he wasn't confident in his ability to condense higher-level formations, he felt the increased speed would make up for it.

He painted as he ran up the mountain with Stormchaser Steps. The last mountain lit up with colors that complemented the natural flow of energy. Soon, he arrived at the peak of the mountain, where he was greeted with a corpse-littered battlefield. Man and beast alike had killed each other in cold blood.

I can stop this, he thought. *I can make the difference.* He took his brush and began painting the last formation.

The loss of his tactician frustrated Guo Jia. With his disappearance, Guo Jia had no choice but to divert some of his attention to commanding instead of laying down formations. It was this increased perspective of the battlefield that alerted him to the figure at the peak of the mountain. He was painting a large formation, but from what Guo Jia could see, it was only a piece of a much greater whole.

His eyes narrowed.

Help me break through to the peak of the mountain no matter the cost, he yelled. *If that man finishes the formation, we're done for!*

The battlefield erupted around him. Core-formation cultivators increased their efforts and pushed the defenders aside. One by one, the many forces in Guo Jia's way fell apart.

I can make it!

Suddenly a young woman appeared in front of him. She kept her eyes closed, but she seemed familiar to him. He smirked. "So, the little girl Master picked up has become such a beautiful young woman," he said. "Move aside. I'm not interested in you. Just that man behind you."

"I don't care to move aside for the man who betrayed Master," she said. "His heart was broken when you went to the Obsidian Syndicate. Just like his brother before him did."

"He just didn't understand that life isn't worth living if you don't pursue the peak of power and wealth," Guo Jia said. "Now stand aside, or I'll be forced to kill you." A seventy-two-sigil combat formation manifested in front of him. It was an earth sigil, perfectly countering Xuehua's strengths.

"Then it's time that I use a few trump cards Master gave me," she said coldly.

Guo Jia shivered as dozens of talismans flew out toward him, each with increasing levels of power. He was forced to retract his combat formation. He then threw down seven successive lower-level defensive formations. Then, seeing that the rain of talismans would breach his defenses, he threw out three talismans of his own. These had been provided by his master. His *new* master. At a cost, of course. Everything had a price.

Ice was shattered apart by mountainous spikes, causing Xuehua, who was caught in the aftershocks, to cough up blood as she was thrown aside. Guo Jia didn't focus on her. Instead he rushed to stop the young man who was painting at the peak of the mountain.

As the man painted, the mountain began glowing with a pure jade luster. It hurt Guo Jia's eyes, but he couldn't help but press forward. Soon, he arrived before the man, who was holding his brush and staring at him.

"So we meet again," the young man said.

Guo Jia's eyes were still adjusting, so he couldn't make out his features.

"What do you mean, meet again?" Guo Jia asked. He rushed

forward to stop the man as he painted the last formation line. The entire mountain took on a jade luster as a large dome suddenly appeared over the Silverwing Mountain Range. At this moment, he finally saw the features of the man who had activated the grand formation. He was a young man with unusual brown hair and jade and purple eyes. His facial structure was also unusual, that of a foreigner. He gasped when he remembered the face, his eyes flickering to the man's forehead. He remembered that forehead.

He had placed a slave rune there a few years ago.

Cha Ming gazed at Guo Jia intently. His hands clenched in rage as he recalled the degrading treatment he had endured at Wei Chen's hands. Guo Jia, Wei Chen, and Xiao Heilong. One had died, and the others would soon follow. He would start with Guo Jia.

"So what if you've set up this formation?" Guo Jia said, bringing out dozens of formation flags. "Do you think you can win against me? I can tell at a glance that you merely completed an existing formation and aren't the original builder."

Cha Ming shrugged and quickly cast a Stormchaser Steps combat formation beneath his feet. He then charged at Guo Jia, who was in the process of materializing a fire-based high-grade formation. While his tone was aggressive, Cha Ming could see that he was just putting on a strong front. The ochre aura oozing out of Guo Jia was rapidly being eaten away by the defensive formation. After all, Cha Ming was the one who had activated it. He had taken special care to imbue it with his Devil-Sealing Intent.

"Too slow," Cha Ming said, throwing out thirty-six ice sigils. He quickly laid a combat formation down, its energy lines clashing with Guo Jia's. It ended in mutual annihilation. A look of shock appeared on Guo Jia's face as he saw his formation disappear, but it didn't last for long. He shot out seventy-two earth-type sigils. Cha Ming's Dao sigils rapidly changed to a wood formation, but he saw it would be a tad too slow. Therefore, while attacking Guo Jia with his Clear Sky Staff, he quickly shot out dozens of mortal-grade talismans, which landed at key points. Both formations were destroyed.

"Interesting," Guo Jia said, quickly dodging Cha Ming's staff while making another formation. It was a close matchup. Cha Ming had his speed and talismans, and Guo Jia had higher-leveled abilities. Cha Ming had a limited number of talismans, but Guo Jia's aura was slowly being eroded by the grand formation. The first to falter would perish.

Great power suffused Huxian's fur and bones, granting him an aura one sub-realm higher than before.

What a powerful formation, Huxian thought in amazement. Not only he, but Silverwing, Lei Jiang, and many others were propelled one level higher. Huxian and Silverwing joined the other remaining sovereigns to fight the core-formation cultivators in the high-level battles. Meanwhile, the kings and many lords began attacking stronger opponents, rapidly changing the flow of battle.

The human cultivators had not received any augmentations, but the increase in the demon beasts' battle prowess rapidly reduced the pressure they felt. At the same time, Huxian could see the ochre auras being suppressed by the jade shield. The devils should have retreated, but their commander was currently battling Cha Ming. They were like puppets with no one to pull the strings.

Huxian turned his attention to one of the core-formation cultivators who had killed the Reptilian Lion Sovereign.

Silverwing, cover me! he yelled.

Silverwing, who was nearby, flapped his silver wings and forced Huxian's opponent to deflect the blades of wind. Huxian took advantage of the opening and swiped out with a white claw in a sea of darkness. It cut through armor and qi shields like wet paper, instantly destroying the initial core-formation cultivator.

He surveyed the battlefield, looking for his next target. That was when he saw Xiao Heilong, a mountain of a man, sneakily escaping the battlefield. He didn't have a chance to intercept him, though. Yet another core-formation cultivator, more powerful than the last, engaged him in close combat.

Wang Jun, Huxian sent, *Xiao Heilong is trying to escape.*

Already on it, he heard back. He dodged one blade after another and continued looking for an opening. Time was on their side, and they had the initiative.

Xiao Heilong snuck out like a thief. Regardless of how this started or how he got involved, he could tell one thing for certain: They were losing. Badly. And he wanted nothing to do with it. Sure, he would get punished lightly for escaping, but that was the least of his concerns. It was nothing killing a few people couldn't solve. It never was.

Almost out, he thought, looking at the edge of the shield just outside the mountain. He activated his best movement technique and carefully slid through, breathing in the fresh air that didn't corrode his devilish powers.

Clap. Clap. Clap.

A figure walked out of the shadows behind a large rock. It was a young boy with blond hair. Wang Jun, the second young master of the Wang clan. The bounty on his head was extremely high, which made tussling with him an enticing but fearful proposition. Targets that were easy to kill never had high bounties, no matter what anyone told him.

"I suppose you've come here to fight me?" Xiao Heilong said, drawing his daggers. Now that he was outside the jade shield, he no longer had to fear exposing his devilish form. The air turned cold around him as he lost his temper. The rage he normally held within him disappeared, eaten away to be converted into pure strength. He fed off rage. It made him grow stronger. But one always had to pay a price for power. Especially if the power was instantaneous and so useful.

"Heavens no, I think you've got the wrong impression," Wang Jun said, chuckling. "I'm here to *kill* you. Which is quite different, you see? One implies the ability to resist." Suddenly, Xiao Heilong realized that he couldn't move a muscle. He was surrounded by shadowy strings that had clearly been laid out beforehand. The young man walked toward him. His gaze caused him to shiver.

"Do you know why cultivating fate is so difficult?" Wang Jun asked. He now stood two feet away from Xiao Heilong. "It's because it's so hard to find proper cultivation subjects. You see, to cultivate the fate aspect, I need to establish karma and sever karma. The stronger the karma, the more benefit I gain. For example, establishing a trade contract would generate a small amount of karma, but karma of a blood debt... well, that's much stronger. Do you understand?" The young man pulled at the air, and soon he revealed a red thread. Xiao Heilong recognized it. It was the thread of vengeance.

"You tried to kill my brother Cha Ming," Wang Jun said. "Twice. And your men caused him untold anguish, both to him and the people close to him. The organization you belong to has caused a war against my brother's brother. That's why the string is so thick, you see."

A black sword pierced through Xiao Heilong's chest. His knees sagged as the last of his life left him. The last thing he saw was a shadow with a gaping maw. It slurped up the thread of karma like a tasty snack before Wang Jun sent him on his way.

"You're losing this war," Cha Ming remarked, "and you have no one to blame but yourself." He was panting, exhausted, and he was running low on talismans. Another formation sprang up, causing Cha Ming to set up his own quick formation and throw out some lightning talismans to complement.

"Fire with lightning?" Guo Jia yelled. "Seriously? I would have thought that Master would have trained you better. Or are you out of your precious talismans finally?"

"Master?" Cha Ming asked, concentrating more on undoing the next formation. It was getting increasingly difficult to maintain his lead. It was slipping, and soon Guo Jia's formations would get through.

"Of course," Guo Jia said, panting. "There are only three other mortal formation artists in the city. Someone in the Alabaster Group, some guy in the royal family, and me. Who do you think taught all of us in the first place?"

Rage boiled in Cha Ming's stomach, and his expression turned cold. "No wonder he's so strict on recruiting students. Scum like you somehow managed to sneak through."

"I was his pride and joy," Guo Jia said. "But I definitely see his mark in your fighting style. He taught you well, but unfortunately, you're just too young."

"I highly doubt he's very proud of you," Cha Ming said with his teeth clenched as he countered yet another formation. "When I mentioned blood formations in the Song Kingdom, he immediately thought of you. The disappointment he has for you probably tops anything else in his life."

He used his staff to bat aside another formation line, causing it to deviate slightly. Another line quickly took its place.

"You know nothing of the disappointments he's faced," Guo Jia said. "I think his brother founding the Obsidian Syndicate was definitely his crowning shame. But regardless, it doesn't matter much. Because I now have the advantage, and you're dead."

A bright array of blue lights materialized around Cha Ming, trapping him. Cha Ming summoned an earthen formation, but unfortunately it couldn't cause enough damage to shatter it. Thousands of icicles pierced from the ground, slicing apart his strong flesh. Fortunately, his bones were as hard as magic treasures, and they didn't break like the rest of his body did.

He rapidly activated his last remaining Hardening Talisman and Resistance Talisman, both toughening his skin and preventing himself from getting trapped. Then he threw his last remaining Crumbling Talisman at Guo Jia's body. Finally, he threw out his single Sharp Talisman.

Unlike the others, which were buffing and supportive talismans, the Sharp Talisman attacked directly. He also followed up with his last remaining Nine Heavens Lightning Talisman, the last one he had in stock. Unfortunately, Guo Jia suddenly transformed. The most highly concentrated ochre aura Cha Ming had ever seen appeared. It was rapidly being eroded by the Devil-Sealing Intent in the protective formation. Guo Jia grimaced as he appeared in front of Cha Ming, slamming down his boot on Cha Ming's head.

"It's such a shame," Guo Jia said with a distorted voice. "You would have made an excellent greater devil with your mastery over the five elements. But you've used everything you have. And I don't like competitors."

I've used everything I have, Cha Ming thought. No, that wasn't accurate. He still had one trump card, but it was very risky, very damaging. Also, he had never tried it out of fear of destroying his sigils. *It's now or never.*

He couldn't look up due to Guo Jia's heavy boot, but he sent his resplendent force out to guide five sigils, substantially less than normal. Instead of transforming them into formations, however, he quickly expanded them to a larger version of their original shape. Five elemental sigils shone brightly around Guo Jia.

Cha Ming felt the pain in his skull intensify as the boot shoved him further down. He poured his foundation qi into the sigils despite his debilitating condition. He didn't use five-element qi. Only black qi poured in. The five elements created, but they also destroyed. He was gambling that five sigils could make a complete formation and support the destructive black star that linked them. At the center of the black, starry matrix was where Guo Jia was currently standing.

Guo Jia grunted and threw out thirty-six sigils to ward away Cha Ming's seemingly pathetic attempt, but the runic lines fizzled when they met the five sigils. This caused Guo Jia to force down with all his might, trying as hard as possible to crush Cha Ming's unreasonably hard skull.

Seventy-two flags flew out, and Guo Jia rapidly attempted to consolidate a high-grade formation. It was a gold formation, best for slicing. Five giant swords appeared beside him, striking down where the black connecting lines were forming. The gold swords shattered when they hit those black lines, unable to resist their suppression.

Guo Jia lifted his foot to flee, but it was too late. Cha Ming rapidly poured in the rest of his qi, instantly completing the formation.

"No!" Guo Jia shouted in agony as his body was bisected by the black star. His body collapsed, and so did Cha Ming. The mental energy he had consumed was staggering. He could tell that if he hadn't broken through to the resplendent soul realm, he could have easily ended up as a vegetable after activating the formation.

Huxian, Wang Jun, Cha Ming sent. *I'm out. Make sure you win.*

Epilogue

The battle's outcome was as expected. The Silverwing beasts and the Alabaster Group won, but at a terrible cost. Over half of the members sent by the Alabaster Group had perished, including their higher-level forces. Only a third of the allied beast forces remained.

There was a silver lining, however. The Pure Jade Defensive Formation had been activated, and it would remain activated for the foreseeable future. The price to maintain the formation was steep but worthwhile for the Silverwing beasts.

After the battle was completed, the Alabaster Group conducted an investigation and found the traitor. It was an inconspicuous member who wasn't around too often. They weren't sure how he got past their screening process. Unsurprisingly, the punishment for treachery was death.

Unfortunately, the owl monarch perished from his wounds shortly after the battle. Before dying, he passed on his inheritance to the last True Seer Owl on the mountain, the one Wang Jun had effectively used as a monitor to manage the battle. Then, seeing that the owl was clearly not leadership material, the owl monarch appointed Huxian as leader.

Huxian, not wanting to disappoint the monarch, accepted, but he abdicated shortly after the monarch's death and nominated Silverwing, who bluntly rejected. Eventually, the Geomantic Sovereign took on the role as monarch. As a formation expert, she was best suited to controlling the defensive formation. In addition, her contributions to the war and to their survival far eclipsed that of any other beast. Everyone unanimously approved her appointment.

Two weeks passed before Cha Ming, Huxian, and Wang Jun took their leave. They were sent off with a celebration and a large gift of medicinal herbs—useless for the beasts but useful for Cha Ming. Coincidentally, all the ingredients required for his next two pills had been gathered. After one day, they finally departed and left the Silverwing Mountain Range behind them.

"We really made off like bandits," Huxian said, merrily skipping along. Lei Jiang sat on his head, keeping his paws to himself, lest Cha Ming and Wang Jun scold him once more.

And I thought Huxian was a handful, Cha Ming thought. *And he says he's going to recruit seven more friends? What am I, a zookeeper?*

Worse, Huxian had no way to earn income. Therefore, Cha Ming gained an extra mouth to feed with every new companion Huxian gained. He only hoped that their appetites wouldn't be as overwhelming as the little fox's.

Suddenly, Huxian's ears pulled back. "Someone's coming!" he yelled. Cha Ming, who had known this long before, held his hand out and motioned for Huxian to stop.

"He's a messenger from the Song Kingdom," Cha Ming said. "Likely here for Wang Jun."

Sure enough, the man who came was a soldier. He immediately bowed to Wang Jun before delivering a letter. The latter grimaced after reading the contents.

"It seems my absence had some consequences," Wang Jun said. "We secured funding on this expedition and weakened the crown prince. However, a major event happened while we were gone. The king, who has been in poor health of late, collapsed."

"What coincidental timing," Cha Ming said.

"Indeed," Wang Jun replied. "And naturally, the doctors all think nothing is wrong with him."

Cha Ming held his hand to his chin. "Is it possible for me to take a look at the king?"

Wang Jun raised his eyebrow. "You're a spirit doctor now? There are human limits to success, you know."

Cha Ming flushed in embarrassment. "By no means am I a spirit doctor, but I studied under a mortal doctor for some time, so I am familiar with human physiology." He looked back toward the Quicksilver Empire, recalling the lavish buildings the spirit doctors occupied. "Besides, I don't think I trust spirit doctors anymore. They are conceited and think themselves infallible."

"Very well," Wang Jun replied. "A small matter. I'll make it happen." He looked at Huxian and Lei Jiang. "What about you two?"

"We're following Brother Cha Ming, of course," Huxian said.

"I'm following Brother Huxian," Lei Jiang replied.

Wang Jun massaged his forehead. "Fine. I'll arrange something for you to appear like Cha Ming's tamed beasts." Cha Ming frowned when he heard this. "It's just the way of the world, my friend," Wang Jun said. "Every human empire has a rule—all beasts, if not imprisoned, must be tamed. Otherwise, they are to be killed on sight."

"It's fine," Huxian said. "It's far better than being separated again."

Cha Ming's expression softened after getting Huxian's approval.

A day passed, and they finally exited the forest and saw their first glimpse of civilization. There were villages and a large city nearby. Farmers were tilling their fields and sowing seeds during these first few days of spring. Just as they were leaving the forest, a silver glint appeared overhead. Soon, a tiny bird was perched on Huxian's now enlarged form.

"Are you tagging along too?" Huxian asked.

"Of course," Silverwing replied. "What kind of friend would I be if I stayed behind?"

Cha Ming could barely discern a softly glowing "friend" character on his forehead.

Make that three mouths to feed, he thought. Then he looked to Wang Jun, who chuckled. "Three fake beast-taming collars won't cost much more than two," he said lightly. The remainder of their trip was naturally spent housebreaking Silverwing, who was just as bad as Huxian and Lei Jiang.

Feng Ming was annoyed. All he wanted was to kill devils while leading the army. And now he was confined to barracks until his father arrived. Naturally, there was nowhere to run. He was surrounded by good men, and he didn't want them to suffer if he escaped.

Just what could make my father act like this? he thought. His father had given him free rein until recently. Now he had chosen to swiftly retract Feng Ming's leash. As a senior general in the army, his father's orders weren't questioned.

He slept on his flat bed, not touching any food or drink as he waited miserably for his father to arrive. While waiting, he heard some interesting rumors. Was the king dead? No, he had only collapsed. He had been sick for a long time. But who would take over as king now that he was incapacitated? The crown prince? The third prince?

He heard conversations and questions from every angle. Apparently, troops were getting pulled back from all corners of the Song Kingdom. All the great generals were convening their colonels and stationing their troops in ways that indicated their political position.

So that's what it is, Feng Ming thought. *Political games while the kingdom is falling apart.* In his opinion, politicians and devils were of the same breed. They spoke sweet words but veiled their true intentions. They deceived the world while accomplishing their greedy goals.

Well, he thought, *I won't have it. I refuse to participate in these lousy games.* There was a war to be fought, and people had forgotten it far too soon.

The final ghost dissipated as Gong Lan decapitated it with a blade of light. The surrounding air was purified. With time, the trees would grow near the decrepit graveyard. Just like it would with the 107 others.

"Where do we go next, Bodhi?" Gong Lan asked, wiping the sweat from her brow.

"Next, we go to the most central location in the kingdom," the bodhi seed said. It appeared on her shoulder. This time, its expression was serious.

"You mean the capital city?" Gong Lan asked.

"Heavens, no," the bodhi seed replied. "The capital is relatively new. We must go somewhere older. Somewhere ancient. We must go where the destiny of the nation accumulates, where the spirits of its kings are buried. We must follow the path of corrupting crimson and stop the enemy where the evil spirits gather."

"But what are they after?" Gong Lan wondered.

The bodhi seed sighed. "The Ancient Emperor's Seal of Pure Jade."

– End Book 4 –

A Note to Readers

If you've enjoyed this book, I would greatly appreciate it if you left a rating on the site where you purchased it. Ratings lead to credibility in this competitive marketplace, and by leaving one, you signal to the world that this book is worth reading.

As some of you might know, I release each book as I write it. It wasn't necessary for you to buy this book, but your support is greatly appreciated. If you are so inclined, you can continue reading as I write at:

https://royalroadl.com/fiction/16320/painting-the-mists

I can't promise fully edited or proofread content, but I will do my best to continue maintaining frequent and high-quality releases.

If you would like to receive bimonthly updates on writing progress, releases, and the life of Patrick Laplante, subscribe to the Painting the Mists newsletter at:

http://eepurl.com/dymvO1

You can also find a link to the newsletter at www.paintingthemists.com. As a bonus for subscribing, you'll receive exclusive biography sketches for each of the key characters, starting with Huxian!

Other ways to contact me or keep in touch:
Facebook: https://www.facebook.com/RedMiragePtM/
Twitter: @RedMirage_PtM

The Cultivation Systems

Qi Cultivation
- Qi Condensation – condense the qi of heaven and earth into a liquid in your dantian
  o Stages 1-3: form a qi pool
  o Stages 4-6: form a qi lake
  o Stages 7-9: form a qi ocean
- Foundation Establishment – form pillars from your qi, setting a firm foundation for your future cultivation.
  o Traditionally, a cultivator forms between one and nine pillars, which are affixed to the bottom of the qi oceans.
  o The liquid qi in this stage is more viscous, its quantity and quality is dependent on the number of pillars.
  o Pillars are grown from the bottom up, gradually forming the foundation with which to form your core
- Core Formation – condense your foundation into a core, the basis of your future growth
- Rune Carving – ???

Body Cultivation
- Body Strengthening – basic body strengthening and purification. Typically, the body is fed with qi and then refined with an opposing qi, removing any impurities
- Bone Forging – bones are the basis of strength and durability. The strongest body is nothing without strong bones supporting it.
- ???

Soul Cultivation
- Innate Soul – cultivators are born with an innate soul, and it grows as the cultivator advances in qi condensation. Eventually, the soul will make a rapid breakthrough into incandescence.
- Incandescent Soul – the soul begins to shine with incandescent light. Advanced soul manipulation of objects and mental communication is now possible.
- Resplendent Soul – wrap the soul in a resplendent vestment

Acknowledgments

As I continue to write, I find that this list of acknowledgments grows. There are far too many people to thank—if I missed you, I'm sorry. It wasn't intentional.

This time, I'd like to specially acknowledge this book's beta readers: Denis Laplante (my brother), Dave Yeung (who has been providing feedback since the start of the series), Sarah, Psiioniic (RR), Astrael (RR), and Savane (RR).

Just like before, I would like to acknowledge my parents and my wife, Xing Wen, who continue to encourage me on my journey in writing this novel series. Likewise, thanks go to my two brothers and my sister. Thank you once again, Denis, for joining the beta team, and thank you, Levi, for finally starting to read the novel.

Thank you to all my friends once again. I recently took some time off work to focus on writing, and after talking to them, I'm convinced that I've made the right decision.

Many thanks to Crystal Watanabe for her excellent support while editing my novel. My writing continues to improve with her help, so I'm glad to have her on board.

Thank you once again to Samuel Alves for the excellent cover. With this cover remake, the series finally looks like a set.

Finally, thank you to my readers. I write to tell stories to people, and a story is worth nothing if it isn't shared.

About the Author

Patrick Georges Laplante was born in a small town in the Canadian prairies in 1987. He began publishing *Painting the Mists* online under the pseudonym RedMirage in January 2018.

An engineer by trade, he graduated from the University of Alberta in 2009 and completed his master's degree in 2011. While writing and engineering have little in common, he actively utilizes his experiences and attention to detail in fleshing out a vivid world and answering the "whys," which are often left unanswered in Xianxia fiction.

As an avid vegan, he aims to prompt internal reflection in his readers through various themes like non-violence, choice, and begging the question: Is personhood restricted to humanity? And what is proper conduct, morality, and love?

His work is inspired by a combination of Western fiction, *Dungeons and Dragons*, Chinese web novels, and various Japanese, Korean, and Chinese comics and illustrated novels.